Chris Haslam has pursued a variety of bizarre c̶___ns all
___d the world and currently writes for the ___ *Times*.
___ is his third novel. His first, *Twelve Step Far___* ___as short-
lis___d for a prestigious Edgar Allan Poe Award.

Also by Chris Haslam

Twelve Step Fandango
Alligator Strip

el Sid

CHRIS HASLAM

ABACUS

ABACUS

First published in Great Britain in 2006 by Abacus

Copyright © 2006 Chris Haslam

The moral right of the author has been asserted.

A CIP catalogue record for this book
is available from the British Library.

ISBN-13: 978-0-349-11886-4
ISBN-10: 0-349-11886-8

Typeset in Bembo by M Rules
Printed and bound in Great Britain by
Clays Ltd, St Ives plc

Abacus
An imprint of
Little, Brown Book Group
Brettenham House
Lancaster Place
London WC2E 7EN

A member of the Hachette Livre Group of Companies

www.littlebrown.co.uk

To Annabella,
my treasure

Acknowledgements

With grateful thanks to David Hooper, who served with the British Batallion at Jarama, to Pablo Ugana Prieto, who was on the other side, trying to kill him, and to Jack Slater, who lost his fingers at Tereul. Thanks too to Professor Paul Preston, the foremost expert on the Spanish Civil War, and Gerry Blaney, of the Cañada Blanch Centre for Contemporary Spanish Studies. I'm grateful to all at the Marx Memorial Library for granting me access to the International Brigade Memorial Archive, to Gail Malmgreen at the Abraham Lincoln Brigade Archives in New York City for letting me through the door and to the volunteers at the superb Centro de Estudios de la Batalla del Ebro in Gandesa for standing up to prolonged interrogation. I thank John Sayles, who inspired Sidney's last-tree-on-the-battlefield-speech, Tim Whiting for letting me off the leash, Kate Shaw for her advice and Steve Guise for his patience and his practicality. Most of all, though, I thank Natalie for her love, her support and her willingness to learn more about the battlefields of the Spanish Civil War than any girl truly needs to know.

'The only thing that gives any purpose to life is to move humankind along to a better world, the struggle to eliminate homelessness, hunger, disease and most of all, to eliminate the greatest insanity, war. That is the good fight' – Milt Wolff, Commander of the Abraham Lincoln Brigade.

Between 1936 and 1939 more than thirty-five thousand men and women travelled to Spain from over fifty countries to fight for the Republican cause. Over 2300 of these were from Britain and Ireland, and more than five hundred of them were killed. The International Brigades Memorial Trust (www.international-brigades.org.uk) exists to preserve the memory of those men, of whom just twenty-three remain alive today. They were all better than most of us.

1

Lenny Knowles knew he was late, but he didn't conform to traditional models of punctuality. Turning up on time was a sign of weakness that showed an eagerness to please. Jobseekers and salesmen did it. Mercurial geniuses didn't. If Lenny said he'd be with you by three it was merely an indication of vague intent. You didn't get ahead in his game by sticking to routine or keeping promises – you flowed like a river, seeking the path of least resistance and greatest profit, sliding around obstacles and plunging down precipices as you moved inventory downstream to the punter. He stepped on the brakes, raising his eyebrows as the clapped-out van he called Sick Transit Gloria slithered to a stop on the snow-covered road. It didn't pay to think about rushing rivers after six pints.

'Got to have a Jimmy,' he muttered to his passenger, sliding out of his seat and into the night.

Nick Crick opened one eye and sighed, his breath a puff of steam in the frigid cab. Then he opened the other eye and sat upright. Lenny hadn't bothered pulling over – he'd just left the rusting white Transit in the middle of the road on an icy blind bend.

'You worry too much, Nickle-Arse,' opined Lenny when he returned, wiping his hand on his T-shirt. 'Gloria's charmed.'

'Living on borrowed time, more like,' muttered Nick. The blizzard was thickening now, the fat flakes falling like feathers, spinning in the freshening wind. The single-track road stretched straight into the snowstorm, and the empty fields on either side were hidden behind a flickering veil. Nick shivered as he stared through the windscreen wipers, imagining that Sick Transit Gloria was a rocket and the snowflakes that disintegrated against the screen were asteroids. The sense of solitude was encouraging, the notion that he was embarking on a journey without end through an empty universe somehow comforting. Given the chance, he would keep going for ever but he didn't fancy Lenny as his companion to infinity, and beyond. He glanced to the side, wondering how long it would take him to die of exposure out there in the frozen field if he stripped off and lay down in the night. The notion of curling up in a hole in the snow and shivering to death was certainly more attractive than tonight's alternative. 'Who is this bloke then?' he asked at last.

'Mr Starman?' replied Lenny. 'He's a nice old boy. You'll like him.'

'You said he was a boring old fart.'

'To me, yes. But you'll like him. He's into history and art and all that bollocks.'

'All that bollocks?'

'You know what I mean,' said Lenny. 'He reads books and stuff.'

'How old is he?'

'He's getting on a bit. Got all his marbles, though. The full ticket.'

'Why are we wasting my birthday driving into the sticks to visit some miserable old git?' protested Nick.

''Cos it's more fun than anything you had planned,' retorted Lenny.

Nick bit his lip. He had nothing planned. He lit a cigarette. 'You're up to something.'

Lenny focused on the road as a squall reduced visibility to a few feet.

'I said you're up to something, aren't you?' persisted Nick.

2

'I'm warning you now: I'm not getting involved in any thieving from the elderly.'

Lenny shook his head sadly. 'Nicholas: please. Try not to be so negative all the time, and don't be so distrustful. It really hurts me that you think I'd rob a pensioner.' He threw a wet-eyed glance at Nick. 'You should apologise.'

Nick tried to turn up the heater. 'So why are we visiting him?'

'Because I'm the sort of geezer who cares for his fellow man,' sniffed Lenny. 'I saw it was going to snow, and immediately thought of all the poor old folk who would die of cold and star-vation in the big freeze.'

'You said it wouldn't snow, as I recall,' interjected Nick.

'Just trying to keep your morale up. And anyway, if I thought it wasn't going to snow, why did I lay out all that cash at Tesco's on pensioner food?'

Nick sighed. The flakes were racing past like galaxies at warp speed.

'Eh?' insisted Lenny. 'Can't answer that, can you? You just can't accept that there are some people out there – doctors, aid workers, vicars and people like me – who care for those in need and don't think about themselves all the time.' He wriggled self-righteously in his seat. 'I was going to buy you a birthday present, Nickle-Arse, but I think I've just given you something that's not available in the shops.'

'Cheers for that,' muttered Nick, but Lenny wasn't finished.

'I'm a wasted asset is what I am,' he sighed. 'I could be work-ing for the UN or Jeux Sans Frontières instead of looking after you.' He pulled Gloria to the side of the lane, lifted the hand-brake and killed the engine. The van rocked beneath the angry punches of the east wind. 'This is it,' he announced.

Nick stared into the night, his breath steaming the window and fogging his scepticism. 'This is what?'

Lenny pointed through the windscreen. 'It's over there, down a footpath a little way. Can't get Gloria down there so we'll walk.'

Nick shook his head and let each syllable fall with its proper, desperate weight. 'Fuck . . . ing . . . hell.'

There was only one chair in Sidney Starman's drawing room. It sat on a faded carpet in the middle of the floor, a greasy sheen on its threadbare upholstery. Its partner was a Victorian side table, once pretty and delicate and now old and wrinkled, the flaking veneer hidden beneath a veil of yellowed lace. Three photographs in tarnished silver frames stood on the tabletop, the monochrome pigment faded until the three faces seemed like ghostly whirls in a fog. The furthest from the chair was a formal photograph of a soldier, a tall sergeant in a tight uniform that made him look fat. Beside him was a portrait of a sad-looking woman in a black hat and a rabbit-fur collar who stared straight at the lens as though awaiting a straight answer to a straight question, and nearest to the chair a pretty girl was looking up and away with wide, fearful eyes, her gaze seeming to fall upon the old man sitting in the chair. Nobody had ever called Sidney Starman a handsome man, but he had the soldier's firm jaw line, the sad woman's unwavering eyes and a thin grey moustache that suggested a fast wit. He wore a frayed collar and a tightly knotted tie every day except Sundays and spent an hour a week polishing his two pairs of shoes. Like most men of his age, Sidney Starman took comfort from routine, but of all his habits drinking was his favourite. He poured himself a glass of red wine and raised it to the pale faces in the photographs, toasting his father, his mother and the scared girl who had looked away as the shutter fell. Outside the north wind slammed into the house, blowing smoke back down the chimney, rattling the doors and hurling snow flurries that whirled around the windows like Arctic moths in the Norfolk night. The old man finished his wine in three gulps and poured himself another

4

glass. He had drowned his conscience in drink every night since the end of the war, sat in this chair, beside that table, and watched by those three sober faces, and every morning he came round to find his conscience resuscitated. Sometimes he awoke in his bed, but more often than not it was in this chair, his head on one side and a glass in his lap. He expected to be found dead in the armchair, his face faded like the photographs and an empty bottle of Scala Dei at his feet, but then he had never really lived up to expectations. He pulled himself to his feet, wincing as his hip clicked, and crossed slowly to the fireplace. The wooden clock on the mantelpiece lost three minutes a day but Sidney couldn't begrudge it that shortcoming: he'd lost entire weeks sitting in that chair, staring drunkenly into the past. He pulled a green log from the basket beside the hearth and dropped it in the fire, watching the ivy that clung to its bark wilt in the low flames. A gush of sparks flew up the chimney like departing souls and as he turned to warm his backside Sidney Starman told himself again that his mind was at last made up. In 1937 he had made a promise to the girl in the photograph and while the vow was still unbroken it was as weak as his grasp on life. He had poor reasons and no excuses for his failure, knowing simply and above all that it was fear that had cheated him of his destiny. Had he been the romantic hero of book or screen he would have fought man and mountain for the sake of what he supposed was love but in real life time, distance and petty practicality had conspired to make his life one of guilt and regret. The cottage shuddered under another blow from the storm and the room filled with smoke. Sidney pushed himself away from the mantelpiece, wiping acrid tears from his eyes as he groped for the bottle. The plain truth was that he was a weak and frightened man who had sought out reasons not to return. He had hidden behind obstacles between England and Spain, exaggerating their impassability and, like a nervous mountaineer thwarted by bad weather, he had drawn thin comfort from impediment, always knowing that when the skies cleared Spain, like a vicious mountain, would still be there. He topped up his glass with trembling hands under the gaze of his parents. His mother had lost her husband to a tiny sliver of German steel in 1918, the year of Sidney's birth, and ever after she had taught her son never to put any person or cause before himself. In the end the lesson had been well learned, reflected Sidney as he drank his wine, glad that he didn't have to look the girl in the eye.

The desire to return to Spain had finally overwhelmed his fear last summer. It had introduced itself as a serious proposition one wet afternoon as he was walking home from the bus stop, and it had inveigled itself by asking what harm could be done by going back. He was old, she was old, and their lives were almost behind them. Revisiting the past would merely mend a broken circle and right unnecessary wrongs, it insisted, but Sidney wasn't so sure. Nevertheless, he had entertained the idea, allowing it to occupy his mind, to make itself at home. It wasn't long before the notion had taken him hostage, threatening to kill him if he didn't accede to its demands. Sidney's sense of betrayal was diminished only by the knowledge that the idea was right and that it would kill him whatever he did.

Opportunity was knocking.

Time was short.

Life was trickling away and if he was going to keep the promise, he would have to do so very soon, with whatever help he could rally. That help, he realised, with a glance at the ticking clock on the mantel, was already two and a half hours late – a loutish oaf whose only assets were a van, a pair of strong arms and the single-minded desire to charm himself into Sidney's last will and testament. It was a woeful muster, but it was all there was at short notice. He wasn't even certain if the fool would take the bait, even if it was the second most enticing lure known to man. He sighed and leaned back in the chair, his bones numbed by dark Catalan wine and his head spinning. Old buggers couldn't be choosers.

The knock came thirty minutes later.

'You're three hours late,' growled Sidney, his face flushed with wine and heat.

Lenny brushed the snow from his crew-cut and frowned. 'Naughty, naughty, Mr Starman,' he intoned in the half-witted voice one might reserve for the very deaf and the very stupid. 'What did Lenny tell you about the security chain?'

Sidney ignored him, peering to inspect the narrow man stood shivering beyond the porch light. 'Who's that?' he asked.

'This is Nicholas,' said Lenny. 'One of my staff.' He held up the Tesco's bag. 'Lenny's brought you some of your favourites.'

'Unlikely,' murmured Sidney with weary resignation. 'Come in before you let all the heat out.' The stranger, he noticed, had the decency to stamp the snow from his boots at the threshold, unlike his uncouth employer. His skinniness gave the impression of height, and he had a narrow, downcast face half hidden behind an unkempt mane of indeterminate colour. 'I'm Sidney Starman,' he announced. 'Go into the parlour and sit down.'

The stranger didn't offer his hand – they didn't, these days – glancing up instead with the haunted eyes of an insomniac. 'Thanks. I'm Nick Crick.'

The Rayburn's fire door was open and the heat sucked the blood into Nick's cheeks as he pulled a chair across the tiled floor and sat down. Lenny was on his feet, scoping the shelves, lifting ornaments and reading their bases.

'I take it you want a pot of tea?' grunted Sidney.

'Drop of something stronger would be nice, considering the implement weather,' replied Lenny. 'Look what I've brought.' He tipped the contents of the carrier bag onto the table. 'Couple of packets of lovely fig rolls, a nice Fray Bentos pie . . . oh, look, some mint imperials and two tins of your favourite London grill.'

Sidney placed a decanter and three glasses alongside the groceries. He looked like an old soldier to Nick, with what was left of his hair as grey and as closely clipped as his military moustache. His temper seemed slightly shorter. 'How much do I owe you?' he muttered.

'Owe me?' cried Lenny. 'Nothing! It's a gift, Mr S, and you only need two glasses. Nick's a lightweight.'

'He's a what?'

'I don't drink alcohol,' explained Nick.

'Good God!' exclaimed Sidney with a look that was part wonder and part suspicion. 'How unusual. I'm not making tea just for you.'

'That's all right,' smiled Nick. 'We're not staying long.' He urgently wanted to go back to his bedsit, lock the door, draw the curtains, light a candle and get the party started.

'It's his birthday,' explained Lenny. 'He's thirty-three. He wants to go home and crucify himself.'

'Well, happy birthday to you,' said Sidney, raising his glass solemnly. 'Are you sure you won't join—?'

'Nice drop of sherry,' interrupted Lenny. 'Harvey's, is it? Emva Cream?'

'Actually it's a manzanilla from San Lucar,' replied Sidney archly. 'Drink up. I need you to look at the plaster in the drawing room.'

'Now?' asked Lenny.

'When were you thinking?' asked Sidney. 'And another thing: there's a terrible draught coming through the window in the back bedroom. Have you brought any tools?'

Nick watched Lenny as he promised to return first thing. Then he watched Sidney as he shrugged with the disappointment his generation reserved for their progeny. And he considered the dynamic.

'Come in here and have a look at the wallpaper,' Sidney was saying, and Lenny was nodding, eager to please. He gave Nick the wink as he followed the old man out of the parlour. Nick rose and went after them.

'There, in the corner,' said Sidney, ushering them into a richly decorated drawing room that smelled of liquorice and camphor. 'It's coming away from the wall. Must be damp.' He glanced at Nick, who was gazing around the room. 'Do you like art, young man?' He tapped a framed drawing, a scatter of lines and a clutch of ovals. 'That's a sketch by Miró. Quite valuable.'

Lenny sucked air through his teeth. As a cowboy jack-of-all-trades he was obliged to do so when examining a job. 'Plaster's gone live,' he surmised. 'Long job, that is.' He began tapping the wall and Sidney pointed at an alabaster bust.

'French. Late eighteenth century. It's signed but untitled.'

Nick had already seen it. A large-scale map hung opposite the fireplace, a monochrome jumble of spidery contours and foreign place names, but almost every other square foot of wall space in the room was covered with works of art. There were oils, water-colours, woodcuts, engravings, landscapes, portraits, miniatures and lithographs, but not a single photograph. The top of a huge sideboard was stacked with leather-bound books, ceramics, antique glassware and a large stuffed rook, but again, there were no photos on display. The shelf space in front of the volumes in two mahogany bookcases was crammed with valuable-looking knick-knacks and curious artefacts, and, yet again, not a single snapshot of anyone who could possibly have been friend or family of this strange old man. Then he saw them: three silver photo frames in art deco style, standing on an antique table beside a worn armchair, holding three faded pictures – two women, one soldier of the Great War, all black and white, all long dead, by the look of them. He looked back at the alabaster bust. 'Reason,' he said. '*L'esprit de Raison.*'

Sidney looked at him for a moment. 'You surprise me,' he replied at last. 'So how much is this job going to cost me, Mr Knowles?'

Lenny climbed awkwardly to his feet, rubbed his hands on the seat of his pants and frowned. 'It's not the money, Mr Starman, it's the time. I'd only charge you for the materials – bag of bonding coat, really – but it's sorting out the time to do it.'

The old man sighed. 'I want to know when, not why.'

Lenny rubbed his chin. 'Yeah, yeah, I know . . . I'll have to do a bit of juggling about, you know?'

'Well juggle away.'

Nick let his finger brush the cheek of Reason and smiled. A defenceless man was being shamelessly exploited before his eyes, yet he couldn't work out who was the victim.

Outside the sheet of snow lying across Norfolk had become first a blanket, then a thick quilt. Bulldozed by an Arctic air stream, the snow drifted high against hedges, banks and parked vehicles, spilling over frozen fields and the sunrise sides of tree trunks in a hard, white rime. TV newsmen warned against all but the most essential travel and promised the folk of East Anglia a winter night to remember, but Sidney and his guests heard none of this. There was no television in the Starman abode, and it was only when Lenny made a trip to Gloria to fetch more fags that the impossibility of travel became clear.

'You'll have to stay,' sighed Sidney, secretly surprised by the storm's apparent collusion in his scheme. 'I suppose you'll want feeding.'

Lenny lit a superking. 'What's the name of the drink you offer people before they have their tea?'

'Aperitif?' hazarded Sidney.

'Love one, thank you, Mr S. Drop of that sherry will go down lovely. What's the matter with you, Nickle-Arse?'

'Nothing,' replied Nick. In truth he was dismayed and disturbed at the thought of spending a night in the old man's house, and he could feel a sore throat coming on. Unannounced changes of plan upset his finely balanced, highly strung sense of wellbeing

10

and he was concerned that he had neither toothbrush nor change of clothes. His urgent desire to hole up with his sacred relics and spend the night in solemn contemplation had been thwarted by nature, and when Lenny agreed with Sidney that they would spend the night at the cottage he had no choice but to concur.

'Rabbit,' announced Sidney.

'Where?' asked Nick.

'Eat it?' replied Sidney. 'Do you eat rabbit?'

Nick shrugged. 'S'pose so. Don't know.'

Sidney nodded abruptly and lifted the lid on a saucepan. 'Thought you might be vegetarian as well as teetotal,' he grunted. 'This'll need more potatoes in. I'll just nip down the shed and fetch some.'

Lenny started to say something, glanced outside and changed his mind as Sidney unlocked the back door and shuffled out into the snowstorm. 'What do you think?' he grinned, taking a long slug from the sherry bottle. 'Treasure trove or what?'

'Lot of nice stuff,' agreed Nick. 'What's the plan? Knock him on the head and load up the van?'

Lenny gave him a long, hard look. 'You're a nasty piece of work.' He took another three swallows, wiped his mouth and replaced the bottle. 'Anyway, we won't have to.'

'I know. I noticed.'

'What?'

'No family. There's only three photos between here and the front room and they look like they all died years ago. The old fella's either fallen out with his heirs or he doesn't have any. Either way . . .'

'Well spotted, Nickle-Arse,' nodded Lenny. 'You're learning fast. He's got this lovely little cottage full of quality pieces and no one to inherit it. It's a crying bloody shame to come to the end of your life, surrounded by the fruits of your labours and have no one to leave it to but the sodding taxman. That poor old geezer. If it wasn't for me . . .'

11

'How do you know the house is his? He might be renting it.'

'He's not.'

'You asked him?'

'I asked him what his plans were for the house when I was pricing up the gutters, and he said it was all part of his estate. And I reckon that if you added up the value of all them paintings and stuff they'd probably be worth another ten.' He jumped to his feet and ran his hand along the Rayburn's chrome rail. 'First thing I'll do is strip this crappy old kitchen out and throw some quarry tiles down. Knock that wall through and stick a fitted kitchen in, bung a conservatory out the back and offload it to some yuppies from the Smoke.' He pointed at Nick. 'One thing: don't go and spoil it by mentioning the past.'

'You mean that we've both been inside?'

Lenny winced. 'Exactly. He's bound to grab the wrong end of the stick if he finds out we've done time. He'll think we're criminals or something.'

'I think it's better out in the open,' began Nick, but Lenny cut his protest short.

'Nicholas: you've been in prison. You are out on probation. You are an ex-con. Wrap it up any way you like but at the end of each and every day for the next five years you are subject to the Rehabilitation of Offenders Act of 1974, so keep your bleedin' gob shut.'

The back door was thrown open by the wind as Sidney returned, snowflakes whirling around his head like confetti.

'Let me help you with those, Mr Starman,' cried Lenny. 'I was just telling Nicholas how well you've kept this old house up.'

The rabbit stew was hot, and as far as Lenny was concerned, that was all it had going for it. Rich and orange, it was full of whatever grew in the fields round here, but the stringy meat could have been cat for all he knew. Whatever it was appeared to have been shot at close range with a sawn-off, execution-style, and hard black pellets of lead shot lay on the edge of everyone's plate like forensic evidence. He watched as Nick and the old man sucked bones and dipped bread into the greasy gravy, wondering if it would be rude to cook up the Fray Bentos he'd brought. He helped himself to another glass of wine, studying the label like a connoisseur and wishing he'd bought some of the moody Stella he'd been offered down the market.

'Scala Dei,' nodded Sidney. 'The stairway to God.'

'Stairway to heaven,' suggested Nick, loading more stew onto his plate.

'Quite, er, robust,' offered Lenny, 'wouldn't you say?'

'Like a nun's underwear, Mr Knowles,' agreed Sidney. He picked up the bottle and waved it at Nick. '*Mei confii gens en a home que no beu.*'

Nick looked up. 'Pardon?'

'Old Catalan proverb: never trust a man who doesn't drink. Probably comes from the time of the Moorish occupation, but it still holds true.'

Nick shrugged. 'Don't trust me then. I never asked you to.'

Sidney smiled and refilled his glass. 'What was your name again?'

'Nick Crick.'

Sidney nodded. 'Mr Crick.'

'Nick'll do.'

The old man shook his head. 'I'll stick with Mr Crick if it's all the same to you.'

'Tell you what,' said Lenny. 'I'll have his wine and he can have my stew. Fair enough?'

Nick wiped his mouth with his napkin and tore off more bread. 'Have you lived here all your life, Mr Starman?'

'Not yet, Mr Crick,' replied the old man.

'You ever been out of Norfolk?'

Sidney covered his mouth with his hand and looked at Nick for a moment over his glass. 'A couple of times,' he replied at last.

13

'Ever been down the Smoke?' asked Lenny, refilling his glass.

'London? Of course. I've been to Kilburn, Limehouse, Camden Town and Victoria.'

Lenny hadn't lived in London since he was seven years old but considered himself an expat cockney. 'I know geezers in all them manors,' he lied.

'Where else?' asked Nick.

'Oh, I've been to Germany a few times,' smiled the old man. 'Berlin, Cologne, Hamburg – all the best places.'

'I went to a conference in Cologne once,' said Nick. 'It's nice in the Altstadt, where all the beer halls are.'

Sidney frowned. 'I thought you were a teetotaller.'

'I wasn't then,' replied Nick. 'What were you doing in Cologne?'

Sidney took a sip of Scala Dei. 'Bombing it flat,' he replied. He stood up and tipped the dregs of the bottle into Lenny's glass. Their eyes met for a brief moment before Lenny looked away. Sidney maintained his gaze, studying the round and ruddy pretender to his estate. Mr Knowles was but a few licks short of insufferable: an overweight, uncouth, ignorant, opinionated, bullying drunkard with the intellect of a donkey and a convict's haircut. His companion seemed to be a malnourished neurotic, but he clearly had both intelligence and education. That he didn't drink showed a distinct lack of moral fibre, a limp-wristed untrustworthiness, but his presence, in some small way, was undoubtedly beneficial. Sidney shook his head at the prospect of embarking on an adventure with this pair of clowns, but it was now or never, and there was still no guarantee that they'd agree.

'Fancy a game of cards, Mr S?' asked Lenny. Stealing the old boy's pension was one thing; winning it over a few hands of three-card brag was another thing entirely.

'Perhaps later,' replied Sidney. 'First let me give you both something.'

He rose painfully from his chair, his hand on his aching hip. 'Join me in the other room, gentlemen.'

The drawing room was blue with smoke when they entered. Nick sat on the floor at the hearth, wondering who the girl in the picture was. It was a reasonable guess that the other two were Sidney's parents, but the big-eyed girl in the cheap dress had a poor and foreign look about her. She wasn't looking directly into the camera but off to one side, as though something had distracted her, frightened her just as the shutter closed. It was the sort of photograph that a man would reject if he had a choice, yet Sidney seemed to cherish it as much as the portraits of his parents.

He wondered if Sidney talked to his photographs. 'Who's the girl?' he asked.

Sidney glared down his nose like a magistrate. 'None of your bloody business. Now, I may be making a mistake but at my age all one's eggs are best kept in one basket.'

'I'll grab a refill if there's going to be a speech,' said Lenny, stabbing a corkscrew into a dusty bottle of Rioja.

'Take these,' said Sidney, handing each a small item wrapped in old newspaper. 'Open them. They're yours to keep, or sell, or give away, if you so desire.'

Nick unwrapped his parcel. It gleamed like sunlight. 'It's a coin,' he said.

'It's a bleeding gold coin,' exclaimed Lenny.

'How old is it?' asked Nick.

'Probably three hundred and fifty years.'

'How much is it worth?' asked Lenny.

'Perhaps a couple of thousand pounds to a collector.'

'Where did it come from?' asked Nick.

'Peru, originally.'

'Are there any more?' gasped Lenny.

Sidney chuckled. Gold fever was like hunger – no man was immune. He took a long pull on his wine, looking from one open-mouthed idiot to the other. 'Oh yes, Mr Knowles. Thousands of the buggers.'

They had taken the bait and now they gaped at him like gold-fish.

'Whereabouts?' asked Lenny.

Sidney looked sideways at the girl in the photograph. 'In Spain,' he said.

2

They'd been on the road since before dawn and Sick Gloria was touching seventy on the southbound carriageway of the M5.

'Did you remember to pack your toothbrush, Mr S?' called Lenny, swerving to overtake a coach.

'Of course I did, Mr Knowles.'

'Well done. Spare grundies?'

'Yes, Mr Knowles.' He had found more comfort than should have been available as the third man on the bench seat of a Transit.

Nick, squeezed between the old man and Lenny, pushed half a KitKat into his mouth and shook his head. 'I haven't got any spare grundies.'

It had been four days since Nick had met Sidney, and the snow still lay in dirty drifts across the fields. The old man's gold had entranced them and his promise had trapped them. The scheme was as simple-minded as they came: they would drive down to Spain, and dig up the gold. End of story. There were no plans for its disposal, and as far as Nick knew, no agreement had been reached on the distribution of profits. It was a most unlikely venture, but he really didn't care. Any adventure was better than none.

'Got your wallet?' called Lenny. 'We'll need lots of cash on this trip.'

'Yes,' sighed Sidney. Lenny was beginning to irritate him now. He'd been shouting out random questions since Reading, and

Sidney could understand why the man was divorced, or separated, or whatever they did these days.

'Alka Seltzer?'

'You alredy asked, Mr Knowles.'

'Passport?'

Sidney stared out of the window. The sun was low over Glastonbury but the motorway was already busy with fast-moving traffic that raised an ugly black spray.

'I asked if you remembered your passport, Mr S?' called Lenny.

'I heard you,' replied Sidney.

'Well did you?'

A blue sign whizzed past: 'Exeter 45, Plymouth 87'. Sidney's silence said more than words.

'Oh fuck,' moaned Nick.

'You've left it at home, haven't you?' sighed Lenny.

'I don't have one,' shrugged Sidney.

Sick Gloria swerved into the slow lane. 'Don't slow down,' said Sidney. 'We'll miss the boat.'

'Course we'll miss the bleeding boat,' said Lenny. 'We'll have to go back, that's all.'

'Not at all,' insisted Sidney. 'Just drop me off somewhere near the port entrance and I'll see you on board.'

'Unlikely,' sighed Nick.

'Yeah, unlikely,' agreed Lenny. 'That's Plymouth we're talking about. It's not like it was in the good old days, you know, and you're a bit old to be doing the James Bond stuff. It's a post-seven-eleven world now, Mr Starman. Take it from me – Lenny knows.'

'Nine-eleven,' interjected Nick.

'Whatever. They've got cameras, coppers, sniffer dogs, X-ray machines, Customs, Immigration, private security guards, squaddies . . . ' His words dried up as he began to scare himself. There was bound to be something in the terms of his probation that banned overseas travel, but he hadn't checked because he really hadn't believed they would actually make it this far. The best thing to do was to turn back and put the whole affair down to experience. The record would show that Lenny had once again gone out of his way to help a poor old man with no beneficiaries to his estate and that was all that mattered.

'Drop me at the gate,' repeated Sidney with a smile. 'I'll see you both on board.'

Two and a half hours later he wandered into the bar on the Brittany Ferries *Pont-Aven* wearing his cap and his gabardine overcoat, and carrying a bag from the duty-free shop. He dressed like Eric Morecambe, thought Lenny, raising his glass in salute.

'Well, fuck me, Mr S,' he declared. 'I'm impressed. I'll have another Carling, if you're getting them in.'

Sidney surveyed the bar, then his watch. It was 10.10 a.m. 'I was hoping more for a decent cup of tea,' he said. 'Where's Mr Crick?'

'Buggered if I know. Probably up on deck moaning at the seagulls. Nice watch you've got there.'

'It's German,' explained Sidney. 'It hasn't lost a second over sixty years.'

Lenny nodded. 'Mate of mine got a Sekonda off a bloke in a pub that's accurate to a hundredth of a second for a thousand years or something. Might even be a millennium.'

'Or your money back?'

'Wouldn't have thought so,' replied Lenny. 'Not from Roger the Dodger, anyway.' He lit a fag and blew smoke through the downlights.

'A bag in a cup of warm water does not qualify as a cup of tea,' Sidney informed the barmaid. He pointed at a cloudy coffee jug. 'I'll have a cup of that brown stuff instead and my colleague here will have another pint of beer.' He counted coins from a leather purse and turned to Lenny. 'Mr Crick seems to be a melancholy chap.'

Lenny took a long swig from the back end of his fourth pint. He was feeling quite pleasantly pissed. 'Miserable bastard is what he is. Living in the past, Mr Starman. He wants to let go of what's gone and move on. That's what I done.'

'Move on from what, exactly?' asked Sidney, struggling to tear open a sugar sachet.

Lenny flicked his ash. 'Things what you wouldn't believe, Mr S.'

Sidney gave up on the sugar and examined his coffee. He'd forgotten the rules – the most important of which was not to become involved in other people's life stories – but then he'd been out of the game for a long time. The last time he had crossed the Channel by boat had been in late October 1936. The ferry service had been running for only a few weeks, Franco had been declared *Jefe de Estado*, the Marx Brothers' *Night at the Opera* was all the rage, and the Jarrow Marchers were heading south. Sidney was heading further south, to Spain, with his friend Joe Kirow. The pair had enlisted in the International Brigade up in Kilburn a week previously and neither could believe that they were on their way to war. The speed at which the modern world allowed one to change one's life had astounded Sidney as he walked to the stern deck of the SS *Ford* to watch the white cliffs of Dover recede in the autumn haze. He felt like a boy among men, a naïf who would surely be rejected upon arrival in Spain as too young to kill fascists in the name of democracy. He found Joe leaning on the rail. 'Not having second thoughts, are you?'

Joe looked even younger, his pale face, thick spectacles and consumptive frame belying his twenty-two years.

'Just bidding Albion farewell,' he said. 'How long will it be before we're back?'

Sidney shrugged. 'Don't know. Do you reckon they'll take us?'

'At least you can shoot,' said Joe. 'I don't know one end of a rifle from another. I've never slept outside and I can't even speak Spanish.'

Joe, though, spoke the language of revolution, and seemed destined to prove that the politically committed made the best soldiers. His reading of the Iberian situation was that the democratically elected Republican government of the Popular Front under President Azaña and Prime Minister Casares Quiroga was fighting a desperate and righteous war against an illegal coalition of reactionary right-wing organisations supported by a cynical Catholic establishment and led by a brutal army aided and abetted by Hitler and Mussolini. Sidney's understanding was that Spain was hot and was where oranges came from. Both were bound for disillusion and disappointment.

Sidney had watched Joe rousing the rabble round the fringes of Cable Street three weeks earlier, his passionate words inspiring volleys of cobblestones to be launched at the police, and he knew his new friend was wasted as a mere foot soldier. 'Do you reckon they'll let us stay together?'

Joe patted him on the back. 'Wait and see, chum.'

Back then they served proper tea from a shiny steel urn, milk from jugs and sugar from bowls.

Seventy years later Lenny was still seeking sympathy. 'It's been nothing but rough seas for me the past five years,' he muttered.

'I'm sure it has,' agreed Sidney absently.

'I tell you, if it hadn't been for bad luck, I'd have had no luck at all. I could tell you stories that would make your hair go grey.'

'It already is,' sighed Sidney. 'Would you excuse me?'

He left his coffee on the bar and went out on deck. The wind stung his face, driving spray before an inauspicious day. He found Nick stood in the lee of the funnel, his back pressed against the warm steel.

'Blimey!' cried Nick. 'You made it!'

'Not as old and stupid as I look, am I? What are you doing out here in the cold?'

Nick shrugged. 'Saying goodbye to England. How long do you reckon before we're back?'

Sidney turned to face the open ocean, tasting salt and diesel in the wet air. 'I doubt I'll be back,' he murmured.

The crossing from Plymouth to Santander takes twenty hours and twenty minutes on a good day. That Sunday in March, however, was a bad day. A wet westerly blew up the Channel, soaking the ship with cold rain and spray as a heaving sea rolled past like greasy quicksilver. Nick tried focusing first on the horizon, then on his churning belly and finally on reaching the rail before he hurled. He failed on all three counts, compounding his misery by slipping on his own vomit as he descended a ladder.

Sidney had gone below as soon as the English coast had disappeared behind the low curtain of rain. He chose the seat closest to the centre of the ship, a position he felt sure would minimise his suffering, and sat upright, his raincoat tightly belted against his churning belly and his eyes squeezed shut in a counter-productive attempt to ride the waves of nausea induced by the pitching ferry. That cup of stale, over-brewed coffee sat in his stomach like a pool of acid and his moustache itched with prickles of sweat. The last time Sidney Starman had been in the Bay of Biscay was when he had returned from Spain in the summer of 1937. Then he'd been so sick he had vowed never to set sail again. He swallowed bile as the ferry shuddered from stem to stern, realising that he had broken one promise to keep another. It didn't seem so noble now.

'Nineteen hours to go.'

He opened his eyes. 'If that's the best news you can offer, Mr Crick, I'd prefer ignorance.'

'Sorry,' murmured Nick. His face was the colour of a day-old corpse and his trousers were stained with vomit. 'Mind if I sit down?'

'Not at all,' groaned Sidney. 'As long as it's nowhere near me.'

'I don't think I can survive another nineteen hours of this,' announced Nick, slumping into the seat behind. 'I don't see why we couldn't have just nipped across to Calais and driven to Spain.'

From the seat in front Sidney let out a long sigh. 'I'm sure Mr Knowles had good reason,' he said.

As it happened, Lenny had five good reasons for taking a long sea voyage to Spain. First, Sick Gloria's clutch was hanging on by a thread and, second, she was uninsured. Third, she was untaxed and unregistered and, fourth, there was some small disagreement over her title with a family of tarmac tinkers from up King's Lynn way. Even though Lenny had long since changed the plates he was uncomfortable driving a death-trap of disputed ownership – he didn't like the word 'stolen': Gloria had been appropriated in lieu of payment for services rendered – across country with the attendant risks of breakdown and arrest when there was an easier option. That brought him to reason number five: twenty hours in a bar with a sea view. He fed another handful of pound coins into the fruit machine and held the bells, exchanging Cashpot for Features and gambling up to Runaway Sevens. There was one drinker left in the bar, a florid trucker from Lincolnshire bound for Valencia to collect carrots, but as the ship nose-dived like a gluttonous pig into another trough he shook his head, stubbed out his cigarette and wobbled away, leaving an untouched pint of Guinness on the bar. Lenny sipped his lager and considered the options flashing before him. Runaway Sevens guaranteed a minimum payout of fifty-odd quid, but one more gamble would give him the two-hundred-pound jackpot. No question, he thought, hitting the gamble button. He lost, but succeeded in catching the red-faced trucker's pint of Guinness as it slid along the bar, tasting a strange kind of luck in the air. Despite his firm belief that life was like a river, he had noticed that his own had seemed much more like an ocean of late. During the four and a half years he had served for a crime he hadn't committed he had been forcibly becalmed, slowly dying of thirst in Her Majesty's doldrums. The wind had picked up since his release, but it had been an ill one, blowing him from one disaster to another as he struggled to put his life back on course. In a fair world Lenny Knowles would have been a successful property developer by now, or a respected scrap-metal merchant, or the much-loved CEO of a waste-disposal empire. He was nearly forty-five years of age and by rights he should have been driving a classy motor like a Beemer or a Merc, hobnobbing with the leading influencers and decision-makers of his day and taking his holidays in Barbados and Tenerife. Instead he was driving a clapped-out Transit, hanging around with a half-witted college boy and an eccentric geriatric and taking his holiday in Spain. He downed his Carling and started on the Guinness, reminding himself that these minor setbacks were all in a life's work for the talented entrepreneur, and the rewards far outweighed the effort. Lenny could have stayed in school if he'd wanted to. He could have taken O levels and A levels and gone to university like Nick Crick, but where would that have led him? To a desk in an office somewhere, a two-hour commute and a life of debt and taxes? Lenny sniffed and threw an admiring glance at his bright white Reeboks. You didn't need a Next card to look good, even if the trainers were snide. He fed another fiver into the fruit machine, accepting that if he had gone to university he would no doubt have been head of his department by now, running finance for a major corporation or developing cutting-edge marketing strategies for blue-chip enterprises, but at the end of the day how many of those sharp-suited desk jockeys could truly say they were free?

The ferry lurched, as though hanging in mid-air, then crashed into the gutter of a thirty-foot wave in an explosion of spray. Lenny lit a cigarette, lost seventy-five pounds on a fifty–fifty gamble, belched and summoned the sickly barmaid. 'Give us a large vodka Red Bull and a pint of Carling, darling,' he called cheerily. 'Anywhere round here I can get a kebab?'

It was eight hours before he saw Nick and Sidney again. They met in the ship's grim cafeteria, where Sidney sat staring at a storm in a teacup and two slices of dry toast. Nick sipped from a bottle of troubled water, grimacing with each swallow as though he was forcing down mouthfuls of cod-liver oil. Lenny, who had won and lost a couple of two-hundred-pound jackpots and half a dozen lesser wins during the day, sipped Stella from the can before smothering a grey slab of steak with ketchup. Sidney clapped a hand over his mouth as the vessel lurched, spilling tea, water and lager. A waiter in a stained jacket smiled weakly as he mopped up the mess and Sidney thanked him feebly.

'I see you speak the lingo, then,' said Lenny, chewing on an onion ring. 'Where did you learn French?'

'From a Frenchman,' replied Sidney.

'Were you there in the war?' asked Nick.

Sidney nodded. 'Over it, but never on it. I was an airman.'

'Ever kill anyone?' asked Lenny. 'Shoot down any dirty Fokkers?'

Sidney gave him a look as long as a dagger in reply.

'I bet you killed loads of Germans, you old sod,' continued Lenny, forcing his words through a mouthful of beef. 'The quiet ones are always the worst.'

'So what's the story on the gold?' asked Nick.

Sidney switched his glare, put down his teacup and rose,

placing his bony fists on the swaying tabletop and leaning forward. 'I'll remind you once more, gentlemen, and then no more. We never, ever, discuss the nature of our business in public, and we do so in private on my instigation alone. In other words, I'll tell you what you need to know, when you need to know it, and you two keep your big mouths shut. Do you understand?' He pulled on his flat cap and wobbled purposefully out of the cafeteria.

Nick watched him go, then turned to Lenny. 'I feel terrible,' he moaned.

'And so you should,' sniffed Lenny. 'You were bang out of order upsetting an old man like that.'

Sidney appeared to be sleeping when they returned to the saloon. Beyond the salt-streaked windows sea and sky had merged in washed-out shades of grey as Biscay raged like Charybdis. The odour of Lenny's onion rings lingered in Nick's nostrils like toxic waste and his throat was sore from retching. He slumped miserably in his wipe-clean seat, pressing urgently on the acupressure spots on his wrists and wishing the whirlpool would suck them all down. Lenny settled into a nearby seat and poured himself a post-prandial drink. He'd invested some of his fruit-machine winnings in a two-for-one deal for Smirnoff Blue Label, and as he sipped the clear spirit he wondered out loud if vodka counted as an after-dinner liqueur.

'It does not,' growled Sidney, his eyes still closed. He pulled a battered flask from his overcoat pocket and unscrewed the cap. 'Armagnac is what one might call a liqueur.'

'Give us a sip,' asked Lenny.

'No,' replied Sidney. He sat forward, replacing the cap. 'Instead I'll show you the route we'll be taking.' The ship groaned as she climbed another monstrous wave. An orange bucket slid past their seats.

'Fair enough,' shrugged Lenny.

Sidney rummaged in his carrier bag and produced a map of Spain. He spread it across his lap and pointed at the top left-hand corner with a trembling finger. 'We land here, in Santander.' He traced the line of the A8 to Bilbao. 'We're going here, where we'll stop for the night. Then to Zaragoza in the morning, then across the desert and over the mountains to Montalban.'

Nick peered around the seat to study the proposed itinerary. 'Can I suggest something?' he asked.

Sidney smiled like an elderly *Gruppenführer*. 'No, you may not, and that leads me to my next point. More so than either of you, I believe in a socialist democracy in which the voices of all are heard, but in order for that model to work its members must display, shall we say, good faith. Now while I seek neither to oppress nor to offend, I am also aware of the need for this mission to have one leader and two followers – one chief and two Indians, if you like. First off, I'm the only one of us who speaks Spanish. Second, only I know where we're going and why we're going there. And last, but not least, because I'm the oldest, I'm in charge. There'll be no dissent – consider yourselves subjects of a benign dictatorship. If you don't like it, you can leave.'

Lenny fumbled with his fag packet. No one told him what to do and got away with it. 'I thought this was supposed to be an equal partnership,' he mumbled.

'It will be,' replied Sidney. 'When all's said and done we'll split the profits three ways.'

Nick had his doubts. 'And what if there are no profits?'

'Yeah, what if we never find the gold?' nodded Lenny. 'What then?'

Sidney pulled two white envelopes from his blazer pocket. 'One each,' he said. 'I take it you can both read?'

Three giggling children scurried past, leaning at seemingly impossible angles to counter the sway of the ship. Lenny watched as Nick opened his envelope and withdrew a folded note.

'Look upon it as your travel insurance,' suggested Sidney.

Lenny scanned Nick's document, then read his own.

'They're both the same,' said Sidney. 'I've made you the sole beneficiaries of my estate.'

'You haven't signed mine,' noted Lenny.

Nick reopened his. 'Nor mine.'

'Of course I haven't,' smiled Sidney, with a slightly sad shake of his head. 'I'm a poor, vulnerable old gentleman stuck on a ship with no passport and you two ruffians for company. Of course I haven't bloody signed it, but I promise you that when the time comes, I will happily do so. Shake on it.'

Lenny sighed as he took the old man's bony hand. 'A handshake means nothing.'

Sidney looked him straight in the eye. 'It does in my world, Mr Knowles.'

Nick accepted Sidney's leadership with a certain amount of glee. The old man's assumption of power had thwarted Lenny's ambitions to embark on an extended booze cruise and imbued the journey with a certain purpose. Until now the trip had felt like a Help the Aged outing of the type he'd done as part of his community service at the back end of his sentence. Sidney's vagueness in the days before they'd set off had compounded Nick's suspicions that they were embarking upon a fool's errand, a pair of Sancho Panzas to a doddery Don Quixote. The old man had repeatedly assured them that he knew where several thousand gold coins were hidden, but that was all he'd said, and Nick had suspected that the story was merely an incentive to a wild-goose chase. Sidney's brusque assumption of command, however, lent credibility to his claims and allowed Nick to entertain the pleasure of speculation.

Lenny was less pleased. The last time he'd taken orders from anyone who wasn't a prison officer or a copper had been in June 1976, one month after his fifteenth birthday. His uncle had found him a job as a hod carrier on a building site in Thetford and he'd stuck it out for three days. It wasn't that he was naturally rebellious or that he was hostile to authority, just that he was naturally incapable of taking orders from anyone less intelligent than him; boastful though it seemed, he rarely came across anyone who wasn't. He glanced at the map. Here was a case in point. Old Starman had chosen the most obvious route from wherever it was they were landing to wherever he reckoned this treasure was buried, but life was rarely that easy. Gloria just wasn't suitable for smooth, fast, heavily policed motorways. Her ideal road surface was one rarely travelled by the Bill – country lanes, by-roads and backwoods tracks – and Lenny saw no need to rush. Handled properly, this adventure could become a gentle meander through the Spanish countryside punctuated by leisurely stops at whatever fine hotels and well-appointed bars they encountered. What was certain was that the only gold he'd see on this trip was filling a hole in his back teeth, so it made sense to mine the old man's wallet until he could honestly stand up and say he'd done his duty. He folded his copy of the Starman will and slipped away to the bar to have a quiet think.

Sidney lost his battle against seasickness a couple of hours later. The malodorous atmosphere of the pitching ferry, redolent of stale vomit, diesel oil and deep-fried food, crushed his resistance in a devastating attack that left him sprawled on his bony hands and knees beside a blocked toilet bowl. Nick hovered near by, holding his nose with one hand and passing wads of paper towel with the other while the old man heaved himself hoarse, his croaking retches like death rattles in the flooded toilet stall.

By midnight, empty and exhausted, he slipped into a sweaty slumber, leaving Nick sitting in the low-lighted saloon, listening to his snoring. There were few other passengers aboard: a group of hyperactive kids seemingly unaffected by the rough voyage and a handful of grim-faced truckers who had bedded down with air mattresses and sleeping bags on the stained floor. Outside the swell seemed diminished, as though the ship had sailed through the storm and out the other side, and an atmosphere of quiet yet purposeful exhaustion had spread along the darkened decks.

Weak and tired, but unable to sleep, Nick left Sidney and crept out on deck. It was still raining and as black as blindness but as his eyes grew accustomed to the night he saw faint streaks of phosphorescence racing past the dripping hull. This, thought Nick, was the true heart of darkness. A man could climb the safety rail and disappear for ever on a night like this, emerging shocked and spluttering from the ferry's wake to see its navigation lights and the yellow cabin glow disappearing into the murk. Staring down at the hissing sea, Nick wondered how long he would wait for death in that icy black horror. A minute? An hour? However long it took, it was a lot quicker than not jumping. He walked slowly around the deck, his trainers squeaking on the wet steel, passing solitary smokers whose faces glowed like ghosts in the murk before stepping back into the ship. Inside was like his old life: warm, light and safe from the elements. Outside was like his new life: dark, cold and unpredictable. He preferred to be inside, he decided, wondering if the aches in his legs meant he was coming down with a dose of flu. He slipped into the toilets to wash his face and met Lenny as he was drying his hands.

'Silly old bastard,' muttered Lenny, draining a quart of lager into the urinal.

'Who is?'

'El Sid is.'

Nick smiled. Unlike Nickle-Arse, El Sid was a fine example of Lenny's talent for nicknames, but he didn't tell him.

'I think he's wishing we'd driven to France instead of listening to you and taking the boat,' said Nick.

Lenny wiped his hands on his shell pants and examined his nose in the mirror. 'Yeah, but it's my van and I'm in charge here, not him.' He leaned closer to the dirty glass to inspect his pores. 'I'll let him think he's the boss for as long as it suits my purposes.'

'What purposes are they?'

Lenny turned and winked with a bloodshot eye. 'Lenny knows, Nickle-Arse. Lenny knows.'

Nick swallowed a sigh. That irritating catchphrase had been the first thing Lenny had ever said to him, two years ago in a cell in Bedford prison. Looking back, it always seemed like a scene from *Porridge* – Nick's anaemic Godber arriving in Lenny's Fletch-like abode – but at the time it had been less amusing. A mustachioed warder with stained armpits and bad breath had introduced them, and Lenny, stretched out on the bottom bunk in a pair of sweaty grey underpants, had shaken his head in disgust. 'Lenny knows,' he had muttered, pulling a roll-up from behind his ear. In common with most of his fellow inmates Lenny was an innocent man serving four and a half years for a crime he hadn't committed. When Nick arrived he took him on as the Birdman of Alcatraz might have adopted a wounded crow, teaching him new tricks and raising his own self-esteem through a combination of utter bullshit and practical advice. Lenny had met the Krays – of course he had – and he knew how to forge a dodgy MOT with a tray of brake fluid and a hairdryer. He had done business with the Colombians – implausibly meeting with the Medellin cartel in the snug of the White Lion on cribbage night – and he knew how to screw maximum disability benefit from the DWP. Nick had missed Lenny after his release and had been astonished to find him waiting with Sick Gloria at the prison gate upon his own discharge, six weeks later.

It had taken him a few days to realise why Lenny had come back for him: on the inside life had been safe, warm and predictable. Lenny had been someone on C Wing, and Nick had always deferred to the big man's greater wisdom. He had done so partly out of fear but mainly from a sense of propriety, feeling that their respective roles were the prescribed elements of a symbiotic relationship. Nick had felt lost and alone after Lenny's parole, but he hadn't realised that the feeling was mutual – that the fat, swaggering loudmouth's confidence was partially built on Nick's back. Once outside, in a one-room bedsit on maximum benefits, far from the family that had deserted him, Lenny discovered that existence had become dark, cold and capricious. Old friends had moved on, and new friends were hard to find in a small town where reputations died hard. On the long drive home from Bedford Lenny had explained to Nick that he was merely keeping an eye on him until he got back on his feet, but the truth was less altruistic. That last stretch inside had succeeded where all Lenny's previous sentences had failed, robbing him of his self-worth and stealing his self-confidence before throwing him back on the street. With no job, no home and no family, Lenny's easiest option would have been to secure himself another long stretch, but instead he'd taken a little bit of prison home and set him up in a bedsit across the hallway.

The ship rolled, tipping Nick into the scratched electric hand-dryer. He took a deep breath in an effort to keep down the vomit and leaned against the wall. 'What do you reckon on this will business?' he asked.

Lenny squeezed a blackhead from his nose and smeared it on the mirror. 'Ain't worth the paper it's written on without a signature. It's just something to string us along.' He poked out his tongue and farted.

'You think he's stringing us along?'

'Of course he is. Do you really believe he's going to lead us to a crock of gold? Wake up, Nicholas. This is the real world.'

'What about the coins he gave us?'

'Probably bought them at an antique fair.'

'So what are we doing here?'

Lenny lit a superking and raised his eyebrows. 'We're making an old man very happy. We'll have a little drive around Spain, stay in some nice hotels, have a few drinks, maybe meet a few *señoritas*. Then we'll take him home for his tea.'

'Then what?'

'Then I'll get my mate Eddie the Legal to come round and see him, get that will all legit, sit back and wait for the inevitable to happen. And don't be giving me that holier-than-thou routine. You're in this too, though Christ knows you're a spawny bastard.'

Nick shook his head. 'It doesn't add up. Why drag us all the way down to Spain if there's no reason to go?'

Lenny sighed. Nick had a long, long way to go. 'I never said there was no reason, only that there was no gold. Maybe one of his mates or someone got killed there in World War Two and he wants to see the grave one last time. Maybe he got some bird up the duff there – I don't know. He's got his reasons and he wanted us to come along to keep him company and the only way he was going to do that was by dangling a rabbit.'

'Carrot,' said Nick, 'and Spain wasn't in World War Two.'

'I meant World War One.'

'Wasn't in that one either.'

Lenny raised his eyebrows and pointed a finger.

'Check your history, sonny. World war – as in the whole world, at war. Everyone was in it. Otherwise it wouldn't have been a world war. Anyway,' he continued, changing the subject before Nick could object, 'who says it has to be a war? Could be anything . . .'

'Could be a bloody huge pile of gold, like he told us.'

'Except that. Get out on deck, Nickle-Arse. Feel that cold rain and that biting wind. This is the real world, not Nicky Crick's Wonderful World of Fluffy Unlikelihoods. Didn't you learn nothing inside? If you want happy endings out here you've got to make them happen at someone else's expense. This time Sidney gets his at our expense, then we get ours at his. It's a rare thing that's happening here – it's called a probiotic relationship.'

'Symbiotic,' said Nick.

'That's what I said,' replied Lenny. 'I'm going back to the bar.' He stepped out of the toilets and hesitated before leaning back through the door. 'One more thing: just because you and him are getting all chummy, doesn't mean you have to spill your guts to him.'

'About what?'

Lenny tapped the side of his nose. 'Lenny knows, and you know he knows. I don't want you using your jail sentence to gain sympathy.'

Nick was aghast. 'Fuck off!' he spluttered.

Lenny tapped his nose again. 'As long as we're straight on that.'

The more he drank in that empty bar, the more Lenny realised that he was going to have to keep a close eye on Nick over the next few days. The little sod had already taken a nominal 50 per cent of Sidney's estate, and Lenny could see him walking away with the lot if he wasn't careful. Lenny very rarely made mistakes in life, but he'd made up for past infallibility by bringing Nick in on this. Then again, what else could he have done? How was he to have known that Sidney would choose the one night he turned up with the staff to lay his cards on the table? Clearly the old man had been assessing Lenny's abilities and trustworthiness for a long time, and he had chosen that night to tell him about the imaginary gold. Why the fuck he'd invited Nick along was a complete mystery to Lenny – admittedly 33 per cent of non-existent treasure was neither here nor there – but what the hell was the old sod playing at with the last will and testament? He'd known Nick for less than a week and he was giving the miserable loser half of his estate. If Lenny hadn't been promised the other half, he might have challenged Sidney Starman's soundness of mind, but as it stood he was probably better to play along. This was a situation which required subtle and precise management, and subtlety was just one of the finely honed tools in Lenny's toolbox. He winked at the barmaid, a plump little French girl with hazel eyes and acne, and she frowned in reply, doing all she could to hold herself back. Many envied Lenny, but his effect on women was another curse of his cockney blood. Chasing his lager with another vodka Red Bull, he heaved himself from his stool and resumed his assault on the fruit machine. The barmaid would still be there when he finished.

Sidney Starman awoke to his second morning at sea with a stiff neck and a sore throat. He stood up slowly, rotating his head until the pain eased, then took a drop of Armagnac to soothe his throat. It was light outside — the salt-smeared windows told him no more than that, but when he went out on deck a pale sky was studded with the wind's ragged rearguard and the sea rolled like oil. The Iberian coast lay dark on the horizon like an advancing storm front, low and threatening, and Sidney grabbed the wet rail, standing on tiptoes to sniff deep lungfuls of Biscayne air in the hope that the faint smell of Spain would refresh his memory. He watched the Cantabrian shore with the fear and excitement of a wayward father returning to an abandoned family, his nervous apprehension tempered by the belief that his intention was righteous. It was almost disappointing that a country it had taken sixty-nine years of mental anguish to revisit had been reached after just twenty hours of physical misery. Certainly the sea had opposed his return. Would the land want him back?

He moved for'ard to where Nick stood in the bows of the ferry, his lank hair lifted by the slipstream. 'Thank you for tending to me last night,' he said, holding his cap on his head.

Nick shrugged and looked ahead. 'You're the boss.'

Buildings were visible on the shore now and small fishing boats were returning to the harbour.

'What is the provenance of that thing Mr Knowles does — you know, when he taps his nose, like this?'

'You mean "Lenny knows"? He read a book about Bernard Matthews and decided he needed a catchphrase like "bootiful" as a marketing tool. "Lenny knows" is supposed to be a bit like *Lenny Knowles*.' Nick looked round. 'Irritating, isn't it?'

Sidney nodded. 'I think it wears one down in the end.'

He leaned on the rail and looked at Nick. Gulls were wheeling around the trawlers and the first resinous tang of the land was in the air. The younger man was trying to look disinterested, bored even, but his mouth betrayed his excitement. It was an encouraging sign.

'Would you like to know more about the gold?' asked Sidney, wiping his glasses on his handkerchief.

'Up to you,' shrugged Nick, feigning nonchalance.

Sidney smiled and leaned closer, checking left and right for eavesdroppers.

'Like I told you back in Norfolk, it's mostly old coin. Very few ingots. It came from Spain's territories in Latin America and formed the greater part of the gold reserve of the Spanish state in Madrid. In 1936 the Spanish army, under Generals Franco, Mola and Quiepo de Llano, rose against the government to protect the state and the Church from what they perceived to be the "red Menace". The Germans and the Italians sided with them, while the legitimate government was backed by Mexico and the Soviet Union.' He looked up at a petrel that seemed to hover overhead. 'Do you enjoy history, Mr Crick?'

Nick watched surf breaking on the curved trigger of Somo beach, smelled strange food and smoke, heard the ship's Tannoy, the rip of the sea beneath the bows, the excitement of the gulls overhead and the distant clang of the approaching port. 'I enjoy freedom, Mr Starman,' he replied. 'Wasn't that what the Spanish War was all about?'

Sidney sighed. 'Didn't seem that way to me.'

'So what about the gold?'

'Ah well,' nodded Sidney slowly, 'that's the thing. The Spanish reserve was held in the vaults of the Bank of Spain, in Madrid, and by late summer 1936 Franco's forces were on the outskirts of the city. The Republican government was in panic – the future seemed to hold little but blindfolds and last fags – and any advice seemed better than none. Joe Stalin had plenty of advice. He pointed out that the loss of Madrid would not necessarily bugger the country, but the loss of its capital most certainly would. He recommended that the entire gold reserve be transferred to Moscow, for safe keeping, from where it could be used as a sort of current account against which to buy arms and equipment. Look at that gunboat.'

A pale grey frigate was alongside the Muelle de Puertochico, white-uniformed sailors leaning on her seaward rail.

'F73,' read Nick from her bow. 'The *Cataluña*.'

'My eyesight was that good once,' said Sidney with grudging admiration.

'Your memory seems all right,' replied Nick. 'Did the Spanish government go for Stalin's plan?'

Sidney nodded. 'What else could they do? They were being crushed between two ideologies, and only one seemed friendly.' He took off his cap and ran his hand across his scalp. 'Stalin had a vicious sod called Orlov working as a security adviser to the Republican government and charged him with the supervision of the transfer of the gold. He was supposed to be cooperating with a Spanish fellow called Negrin, who was then the Minister of Finance, but I think Orlov did as he pleased. Negrin had arranged for the gold to be transported in great secrecy from Madrid to the Mediterranean coast. There were five hundred and sixty tons of the stuff and they hid it in caves in the Naval Arsenal at Cartagena. Orlov had four Russian ships sail from Odessa to pick it up, and on the night of 26 October 1936 forty trucks shuttled the gold to the docks. No one knew what it was, and if anyone had their suspicions they either swallowed them or choked on them. They say Stalin laughed his head off when it arrived in Moscow. "Just as they cannot see their own ears," he said, "they shall not see their gold again."'

Nick smiled. 'Good story. So why are we going to Spain if the gold went to Russia?'

The air was split by a thunderous, baritone belch. Sidney glanced around: Lenny was on deck. He leaned close to Nick. 'Because one hundred boxes never made it to the docks. And if you can tell a better tale, Mr Crick, I swear to God you'll have to tell a lie.'

3

Sidney disembarked as a foot passenger and succeeded in slipping through Spanish Immigration as easily as he had evaded Passport Control in Plymouth. He was waiting at the port gates as Sick Gloria wheezed past.

'I'm not having this forgotten-passport bollocks,' announced Lenny as the old man climbed aboard. 'I reckon you've got one and you're just doing this cloak-and-dagger stuff to impress us.'

'Why on earth would I want to impress you, Mr Knowles?' asked Sidney.

Lenny lit a fag while he searched for a riposte, somehow making eye contact with a pair of motorcycle cops passing the van from the other direction. 'What're they looking at?' he growled.

Nick leaned forward to watch the motorcyclists in the wing-mirror. 'Nothing,' he reported. 'They've gone.'

'Best not to antagonise the Spanish police, gentlemen,' warned Sidney.

'I couldn't half go for a full English,' muttered Lenny. 'I'm Hank Marvin. What do they do for breakfast round here?'

'Bread, olive oil, tomatoes,' replied Sidney 'Bit of cheese, I suppose, and some sausage.'

Lenny shook his head. 'It's fucking pitiful how people have to live in these Third World countries. It's a global economy now – you'd think the fry-up would have made it to the four corners by now. S'pose we'll have to go for McDonald's.'

'I'm not having McDonald's,' declared Nick.

'You can't be poncey about your food now, Nickle-Arse,' countered Lenny. 'When you're abroad it's all there is, unless they've got Kentucky.'

'Stop there,' ordered Sidney, pointing at a roadhouse called La Casa Pepe.

'It's foreign,' protested Lenny.

'Of course it is, Mr Knowles. It's all there is when you're abroad.'

'I'm not eating no foreign muck,' warned Lenny.

'Fine,' nodded Sidney. 'Will you join me, Mr Crick?'

Lenny watched as Nick and the old man went into the transport café, feeling a headache coming on that Anadin couldn't handle. Nick's disloyalty was going beyond mere pain and threatened to become a terminal condition. He'd had quiet words with the lad back in Norfolk, on the road, and aboard the ship, letting him know exactly what was expected of him, and the little sod still refused to take heed. As his official sidekick, Nick's place was at Lenny's side, not at that of a doddery old sod who insisted on eating dodgy foreign rubbish just to be different. Nick didn't even like foreign food – he never went near a kebab house back home – and his going along with this continental breakfast non-sense was nothing less than a betrayal. They were probably in there right now, eating olives, anchovies and other fancy stuff, plotting how they would leave Lenny behind next time he went to the toilet. Lenny tapped his nose subconsciously – he would-n't be laying any long cables while these two were around. Two was company and three was a crowd, so someone – someone sneaky and untrustworthy – would have to go. He hitched up his shell pants, locked the van and sashayed into the café, wrinkling his nose against the hot blast of black tobacco smoke, garlic and loud chatter that met him on the threshold.

A table of truck drivers paused in their discussion to watch Lenny as he passed, their casual interest instantly detected by Sidney. He glanced at Nick, noting with disappointment how road soiled the pair had allowed themselves to become after such a short time. While Sidney himself was washed, shaved and wearing a clean shirt, neither of his employees had made the slightest effort and both appeared to be wearing exactly what they had worn when they had left Norfolk two days earlier. They looked dishevelled, seedy and poor, and while that didn't matter, the fact that they were conspicuous did.

Lenny pulled out a chair and sprawled, his arms crossed and his legs stretched deep into Nick's personal space. Nick responded by shifting his chair to the right, nonchalantly pushing a slice of *pan con tomate* into his mouth.

'Are you going to eat, Mr Knowles?' asked Sidney.

Lenny shook his head. 'Not that shite, Mr S. Anyway, I'm jurassic.'

'I beg your pardon?'

'Jurassic. Boracic lint. Skint.' A cruel run of early morning luck on the ferry's fruit machines had robbed him of his funds.

'What about you, Mr Crick? How do you intend to pay for your breakfast?'

Nick looked up, startled. 'I thought you were paying,' he mumbled through a mouthful of bread.

Sidney sighed. 'Well, you may be the subjects of a benign dictatorship but you shouldn't be dependent on me for your day-to-day needs. What's the standard *per diem*?'

Nick had no idea. He looked at Lenny. Lenny didn't know what *per diem* meant and Nick guessed so from his expression.

'Daily rate,' he explained. '*Per diem* means "per day".'

Lenny glared at him. 'You're not the only one who speaks French round here mate!' He scratched his chin. 'I normally charge anywhere from three upwards, depending.'

'Three what?' asked Sidney.

'Hundred.'

Sidney smiled. 'And what does one get for three hundred pounds a day, Mr Knowles?'

Lenny slid open a box of matches and started splitting them lengthways with his thumbnail. 'General building, plastering, third fix, groundwork, waste disposal, er, roofing, guttering, chimney-sweeping.'

'Pest control,' added Nick. 'He's good with wasps.'

Lenny nodded. 'Yeah, wasps, rats, mice, cockroaches, ants, rabbits, pigeons, stray dogs, donkeys – anything like that.'

'What else?' asked Sidney.

'Consultancy work: you know, your marketing, brand image, product placement, PR, all that sort of thing.' He lit a superking with a split match and took a long drag, his hand over his mouth and watching for the moment when Sidney took the bait. Sidney sent his glance straight back at him, an expression of cold bemusement on his papery face. Lenny took another suck. 'IT,' he continued. 'I'm a bit of a whizz on computers, faxes, tellies, microwaves, washing machines – anything technical.' He waited for a response from Sidney. None came, so he continued. 'Motors: private and commercial. MOTs, resprays, bit of buying and selling. Got a good eye for a bargain.'

'I take it Sick Gloria is the exception to that rule?' asked Sidney archly.

'Sick Gloria is a special case,' replied Lenny. 'Anyway, you're a man who likes the finer things, Mr S. What about art and antiques? You know Lovejoy, off the telly? Lovable East Anglian antique-dealing rogue? Based on me, that show was. I sold a fireplace to some TV people who had one of those barn conversions in Suffolk and next thing there's a series on the telly. Not a coincidence. So, art and antiques – I'm your man.'

Sidney was watching him with a thoughtful expression. He switched his eyes to Nick. 'And you, Mr Crick?'

'Er, insurance. I was assistant to the deputy regional risk services manager.'

'He had his own desk,' added Lenny.

'Sounds riveting,' said Sidney. 'Your current rate?'

42

'Whatever I can get,' shrugged Nick. 'Don't have my own desk any more.'

'Tell you what,' said Sidney. 'Since I'm paying for your hotel accommodation and most of your meals, and seeing as I have no need of any of your many professional skills, I'm going to pay you thirty euros a day for incidentals.'

Nick was delighted with the deal. Lenny was furious, but he bit his tongue, choosing to wait until he had Sidney on his own before negotiating a rise. Nick was overvalued at thirty euros a day, but Lenny was a skilled professional. Paying him the same as Nick was an insult, and Lenny suspected it was intended. He took a deep breath as he relieved himself in a cracked urinal. Rocks had been thrown in his face but mighty rivers flowed around them, over them, and ultimately wore them down to silt.

The conversation in the restaurant died away as he returned from the gents', and he half expected to find Nick and Sidney gone and a roomful of grinning foreign faces. No one was smiling, however, and the eager chatter had been replaced by the scraping of chairs against the tiled floor as the Spanish drivers rose to leave. Two motorcycle cops stood at the bar, their backs to the counter as they surveyed the room. Lenny recognised them as the leather-clad pair who had passed the van at the port gates. Of all the bars in Santander they had to walk into this one. If a man was inclined to paranoia he might well be afraid, but Lenny was long used to the unexpected and coincidental appearance of policemen. He raised his eyebrows to his companions and jerked his eyes towards the door. Sidney nodded, dropped payment on the table and rose. Nick followed. The cops watched as they passed.

'That was a bit tense,' said Nick as they stepped into the pale morning sunshine.

'Guardia Civil,' explained Sidney. 'Professional bastards created by the Second Republic to keep the people in their place. Did you see how the restaurant emptied when they came in?'

'No such thing as an innocent trucker,' observed Lenny, fumbling with the van keys.

'Let Mr Crick drive, Mr Knowles,' ordered Sidney quietly.

'You're all right, Mr S,' insisted Lenny. 'I'm fine.'

'You're drunk, and you smell like a distillery. If those policemen see you drive away they'll have us all. Let Mr Crick drive and don't question my decisions.'

Lenny heaved a deep sigh and tossed the keys to Nick. 'You'll be sorry,' he warned.

Gloria started first time but refused to roll. As Nick struggled to engage first gear the cab filled with the acrid smell of burning clutch. 'Can't get it in gear,' he complained.

'Try reverse first,' suggested Lenny. 'Sometimes she likes to go backwards before she goes forwards.'

Nick stirred the gearstick and nodded. 'Got it.' He released the clutch and Gloria rolled slowly backwards, her rusty rear step making gentle contact with the front wheel of one of the Guardia Civil motorcycles. Unaware of its presence, Nick stepped on the accelerator and Gloria jumped back another four feet, knocking both bikes off their stands and pushing them across the parking lot.

'Hold up a minute, Nickle-Arse,' called Lenny. 'You've hit something.' He opened the passenger door and stepped out just as the two horror-struck cops exited the bar.

'Have I done any damage?' called Nick breezily.

Lenny made a swift appraisal of the situation. His unregistered, untaxed, uninsured van had just flattened two police bikes while being driven by a parolee under licence not to leave the country. He was subject to similar restrictions himself and the third member of his party was apparently travelling without a passport. Neither of the two rapidly approaching coppers appeared to have a sense of humour, and Nick seemed to have succeeded in engaging first gear. Lenny leapt back into his seat. 'Leg it,' he suggested. The cops' expressions of grim dismay turned to open-mouthed shock as the rusting Transit leapt onto the highway in a low cloud of pungent blue smoke.

'What on earth are you doing?' cried Sidney. 'You're heading back towards the docks!'

'Don't question my decisions,' retorted Lenny. 'Nick: pull over and let me drive.'

Three hundred metres behind them the two furious policemen were struggling to right their bikes as Lenny slipped behind the wheel. 'I can't believe it,' he gasped. 'We've only been here five fucking minutes.'

'Couldn't agree more,' nodded Sidney. 'It's like travelling with Laurel and Hardy.'

'Stay cool,' advised Nick.

'Nickle-Arse?'

'Yes?'

'Shut the fuck up. Lenny knows.' With one eye on the road and another on his wing-mirror, he judged the moment perfectly and swung a right-hander into a garbage-strewn side road leading towards the wharf. Accelerating, he took the first left into a canyon of abandoned warehouses before bumping over the kerb and gunning Gloria through a gap in a rusting chain-link fence.

Sidney raised an eyebrow as he polished his glasses. 'Was that strictly necessary, Mr Knowles, or are you merely trying to impress me?'

'Strictly fucking necessary, Mr S,' nodded Lenny, reversing into a derelict loading bay and killing the engine. 'Michael bleeding Schumacher here just ran over two police bikes and Gloria can't afford to pay for the damage.' The throb of motorcycle engines and the crackle of police radios echoed through the crumbling brick gullies as he spoke. 'As I was saying,' he continued, 'Nickle-Arse here is just along for the ride. In future, Mr S, you'd be well advised to leave the clever stuff to Lenny.'

Sidney bit his lip and tried to recall past examples of the clever stuff to which Mr Knowles referred. The adventure seemed doomed to end in a Spanish jail before it had even started, but then failure was always a possibility where these two were concerned.

'Nip out and see if they've gone,' whispered Ollie.

'Sod off,' replied Stan. 'You go.'

'Is this van stolen, Mr Knowles?' asked Sidney. 'I have a right to know.'

Lenny winced. 'Not stolen. Taken in lieu of services rendered.'

'Meaning?

'The pikeys from what it was procured nicked it, if you must know.'

'From other pikeys who stole it from tinkers who nicked it from a building firm in Diss,' added Nick. 'Gloria's been passed through the underworld like one of those Eastern European sex slaves you hear so much about.'

'And never seem to meet,' said Lenny ruefully.

'And now the Guardia Civil are part of her sad history,' observed Sidney.

Lenny blew smoke at the windscreen. The old man was beginning to get on his mammaries with all his questions, and he clearly knew nothing about cops. Lenny had been running from policemen since he was eleven. 'I think they'll be more concerned with giving Nick a kicking for crushing their bikes. Gloria's tragic past will be a secondary concern.'

'Do you think they'll call for back-up?' asked Nick.

Lenny nodded. 'They'll probably call up a helicopter, get dogs out here, set up roadblocks . . .'

Nick bit his lip. 'Why did you tell me to drive off? We could have talked our way out of it. Mr Starman speaks Spanish – I'm sure they'd have understood.'

Lenny let a long sigh fog the windscreen. 'Do you know what you are, Nick?'

'Don't start.'

'You're a bleeding liability is what you are. The best thing you could do is get the next boat back home and leave the treasure-hunting to the professionals.'

'So you're a professional treasure-hunter now, are you?'

'We're not talking about me, Nickle-Arse. We're talking about you, and if you were making the decisions we'd all be banged up in some Spanish nick right now. I did what I had to do as the situation presented itself, and bleeding good thing too.'

'Hear, hear,' called Sidney, somewhat flippantly. 'Drop of Armagnac anyone?'

A long-forgotten feeling was rippling through his body, travelling beneath his skin and lifting the hairs on his arms. It made his knees weak, his stomach shrink and his throat dry, exactly as it had the last time he had entered Spain illegally. That time there had been thirteen of them, six nationalities and all varying shades of red. They had travelled overland from Paris in the back of a furniture van, disembarking stiff-legged and sore-arsed some time after midnight in a silent, cloud-bound village of dripping stone high in the Pyrenees. Some of the men carried suitcases, others canvas kitbags stuffed with possessions they would curse as they struggled to haul them over the mountains and into Spain. A short-haired French girl fed them stale bread and hard cheese and poured tiny glasses of *eau de vie* from a painted bottle in a barn on the edge of the hamlet before they stumbled onward and upward through the overcast, hobnailed boots wrapped in sacking and leather soles slipping on the wet scree. Outwardly the men maintained a dispassionate air of long-suffering boredom but inside surely each had been grinning as hard as Sidney. From Calais to the border no one had spent a farthing on food or drink and everywhere they went they had been welcomed, albeit discreetly, as heroes. Their cause was righteous, their intentions noble and their victory assured. Despite their overt atheism, the men of the International Brigades had been modern-day crusaders, fighting for the new religion, and one day, Sidney had been absolutely certain, gentlemen in England would think themselves accursed they were not there.

Lenny insisted they wait an hour before leaving their hiding-place and then passed the time berating Nick, drinking vodka and smoking. At last he checked his imaginary watch and nodded. 'That'll do it. Let's go and get some lunch.' He screwed the cap back on the Smirnoff and leaned forward to turn the key, catching Sidney's concerned eye as he did so. 'What now?'

'You're drunk,' announced Sidney. 'You can't drive.'

Lenny shook his head. 'Don't you worry yourself, Mr S. You'll—'

Sidney cut him off. 'You're drunk, and you're not driving. Take his place, Mr Crick.'

'After what happened last time?' gasped Lenny. 'He'll probably blow the fucking thing up this time . . .'

Sidney silenced him with a threatening finger as Nick started the engine.

'Get on with it!' urged Lenny.

'Won't go into gear,' replied Nick through clenched teeth.

'Don't force it,' warned Lenny. 'You'll bugger the clutch.'

Nick put both feet on the clutch pedal and both hands on the gearstick, applying maximum force at both ends. At last there was a gentle but unfamiliar clunk from deep within the gearbox.

'Got it,' grinned Nick, stepping on the accelerator. The engine roared and then there was a sickening, smoky bang as the entire clutch assembly exploded. Nick looked at Lenny. 'Oops,' he said.

It was an inadequate response to a discouraging situation. Lenny scratched his backside, looked in the wing-mirror and then at Sidney. 'He's only gone and killed Gloria,' he sighed. 'Lenny knows, you know.'

They gathered around Gloria's corpse, furtively glancing at

her mortal wound like men who'd never seen death before. A look beneath her smoke-blackened bonnet was enough to confirm her demise – the overheated, seized-up clutch assembly had blown a hole through the engine block, draining black oil to pool among the weeds like blood from a severed artery.

'What now?' asked Nick.

Sidney shrugged. 'We walk, I suppose.'

'Walk?' cried Lenny. He never walked. Walking was for women and children. Geezers drove. 'Why can't we rent a motor?'

'From where?' asked Sidney, glancing around. 'We still have to walk to the rental office.'

Lenny shook his head. 'Nickle-Arse walks to the office. We wait here with the luggage.'

'I don't have a credit card,' said Nick.

'Borrow El Sid's.'

'El Sid?' repeated Sidney. 'I rather like that.'

'But my licence is in my name.'

Lenny shook his head and looked at Sidney. 'He always has to make things difficult. Always dragging others in to sort out his mess.'

'I'll have to go with him,' replied Sidney. 'You can wait here if you like and we'll come back for you.'

Lenny smiled. He was working with amateurs, and they wouldn't lose him that easily. 'Tell you what,' he said. 'Let's all stick together.'

They were in the dead margins of a once-busy port, a neglected warren of broken glass, burned-out cars and graffiti. Rusted signs on broken fences issued empty threats of pursuit by wolf-like Alsatians and prosecution by grim-faced judges, and the only life apparent in the area was a railway track along which long lines of wagons awaited discharge at the dockside.

'Probably safest if we follow the line,' suggested Sidney as they came to an unguarded level crossing. 'It's the best way of avoiding the police.' His possessions were packed in an old canvas rucksack that hung easily from his narrow shoulders.

Nick followed, lugging a small suitcase. Lenny, carrying an enormous Nike sports bag, was at the back. The tracks curved gently between abandoned warehouses adorned with the faded paint of outdated advertisements before branching out into a crowded goods yard.

'Maybe we could jump a train,' opined Nick, peering into an empty goods wagon.

Sidney paused to look at him. 'Maybe we could,' he nodded.

Lenny pushed past, shaking his head. 'We're not jumping no bleeding trains. We're renting a Corsa. End of.'

Nick shrugged and shuffled along the roadstone. Sidney remained standing by the open door of the goods wagon. 'It's not such a bad idea, you know,' he said. 'These plates here say the train is going south to Palencia. It would save us a great deal of money, and it would be fun.'

Lenny kept walking.

'You don't strike me as a man who's had an awful lot of fun in your life, Mr Knowles,' called Sidney. 'When I was your age . . .' He didn't finish the sentence.

When he was their age adventure was more than a product one bought from a travel agent. Jumping trains was a forgotten skill these days, but back in 1937 Sidney had been taught by men who had learned the craft from those who'd ridden the world's rails from Berlin to Biloxi, from the Caucasus to the Dust Bowl. Those men had long since become dust themselves, but after seventy years Spanish rolling stock seemed all but unchanged. He ran his fingers along the rusted rungs of a roof-access ladder, his aged senses reinvigorated by nostalgia. The iron, the wood and the grease smelled and felt the same, the heavy doors could still chop your fingers off and where once had been stencilled the advice not to exceed one hundred men, or twenty horses, was now painted a warning prohibiting the transport of hazardous substances. Beyond this grimy yard Spain too would be unchanged but for new signs on old roads and modern houses in ancient towns. The people would look no different, the language would sound the same and the bread would taste as it had before – if anything, the land was safer than it had been in centuries. Sidney rested his hands on the cold door runners, turning his head to the right just in time to see Lenny shove Nick before the bickering couple disappeared around a curved wall of wagons. He wondered if he should let them go and carry on alone. Then he glanced to his left and wondered how long the three youths in hooded tops had been watching him.

'Your problem', declared Nick, 'is that you're paranoid. You think everybody's trying to rip you off all the time.'

'Who told you I was paranoid?' demanded Lenny, his trainers crunching on oil-stained track ballast. 'You can't go around making great sweeping statements on people's mental health, Nickle-Arse. It's rude.'

'And shoving me in the back isn't?'

'You deserved that for being a tosser.'

'So I'm a tosser now, am I?'

'You'll always be a tosser, Nick. You've got no loyalty. We've only been here two minutes and you've already betrayed me.'

'Betrayed you? Voting for a continental breakfast rather than a McMuffin hardly constitutes treachery.'

'Doesn't matter what you did: you were siding with El Sid and it means I can't depend on you.'

'Depend on me for what?'

Lenny paused, his fat face red in the morning sunshine. 'You see, Nickle-Arse? The fact that you have to ask that question says it all.' He strode away in haughty dismay. 'Lenny knows, and he's very, very disappointed.'

Nick shook his head. 'Not as disappointed as Sidney. He must think he's fallen in with a right couple of clowns.' He looked back down the track. 'Where is the old boy anyway?'

'See what I mean?' seethed Lenny. 'You can't even keep tabs on a bloody pensioner. Go and find him.'

Nick dropped his bag and headed back down the track. Lenny Knowles never admitted liability, never accepted responsibility and never, ever, apologised. He was an obdurate adherent to an unwritten rule of pig-headed, working-class obstinacy, and Nick found it easier to comply than to contend. There would have been no pleasure in his company whatsoever had it not been for the certainty that, like Wile E. Coyote, Lenny would always succeed in bursting his own bubble. He kept all his eggs in one basket, and the higher and faster he juggled them, the sooner he would be wiping them off his face. That alone made it worth sticking around. At least that's what Nick told himself.

He started to smile as he rounded the curve but got no further than a gasp. Sidney was sprawled in the siding, a huddle of worn flannel and gabardine in the gravel. Three youths, heads hidden in grey hoods, were standing over the old man, their legs spread wide and their bodies bent low as they rifled his pockets. With the instincts of a rat, one of the three caught Nick's horrified stare and returned it with menaces, his eyes glinting like a dagger in the dark above a long nose and a daintily bearded chin. Like a bloody-snouted hyena eyeing an indignant fawn, the mugger seemed to be inviting Nick to make a move, but Nick couldn't feel his legs. The terror was like cold mercury in his stomach and his veins, its weight pushing him into the ground.

He watched as his observer reported his presence to his accomplices, shaking his head in mute terror as they left the old man in the dirt and advanced slowly, casually, upon him, calling soft words in a harsh language. Suddenly Nick's sympathetic nervous system woke up and offered him the option of fighting or flight. To Nick, this was no choice at all, and he took off as fast as his leaden legs could carry him. The robbers followed, their trainers crunching on the ballast as they fanned out in his wake.

'Help!' screamed Nick, and two hundred yards up the line Lenny saw him coming. He shook his head wearily, took a long drag on his superking and pushed himself away from the wagon he'd been leaning on. He waited until Nick was twenty feet away before stubbing out his cigarette, and as his three pursuers came into view Lenny stepped into theirs. He grabbed Nick's arm as he ran past. 'What are you running from, Nickle-Arse?' he hissed.

'Have a wild guess,' gasped Nick.

'These wankers?' He pushed Nick aside and took a step forward. 'Where's El Sid?'

'I think they mugged him.' The muggers were still advancing, but slowly now, issuing threats and challenges in a strange language.

'Did you see him?'

Nick thought for a moment. He'd seen an old man being robbed and beaten and he'd done nothing to save him. 'No,' he replied. 'I was nearly there when I met these three coming the other way. They looked like trouble, and when I turned to come back they chased me.'

'Whatever.' Lenny knew when he was being lied to. The pause was too long, the answer too detailed. Nick had never been called upon to fight before, not even in prison. Fights had been Lenny's responsibility when they were cellmates. Nick had already told him that the last time he'd been involved in a punch-up had been when he was eleven, and since then he'd become an upwardly mobile young professional happy to compensate for his inability to defend himself by playing football every other Saturday with like-minded young men. Like so many of his generation, he could talk the talk in a lagered-up mob of his peers, but when faced with true thuggery too ugly, too trivial and too dull to have been vicariously experienced in the multiplex or on TV, he found himself unable to walk the walk. Lenny, on the other hand, had grown up with violence.

Beaten by his mother, by various uncles, by his cousins and by his neighbours, he had long ago learned that it never hurt as much as you thought it would. Lenny was not the sort of man who gave up after experiencing the nauseating shock of a punch in the mouth, the blinding pain of a well-placed head-butt or the stomach-churning ache of a knee in the balls, and his tendency to be the last man standing had earned him an unenviable reputation at home. Rural policemen treated him as a training exercise, and any village idiot who fancied himself would have a pop at him before closing time. In short, Lenny Knowles was a useful scrapper.

'Look,' pleaded Nick, 'it's not worth anyone else getting hurt over this. Let's just give them something and they'll leave us alone.'

'Bollocks to that,' scoffed Lenny, striding towards the tallest of the three, his voice rising to a bellow. 'I'm going to tear their fucking heads off!'

His target stood his ground, holding up his palms as though asking what on earth he had done to offend this big, red-faced man.

Lenny came chest-to-chest with him, leaning into his hood. 'Give it back,' he shouted.

'Lenny! Leave it!' cried Nick.

The mugger screwed up his nose as though offended by Lenny's breath and grinned at his companions. It wasn't a particularly smart move. Lenny tipped his head back and snapped it forward, hammering his brow into the thug's nose. There was a wet crunch, like a cabbage dropped from a great height, and the mugger collapsed.

'That took the twinkle from his eyes,' observed Lenny, pinching the bridge of his nose. He sniffed, eyeing the remaining pair as one fumbled with a short knife. 'Want some respect, do you?' he growled, stepping over the fallen robber and lunging for the knifeman. The blade, a cheap Chinese lock-knife, clattered to the gravel as Lenny's wildly aimed roundhouse caught the youth on the side of the head. He staggered sideways, hands raised in surrender, then turned and followed his fleeing companion. 'Not like the films, is it, Nickle-Arse?' panted Lenny, bending down to retrieve the knife. 'This is real life now, my son. One or two whacks and it's all over.'

The head-butted mugger had rolled into the foetal position, hiding his bloody face in his hands and drawing his knees up to his chest.

Lenny snatched the skinny brown fingers away and tore the hood from the shaved head. 'I asked you nicely first time,' he said. 'Now I'm asking you again: give back what you nicked.' The youth tried to reply but Lenny cut him short with four wickedly placed kicks to his skull, his face, his throat and his ribs before dragging the grey sweatshirt from his body and inspecting the pockets.

'What you waiting for, Nickle-Arse?'

'I'm waiting for you.'

'Come over here and give him a slap.'

Nick shook his head. 'I can't.'

Lenny sighed. 'Tosser.' His search had turned up a bunch of keys, a packet of condoms, a tiny bottle of breath-freshener and half a packet of Camel Mild. 'No wallet,' he announced. 'Those other fuckers must have had it. Let's go and rescue El Sid.'

Huffing and puffing like a steam train, Lenny marched down the tracks with Nick shuffling behind him like a dog in need of tranquillisers. They found Sidney propped against the rusty wheels of a goods van, dabbing a split lip with a beige handkerchief.

'They got my wallet,' he croaked. 'Three of them. They weren't Spanish – maybe from the Balkans.'

'We met them,' said Nick. 'Lenny laid one of them out up the line.'

'Good for you, Mr Knowles. You just missed the other two. They ran past a couple of minutes ago. I presume—'

'You presume all you want, Mr S, but it won't bring your wallet back. I went for the most likely contender but he'd already shifted it. Was that all the cash we had?'

'Regrettably, Mr Knowles.'

'They'll be long gone by now,' muttered Lenny.

'Let it go,' pleaded Nick. 'We'll manage.'

Lenny looked at him. 'How?'

'Yes, how will we manage, Mr Crick?'

'Ignore him, Mr S,' advised Lenny. 'It's like talking to Rain Man. I bet we haven't even got enough cash to catch the ferry home.'

Sidney rummaged through his trouser pockets. 'Six euros,' he announced.

'Fucking marvellous,' seethed Lenny. 'This is all your fault, Nickle-Arse.'

'My fault? How do you reach that conclusion?'

'If you hadn't run over the police bikes . . .'

'Yeah, and who didn't tell me they were parked behind Gloria?'

'Who didn't fucking look where he was driving?'

'And who told me to run away when an apology would probably have been enough?'

'And who couldn't be arsed to look after Mr S in a dangerous, crime-ridden dockyard?'

'Gentlemen!' yelled Sidney. 'I'm fine, thank you for asking. Backside's a bit sore and I've cut my lip but otherwise I'm fighting fit. I suggest we give thanks for our physical wellbeing and throw ourselves at fortune's feet, particularly since we have no means for repatriation.'

As Lenny struggled to comprehend the old man's meaning a distant impact sent a squeal of anticipation through the line of wagons.

'Fortune has smiled,' cried Sidney. 'All aboard!' He clambered to his feet, wincing with the effort and brushing the dust from his coat. 'This one looks as good as any,' he declared, inspecting the open goods wagon. 'Nice and clean and no holes in the sides.'

'Have you done this before, Mr Starman?' asked Nick.

Sidney smiled. 'I've done a lot of things before.'

Three hundred yards ahead, the signal light flashed green and the driver released the brakes. The train seemed to sag, rolling backwards with hydraulic sighs and steely creaks before straining against its couplings.

'Off we go,' cried Sidney, feeling the resurrection of a long-dead adolescent excitement. 'Make a step.'

He cupped his hands to show Nick what he meant. Nick shrank away from the possibility of human contact passing responsibility to Lenny with a fearful glance. Lenny sighed and heaved Sidney and the bags aboard.

'Throw up some roadstone, Mr Crick,' called Sidney, 'for the fire.'

Nick grabbed a handful of ballast and placed his hands on the step to haul himself aboard. Sidney pushed him back.

'We'll need more than that – enough stones to bed a fire or we'll freeze. Quick, and see if you can find some wood!'

'Bloody hell,' seethed Nick, scooping handfuls of the egg-sized stones into the boxcar.

Lenny hauled himself aboard, pulled his vodka from his bag and lit a Camel. 'There's knights,' he observed, then he nodded towards Nick, 'and there's serfs.'

'I see you more as a yeoman, Mr Knowles, but I catch your drift.'

'What's a yeoman?'

'A kind of knight,' lied Sidney.

'In shining armour, Mr S.' He winked and touched his nose in a knowing gesture. 'Get a move on Nickle-Arse.'

The train lurched as the driver threw the deadman's handle, throwing Lenny off balance and sending Nick sprawling as he bent to lift a pallet from the trackside. Sidney saw him rise to his knees, rubbing the back of his head with a pained expression before a lamp bracket on the following car knocked him down again. He rolled clear, staggering to his feet as the last car passed him, leaving him standing in a weak beam of sunlight.

Lenny joined Sidney at the door, cigarette ash and vodka staining his shellsuit, and watched Nick diminish by the curving line. The train was still gathering speed, and a fully committed sprint might have made it attainable, but Nick had already surrendered to despair.

'Run, you silly bastard!' called Lenny.

'He's not going to catch us now,' observed Sidney.

'Where are we going?'

'God knows,' admitted Sidney. 'Tell him to meet us in Palencia.'

Lenny held on to the door frame and leaned into the slipstream but Nick was hidden behind the curve of the train.

'Valencia, Nickle-Arse,' he called. 'We'll wait for you in Valencia.' He could have shouted louder, but as Sidney had pointed out only minutes before, fortune had smiled. 'He's gone,' he told Sidney, shaking his head.

The old man pushed his suitcase into a corner with the toe of his brogue and sat on it, his arms crossed. 'Can we manage without him?' he asked.

Sidney Starman had grown up in a time of sudden loss and he spared no sentiment for absent friends. His concerns were purely practical, and since Nick had proved himself singularly lacking in any practical skills whatsoever Sidney had few concerns over his disappearance. The young man had been affable company and had offered an attentive ear but his presence seemed superfluous to the needs of the mission.

Lenny was slightly more emotional in his response. 'I suppose we'll manage, Mr S,' he nodded. 'Nick was a lovely lad but he was out of his depth. If he's got any sense, he'll make his way back to the ferry terminal and scrounge a passage home.' He glanced at Sidney, checking to see if his words were pressing the right buttons. 'I'll miss him though.'

'I'm sure you will,' sighed Sidney. 'Pull that door closed and I'll kindle a fire.'

Lenny watched in the gloom as Sidney arranged the rocks in a circular bed the size of a tea tray. Fortune, he reflected, was a funny old bird. Two hours ago it looked like it would be he who was abandoned on the wrong side of the tracks, left behind because he didn't like foreign food and couldn't talk about poxy wars that no one had ever heard of. Now, by dint of a chain of events he would never have predicted, he was sole heir to the Starman estate, just as long as the two of them didn't perish in a railroad blaze. 'I'm not happy about lighting a fire in here,' he said as the train headed south at a steady sixty miles per hour.

'It's perfectly safe,' replied Sidney, slicing slivers from the floorboards with a worn-out pocket knife. 'I learned this from a man who was taught by hobos on the Union Pacific in the 1890s.'

'Fascinating,' muttered Lenny. The luxury, all-expenses-paid European tour was going distinctly pear-shaped. He watched as the old man arranged the kindling in a fragile, tent-like heap and stuffed shaved splinters into its heart. 'How long will we wait for Nick in Valencia?'

Sidney looked up. 'It's *Palencia*. Valencia's on the other side of the country. I think we should give Mr Crick a day or so to rejoin us. Alternatively, we could try to jump a train back to Santander if you think he might be waiting for us. What do you think?'

Lenny shook his head. 'Nick'll be on the next boat home. Trust me.'

'We'll give him twenty-four hours. Lighter?'

'Try these,' offered Lenny, throwing a box of matches. Each had been split in two, offering two flimsy lights for the price of one, and they snapped in Sidney's trembling hands before he could kindle the fire.

'Give 'em here,' said Lenny, and in moments an eager yellow flame threw crazy shadows against the boxcar's walls.

'Lovely,' smiled Sidney. 'These floors have some sort of treatment on them – makes wonderful kindling – and see the rocks? They absorb the heat – stop the whole carriage going up – then they act like a radiator.'

'T'riffic, Mr S,' nodded Lenny distractedly. He was staring into the flames and all he could see was that tidy little Norfolk cottage with UPVC windows, oil-fired central heating, new kitchen and bathroom and a pretty little sign saying 'For Sale' in the lane. As soon as the mad old bugger's hip started hurting he'd abandon this half-arsed adventure and they could head home, ideally at the expense of Her Majesty's government.

'No smoke, neither,' boasted Sidney, shuffling closer to the flame. 'It's because I chose the right spot and it all gets sucked away.' He pointed at an irregular charred circle overlapped by his own fireplace. 'See that? Others have ridden the same car.'

'Well I never, Mr S,' muttered Lenny, unscrewing the cap from his bottle and taking a long swig.

They'd have to file a snidey robbery report in order to explain Sidney's lack of a passport, and even if the authorities were able to check whether he'd had one in the first place they wouldn't leave a doddery old sod stranded in a hostile land. Lenny took a thoughtful sip of his Smirnoff and released a thunderous fart. He could pass himself off as Sidney's carer, a role he had been quietly fulfilling for months until Nick had muscled in at the last minute like some smooth-talking insurance salesman, snatching 50 per cent of the reward for zero per cent of the effort. Lenny had invested hundreds of hours running up and down ladders, clearing drains, pruning fruit trees and stomping round Tesco's with the old man's shopping list to secure this legacy, only to see half of it given away on a whim to some poncey college boy who knew a bit about wine and art. Nick was probably sobbing on a kerb in Santander now, too blinded by bitterness to see that he'd learned a valuable lesson. In this life a man's missus, his family, his dog and his business were sacrosanct, and if you interfered with any of them you deserved what you got. They didn't teach you that at university, and that was the problem, thought Lenny. He lit a fag with one of his split matches and blew smoke across the fire. It was important that he established a rapport with Sidney similar to the one he'd seen between the old man and Nick. Pensioners loved rabbiting on about the good old days and all you had to do was pretend to be interested.

'I bet you went to university, didn't you, Mr S?'

Sidney pulled his hip flask from his pocket and took a sip. 'I had no time for university.'

'Me neither,' replied Lenny. 'We've got a lot in common, you and me.'

Sidney looked up from the flames, eyes widening. 'No we don't.'

'Yes we do.' Lenny scratched his armpit. 'We're both art experts.'

'And?'

'We, er, both live in Norfolk.' Sidney was still looking at him. Lenny raised his bottle. 'We both like the odd tipple from time to time.'

'Leave it, Mr Knowles,' warned Sidney, placing another splinter on the fire.

'We both enjoy the finer things in life.'

'I said leave it.'

'I could be the son you never had.'

'Mr Knowles!'

Lenny let another one rip. 'Shall we talk about history, then?'

Sidney glared at Lenny. 'History?'

'Yeah, you know: the olden days.'

'What period?'

'One with a war in it. A war you was in.'

Sidney sighed. 'I presume you want to hear about the gold?'

Lenny shrugged, 'Whatever,' and Sidney told him exactly what he had told Nick early that morning, coming up with the same shortfall of a hundred boxes. Outside, the suburbs of Santander were already far behind as the goods train rushed through the rain and south towards the Cordillera Cantabrica and Palencia. Lenny took three full drags on his fag before he replied. 'How come you know so much about it?' he asked at last.

'Because I've seen it,' replied Sidney. 'I'm almost certainly the last living man on this earth to have seen it. One hundred boxes, each one measuring nineteen by twelve by seven inches and weighing one and a half hundredweight . . .'

'Where did you see it?' demanded Lenny.

'Here in Spain, in the Maestrazgo, in Alto Aragon.'

'When?'

'In the early summer of 1937.'

'And you reckon it'll still be there?'

Sidney took a hit on his flask. 'I know it will.'

Lenny leaned forward to light a fresh cigarette from the embers. 'What were you doing in Spain in 1937?'

Sidney tipped back his head in a gesture that defied challenge. 'I was trying to kill Germans,' he replied.

Lenny looked at him, the Smirnoff bottle poised at his lips. 'You're a bleeding psycho, you are,' he announced.

'You're very kind,' replied Sidney with a lethal grin.

4

In July 1916, in one act of conspicuous gallantry in the battle of
Bazentin Ridge, Big Bill Starman did more for the child he was
yet to father than he could ever have managed had he stayed at
home. His Military Medal, one of thousands awarded during the
Somme campaign, and his death, two months before Sidney's
birth in November 1918, promised the fatherless infant a golden
future. Perhaps it was easier to recognise a hero on the modest
memorials of the countryside than it was in the towns and cities,
where the rolls of honour ran for yards and yards, but the pain
was the same and the loss of men like Big Bill would send the
Rutherford estate and others like it across rural England into terminal decline. Perhaps Lady Rutherford had known this when
she visited the widow Starman in the gamekeeper's cottage two
days after the Armistice. Her two sons had fallen within a week
and a mile of each other on the Ypres Salient in 1917, leaving
the estate without heirs. Silly talk had been heard of revolution
in the months before the end of hostilities, and even if the
rumours proved false the truth was that nothing would be the
same in the future as it had been in the past. She passed an
envelope to Mrs Starman. It contained a notarised letter ceding
the tied cottage to Sidney Starman for the duration of his natural
life, or, God forbid his mother should she outlive him. After that,
it would revert to the estate, but furthermore a sum had been
lodged with Agnew and Ricker, solicitors, to pay for the child's
education, and this was in addition to his Lordship's pre-war
undertaking to pay five years' full salary to the widow of any

estate worker killed in the service of the King. Her Ladyship, who would drown herself in the Bure before those five years were gone, hoped that these little things might in some way assuage the grief she knew the young widow felt.

At the age of seven, Sidney Starman enrolled as a day-boy in the lower house of a minor public school in Norwich. By taking him from the estate and placing him in the company of the sons of the prosperous middle class, the move further isolated an already solitary child and he passed through the early years of school like a ghost – invisible to the insensitive and appearing to those who noticed his presence as belonging to a different time and place. At home he divided his time between his father's shed, where he built traps, and the woods, where he set them, catching rabbits, hares, foxes, weasels and even the odd deer. His father, a professional gamekeeper and a pragmatic trapper, would have been disturbed by the cold-blooded ingenuity of his son's contraptions.

In 1929 Sidney moved to the upper school, where he maintained his utter lack of renown. Polite and inoffensive, he played no field sports and had no real friends. He was rarely invited to birthday parties and despite his mother's insistence he never once invited another boy home. In the evenings and at the weekends he now prowled the woods armed with a single-barrelled .410, a poacher's gun, and his mention of this at school brought him to the attention of the one-legged Captain Parker, who taught scripture and shooting. The country boy, it seemed, was a born marksman, but his innate talent brought him little joy. By the time he was thirteen he was recognised as a reasonably gifted draughtsman, but the rest of his schoolwork had dropped from mediocre to inadequate, and despite his aptitude for invisibility, his absence from class was noted with increasing frequency. When the school called his mother in, she embarrassed all present by curtseying to the headmaster and calling the porter 'sir'. When asked to account for his absences, Sidney replied that he spent most of his time in the cathedral, just sitting and thinking. The headmaster, an oily man who licked his lips before uttering predictable aphorisms, told Sidney sternly that school was traditionally the place for thinking. 'Not about the bastards who killed my father,' replied the boy.

Following this meeting it was tacitly agreed that Sidney should continue to attend the school, as best he could, and for as long as Agnew and Ricker were paying the fees, and that a further view would be taken consequent to the results of the General Schools Examination when he was sixteen. He never made it that far.

The bastards who did the killing were rarely discussed in the Black Horse, a run-down pub on the poor side of Castle Hill. The limbless and listless veterans of the Norfolk Regiment who wasted days in a fug of smoke beneath its low yellow ceilings were more concerned with the victims than the perpetrators. The landlord himself had been a New Army man, conscripted in 1914 into the 8th Battalion and killed during the same battle in which Bill Starman had won his Military Medal. It was perhaps for this reason that his widow allowed Sidney to spend so long in the pub, providing a pair of eager ears to catch whatever slurred nonsense was spilling out of the regulars' mouths. He made himself useful, too – collecting glasses, running errands, rolling fags for the men who'd lost their hands – but he annoyed some of the old soldiers with his unending questions.

On 12 November 1932, the day after Armistice Day, Sidney left school. He was only just fourteen and his mother was distraught. She made an appointment to meet with his Lordship up at the big house in the belief that he would lend his influence to her attempt to persuade Sidney to return to his studies. She was greatly mistaken. Rutherford had never shared his late wife's sentimentality and had been angered by her meddling in the affairs of the estate staff. Not only had her ludicrous generosity sacrificed funds and properties for the sake of goodwill but they had overshadowed his own arrangements, which were measured, appropriate and fair. He was grateful indeed that of the eleven who had left the estate to fight, only three had been killed and just one had been married. The gamekeeper had been a good man, but sending his son to public school had been indicative of the madness that had crept in through his wife's broken heart and seized her mind. She had embraced the spiritualist fad with a convert's zeal, causing sadness and embarrassment on social occasions by relating, with a feverish glitter in her eyes, the conversations she had enjoyed with her sons. Lunacy was everywhere these days, and the Starman boy was a case in point. Staff had complained on more than one occasion about his creeping about the estate at all hours with a loaded shotgun, hanging up carcasses like a bloody Cherokee. His early removal from his proper social context had only exacerbated his alienation, and now his mother was begging an extension to his exile. Rutherford had a far more practical idea, and the following Monday at six-thirty in the morning, Sidney Starman began his apprenticeship with Ernie Warren, head keeper.

There was little sympathy for Sidney among the estate workers, and Warren, who had suffered for his laziness and dishonesty under Bill Starman, was especially keen to spice up the traditional humiliations suffered by apprentice boys with a little personal venom. His own boys, both older than Sidney and engaged as field workers, did what they could to darken his days, and Cedric, after Little Lord Fauntleroy, was the least offensive of his nicknames.

At the staff Christmas party in 1935 Sidney was approached by Mary Foulden, daughter of the cook and the chauffeur. An intelligent girl who considered her position as maid to be temporary, she was attracted to Sidney by his aloofness and his education, and pestered him well into the spring of 1936 to take her out. Their first date was a visit to the Regimental Museum of the Royal Norfolks, in Norwich Castle, followed by a cup of tea and a slice of cake, and their second was to an art exhibition, also at the castle. When Mary asked if they could go somewhere else next time, Sidney replied that there was nowhere else to go in Norwich.

'There's the pictures,' mentioned Mary.

'Don't like the pictures,' replied Sidney. The last film he'd seen at the Gaumont had been *All Quiet on the Western Front*, three years before, and he had found it to be a shameful piece of pro-German propaganda. Mary suggested that he should join her father, Tom Leverett the blacksmith's boy and herself on their Wednesday night outings to the Labour Club.

'Don't like politics,' replied Sidney.

'It's not a matter of liking it,' said Mary. 'It's like gutting rabbits: no one likes doing it, but you have to roll up your sleeves and get on with it. Anyway, we get speakers come along and tell us about the workers' struggle in other places.'

Sidney refused her enticements and thereby, very slowly, he lost her. Their courtship continued in a desultory fashion – she swallowed her conviction that the artists of the Norwich School were alienated bourgeois propagandists and he shelved his argument that cinema was electric laudanum – and considering they had so little in common it surprised Sidney how much it hurt when he learned on Sunday, 19 July 1936 that Mary Foulden had been seen kissing Tom Leverett outside the White Swan. It was also reported on that day that the Spanish garrison on Morocco had risen against the government in Madrid. Word had it that the Republican government was corrupt.

Sidney asked Mary about the kiss and she laughed. 'Just a peck on the cheek,' she cried. 'I've known Tom Leverett all me life!'

He believed her, and in August he took her to see *The Thirty-Nine Steps*, but it was the Pathé newsreel preceding the feature that seized his attention: Germany had sent aircraft and men to assist the rebels in Spain. Mary already knew that. Later, as they ate chips beside the river from a newspaper that showed French Prime Minister Léon Blum arriving in London for crisis talks with the Foreign Secretary, Anthony Eden, Sidney announced that he was joining the army.

'To fight the fascists?' asked Mary.

'To fight the Germans,' corrected Sidney.

'Well if you join the British army,' huffed Mary, 'you'll never get to fight your stupid Germans,' and then she outlined the non-intervention policy under discussion between Britain and France. Tom Leverett, she said, was totally opposed to any non-intervention policy, a belief he expressed by interfering with Mary on a muggy Bank Holiday Monday while Sidney slept off the beer he'd drunk at the annual estate workers' picnic.

Sidney attacked Tom, blackening his eye and bloodying his nose to the cheers of drunken onlookers. Mary was furious, and as she knelt at Tom's side, she told Sidney that she never wanted to see him again. Sidney left without speaking and walked in breathless fury to the Wheatsheaf, where he sat alone at the bar and drank until closing time. As he left, staggering beneath an orange harvest moon, he met Tom Leverett and his two cousins, who had been drinking in the White Swan. They left him bleeding in a ditch full of duckweed.

The next morning, Tuesday, 1 September 1936, Sidney should have reported for work at six-thirty. The St Giles Day shoot was a tradition on the Rutherford Estate that went back over a century, the parish church of the same name lending an air of divine priority on this the first day of the partridge-shooting season. For many of the visiting shots, down from the City, it was an opportunity to get their eyes in before the pheasant season opened; and for the beaters, up from the village, it was a salutary time to remember that St Giles was the patron saint of cripples. Sidney's task was to organise a platoon of men armed with sticks, rattles and whistles to drive the hapless birds before a barrage of aristocratic gunfire. He arrived for work exactly two hours late, his battered face and limping gait compounding the poor impression he had made by his tardiness. Called to account by Lord Rutherford himself, before a faintly amused audience of the great and the good, Sidney slipped on the gravel and discharged his shotgun into the side of the Duke of Bedford's car. Attempts by an excitable society columnist to call the negligent discharge a Marxist assassination attempt were defused by Rutherford, who pointed out to his guests that the gunman in question was the son of a war hero and had only yesterday beaten up the only Red in the village. Nevertheless, his turnout was shabby, his timekeeping abysmal, his attitude suspect and his popularity undetectable. Sidney Starman was sacked on the spot. If he had waited a week or so, written a letter of apology to the Duke and to his Lordship and been prepared to beg, he would have been given his job back, not least because Ernie Warren couldn't manage without him, but Sidney, with the impetuousness of a youth two weeks short of his eighteenth birthday, could not wait. He packed a bag, kissed his mother goodbye and took the bus to Norwich station. That night he was in London.

5

It was early afternoon in Santander and Nick Crick was walking out of town. The thin sunlight had been dowsed by a thick overcast and the damp air smelled of the woods and the sea. A chill southerly sighed down from the sierras, lifting litter from the empty streets in tiny spirals but failing to cool the sweat on Nick's creased brow. His head ached and he was certain he was sickening for a fever, but he had neither the time nor the money to take care of himself. Like a doubtful soldier marching to an unjust war, he was unconvinced of the usefulness of his actions, but he was too frightened to stop and reconsider. The sign on the goods wagon had said Palencia – a browse through a road atlas in a Texaco station had revealed the town to be 120 miles south and slightly west of Santander, two-thirds of the way between Burgos and Valladolid. The railway followed the crow's route, a taut bowstring to the curve of the road that bent east via Bilbao, Miranda del Ebro and Burgos. Nick knew that the smartest move would have been to hop the next train south, riding the same rails down which his companions had disappeared, but he'd been too scared of running into the muggers again. His flight from the rail yard in the minutes after the train's departure had been, he was certain, an escape from certain death. The muggers were probably long gone but every trembling step along the broken roads between the derelict warehouses had been fraught with the dread of confrontation. 'Briton found dead in Spanish port' – two column inches that would elicit neither sympathy nor sorrow.

Spanish police have confirmed that a body found in the dockyards at Santander is that of Nicholas Simon Crick, 33, unemployed, from Norwich in Norfolk. Mr Crick was recently released from prison after serving an eighteen-month sentence that was nowhere near long enough to compensate for what he'd done to his family, and justice was finally served in multiple blows from a cheap Chinese lock-knife. It was what Crick, a former insurance salesman, would have wanted.

Death was life's most effective painkiller but it was a hard pill to swallow. Nick had craved oblivion every day for two years, one month and five days, and every time the opportunity had presented itself he had flinched.

Two years, one month and six days ago, Nick Crick's life had been proceeding according to a comfortable and unambitious plan. Already skilled in deriving an acceptable, if mediocre, return from minimum effort, he had sunk slowly into the sofa of suburban consumerism. His wife was a sharp-dressed, fast-talking accountant with a blonde bob and a company sports car who had been devastated when she fell pregnant after just eighteen months of dinky affluence. They traded their riverfront flat for a smart three-bedroom executive home with a Shaker-style fitted kitchen on a landscaped estate on the edge of the city. Nikki claimed one of the bedrooms as an office on the grounds that she would be able to work from home when the baby was born. Nick bought a forty-two-inch plasma TV with Total Cinema features on the grounds that he wouldn't be able to afford it after the baby was born. They were so happy.

One night Nick took a call from his old friend Danny Mann. They'd been at college together, but when Nick had gone to work in risk assessment for Anglia Assurance, Danny had taken off to Thailand to see if he could find himself. As Nick completed his graduate training and joined the regional risk department, Danny drifted through South-East Asia, sending *schadenfreude* by e-mail from one exotic location after another. After three years in which Nick had attained the position of assistant to the deputy regional risk services manager, married his long-term girlfriend and become a father, Danny returned, poorer, wiser and blonder, and moved in with his ex-girlfriend, a hippy called Heather who almost made a living as an alternative healer out in the countryside. They were throwing a Winter Festival homecoming party and the Cricks were invited. Locked down since the birth of their daughter Chloë four months previously, and already feeling like he'd done too much too young, Nick begged his wife to let him go to the party. Surprisingly – for she considered both Danny and Heather to be slacker potheads – she agreed, announcing that she was coming too.

'What about the baby?' asked Nick.

'We'll take her with us,' replied Nikki. 'Heather's got a two-year-old, and I'm sure there'll be other kids there.'

'Where will she sleep?'

'In her carrycot, and if she wakes up it'll give us a good excuse to leave.'

Nick didn't want a good excuse to leave, but, as Nikki pointed out, his lost nights on strange sofas were long gone. There was one more thing: Nick was driving. Whereas he had managed to go to the pub after work at least twice a week since the baby had been born, Nikki had been in sober solitary confinement for the past sixteen weeks and she felt that she deserved to let her short hair down.

'You can have two pints,' she advised him outside Heather's remote country abode.

'I'm a risk assessment analyst,' replied Nick icily. 'I know exactly what my limitations are.'

'So pace yourself,' advised Nikki.

If Nick had been looking forward to a reprise of the raucous nights for which Danny Mann had been famous as a student, he was disappointed. The candlelit atmosphere was more akin to one of Nikki's network dinners, with music chosen to reflect lifestyle choices and a selection of wholesome vegetarian snacks. Smoking was not allowed in the house, and as he shivered over a spliff in the back garden with Danny and a marketing executive called Tom, Nick admitted regret. He should have hit the road after graduation and seen a bit of life before giving himself up to corporate living. He drained his Shiraz and sucked on the skunk, shaking his head. He didn't want to give the wrong impression: fate had been very kind to him so far. He had earned 50K plus bonus last year, had two weeks booked in a four-star hotel in Barbados and watched the latest movies on his big-screen. He drove a Vauxhall Omega, carried a Nokia 8510 with Bluetooth and a Donna Karan wallet full of credit cards, and he had his Paul Smith shoes firmly planted on the third rung of the property ladder. Life was pretty secure, but he sometimes felt that he had paid for its many comforts with his freedom, and when he compared himself with Danny he wished he could have a little of that freedom back. Tom agreed, and Danny refilled their glasses. They were both married now, with kids, he reminded them gently. Their freedom was gone for ever.

Back in the warm, the Chardonnay had gone to Nikki's head, and both she and her daughter were sound asleep as Nick drove home along icy roads. She woke just as he clipped the verge at seventy miles per hour on the A47 at the Halvergate junction, but Nick didn't catch what she said. The car flew briefly and landed on its roof in the River Bure, where it sank in six feet of freezing, fast-flowing water. The autopsy report stated that Nicola Alison Crick, twenty-nine, died of a broken neck; her daughter, Chloë Madison Crick, four months, strapped into her child seat, died of drowning. The newspapers reported that Nicholas Simon Crick had escaped with minor abrasions. His blood alcohol level was 123mg/100ml. Nikki's father dropped dead from a heart attack when he heard the news. Her brother, a soldier, was charged with common assault and contempt of court after leaping from the public gallery and knocking Nick unconscious on the day a red-faced judge sentenced him to thirty-six months for causing death by dangerous driving. Such was the price of freedom.

Nick had spent much of the past two years, one month and five days pondering the astonishing power of small things and the absurd fragility of life. A small quantity of red wine and a single joint had achieved the same effect as a tsunami, washing away his cosy little world and leaving his life beyond repair. His wife and daughter had been buried in the same box, but no headstone marked their tomb. Nikki's family had insisted that their daughter was remembered by her maiden name, and while Nick, had he been asked, would have been willing to concur, the law insisted otherwise. If Nick had been a decent, brave and noble man, he wouldn't have allowed himself to live this long, wasting days, weeks and months in semi-catatonic contemplation of all the if-onlys. If only he hadn't kept in touch with Danny Mann. If only he hadn't accepted the invitation to the party. If only he had cared enough to forgo that meaningless wine and that pointless fucking spliff. If only he'd listened to the sober voice in his head that had warned him to slow down on that icy road. And if only he'd had the balls to cut his own throat on the day of judgement.

He'd attempted suicide three times while awaiting trial, but neither competently enough to succeed nor with enough determination to be diagnosed as anything more than a remorseful attention-seeker. In prison death should have been easy to find: insults weighed heavy on the inside and egos were easily bruised. The visiting psychiatrist, in her earnest Edinburgh brogue, had told Nick that if he really wanted to die, he would always find a way and no one would be able to stop him. All it took was commitment, but that, along with bravery, decency and nobility, was a quality missing from Nick's character. He had planned to kill himself in the same half-arsed way he'd once been determined to save money, or to learn to sail, and had justified his failure on the spurious grounds that it was probably harder to live with his guilt than to die with it. He had allowed Lenny Knowles to deliver him from evil on the inside and lead him into temptation on the outside because it was easier to surrender his will than it was to be a free man. As long as Lenny was calling the shots Nick wouldn't have to bite the bullet, and that was why he was dragging his bag south out of Santander: a cowardly emotional cripple crawling in search of his crutch. Lenny Knowles had looked after Nick for the past two years, carrying him through a period of numb apathy and making decisions that seemed irrelevant, like what to eat and where to live. Without Lenny to speak for him, Nick would have been mumbling if only, over and over again in a Norfolk sanatorium; and without Lenny to hold him up, he would have been on his knees.

He winced as a passing Scania hurled a gritty backblast in his face. The narrow pavement was more of a sill to the carriageway than a safe path for pedestrians, its grimy slabs scattered with the shredded remains of blown tyres, discarded fast-food packaging and the odd shoe left like the undiscovered evidence of a late-night hit-and-run. These roads weren't made for walking, decided Nick, his head down to avoid the suspicious stares of passing motorists. He wasn't even sure if the law permitted his presence on the hard shoulder of the N365, but in the feverish panic after the train's departure hitch-hiking to Palencia had seemed like the best option. Now he wasn't so sure. He hobbled on miserably, and dropping his bag beneath a sign that said, 'Bilbao 100, San Sebastian 197, Valladolid 377, Madrid 492', stuck a desultory thumb into the passing traffic. You didn't need a signpost to know when all was lost.

★

Far away, south of the Cantabrian Mountains and over the flood-swollen froth of the River Cueza, the train rattled over rusting rails to Palencia. Inside the fourth wagon from the back Lenny lay beside the low fire, propped on one elbow and studying his bottle like a one-night stand. The great thing about vodka was its imperceptibility. It tasted of nothing, had no smell and was almost invisible. If it hadn't been for its giveaway physical and psychological effects, vodka, reckoned Lenny, would have been the perfect human refreshment. The train had slowed to a speed of forty miles per hour, and the wheels clattered on the fishplates like an unhealthy heartbeat. The effect had proved soporific for Sidney, who lay as he would in his casket, his overcoat spread over him like a shroud and his head pillowed on his bag. Suddenly, though, he threw off his covering and fumbled for his glasses.

'Are you awake, Mr Knowles?'

'I am,' nodded Lenny.

'Would you help me up? I need you to hold me while I pee.'

Lenny's eyes widened. 'You what?'

'I need to pee. I need you to hold me.'

'Er, can't you hold yourself?' asked Lenny, horror-struck.

'Hold on to me while I pee, you berk,' growled Sidney. 'So I don't fall out of the bloody train.'

Lenny shook his head, sighed, and helped the old man to his feet. He slid back the door and placed an unwilling hand lightly on Sidney's shoulder.

'Grab my belt, fool,' barked Sidney. 'I need security, not encouragement.'

He pissed long and hard into the slipstream, turned and sighed, his bony fingers fumbling with his zip. 'Thank you,' he smiled. 'I suppose it won't be long before I need you to sort out my fly.'

Lenny smiled back, shuddering inwardly.

Sidney leaned against the boxcar wall and pushed his hands

into his pockets. 'I was coming back from the front once, and we were riding in one of these, going at full speed through the night to escape the planes – *jabos*, we called them. There was this big Hungarian, huge chap with enormous warts on his face, quite a famous poet, apparently, and he was stood in the doorway taking a leak, singing some hideous Magyar folksong. Then he stopped, and as we turned to thank him for his consideration, he was gone.' Sidney laughed at the memory. 'Gone. Never saw him again. Silly sod had fallen out. Lesson learned.'

Lenny put a match to a fag and sucked. He'd come for remuneration, not education.

Sidney tapped the fire with his foot. It had less life left in it than he did. 'So how long were you in prison, Mr Knowles?'

The smoke caught in Lenny's throat and he went hot, then cold. That bastard Nick had broken the golden rule. He rubbed his chin, glancing shiftily at Sidney, wondering if there was a chance of a successful denial. Sidney's steady, impassive gaze suggested otherwise.

'Did four and a half years for a crime I never committed,' he replied. It was an answer that worked wonders on divorced barmaids and bored housewives.

'Whereabouts?'

'Bedford and Norwich.' He wished Nick was here. The snidey little sod had probably sworn Sidney to secrecy, but the beans were well and truly out in the open now. There seemed no harm in spilling a few more.

'Bedford was where I met Nick,' he said.

Sidney swung around in surprise. 'So he's a jailbird too? How delightful. What was the crime you were unfairly accused of committing?'

'Didn't Nick tell you?' grunted Lenny. 'I'm surprised.'

Sidney shook his head. 'You're mistaken – Mr Crick told me nothing. It was the matches that gave you away. It's an old lags' trick, isn't it? You get one box of matches a week, so the first thing you do is split each match in two, doubling your lucifer. I've seen you do it on a number of occasions. Men hang for habits like that.' He raised his eyebrows and smiled. Behind the glasses, the watery eyes, the sallow skin and the wrinkled neck, Lenny saw the face of a smartarse kid. It was a face he'd have liked to slap.

'So describe this miscarriage of justice,' said the smartarse.

It was an old story, easily told. Its inconsistencies had long been eradicated, allowing Lenny to concentrate on tailoring the tale to fit the listener's ear. 'I had this mate called Roger. Not the brightest star in the sky, but nice enough. He was an estate worker, like your old man, and me and him used to go shooting – pigeons and stuff mainly.' This introduction was entirely new: Lenny had never been shooting in his life and the only estate Roger had worked on was a stolen Volvo. 'Roger's got this little daughter, five she was, and she's not well.' He bit his lower lip and looked up at Sidney. This was the bit that usually hooked them in the tear ducts.

'Leukaemia. Terminal.'

This was an unholy exaggeration: Roger had no daughter, sick or otherwise. He had two sons, by different mothers, in different villages, to whom the courts occasionally ordered him to pay child support. Lenny had met Roger while serving a previous prison sentence for possession with intent to supply of two pounds of homegrown skunk with the remarkably accurate name of Professional Suicide.

'Roger's a quiet bloke. You know the type: lived for the family, always doing DIY, gardening, that sort of thing.' This wasn't strictly true either. Roger actually lived for drugs, cider, motorbikes and DVD porn. 'I met him one day coming out of the church. I said, "What you been doing in there, Rog? Never took you for a religious man."' That much was true: Lenny had indeed met Roger coming out of All Saints' in Great Cressingham, at two in the morning. He had been carrying a

78

poorly concealed silver chalice. '"Praying for a miracle," he says.' Lenny shrugged. 'You know me, Sidney: I'm one of those born to help others. Can't stop myself, especially when it's little children, so I tells him that whatever he wants, whatever help I can give him, it's his for the asking. You should have seen the gratitude in that man's eyes.'

True again. Roger's ill-conceived plan for the disposal of the chalice involved taking it to a local recording of *The Antiques Roadshow* and trying to sell it in the car park. Lenny touted it to an American acquaintance, who sold it on to a Jewish couple in Baltimore. Since Roger's plan would have resulted in his immediate arrest and conviction, he was hugely grateful when Lenny slipped him two crisp fifty-pound notes as his 50 per cent share of the nine hundred he'd earned from the Septic.

'One night he's asked to borrow Sick Gloria – said he had to move some stuff. Of course I said yes, even offered to help him, but he said he'd be all right on his own. Next thing I know the Old Bill are banging on my door. Sick Gloria has been found nose down in a ditch out near Weasenham with Roger unconscious at the wheel and three rather attractive Regency fireplaces in the back. I suppose that poor, desperate man had turned to crime to pay for his daughter's operation.'

'What about the National Health?'

'Couldn't help,' shrugged Lenny. 'She had to go to the States – Orlando, I think it was. There's a big children's hospital there and the deal is that if they can't save your kid, you get a family ticket to Disneyworld instead, as a sort of compensation. Anyway, you know me. What could I do?' He threw a humble, sidelong glance at Sidney and was rather disappointed to find the old man polishing his glasses. 'What do you think I did?'

'Surprise me,' sighed Sidney.

'Put my hands up, that's what I did. Took the rap for Roger. Told the Bill it was me driving the van, and me who had done the burglary. Told them Roger had nothing to do with it, that I

was just giving him a lift home. You know how it is, Sidney –
you went off to Spain to fight the communists—'

'Fascists,' interjected Sidney.

'Whatever,' said Lenny. 'Sometimes a man has to stand up and
be counted. Remember the Scarlet Pimpernel? "It's a far, far
better thing what I do now than what I've ever done before."'

In fact, Lenny had had no other choice than to own up to the
crime. He had persuaded Roger to join him on a nocturnal tour
of three rooms in an eighteenth-century rectory undergoing
restoration by English Heritage. The premises had been remote,
empty, unguarded and clad in scaffolding that afforded easy access
to every room on three floors. With tools left on the job by
builders anxious to blow their wages in the boozer, and numer-
ous ladders, blocks and tackle surrounding the job, the theft of
three fireplaces had been as simple as it was unambitious. It was
the getaway that had gone wrong, when a stupid argument over
who was going to finish a spliff made from the last of their weed
had descended into a mobile fist-fight between the two hapless
burglars. A lucky left from Roger caught Lenny under the jaw
and knocked him senseless just long enough for him to drive
Gloria off the road and into a tree. A passing patrol car stopped to
assist and Lenny fled the scene, going across country with a crow's
confidence, straight to the nearest pub. There he drank lager and
played pool until midnight, then took a taxi to his house. The
police, who had beaten him home by three hours, were waiting.

'It's a terribly sad story,' observed Sidney, poking the ashes distractedly. 'Did she live?'

'Did who live?'

'The little girl. Your friend's daughter.'

'Course she did, thanks to me.'

'Well, all's well that ends well,' sighed Sidney.

'That's always been my problem, you see, Mr S,' shrugged
Lenny. 'Can't help myself from helping others.'

'Admirable.' Sidney removed his glasses and pinched the

bridge of his nose, glad that the train wasn't going any further than Palencia. Had it been bound for Madrid or beyond he felt sure he would have died from the effects of the noxious gases rising from Lenny Knowles's bullshit. It wasn't the first self-mythologising twaddle he'd sat through, but it was undoubtedly the worst, and it proved why prisons were full of idiots. Lenny Knowles was the best argument he'd ever encountered for compulsory castration. 'You have children, don't you?' he asked.

Lenny nodded.

'Do you miss them?'

'Don't really know them,' shrugged Lenny. 'The missus got custody and put a restraining order on me after I went down for a crime I never committed.'

'The fireplace thefts?'

'Nah,' replied Lenny, shaking his head. 'Another one. Haven't seen the kids for six years now. They're better off without me.'

'What are their names?'

'My daughter – she'll be eleven now – is called Stella and the boy is called Jack. I named them after what I'd been drinking the night they were conceived.'

'Genius,' muttered Sidney.

'Yeah, I thought so,' agreed Lenny. 'Stella is named after the lager – like Paul McCartney's girl – and—'

'Jack is after Jack Daniels, I presume,' guessed Sidney.

Lenny shook his head. 'Scrumpy Jack,' he recalled. 'Twelve pints with white rum chasers, but I couldn't call the boy Bacardi, could I?'

Sidney raised an eyebrow. 'You could have called him Ron.' A squeal of brakes and a violent shudder promised fresh air as the train decelerated to a lurching halt.

'Are we there?' asked Lenny.

'How should I know?' Sidney glanced at his German watch. 'It's been three hours, although God knows it seems longer. Take a look outside.'

Lenny slid the door open and peered through the crack. 'We're in a town. There's loads of railway lines and we seem to be right in . . . fucking hell!' There was a blast of air as a passenger train rushed past, silhouetting Lenny's bulk against its windows like a zoetrope of a man surprised. 'Bastard nearly took my bloody head off,' he declared, backing away from the door.

'Nearly's not good enough,' muttered Sidney. He was beginning to miss Mr Crick.

Nick watched the red van climb the ramp. He was definitely coming down with a virus and his wrist throbbed from what was probably a strained tendon. He'd been experimenting with body language for the past two hours in a series of failed attempts to elicit empathy or sympathy from an apathetic audience of Spanish motorists. As the van approached Nick assumed an air of honest but nonchalant need: he was a fellow-traveller on a common road, a common-worker seeking help from his own. The van whizzed past.

'That's why communism failed, you bastard,' he yelled into its wake.

His outburst spoiled his chances with the three cars following, but the fourth, an ugly sky-blue van, slowed down as it passed. The driver leaned across the passenger seat to stare through steamed-up windows, and Nick glimpsed thick-framed glasses, red cheeks and a black beard. An orange indicator flashed and as the van pulled on to the shoulder Nick sprinted to its side.

'*Donde vas, chico?*' wheezed the driver. He looked like Rasputin and his vehicle smelled of toilet cleaner and pheromones.

'I'm going to Palencia,' replied Nick, smiling in what he hoped was an honest, unthreatening manner. 'Palencia? You know it?'

The driver frowned, his eyebrows meeting beneath the black frames of his glasses. 'English?'

'Yes. I'm sorry I don't speak Spanish.' Nick's heart dropped. This weird vehicle was the first that had stopped since he had stuck his thumb out, and it looked like the driver was regretting his decision.

He stared through the windscreen for a moment, drumming fat, bejewelled fingers on a shiny plastic steering wheel, then he looked at Nick. 'I go to Matamorosa. It's halfway. Get in.'

Nick tossed his case onto a back seat strewn with old newspapers, dog-eared books and cardboard boxes full of loose papers and poorly bound pamphlets. A pair of greasy-looking crutches lay on the floor and as he strapped on his seat belt Nick noticed there were no foot pedals.

'It is a car for cripples,' nodded the big Spaniard. 'My legs are no good, but everything else works fine.'

'I see,' replied Nick, unsure of the appropriate response.

'Brakes and accelerator are hand-operated. The gearbox is automatic.'

'Lovely.'

'So why Palencia?'

'My friends are there.'

'Girlfriends?' leered the driver.

'Er, no.'

'Aha! Boyfriends?'

Nick laughed weakly. The musky smell of pheromones was really very strong. 'Just friends. They're waiting at the station.'

'So why not take the train?'

'I can't afford it.'

'Where is your money?'

The fat man asked a lot of questions, thought Nick. 'I lost it. Left my wallet in a café. When I went back, it was already gone.'

'So you're poor and vulnerable.'

'Just poor.'

'But your boyfriends, they have money?'

'Not my boyfriends, but yes: I'll be all right when I meet up with them.'

'First time in Spain?'

'Yes.' A dirty rain began to fall, softening visibility and raising a spray on the highway.

'Your boyfriends are Spanish?'

'Not my boyfriends,' grinned Nick through gritted teeth. 'Remember? I'm not gay.'

The fat man slapped Nick's thigh with a sticky hand. 'I joke. You're a good-looking guy.' Maybe it wasn't so bad out in the rain.

'My mates are English.'

'Students?'

'Not at all. One of them was over here during the war.'

'*La Guerra Civil?*'

'Er, yeah. The Civil War. In the thirties.'

'I know when the Civil War was, *chico*,' replied the fat man. 'Look in the back. All those papers relate to the war. What is your name?'

'Nick Crick. Pleased to meet you.'

The fat man extended that same sweaty hand. 'Professor Edouardo Vega. I teach history. What side was your friend on in the war?'

Nick shrugged. 'Not sure. Whatever side the British were on.'

The professor laughed. 'The British were on both sides. Officially they were for the Republic. They had no choice. Unofficially they supported Franco and the Nationalists. That's what the non-intervention policy was all about.'

'Wasn't Franco the bad guy?'

'Be careful, young man,' warned the professor.

'But he was a fascist, wasn't he?'

'And what was the alternative?'

84

'Freedom?'

'Ah yes, of course: land and freedom. Like they had in Soviet Russia. What would have happened to Europe if the communists had taken Spain?' The professor pushed the throttle forward and overtook a truck. 'What would have happened to England if France had been the next to fall?'

'So you think Franco was right?'

'Of course he was right. I'm aware this is an unfashionable opinion in these soft-hearted times, but had it not been for him Europe would have gone back to the Dark Ages. Your government knew that. It's just a shame they failed to convince the fools of the International Brigades who volunteered to die for Stalin.'

'I think my friend was one of them,' said Nick.

'And now he's probably still a sentimental old fool,' suggested the professor.

The same thought had already crossed Nick's mind.

'You know why I'm going to Matamorosa?' continued the professor, patting Nick's thigh. 'I'm going to interview a man of eighty years who might be able to tell me where to find the bodies of sixteen Jesuit priests – men of God – murdered by the communists in 1936.'

'I'm sure there were atrocities on all sides,' replied Nick.

'Very diplomatic,' sniffed the professor, 'and so very English.'

The lecture continued through Torrelavega and Los Corrales de Buelna, the fat professor's indignant nasal whine a bitter commentary on a damp landscape of huddled hills, terraced villages and wide, shallow streams. The road shared the valley with the line to Palencia and every glimpse of the track sent a surge of anxiety through Nick's belly. The professor drove with exaggerated caution, rarely exceeding thirty miles an hour on the shiny two-lane blacktop. If the others had made it to Palencia, how long would they wait for him? Would they wait at all, or were they halfway to Madrid or some other destination in this strange

85

and cold land? His first night in Spain was falling and he had no idea where he would spend it, although he felt sure the professor could suggest a sordid little spot.

The professor sensed his hunger, if not his unease. 'We'll be in Matamorosa in a few minutes,' he announced. 'Have you eaten today?'

'Only breakfast,' replied Nick. Lenny would have pulled a rabbit out of the hat by now and the two of them would be holed up in some snug little hotel with cable TV and hot showers.

'You will dine with me tonight,' insisted the professor.

'I couldn't possibly.' Nick glanced at the useless pair of legs crossed under the steering column. At least the fat bastard couldn't chase him.

'Of course you could. I always dine early, and in my country that means I usually dine alone.'

'But my friends are waiting . . .' He wondered if Lenny was drunk yet. The man had spent not one night in a state of sobriety since his release, and poverty would be a low obstacle to his pursuit of oblivion.

'And they'll wait a little longer, *chico*. There are no more trains to Palencia this evening and you see how empty this road is. It's best that you stay with me tonight, and tomorrow I'll buy you a ticket. You may call these friends of yours and tell them to expect you in the morning.' He glanced at Nick, the wet tip of a yellow tongue flicking at his moustache.

'You have a place in Matamorosa?' asked Nick.

The professor shook his head, studying Nick for his reaction. 'We'll get a room. How does that sound?'

A meal and a bed appealed more than a night on the road in pursuit of a lost cause. Nick returned the fat man's gaze and nodded. 'Sounds good, Professor.'

The waiting room on Palencia station was lit by flickering neon tubes that buzzed like dying insects. High in one corner a poorly tuned TV played soundless loops of rolling news, the colours, crowds and urgency of the reports enhancing the sense of isolation in the cold room. A blue screen in another corner switched between *llegadas* and *salidas*, but both lists were empty. No trains would be arriving or leaving in the immediate future, and the platforms were empty but for a huddle of maintenance workers in bright orange jackets.

Lenny slumped on a plastic bench, its slats the same colour as the workmen's coats, defaced with graffiti as inept as it was ugly. He dangled his vodka bottle before his eyes and shook his head. 'I'm beginning to worry, Mr S,' he announced.

Sidney gritted his teeth. He was no longer fit enough for such unexpected exertions and the day had left him feeling utterly drained. His body ached from his heels to his hips and from his ribs to his wrists, the grating, gnawing pain aggravated by a chill that seemed to have seeped into the marrow. He'd always known the journey would be exhausting but hadn't expected to become so weak so early on. If he couldn't find food, sleep and warm shelter soon his health would become a major problem, but despite the discomfort, the clicking in his hips and the new tightness in his chest, Sidney felt alert and exhilarated, just as he had felt after coming under fire for the first time. Without opening his eyes, he pulled his flask from his pocket and took another tug on the Armagnac, silently toasting absent friends. 'No need to worry, Mr Knowles,' he said at last. 'Mr Crick will either make it by morning or he won't. We've given him every opportunity to rejoin us.'

Opposite him Lenny leaned forwards despondently, his elbows on his knees and his head bowed. 'I don't give a toss about Nickle-Arse,' he muttered. 'It's the vodka situation that's worrying me.'

'Charming.'

'It's not that I'm an alcoholic or nothing,' added Lenny. 'I'm like you: I enjoy the odd little drink.'

'Quite.'

'Especially after a day like today.'

Outside the wind wandered through the deserted station with a low moan and the lights flickered in sympathy. Lenny took a sip of vodka and held it in his mouth until he could feel it no more. He couldn't remember ever being this far down and out. 'To be honest, Mr S,' he announced after a moment's reflection, 'if I'd known it was going to be like this, I'd never have come.'

'I've heard that before,' smiled Sidney, hearing himself as though from a great distance. 'Seventy years ago someone else said the exact same thing.'

6

Joe Kirow was lying in mud made of his own blood, as though he was becoming part of the land he had come to defend. 'If I'd known it was going to be like this, I'd never have come,' he whispered.

Sidney bit his lip and smiled. The euphoria of their triumphant arrival in Spain had evaporated early, leaving a sense of frustration, demoralisation and fear that had thickened through the weeks of inactivity at Figueras, the earnest incompetence of training at Albacete and now the criminal sacrifice here on the steep and dusty scarp above the sparkling Jarama. The International Brigades were part of an army run like a trade union, staffed by revolutionaries and speech-makers, its ranks filled with a multinational mix of agitators, aspirants and card-carrying communists. The wayward sons of Europe's finest families sat whey-faced with dysentery on the velvet-covered benches of the Grand Hotel in Albacete alongside hard-drinking Irish republicans come down for the *craíc*. Passionate men from the Rhondda struggled to master the close, crowd-pleasing drill beloved of the Brigade commissars alongside hard-faced refugees from the German labour movement, while the French volunteers passed a vote and sat it out, proclaiming that close-order drill did them no good in battle. The Party loomed over every aspect of life at Albacete, its all-seeing eye and seemingly faultless organisation providing a sense of security, a promise that all the squabbling ineptitude of its human components would somehow come right in the end. Joe took great comfort from the Party, and became angry when Sidney told him he didn't believe a word it said. It was as though they had swapped roles and Joe was now the bright-eyed naïf, nodding along to the polemic as he polished his useless Ross rifle.

None of it mattered now. If they were going to leave, they should have done so when that sinister bastard André Marty gave them the opportunity to do so at the end of his great speech in the bullring. Not one man had stepped out of line that day, and Sidney had wondered what would have happened to anyone who had. The Party threw a long, dark shadow and it seemed that this great mass of believers and adventurers would be sacrificed for an undeclared end. Sidney's absolute certainty that he would survive was matched by an equal conviction that most of those around him would not. He could look into the faces of comrades and see their fates with complete clarity. There was never any doubt: that one would live; that one would not.

He looked at Joe. He would not.

They had been here two days now, out on the flank and tasked with the defence of a British machine-gun post thirty yards to their left. Sidney had abandoned the position he'd been assigned after being bracketed by the first enemy salvo. He knew nothing about the laying of guns, but it didn't take an expert to see that their artillery had his range. Twenty yards to his rear was an outcrop of bare rock. From here it looked exposed and inde-fensible, but Sidney reckoned with a little rearrangement it could become invisible and impregnable. Joe didn't want to move – he'd heard what happened to those who deserted their posts under fire – but Sidney persuaded him, and thereby saved his life. For a while.

They pulled back just in time, pressing their faces into the dust as the left-hand end of the French line ahead of them was blown to pieces under ear-splitting Nationalist artillery fire from the hills far across the valley. Sidney looked up in time to see a French gun position take a direct hit, vaporising the crew. He watched in awestruck fascination, pinching his nose to stop it bleeding, as a shell ricocheted from a boulder and span end over end in a whirl of smoke, climbing towards him like a Catherine wheel until it fell, inert, and rolled back down the hill. He saw the French abandon their posts, falling back in disarray as the Moroccan troops of the Fuerzas Regulares Indigenas arrived among them, punching a bloody hole in the lines before turning to outflank the British Battalion; and as his hearing returned he heard their voices, happy and excited as they regrouped less than fifty yards away, then the urgent pleas and desperate screams of their prisoners as their throats were cut. His heart was hammering hard enough to leave him breathless and Joe was curled in the bottom of the scrape, trembling like a lunatic. This, Sidney realised, was how men died in battle, the faceless, nameless nobodies erased by similarly moribund nonentities wearing different uniforms. Death was close by, sharpening his blade and biding his time, but Sidney knew that no matter how many Moors came for him, he would not die, not here. He inched forwards, parting the thyme with a steady hand and drawing a bead on a signaller who was standing in plain view a hundred and fifty yards down the slope. He had learned no semaphore in Albacete but he guessed the man was relaying fire-control orders to the batteries on the far side of the river. He waited until the flags were outstretched before pulling the trigger but heard only a flat click as his obsolete Canadian weapon misfired. 'Bugger,' he hissed, pulling back into cover and rolling onto his back to clear the jam.

Joe was moaning softly, his voice a trembling whimper muffled by his hands. Sidney kicked him gently in the ribs and he fell silent, sucking air in a great gasp. A slow drumroll of distant thumps came up from the river, followed by the soft, short whistle of falling shells as another barrage fell. The earth shuddered violently under the impact and a hard rain of dirt and rock splattered across slopes as the shots fell short. His ears ringing, Sidney looked out to see a squad of twenty Moors advancing across his position, crouched down and spread apart, their rifles held before them like pikes. He took aim on the last man and dropped him with a shot that hit him in the armpit before drawing a bead on the next. He'd just shot a man, he realised – probably killed him – and the exhilaration was tempered with relief that some hitherto dormant conscience had not been awakened by that first lethal shot. He pulled the trigger again and once more the weapon misfired. Licking sweat from his lip, he worked the bolt, hearing grit in the grooves, and slammed another round into the chamber. The next shot hit a short man between the shoulder blades, spinning him a quarter circle as he was knocked into the weeds.

The cheap ammunition had left a haze of blue smoke and a single enemy soldier, tall, bearded and black as night, spotted it. Unseen by his platoon, who continued their cautious advance, he fell out and scurried towards Sidney's position, moving fast and low, using cover and dead ground to charge the knoll. It was an action as brave as it was stupid, and it almost succeeded. Sidney took aim and fired at a range of ten yards. The Ross misfired. He threw it aside and seized Joe's weapon from his trembling hands, dropping the African at a range of six feet. The man's outstretched hand slapped Sidney's face as he fell, the side of his head blown away. Sidney took his enemy's weapon – a new Lee-Enfield – and his bandolier, and watched in dismay as the Moors rushed the British positions. The poorly trained, badly equipped volunteers stood little chance at close range against the veterans of Spain's colonial wars in North Africa, and as frightened, disorientated men struggled to clear jams and load unfamiliar weapons, the Regulares cut them to pieces. Reeling, the battalion pulled back, but a last-minute rally by the machine-gun company and Sidney's accurate rifle fire into their rear routed the attackers and the line was re-established.

The enemy retreated, but they probed all night, slitting the throats and sapping the morale of the defenders. Sidney was also abroad, crawling through the weeds to rob the enemy dead of weapons, ammunition and water, spending twenty terrified minutes beneath the remains of a French rifleman as three Moroccans paused five yards away to catch their breath and their bearings. By dawn he had a cache of six brand-new short Lee-Enfields and a Luger taken from a dead Spanish officer.

Joe was furious. The rifles were English, so to him were damning proof of British complicity with the fascists. 'So much for the bloody non-intervention policy,' he seethed. 'The bastards are killing us with weapons made in London!'

Sidney held the Luger at arm's length, sighting along the weapon. 'This one was made in Germany,' he said.

'Irrelevant,' raged Joe. 'We're fighting for our lives here.'

Sidney raised an eyebrow: Joe had spent most of the previous day curled into a ball in the dirt and the rest of it vomiting every time he noticed their dead companions' spilled brains. 'I'm the only one doing any fighting,' he said, taking Joe's Ross, drawing the bolt and throwing it aside. 'But I can't do it all on my own.' He handed Joe a Lee-Enfield, showed him how to use the charger and told him to make every shot count.

The Moroccans attacked in battalion strength just after seven, creeping up the dusty hillside like a tide of dirty water, hugging the dead ground and ignoring the impotent crackle of Republican rifles. They mustered at a range of one hundred yards, their voices carrying over the low shrubs and boulders that hid them. Then they advanced, using fire and movement to reach the line before ripping it open with their bayonets. Only the machine-gun company stood its ground, pouring fire into the enemy as the left flank faltered, then fled. The firing died away and Sidney watched as a runner sprinted from the isolated machine-gunners.

'Listen!' cried Joe suddenly, grabbing Sidney's arm. 'Our reinforcements!'

The thyme-scented air swelled with the sound of a hundred voices raised in song, the words indistinguishable but the tune unmistakably that of 'The Internationale', the workers' anthem.

'It's not our boys singing,' said Sidney, pointing downhill. 'Look at those bastards.' A line of nationalist troops was advancing slowly, cautiously, their rifles slung and their fists raised in the air. He crouched on one knee and took aim, but Joe knocked away his weapon.

'They're surrendering,' he gasped. 'It's a mass desertion!' He turned to Sidney and placed a hand on his shoulder. 'We're watching a revolution, Sid! This is history! The workers are leaving the ranks and coming over to us. We've bloody won!'

Along the line Brigaders stood open-mouthed as the deserters came towards them, more confidently now, their voices stronger, their fists punching the hot, still air. Defenders climbed onto parapets of piled rock and began cheering as others joined in the chorus, their parched English voices welcoming their African brothers in arms. Within minutes the deserters were in the British trenches. Then, suddenly, the singing stopped. The machine-gun company had been entranced and encircled, and Joe and Sidney watched like children betrayed as thirty men were led away, coldly aware that they were now utterly exposed.

As darkness fell, with the throaty cackle of Moorish voices carrying on a breeze that smelled of blood and cordite, Sidney crawled out once again in search of water, food and ammunition. Thirty yards out, he passed a Moor going the other way, but neither noticed the other. Ten minutes later, a single shot brought him crawling back, and he found Joe on his back with a dead Moor sprawled at his feet, an embarrassed smile on his face and fifteen inches of bayonet in his belly.

'Bloody done for now, aren't I?' gasped Joe.

Sidney opened his mouth, the lie like a coin on his tongue, then closed it again and swallowed. 'It's not good, Joe,' he said at last. 'Do you want me to get it out?'

Joe looked at the rifle, bobbing up and down in time with his breathing, then at the bayonet, and then at the black stain where it entered his belly. 'It bloody hurts, Sid.'

Sidney seized the rifle, watching Joe wince as he took up its weight. 'Bite your sleeve,' he ordered.

The groove on the side of the British bayonet facilitated its removal, and as it slid from the belly with a fart-like squelch Joe screamed, a high-pitched shriek of agonised disbelief. He passed out before the last of the steel was drawn from his guts, the smell of blood and shit reminding Sidney of the shed at home where he gutted rabbits. He took Joe's bandage from his breast pocket, tore off the cotton wrapping and pushed the folded dressing into the hole. The blood ran around it, trickling like spilled milk from the wound. He ripped the cover from his own dressing and stuffed it into the gash, knowing as he did so that the hole in Joe's back was bleeding just as badly. Sweating in the chill evening air, his hands sticky with blood, he took his handkerchief from his trouser pocket, folded it and rolled it before reaching under Joe's shirt to stuff it into the exit wound.

'You'd better wrap that.' Joe was awake now and staring down at his wound, his breath coming in short gasps.

'I've stuck two dressings on it,' said Sidney. He didn't mention the other hole. 'Hold them in with your hands.' The blood lay like a shadow on the pale dirt. 'If you can keep some pressure on it, you'll be right as ninepence.'

A short stream of soil and shale slid into the hole, as though the land was anxious to bury yet another volunteer, and Sidney shielded his friend's face as it settled. 'At least you got one of the buggers,' he said.

Joe shook his head sadly. 'He's one of us, Sid. Just another poor bloody oppressed worker doing what he's told. I killed him, he killed me, you'll kill his pals and their pals will kill you. The bosses and the shareholders will still see their families at

Christmas and this fellow's children will starve. It's a bloody shame.'

'He hasn't killed you, Joe. You got him fair and square, and now I'm going to get you back over the ridge.'

'Don't be bloody daft.' His lips were blue, his teeth red and his face, covered in tiny scratches that no longer bled but would never heal, was as white as the waning moon.

'It's all right: we'll be safe if we stay in the shadows.'

Joe shook his head. The night belonged to the Moors. 'Forget it. They'll hear us. I'd rather go with my balls attached, Comrade. Did you find a canteen?'

Sidney shook his head. 'Came straight back when I heard the shot.'

Joe winced as gastric acid seeped onto severed nerve. 'Had a feeling this would end badly.' He looked younger without his glasses.

'Hasn't finished yet. Give us that fancy scarf.'

Back in London, Mrs Kirow was famous for her silk scarves. They were six inches longer and a full two inches wider than the nearest comparable product, and were available only from the finest stores. Old Mrs Kirow could never have guessed that a sample from her 'Albion' collection would one day be used to tie the wrists of her mortally wounded son around the neck of a failed gamekeeper. The ridge was three hundred yards uphill and the sunken road that led to the aid station was a quarter of a mile further. Loaded with weapons, Sidney crawled out on all fours, dragging Joe beneath him as he crept through the shadows. They paused for breath behind boulders or under bushes, listening to the pleading, strangely accented cries of '*Sanitario! Sanitario!*' from unseen wounded, the mocking catcalls of the enemy, the whizz, crack and thud of sniper rounds from the Moorish lines, and the panicked outbursts of rifle and machine-gun fire from untrained volunteers terrified by rumours of silent Moroccan knife-work. Through it all Joe joked and mumbled, as

96

though witty repartee would divert Death from the job at hand, but just before the ridge he became serious.

'Promise me something, Sid,' he panted, his breath smelling of the blood that stained his teeth. 'Promise me you'll go home after this and have no more to do with it.'

Sidney's hands and knees were bleeding, and his body, battered by two days of battle, ached like a mule's. The rifles on his back weighed fifty pounds but pride wouldn't let him abandon them and he knew that as soon as he reached the cover of the ridgeline Joe and he would be safe. Sucking great gasps of air he nodded down at Joe. 'I'll promise you anything you like, pal,' he nodded. 'One more big effort and we're home and dry.'

He reached the aid station sixty minutes later with Joe and the weapons slung over his shoulder. His friend had been dead for exactly an hour.

7

The Hotel Alhambra was an unsightly, two-storey pink concrete block on the southern outskirts of Matamorosa. Built to accommodate travelling salesmen, truckers and illicit trysts, it sat back from the roadside spilling sterile neon onto a wasteland of weeds and wind-blown litter. Despite repeated reminders that the wheelchair was electric, Nick had insisted on pushing the fat man through the cold reception and along the bare corridors to their ground-floor room, his hackles rising and his toes curling at even this level of human contact. The professor made no attempt to romanticise the assignation, and the brutal assumption that Nick would be paid for services rendered made what he knew he would have to do only slightly more bearable. The room was as ugly as the exterior, with wipe-clean floors, a double bed and a TV that was bolted to the wall.

The professor sniffed as Nick wheeled him in. 'You want to shower?'

'Later,' said Nick.

'Now, I think,' insisted the professor. 'You stink like a pig.'

The hot water failed to drown his butterflies and as Nick towelled himself dry he shook at the prospect of playing the hand fate had dealt him. Lenny, he realised, as he opened the bathroom door to confront an obese, hairy, naked, disabled academic sitting in an electric chair, would be disgusted; but Lenny wasn't here.

The professor ran his eyes over Nick's semi-naked body. 'That was quick,' he said. 'Did you bother with the soap?'

'Of course,' lied Nick. He could smell his own anxious sweat.

'Nervous, eh?' smiled the professor. 'Not much meat on you, boy.'

Nick smiled back. 'All muscle.'

The professor raised an eyebrow. 'We'll see. Relax on the bed while I take my shower. We'll eat later.'

Nick nodded and stepped aside as the chair rolled past. The room was one of two in the hotel designed to comply with EU disabled-access regulations and as such the shower was fitted with a low seat and handles. There was also an emergency alarm activated by pulling a cord that alerted hotel staff should any of their disabled guests find themselves distressed. By standing on the low seat, Nick had tied this at ceiling level, and as the professor sang Bizet in anticipation of pleasures to come, he wedged the bathroom door shut with an ironing board. Dressing quickly, he tuned in to MTV, turned up the volume and rifled the professor's trouser pockets. There was no wallet – the distrustful bastard must have taken it into the bathroom – but the search turned up the van key, a few euros in change and a pocket-sized can of pheromone spray. Nick took the lot and was pulling out of the hotel car park before the professor had finished soaping his armpits.

He arrived in Palencia an hour later and, as predicted, Lenny was disgusted.

'It's a plastic bleeding Judas,' he cried. The van was parked in the shadows outside the station. 'Look: that's where the wheel-chair goes. At least you left that behind.'

'It's a what?' asked Sidney as orange rain fell softly through the streetlights and onto the empty street.

'Rhyming slang, Mr S,' explained Lenny. 'How could you, Nickle-Arse?'

'It's a car, isn't it?'

'Isn't it a disabled person's car?'

'Try to keep up, Mr S,' sighed Lenny. 'Yes it is a plastic Judas and, yes, Nick stole it from a raspberry.'

'Oh, well done, Mr Crick! It's good to see you again.'

'I knew he'd turn up,' lied Lenny, shaking his head. 'But in a bloody plastic!'

'You don't have to ride in it if you don't want to,' said Nick.

'Where on earth did you get it?' asked Sidney.

Nick opened the passenger door and gestured for Sidney to climb aboard. 'I'd rather not talk about it.'

'I'm sure you bleeding wouldn't,' agreed Lenny. He glanced at the back seat, then up the tree-lined street. 'Quick, Nick, in the back. Coppers!'

Nick looked left and right. A lone carrier bag was lifted by the wet wind and dropped twirling over the pavement. 'Where?'

'Never mind where,' insisted Lenny. 'Hop in. I'll drive.'

They rolled out of Palencia like a runaway shopping trolley, rattling over cobblestones and whirring past empty buses and lonely, troubled-looking pedestrians. Sidney found a road atlas and plotted a straight route east, avoiding main roads and passing to the south of the vineyards of la Rioja.

'You should slow down a little, Mr Knowles,' he warned. 'I don't want to risk capture after we've come so far.'

'Pop a chill pill, Mr S,' suggested Lenny. 'Raspberries go cruising with their mates, don't they?'

'I'm telling you, you're driving too fast.'

'I'm doing twenty miles per hour.'

'I'm not sure this vehicle is going to get us over the mountains,' warned Sidney.

Lenny let out a long sigh. 'Mr Starman,' he began, 'you may be the great dictator, but with all due respect you're not a young man any more and you've had a very long day.' He crushed Sidney's spluttering attempt to reply with a single finger. 'Tut tut! No arguments! Now I'm sure you're delighted to be reunited with Nickle-Arse here, but if it hadn't been for Lenny we'd have still been in that shithole Santander. In hospital, probably.' He glanced over at Sidney and raised an eyebrow. 'Now, I don't want to boast about what happened with those muggers but . . .'

'Yes, yes, Mr Knowles,' nodded Sidney. 'I can't commend you enough for your élan in the railway yard.'

Lenny lit a fag and nodded. 'What's he saying, Nick?'

'That you done good,' sighed Nick.

'Exactly,' agreed Lenny, 'and the point I'm making, ladies, is that you should sit back, relax, and leave the driving to Lenny. All right?'

That shut them up, thought Lenny. Sometimes you had to be firm with the infirm, although Lenny was wary about describing Sidney as such. Sidney Starman was not your usual OAP. Old people were supposed to be miserable, bloody-minded, forgetful, doddery, breathless and incontinent. That was the way Lenny liked them. They were expected to have standards and lifelong habits, to be generally disappointed with the world and to have no understanding whatsoever of the cost of living. Sad as it was, the aged were better off when they realised that they had outlived their usefulness on this earth and moved aside to let the new generation take over and look after them. In return they left their worldly wealth behind, and the cycle continued. It was like gardening, where dead plants fertilised the seedlings. The trouble here was that Sidney was resolutely refusing to play the game. By rights, his main concern should have been whether to have a cup of tea or to have a wee, not playing Napoleon, and Lenny was keen to resolve this anomaly. Tomorrow morning, things would be different. Tomorrow morning, Lenny would make himself the object of a little *coup de grâce*.

It was dark when Nick awoke, papers and pamphlets supporting a fascist history of the Civil War sticking to the side of his face. They were stopped in a lay-by in the woods in what seemed to be the darkest hour before dawn. Lenny was gone, and Sidney was fast asleep, rasping like a rip saw. He looked older without his glasses, thought Nick. He pushed the driver's seat forward and stepped out of the van. Lenny was standing in the shadow of a pile of tarmac, smoking and sipping from his vodka bottle.

'Sleep all right, did you?' asked Lenny.

Nick shrugged. 'S'pose so. Where are we?'

'Just past some place called Soria.' He took a swig of liquor. 'Just having a refreshment break before I wake El Sid up.'

Nick rubbed his eyes and fumbled for a fag. 'Why wake him?'

Lenny gave him a look. 'Oh, so you know where we're going, do you?'

Nick shook his head. 'No need to get shirty. Do you want me to drive for a bit?'

Lenny's laugh was derisive. 'Yeah, right. Get me in the back. Nice try.' He looked at his imaginary watch and pointed to the south-west. 'Some time soon, Nicholas, the sun is going to come up over that mountain there and it will be a new day. You with me?'

Nick nodded.

'Good, and you know why it's going to be a new day?'

''Cos the sun's just come up over that mountain there?'

'Yeah, and because this operation is going to be under new management.' He took another slug of vodka. 'I've got to say I'm disappointed in you, Nicholas. I expected more loyalty.'

'What *are* you on about?' sighed Nick.

'You know very well,' replied Lenny with a tap of the nose. 'Lenny knows, you know. Lenny sees.'

'Sees what?'

Lenny gave a joyless cackle. 'You can't kid a kidder, Nicholas.'

'That's a crap saying, and I'm not kidding you. You're just pissed off because I came back. You thought I'd catch the next ferry home, didn't you?'

'I know you much better than that, Nickle-Arse. Lenny knows.'

'Yeah, and Nick knows Lenny's nose is out of joint because Nick showed a little alacrity in securing transport.'

'That was disgusting what you did, nicking that plastic. I'm ashamed of you.'

'Not too ashamed to drive it though, are you?'

Lenny shook his head. 'Leave it, Nick. You've made me very angry over the past few days, but I'm quite prepared to forget all your disloyalty and to ignore the personal hurt you've caused me if you can insure me that we can move forward together in a mutually beneficial way. It's yes or no, Nick.'

Nick frowned. 'I don't understand . . .'

'Yes or no?' insisted Lenny.

'To what?'

'To us moving forward in a mutually beneficial way. Yes? Or no?'

Nick opened his mouth.

'Yes or no?'

'Er, yeah, but . . .'

'That's all I wanted to hear. Now, when Mr Starman wakes up, he'll be a bit Idi Amin, if you know what I mean.'

Nick nodded. He had no idea what Lenny was talking about.

'And by breakfast time, I'll be the daddy. You with me?'

'You're taking over?'

'Correct.'

'How?'

'What do you mean?'

'Do you know where the gold is?'

'Forget the gold, Nick. There is no gold.'

'How do you know?'

'El Sid told me.'

Nick's jaw dropped. 'Told you what?'

'What I said.'

'That there's no gold?'

'In as many words, yes.'

'What do you mean "in as many words"?'

Lenny put his hands on his hips, holding the neck of the bottle like the hilt of a sword. 'Obviously he didn't actually tell me there was no gold. That would shatter the illusion. He just sort of hinted at it while we were on the train.'

'What did he say?'

'Doesn't matter what his exact words were. You wouldn't understand anyway. It's subtle psychological stuff.' Lenny tapped a finger on his temple. 'The sad whirling of an old man's mind. You should be pitying the poor old sod instead of trying to line your pockets.'

'All I'm saying is that if Sidney's not in charge . . .'

Lenny held a finger to his lips. 'Nicholas! Shhh! Leave it to Lenny.' He weighed up the disadvantages of finishing what was left of the vodka, shrugged and tipped it down his throat, throwing the empty bottle into the woods. 'Let's go.'

As his passengers slept on, their necks lolling like those of hanged men, Lenny smoked superkings and considered his situation. He'd recovered quickly from his shock after Nick had strolled into the waiting room, a smug grin on his face, but the reorganisation of a company of two into a crowd of three twisted the dynamic, putting Lenny at risk once more. This time, however, he was ready for their mischief and had applied strong leadership to the group. His timing had been a stroke of the old Knowles genius: both Sidney and Nick were tired, hungry and cold, and in no shape to argue with him. The trip was once more under his control, and with careful management he would be back in the White Lion by Friday. Nick would do whatever he was told, and Lenny was confident that come the cold light of day El Sid could be gently persuaded that it was time to head home and maybe pop back another time. The mugging, decided Lenny, was the best that could have happened. He glanced at the map. Zaragoza looked like a largish place. Maybe it had an airport, and if they were lucky there would be some cheap and cheerful airline flying back to Stansted for a quid each. The important thing was to bring everybody back to Norfolk as quickly as possible without appearing to be too keen to bail out.

Contrary to Lenny's expectations, the sun rose in the east, a bloody stain on the night sky. A murder of crows flew into its first rays as Lenny waited for a convoy of tractors to pass by a rural crossroads. Sidney stirred, grimacing as he straightened his stiff neck. Harsh white stubble had sprouted from his face as he slept, the coarse hair looking out of place on his sallow skin and giving him a slightly seedy appearance.

'Where are we?' he croaked, unfolding his glasses with trembling hands.

'Near Zaragoza,' replied Lenny. 'Just waiting for these carrot crunchers to shift.' He leaned across and patted Sidney's arm. 'I think you've done very well to make it so far,' he smiled.

'We're nowhere near the end, Mr Knowles,' warned Sidney, 'so let's not be premature. We've acquired a vehicle, and credit is due to Mr Crick for that. We have yet, however, an equally pressing problem of which all our stomachs are well aware.'

'Cash,' nodded Lenny. 'I've been thinking about that.'

Sidney interrupted him with a sigh of exasperation. 'Would you stand down for a spell, Mr Knowles? You've been driving all night, you're tired and you're hungry. Why don't you get your head down and let me do the worrying while Mr Crick drives?'

Lenny took a deep breath that seemed to inflate his frame until he loomed somewhat menacingly above Sidney's frail form. 'Actually, Sid, now you're awake you should know that me and Nick had a chat last night and we think it's time for executive action. Don't we, Nick?' He looked over his shoulder. 'Nick! Wake up.'

Sidney took off his glasses and raised an eyebrow. 'What sort of executive action?'

'A *coup de grâce*, if you like.'

'*D'état*,' yawned Nick.

Lenny scowled. 'Nickle-Arse, please! I know my bleeding Latin! Anyway, Sid, we reckon you're getting a bit long in the tooth for all the responsibility that goes with leadership and we've decided that it's time for you to stand aside and let the younger generation take over. Haven't we, Nick?'

Nick smiled and raised a non-committal shoulder.

Sidney replaced his glasses and released a long, reflective sigh. 'Very well,' he agreed at last. 'I take it that there will be changes around here?'

'A few, yes,' nodded Lenny. 'First off, we drop most of this Mr This and Mr That bollocks. From now on you'll be Sidney, or El Sid. He'll be Nicholas if I'm making a point and Nick at all other times other than when I refer to him as Nickle-Arse.'

'And you?'

'I'll be Leonard or Mr Knowles. What are you laughing at, Nicholas?'

'I'm not calling you "Mr Knowles".'

'You'll bleeding well call me what I tell you,' warned Lenny. 'I didn't start this dictatorship thing, and it's not supposed to be pleasant. Look at Cuba, for crying out loud. Do you think he puts up with people calling him Fido, or do you think he's addressed as Mr Castro?'

'It would be Señor Castro,' said Sidney.

'And it's Fidel, not Fido,' added Nick.

Lenny shook his head. 'That's Fidel Sassoon you're thinking of.'

'The war poet?' asked Sidney.

Lenny hesitated. 'Exactly. Anyway, the point is that I'm in charge, and anyone who don't like it can leave.'

Sidney lowered his head in deference. 'I have no objections.'

'And you can call me Leonard for the moment.'

'I prefer Mr Knowles,' declared Sidney.

'Right. Well, the first thing is that I'm calling the whole trip off. It breaks my heart to do it, because I know how much you were both looking forward to it, but I don't think it's fair on Sid to carry on.'

'I'm perfectly fine to carry on, thanks, Mr Knowles.'

'That's what you think, but Lenny knows.'

'Shouldn't that be Leonard knows?' asked Nick.

Lenny ignored him.

'Anyway, the point is that we're going to Zaragoza airport and we're taking the next flight home.'

'I'm not going home,' declared Sidney.

'Nor me,' said Nick. 'We've only been here a day.'

Vineyards stretched away on both sides of the narrow road, the vines staked out like crucifixes. It was like driving through a huge cemetery.

Suddenly Lenny took a deep breath and pulled the brake lever. 'Like I said, ladies: anyone what doesn't like it can leave any time they like.'

Sidney opened the door and stepped out. 'Would you pass me my bag, Mr Crick?'

Lenny glared at Nick. 'What about you?'

Nick looked at Sidney, then at Lenny, then back at Sidney.

'Too late, Nickle-Arse,' growled Lenny, pushing the throttle. The invalid carriage backfired as it accelerated away.

'Where are we going?' asked Nick.

'Zaragoza airport,' replied Lenny.

'And how are we going to buy tickets?'

'They'll lend us the money. We pay them back when we get home – or at least that's what we tell them.'

Nick shook his head. 'Can't see us two getting charity. Look at us. We look like a right couple of dodgy geezers.'

'Yeah, but we're looking after an eighty-seven-year-old geriatric gentleman. We're carers. Not all people judge others on their appearance, Nicholas.'

'Lenny,' said Nick.

'It's Leonard.'

'Leonard.'

'What?'

'You booted the eighty-seven-year-old geriatric gentleman out of the car half a mile back. I don't think you qualify as a carer.'

The invalid carriage slowed down.

'And what about the will? How's El Sid going to sign the will if he's lost in the Spanish countryside?'

The invalid carriage stopped.

'And I don't think it's a very good idea to tell him he can leave us any time he wants.'

Sidney was walking with some difficulty along the grass verge, his leather shoes leaving dark tracks in the dew. The dampness of the early hours made every joint ache, but it was still the best time of the day. He heard the blue van before he saw it, its engine whirring like a lawnmower between the diagonal rows of vines, and he kept walking as it passed. Then it was alongside him.

'I can't leave you out here on your own, Mr S,' called Lenny. 'It's not in me. Hop in before you catch your death.'

'You should apologise,' whispered Nick.

Lenny ignored him.

'Why should I get in, Mr Knowles? Are you going to try to repatriate me?'

'Course not, you silly old sausage,' cried Lenny. 'Just want to get you back home.'

'That's what he means,' explained Nick.

'Listen, Sid,' tried Lenny. 'Why don't you tell Lenny where you want to go and we'll see if we can sort something out.'

Sidney dropped his rucksack and stuffed his hands in his over-coat pockets. 'I want to go to the Maestrazgo.'

Lenny nodded. He'd never heard of the place but it was bound to have an airport, so it would do. 'Well, why didn't you say?' he cried. 'Let's go.'

Sidney observed him for a long moment. The idiot still thought he was in charge. Perhaps it was time to test his leadership skills. He climbed into the car, hugging his bag to his chest. 'So what do you suggest we do now, Mr Knowles?'

'Right. Well, the first thing is to get some Crosby, and to do that we need to do a robbery.'

'Oh, for fuck's sake,' groaned Nick. 'We do not need to do a robbery.'

'I'm open to alternative suggestions, Nicholas.'

'Perhaps something with a little more subtlety?' suggested Sidney.

'We don't have time for subtlety, Sid. We need to get a tankful of petrol, some grub and get to wherever we're going double-quick time. Then you can be as subtle as you like. We'll do a petrol station.'

'We could get shot,' warned Nick.

Lenny sighed. 'It's very hard working with someone who's so bloody negative all the time, Nicholas. Yes, we could get shot, but we could also run out of diesel or die of starvation, and if you look at it, we could also get run over by a bus just walking down the street.'

'Walking down the street is slightly less risky than robbing a filling station.'

'Forget the risk assessment, Nicholas,' suggested Lenny. 'That was your old job.'

Sidney closed his eyes and took several deep breaths. The operation was falling apart around him, and if the rate of collapse continued it was entirely possible that he might not even make it as far as the mountains. It had all been so much easier in the thirties, although back then one had the benefits of proper organisation and quality personnel. He had always known that a journey in the company of Mr Knowles and Mr Crick would be fraught with irritation, but between them they had endeavoured to exceed even their own high standards of idiocy. They were, however, all he had, and all they needed was feeding and whipping, as Frank Cobb used to say.

The memory of Frank Cobb took years from Sidney. While his swollen prostate, aching back, throbbing joints and failing eyesight reminded him constantly of his age, the image of Major Frank Cobb snatched the carpet from under his feet and put him on his bony backside as an eighteen-year-old boy. He'd first met Cobb in Madregueras, where the remains of the British Battalion had been sent to rest after the mauling at Jarama. Word of Sidney's exploits at the front had spread fast and he sat somewhat bashfully in the special limelight reserved for the slightly insane.

Cobb sought him out and stepped into his billet wearing a long leather coat and a heavy Russian automatic.

'Who are you?' asked Sidney.

'Frank Cobb,' replied the stranger in an American accent. 'Don't bother to stand up.' He was in his forties, with brushed-back black hair and a lupine smile on a narrow, drinker's face. He looked like a film star, thought Sidney, but not one who would ever play a romantic lead. The American picked up the Luger lying on Sidney's cot. 'P08,' he said. 'Where did you get it?'

'Suicide Hill,' replied Sidney.

'From whom?'

'Enemy officer. I shot him.'

'Good for you, kid. What else did you get off him?'

'A map and some orders in Spanish.'

'You speak Spanish?'

'No, not a word.'

'That could be a problem.'

'I've done all right so far, Major.'

Cobb nodded. 'Yeah, but that was in your old job.'

'That'll do jubbly!' enthused Lenny, rubbing his hands together. 'Go up and turn round.'

They had just passed a filling station with a grocery store attached that perfectly matched Lenny's requirement for a small, rural petrol station with little passing trade.

'This is how it works,' he announced. 'We pull up and Nick fills the plastic up to the top. While he's doing that, I'll go inside, scare the shite out of whoever's on the till, grab the cash and we're out of here. Simple as.'

Sidney raised his eyebrows. 'Do you want the gun?'

'What gun?'

The old man calmly unbuckled the side pocket on his ruck-sack and withdrew something heavy and wrapped in a greasy brown cloth. 'This gun,' he said. 'It's a Luger.'

'Blimey! Let's have a look,' said Nick, leaning between the seats. 'Why didn't you use it on the muggers?'

'Because it was in my backpack.'

'Yeah, well, you can put it back in your bloody backpack, for fuck's sake!' cried Lenny.

'So you don't want it?'

'No, I do not want the bleeding gun, you old psycho.'

'And if by chance another customer drives in?'

Lenny frowned. 'We'll improvise.'

The proprietor was a short, dapper bachelor who wore a tweed hat, a navy blazer and a pink tie. His name was Luis Recuero Medina, and he prided himself on the provision of a full forecourt service six and a half days a week all year round. There were three exceptions: the first was the anniversary of his mother's death; the second his saint's day; and the third his birth-day. He touched his hat as the invalid carriage pulled up and retreated to the store. Today was his sixty-eighth birthday, and in recognition of that customers were invited to fill their own tanks, even if they were disabled.

'Think you can handle him?' asked Nick.

Lenny took a deep breath. 'Piece of piss. Leave it to Lenny.' He opened the door and started to climb out.

111

'Wait a minute,' hissed Nick. 'You've forgotten something.'

Lenny dropped back into his seat angrily. 'What?'

'You're driving an invalid carriage.'

'So?'

'So what's he going to think if he sees you strolling across the forecourt?'

'It's a good point,' agreed Sidney. 'Would you like me to go?'

'You stay where you bleeding are,' growled Lenny. 'So what if I walk? He's not going to report me for being able-bodied, is he?'

'No,' agreed Nick, 'but you'll make him suspicious before you're through the door. He might have a panic button or something.'

'He's right,' nodded Sidney. 'You'll lose the element of surprise.'

'Take these,' suggested Nick, lifting the crutches from the floor.

'Oh I say,' said Sidney approvingly. 'What a marvellous prop. They'll lull the bugger into a false sense of security.'

An ex-soldier, decided Luis, watching Lenny hobble across the forecourt. Recently crippled and newly demobbed: he could tell from the short hair and the invalid's ineptitude with the crutches. He looked away as Lenny approached the shop, not wanting to be seen to stare, and busied himself with a bundle of newspapers. The bell tinkled as the door opened, and the ex-soldier walked in.

'Morning,' he said.

Just two weeks previously a tedious young man from Zaragoza had tried to sell Luis a new alarm system. Rural petrol stations were the most vulnerable sector in the business and dozens had been forced to close after ruinous robberies. The new alarm would have been installed and operational in three working days, and included *el boton rojo*, an under-counter device that sent a silent alarm direct to the monitoring company who would then dispatch the police to the site. It was a marvellous idea spoiled by a ludicrous price, so Luis had compromised by fitting a do-it-yourself CCTV system instead. Standing on tiptoe, he aimed the flimsy camera at the big disabled man, surprised by the clarity of the image on the monitor. It wouldn't stop him being robbed, but it was more use than an alarm system that sent the police after the incident.

Lenny watched through the window as Nick filled the car. As soon as he had replaced the pump and started the engine, Lenny would make his move. In the meantime he browsed the aisles, trying to find something that looked familiar to eat.

Outside, Nick was watching the road. A green Citroën was approaching at something less than fifteen miles per hour, its indicator blinking orange. He prayed for it to pass by. In the front, his cap pulled down and peering from behind his fingers, Sidney did the same. Their willpower was too weak, however, and with agonising hesitation the old car finally pulled into the station. The driver was a tiny Spanish woman of Sidney's vintage. Her husband, an enormous man wearing a bottle-green corduroy jacket and a yellow waistcoat, sat beside her, holding a chicken. The old woman, her wiry grey hair gathered in a bun on top of her head, sounded an angry blast on her horn, and inside the store Lenny's heart leapt. He turned and saw the mud-splattered Citroën, then looked at the proprietor. Luis took off his hat and held it before his chest. Everyone knew it was self-service on his birthday, and every year that mad old *chocha* sat there and blew her horn until he went outside to tell her so. Today, however, she would have to work it out for herself.

Nick had relaxed when he saw the elderly occupants of the car. Their body language suggested that all was not well on the domestic front, but their presence would be of little concern to Lenny. He replaced the pump and slipped back into the driving seat. 'Pensioners,' he told Sidney. 'No worries.'

After a thirty-second, battery-draining blast that ended with a whimper, Señora Beatriz Bolaños Chavez ordered her lazy, good-for-nothing layabout of a husband to go into the store and drag that dandified fool of a petrol-pump attendant out to fill the car. Her husband pointed out that he was unable to do so because he was holding a live chicken in one hand and a bottle of *aguardiente* in the other. Disgusted, Beatriz stepped out of the car, red spots of pure anger glowing beneath the powder on her tiny cheeks.

'I do hope Mr Knowles treats her with respect,' muttered Sidney.

'I hope he's locked the bloody door,' replied Nick.

He hadn't, and when the old lady stepped into the shop, Lenny decided to downgrade the robbery by nicking some sweets and doing a runner. Unfortunately for him, both Luis, watching his monitor, and Beatriz, watching the event live, saw him do it.

'That man just stuck something down his trousers!' cried the old woman.

Luis nodded. 'I know. I got it on CCTV.'

'I don't care what you got it on, *señor*. What are you going to do about it?'

Luis shrugged. 'He's disabled. What can I do?'

Beatriz scowled. 'He looks like an anarchist to me. Call the police.'

Lenny had heard the police mentioned, so he slipped what looked like a tube of cheese and onion into his coat and hobbled casually towards the exit. Beatriz beat him to it, locking the door and barring his way.

Lenny opened his jacket. 'Look, it was just a tube of Pringles,' he said. 'Here, have them back.'

'Anarchist!' yelled Beatriz. 'Luis! Call the police!'

Lenny saw the proprietor lift the phone from the wall. 'Hold up, Sancho,' he cried, lifting a crutch and turning towards the counter. Luis knew enough English to know when he was being held up, but as he dithered Beatriz took immediate action, hurling a jar of locally pickled walnuts at Lenny. It hit him on the side of the head, knocking him into a confectionery display. As he sprawled among Skittles and Kinder Surprises, she threw another, which missed. The third was on target, though, ricocheting from Lenny's left ear to smash on the floor in quiet explosion of glass, nuts and vinegar.

Luis winced as she reached for a fourth – the walnuts were four euros a throw – then shrank in horror as the anarchist dragged himself to his feet, covering his head with his arms and bellowing in libertarian rage.

'Hit him with something!' cried the old woman. 'Quickly, you coward!'

Lenny pulled his hands away from his eyes with a yelp as the vinegar on his fingers rendered him painfully blind. He didn't see the walnuts strewn like big brown ball-bearings on the shop floor and had taken no more than a single step towards the light when he fell heavily on his backside in the broken glass. Luis seized the Castile–Leon Yellow Pages in both hands and belted Lenny across the back of the head. Beatriz turned and beckoned her husband from the car. He replied with a shrug that said, 'What?', and she responded with an urgent gesture that said, 'Just get in here, idiot.' Juan Chavez lifted the chicken and the bottle of *aguardiente*, sighed and began lumbering from the car. Luis swung the Yellow Pages again, connecting with the anarchist's shaven head with a dull crack.

'For fuck's sake!' wailed Lenny. 'I was going to pay for them!' He tried to push himself up from the floor and yelped as he pressed down onto shards of glass.

Beatriz found a broom and pushed him onto his back with a jab in the chest.

'Stand back,' warned Luis, 'and cover your mouth!' He leaned over Lenny, his mouth and nostrils hidden in the crook of his left arm, and sprayed a pocket-sized aerosol into his face.

'What the hell is that?' gasped Beatriz. 'Ammonia?'

'Tear gas,' spluttered Luis. 'I might have used a little too much. We should let some air in.'

As Lenny writhed on the floor, blind, wheezing and retching, Juan peered through the glass, the chicken under his left arm as he rattled the door.

'Something's gone wrong in there,' surmised Sidney.

Nick shook his head. 'He'll be all right. It's just a couple of pensioners.'

Sidney gave him a narrow-eyed look. 'Three pensioners,' he said. 'There's a big old chap going in.' He glanced in the wing-mirror, then up the road ahead. 'I'm going to see what's going on.'

'Quickly quickly,' urged Beatriz from behind her hand, opening the door just wide enough for husband, chicken and liquor to squeeze through. 'Why didn't you leave the bloody chicken in the car, you idiot?'

Juan's piggy eyes grew wide as the gas tickled his sinuses. 'Christ almighty, Luis! It stinks in here!'

Luis replied from behind a lace handkerchief: 'It's tear gas. Open the door!'

Juan was staring at Lenny. 'Who's he?'

'An anarchist on crutches,' announced Beatriz.

'Is that why you attacked him?' he wheezed. 'I've got to get this chicken out of here. It smells like hell. What are you going to do with the anarchist?'

'We should call the police,' said Luis, lifting the receiver. 'He'll have to pay for all this damage.'

'Can't trust the police,' replied Juan, shaking his head. Things had changed since Franco had died, and you couldn't trust anyone in uniform.

'Cut his throat, then,' hissed Beatriz.

Juan winced, sucking air. 'Let's just call the Minetto twins,' he said. 'They'll deal with him. I'm taking this hen back to the car.' He turned to confront an old man in a raincoat and a flat cap standing at the door with a handkerchief tied bandit-style around his face. 'Morning,' nodded Juan.

'Good day,' replied Sidney.

'Sorry,' called Luis, the receiver still in his hand. 'We're closed. There's been a robbery.' He fanned the noxious air. 'And a gas leak.'

'My chicken's sick,' added Juan.

'Sorry to hear it,' said Sidney.

'That's a good idea, tying the hankie round your face,' noted Luis, attempting to do the same with his lace-trimmed *mouchoir*.

Sidney pointed at Lenny. 'I've come to fetch him,' he announced.

Beatriz narrowed her streaming eyes. 'The anarchist?'

'I beg your pardon?'

'Him!' She kicked Lenny's ankle. 'This pathetic excuse for a man is an anarchist.'

Sidney raised an eyebrow. 'I don't doubt the former, madam, but the latter is preposterous. This man is a card-carrying apolitical – to him the left wing and the right wing are but menu choices at the KFC.' He glanced from face to blank face. 'KFC. *El Kentucky*. It's a chicken restaurant he favours.'

'What's this, then?' demanded Beatriz, thrusting a crushed tube of Pringles into Sidney's face.

He brushed them aside. 'It appears to be a tube of potato crisps.'

'He was trying to steal them.'

Sidney raised his eyebrows. 'I see. I think he needs to change his medication. The pills he's on tend to make him think he owns everything.'

'Because he's an anarchist!' cried Beatriz.

'If he was an anarchist, surely he would believe that nobody owned anything,' argued Juan. 'Wouldn't he be trying to collectivise the shop?'

'I think he's an anarchist too,' declared Luis, nodding at Sidney. 'He looks like a *pistolero*.'

Beatriz's eyes narrowed as she spied the triangle of unshaved skin not covered by the bandanna, the stained trousers and the muddy shoes. Whoever he was, this man was no gentleman. 'Gas him, Luis,' she growled.

Luis stepped out from behind the counter, the aerosol in his hand. He raised it, then lowered it as the momentum bled from his legs and the will drained from his heart. The elderly anarchist was pointing a Luger at him.

'Drop the gas,' he growled, 'and open the till.'

'Listen, pal,' interrupted Juan, 'I really need to get this chicken some air.'

'Shut up,' ordered Sidney. 'Get over there by the soup and take *la Doña* with you.'

'Barbarian!' spat Beatriz.

Sidney turned to Luis. 'Empty your pockets on the counter.' He plucked a silver mobile phone from the pile of coins, slipped it into his trouser pocket and handed Luis a penknife. 'Cut the receiver from the phone, give me the knife back and empty the till,' ordered Sidney.

'There's less than twenty euros in here,' protested Luis.

'I'll take whatever you can offer,' shrugged Sidney, pocketing the cash. 'Good, now move over there with the others.' He tapped Lenny with the toe of a dirty brogue. 'On your feet.'

The acrid taste of CS gas had seeped through the mask to burn his nostrils and scorch his throat. Only the old woman seemed immune to its effects, and she watched with hands on hips as Lenny struggled to his feet, sucking air in great hacking gasps. Sidney wiped his eyes and glanced around the shop. It appeared to be little more than a rectangular hut with but one door. He moved aside as Lenny groped blindly towards it.

'The keys,' he demanded, the handgun against his chest like a forties villain.

'You're going to lock us in?'

'You won't starve.'

'What about my hen, you vicious bastard?' yelled Juan. 'She's going to taste of tear gas!'

Sidney took two steps forward and snatched the chicken by its legs. 'What's in the bottle?'

'Nothing,' replied Juan. Sidney jabbed him with the pistol. '*Aguardiente*,' he admitted.

'I'll drink a toast to you,' promised Sidney, taking the liquor and stuffing it into his coat pocket. 'Now, if you'll excuse me, *señora y señores*, I have a boat to catch.'

'Anarchist traitor,' muttered Beatriz as Sidney went to leave.

He paused and turned back. 'Madam,' he sighed, 'you have no idea how much that hurts.' He stepped into the fresh air and locked the door behind him.

Lenny was lying on his side in the back of the van, gasping like a fish out of water, his bloody hands held tight against his face. A shard of glass still stuck in his backside sparkled in the sunlight and the van stank of tear gas and vinegar.

'What happened?' asked Nick.

'Just drive,' advised Sidney, the hen still under his arm.

'What's that?' cried Nick.

'A chicken,' said Sidney. He reached over and pushed the bottle of local liquor between Lenny's wrist and his cheek.

'Have a drink,' he advised dryly. 'It will help the tears.'

Lenny groaned and unscrewed the cap with trembling hands.

'I'll reassume command now, if that's all right by you, Mr Knowles,' announced Sidney, his moustache twitching above a tiny smile.

Lenny took a long swallow of the walnut liquor, his eyes swollen, bloodshot and streaming with acid tears. 'Right you are, Mr Starman,' he whimpered.

The chicken clucked uncertainly.

Tom Wintringham was not happy to lose Sidney from his command. More than a third of the 660 men of the British Battalion had been killed or injured on the Jarama, and he could ill afford to lose a talented individual like Starman. While questioning orders was a risky pursuit in Albacete, even for a man of Wintringham's standing, he was determined to establish the provenance and authority of the requisition. The man who had made it, a shifty American with a gangster's etiquette and a flippant disregard of military protocol, had breezed into Battalion HQ and announced that Sidney Starman would be leaving with him. When Wintringham had asked if he might have that in writing, the American had thought for a moment. 'No, you can't,' he had said at last, with a killer's smile.

He raised the matter with the Brigade Commissar and was given short shrift.

'Major Cobb is not under my command,' said André Marty without looking up. 'Nor that of General Kleber.'

His cipher clerk stood in the half light behind his chair, a nervous privy councillor to Stalin's man in Spain. Wintringham took a half step towards the table and Marty glanced up, covering his papers with an arm, squinting through his spectacles in irritation.

'It's one man, Comrade. A carpenter is ill advised to become enamoured of his nails. Surely you have more pressing matters?'

Sidney was already miles away, sitting upright in the passenger seat of an Audi 225 with the nervous suspicion of a child who has left with a stranger. Cobb played the part of abductor like a natural.

'Nice car, Major,' said Sidney.

'You like it? Belonged to the director of the railway company.' He threw Sidney a wolfish leer. 'I inherited it. It's new. Shame about the bloodstains on the back seats, I know, but it only had eight hundred kilometres on the clock when I got it. Front-wheel drive, all the latest German engineering.' He changed down to overtake a convoy of trucks. 'One thing, kid: drop the "Major". We don't have names, ranks or service numbers in my outfit. We're true socialists. Another thing: forget that dumb fuckin' Brigade salute. You want to punch yourself in the head, do it on your own time. Habit like that'll get you killed in the Field Repair Company.'

Sidney frowned. 'Field Repair Company?'

'Welcome aboard. Anything needs fixing, we fix it.'

Sidney scratched a fleabite on his wrist. 'But I came to fight. I don't want to be in a support unit.'

'I think you'll grow to love us.'

An hour later the Audi slowed at a checkpoint across the Valencia road. A trestle barrier, hung with paraffin lamps with red-painted glass, blocked the road. Clusters of villagers stood with the militiamen, cigarettes glowing orange in the darkness. A stone building sat like a tollbooth beside the road, its door ajar and yellow light spilling across the dirt. Cobb pulled over beside the barrier and spoke in rapid Spanish to a consumptive militia-man in a tasselled forage cap. The man nodded and walked with almost mocking slowness to the building, leaving a stench of garlic in the car. Cobb reached under the seat and passed Sidney something heavy, wrapped in an oilcloth. 'Mosin Nagant seven-shooter.'

'I've already got a pistol,' said Sidney. 'My Luger.'

Cobb shook his head. 'Sorry kid, but that Luger has been re-quisitioned for the Republican cause.' He opened his hand. Two fat slugs lay together in his palm, the Russian bullets hidden deep inside their cartridges. 'You'll need these.'

'What for?'

'Your first repair job.'

Sidney followed Cobb into the tollbooth. That same garlic odour permeated the air, now mixed with the smell of farts, sweat, brandy and black tobacco. Hooded eyes looked back at him in the lamplight, the faces expectant and fearful. Only the man in charge rose, one arm outstretched in sycophantic wel-come and the other pouring two glasses of brandy. He looked like a bandit, thought Sidney, dressed in stained striped trousers, a filthy shirt and a greasy sheepskin jerkin. His feet were bare, the toenails long and black. Cobb barked at him in Spanish and he whined in reply, shaking his head as he reluctantly poured a third glass of brandy. Cobb leaned forwards, took a glass and handed it to Sidney. 'Stow the pistol and drink this.'

Sidney pushed the cold, oily weapon into his waistband and sipped the raw *coñac*. It scorched his nose and seared his throat, bringing tears to his eyes that would have made other men laugh in another time and another place, but this assembly merely watched, their teeth brown in their sad, unshaven faces.

'Knock it back,' ordered Cobb, 'and take this.' He held out a second glass.

Sidney shook his head. The numbness he had felt since the bloody chaos of Jarama was melting away, leaving an acid anxiety. 'I can't drink another one,' he said.

'It's not for you,' said Cobb, indicating the third glass. 'That last one's for you and you'll thank me for it. Bring this one and follow me.'

They followed the barefoot bandit into the night. One of his men led the way with a lantern, holding it up until its feeble light fell upon a wall of flaking *cal*. The door was secured with a length of rope, and as the headman untied it he muttered something to Cobb.

'He says he's praying,' said Cobb.

'Who is?' asked Sidney.

The door swung outwards and the yellow light revealed a young man of Sidney's age, at most, his hands bound and his feet bare.

'He is,' said Cobb.

The boy smiled and bowed to his captors, blinking hard, his lower lip trembling.

Cobb leaned against the door jamb and watched him as he might have observed a sick calf. 'How old are you, kid?'

'Eighteen,' replied Sidney.

Cobb nodded. 'That guy's seventeen. He's a deserter. They caught him heading south. Second time, too. He's got brothers in Franco's mob.' He shrugged. 'What are you gonna do with a guy like this?'

The boy kept looking from face to face, smiling and mumbling his prayers in Spanish, as though unsure whether to please man or God.

Cobb watched him for a moment longer then pushed himself off the door. 'Give him the brandy. Then shoot him. Do it outside so you don't mess up the walls, and try to do it clean.' He said something to the headman, then swaggered back to the tollbooth.

Sidney joined him five minutes later. His hands were shaking and the pistol was smoking. He took the third glass and drained it, hoping the alcohol would help the tears.

8

'That was a bloody disaster,' declared Nick as he accelerated past a sign welcoming the stolen invalid carriage and its three fugitive occupants to the Autonomous Community of Aragon. 'What the fuck went wrong back there?'

Sidney glanced over his shoulder to where Lenny lay hunched on the back seat of the van, his hands covering his eyes. 'It all got quite hairy, didn't it, Mr Knowles?'

Lenny groaned. The shame of being beaten up by a camp pensioner and a woman old enough to be his great-grandmother hurt more than the vinegar, the glass, the broom handle and the CS gas combined.

'Mr Knowles couldn't have known that there were two strapping lads already in the shop when he went in,' explained Sidney. 'When I got there, Mr Knowles had successfully subdued the proprietor, the woman and the two, er, bruisers, and I feel I may be to blame for what followed. You see, when I blundered onto the scene I must have distracted Mr Knowles just long enough for the proprietor to spray that awful gas at him.'

'Not your fault at all, Mr Starman,' croaked Lenny.

'How much did we get?' asked Nick.

'Yeah, I'm fine, Nicholas, thanks for asking.'

Sidney fanned the takings. 'Fifteen euros.'

'Brilliant.'

'It's enough for lunch.'

'Only just,' moaned Nick. 'I'm sure I'm coming down with something. I need a hot shower, eight hours' sleep somewhere more comfortable than the back seat of a car and clean clothes.'

'You're right,' concurred Sidney. 'And Mr Knowles should wash that gas from his clothing.' He folded the cash and slipped it into his pocket. 'Gentlemen: I can offer a simple lunch, a bath, a change of clothes and a good sleep. Any takers?'

The *Embalsa de la Tranquera* sparkled in the afternoon sun, its sparsely wooded slopes tinkling with lazy birdsong. The River Mesa drained from the lake's northern end and snaked up a wide valley green with olives and citrus to join the Jalon at Castejon de Armas, a couple of miles away. A chill breeze gusted down from the hills but in the lee of the shore it was warm enough to doze. Sidney directed the van through a thicket of pine to the water's edge.

'Here we are,' he announced.

'What's that?' demanded Lenny, staring through the steamed-up window.

'It's a bathroom,' explained Sidney.

'It's freezing-cold bleeding lake,' announced Lenny.

Sidney stepped out of the van, placed a carrier bag of groceries on a flat stone and removed his overcoat. 'It will be bracing, Mr Knowles.' He loosened his tie and took off his pullover. 'Come along, Mr Crick! Don't tell me you're scared of cold water too.'

Nick smoked like it was his last cigarette, trying to decide whether the sight of a naked octogenarian or the icy water would be the more shocking. Cold water would merely accelerate his infection. 'I'll stay here and guard the clothes,' he said.

Sidney stepped from his trousers, folded them, and placed them on a rock. He wore enormous underpants, noticed Nick.

'You will strip off and bathe,' said Sidney. 'You both stink and I will travel no further until you are both presentable. Now stop arsing around and get in that lake.'

It was cold – so cold that it hurt – and Sidney was clearly immune to its effects. Lean and white, a vivid pink scar traversing one bony shoulder and his flat cap still on his head, he plunged into a pool and spoiled his companions' lily-livered attempts to tiptoe into the water by splashing them with the cruel vigour of an eight-year-old. The ordeal was doubly excruciating for Nick – he loathed cold water as much as he feared nakedness – and he remained immersed just long enough to soap the sweat from his skin. On leaving, however, his skin tight, tingling and curiously warm in the cool air, he was overcome with an elated sense of liberation, as though the lake had washed away more than dirt. He towelled himself down, dressed in clean jeans, T-shirt and fleece and sat next to Lenny, suddenly unable to wipe the smile from his face.

'Fuck knows what's happened to my Jacksons,' muttered Lenny, staring at the crotch of a clean Puma tracksuit. 'It's like a gherkin and half a walnut down there.' He lit a cigarette and pointed at Sidney, swimming slow circuits in the icy pool like an albino otter. 'Look at that mad sod. He'll give himself a heart attack if he carries on like that.'

Nick shook his head. 'It's probably what keeps him so young and vigorous.' He leaned back on a carpet of pine needles and gazed at the sky. 'How's your face?'

'All right.'

'Hands?'

'Fine.'

'Sounded like a hell of a scrap back there.'

Lenny took a drag and gave Nick a scrutinising look. 'It was,' he said.

Sidney was beaming like a man reborn as he crossed the pebbles. Lenny and Nick averted their eyes until he was dressed, then watched as he turned sausage, cheese and a long Spanish loaf into sandwiches. 'Twelve euros this lot cost me!' he said. 'Daylight bloody robbery.'

'You'd know about that, Mr Starman,' said Lenny.

Sidney smiled. 'And you, sir, clearly wouldn't.' He handed out the rations and filled his lungs with fresh air. 'It's good to be back,' he said.

'You been here before?' asked Lenny.

Sidney shook his head. 'Nearest I got was a place called Gallocanta, east of here. It's a salt lake – very different to this one.'

'Was that where you got that scar on your shoulder?'

'Oh no. I got that much further south, very close to where we're going.'

'How?'

'Some bugger shot me. I was damned lucky.'

Lenny scratched the back of his neck. 'I can't understand it, this volunteering business. I mean, what was the point?'

Sidney raised an eyebrow. 'We cared – well, some of us did. My friend Joe cared. He saw that the only way to beat fascism was to confront it and kill it.'

'So he joined the communists?' asked Nick. 'They were even worse.'

Sidney stared up the valley, chewing his sandwich and seeing faces in the clouds. 'They were just as bad as each other,' he said at last.

'Who won?' asked Lenny, swigging from a big brown bottle of San Miguel.

Sidney sighed. He had low expectations of the younger generation and Lenny consistently failed to meet them. 'Franco did.'

'And he was . . .?'

'The fascist. *El Caudillo*.'

Lenny choked on his crust. 'So you lost?' he spluttered. 'That's hilarious!'

'It was complicated,' frowned Sidney. 'We were always the underdogs, and while they had a clear aim, a strong leadership and an experienced army, we were torn by internal divisions, by feuds and plots. And we were alone.'

'Except for Russia, of course,' said Nick.

Sidney took a mouthful of beer. 'Suppose we'd won. Just suppose that we few volunteers had turned the tide and pushed the bastards back to the sea. Suppose we had shown the world that ordinary people could defeat the armies of Spain, Germany and Italy combined. You know what that would have meant?'

'Red Spain,' suggested Nick, remembering last night's lecture.

'Probably, for a while at least. But more importantly we might have prevented the Second World War.' He took another swig. 'Think about that.'

Lenny gave it a moment's thought. 'But you didn't win. You got your arses kicked, and World War Two happened bang on schedule. You should have stayed at home, taken things easy and minded your own business. It's best not to get involved in politics.'

Sidney scrutinised Lenny with a long, hard look. 'You're probably right, Mr Knowles,' he said at last.

Nick stood up and stretched. 'Listen,' he said, 'I've had an idea about the cash situation.'

Sidney stopped him with his hand. 'No more ideas from either of you.' His hip clicked as he dragged himself to his feet, but his skin was glowing and his swim seemed to have washed twenty years from his face. 'We might be over the border, but we're not yet out of the woods. Between us we have committed two rather amateurish criminal offences, and I do not want to be party to any more. From here on we need to be smart, subtle and above all united, by which I mean we do what I say, when I say it.' He looked at his team. 'I suspect that a lot of this won't sink in, but I'm telling you: from now on it's the highway or it's my way.'

'You mean *my way or the highway*,' said Nick.

'Don't interrupt me, Mr Crick. Neither of you has anything

worthwhile to say. I, however, do.' He half turned and pointed towards the sun. 'A few hours' drive in that direction are the Maestrazgo Mountains. It's wild and treacherous terrain, with jagged peaks and sheer drops into deep valleys. The roads probably haven't improved very much and last time I was there it was bloody cold at night – even in June. Somewhere in those mountains there is an old Roman mine, and in that mine, gentlemen, is stored Orlov's gold.' He took a deep breath. 'At last I appear to have attracted your undivided attention. I intend, with your assistance, to recover that gold, but I warn you now that it will not be easy. While I know exactly what the mine looks like, and could draw you a picture of its immediate environs, I have no more than a vague idea of its location. What I intend to do, therefore, is to retrace the route I took in 1937 and hope that something jogs the memory along the way.'

Nick raised his hand.

'Yes?'

'If you don't mind me asking, Mr Starman, why didn't you come back after the war?'

'Before I became a forgetful old man, you mean? In 1946 I would have been arrested, imprisoned and perhaps shot had I returned to Spain. You might ask why I did not return in 1975, after Franco's death, and it's a good question. The fact is that I didn't, and now we're going to do what I left undone.' He looked at Lenny. 'I'm sure you have questions, Mr Knowles.'

Lenny nodded. 'How much gold are we talking about?'

'If it's not been found, and I doubt it has, there will be a hundred boxes less the hoard I took for myself and from which came the coins I gave you.' He looked at Lenny and licked his lips. 'Call it seven tons.'

'And if it's gone?' asked Nick.

'If it's gone then the coins I gave you were the only proof I can offer that I'm telling the truth.'

Nick grinned, pulling his hand from his pocket and flipping

something that glistened in the sunlight as it span. 'Good thing I brought mine with me then, isn't it?'

Sidney watched the coin fall back into Nick's outstretched palm, his disbelief turning to delight. 'Well done, Mr Crick!' He glanced at Lenny. 'Do you still have your coin?'

Lenny hesitated, then shook his head. 'Left it at home,' he said, 'for the kids. You know, in case I didn't come back.'

'No matter,' declared Sidney. 'Nick's donation to the cause should see us through.'

'I feel really bad now,' mumbled Lenny.

'Get over it,' replied Sidney.

'Are we off then?' called Nick.

Sidney looked at his watch. 'There are only two places here-abouts where we will get a decent price for that coin: Zaragoza is two hours north-east of here and Teruel is three hours south-east. We'll make neither by close of business today. That means spending another night sleeping rough in a city and I, for one, simply can't be bothered with it. I propose, therefore, that we remain here for the day.' He stood up and turned to survey the valley. 'It really is quite beautiful, isn't it? You can see why men would die for this country.'

'No you can't,' argued Lenny. 'Holiday home, yes. Violent death, no.'

'There would have to be some personal dividend,' agreed Nick. 'Life was cheap back then. These days it's too precious to risk for an ideal.'

Sidney smiled wistfully, slowly repeating Nick's words as he looked south. 'There would have to be some personal dividend, you say? You know, there are people in this world would have you believe that.'

'I do believe that,' nodded Nick.

'That's cynical. The cynicism of your generation is what impedes human progress.'

'Here we go,' muttered Lenny. 'You've started him off again.'

'And maybe you should listen,' suggested Sidney. 'You two have grown up believing that nothing is worth doing unless it generates a meaningful personal return, and it's not your fault. Two world wars and a decade of Thatcherism taught you that there's no such thing as altruism, no act that is not motivated by greed, or hatred, or fear, and the cynics know that to manipulate society, to make it function, you need to stimulate the desire created by those feelings.'

Lenny released a long sigh. 'You lost me after Thatcher.'

'Well, the cynics would tell you not to worry, Mr Knowles. They'd tell you that was human nature, the animal impetus to prosper, and I agree up to a point. But surely there's more to humanity than that? Every time I hear that argument I want to ask, "What about the chaps in the International Brigades?"' He sat on a boulder and leaned close to his audience. 'I'll tell you what: I get the cynics giving me a load of old guff about idealistic youth and misplaced loyalties and even this ludicrous argument about the last chance. Have you heard that one, Mr Crick?'

Nick shook his head. 'Go on.'

'They say that the young men who grew up after the First War felt inadequate, unequal in quality to their fathers. Many professed pacifism, denouncing war on a cerebral level but feeling, like Sassoon, that they could hardly deplore what they didn't know. No one really believed that the Great War was the war to end all wars, but there was this niggling feeling that it might have been. The last-chancers argue that many of these young men, idealists, communists, pacifists, went to Spain for an intellectual adventure, just in case it really was their last chance to fulfil their innate warrior ambitions. Some did – young Romilly, Hemingway, all the headline grabbers – but most didn't. My old chum Joe didn't.'

'You didn't,' observed Nick.

Sidney conceded the point. 'I was never more than a hired

gun, but when I look back at the men who were with me at Albacete and Jarama . . . someone once said they stand up like the one tree on the battlefield not levelled by the bombing. I like that image – hearts of oak and all that. They came here because they believed in freedom.'

'So?' said Lenny. 'I believe in freedom. I'm sure Nickle-Arse believes in freedom. But we don't have to go off fighting for it.'

'And for all their good faith the International Brigades lost the war,' added Nick.

'That's not the point!' cried Sidney. 'Whether they won or lost is irrelevant. What matters is that they fought, going from Cardiff or Dublin, from London or Glasgow, knowing that their mission brought them no gain and no glory at home and yet seeing it through on principle. Most people in Britain had heard of Spain, but the newspapers and the newsreels told a twisted tale and few sympathised with the Republic. Of course, that all changed after it was too late. Come 1940, you couldn't find a Nationalist sympathiser anywhere in Britain, and the International Brigade was a home for heroes.' He brushed the dirt from a flat stone and skimmed it expertly over the lake. 'The Spanish cause was the last great crusade, the last time ordinary men from all over the world made a personal decision to fight and die for an ideal in a foreign land.'

'Steady on, Mr S,' warned Lenny. 'Let's not get too sentimental about all this. What about al-Qaeda? All those Arab geezers fighting the Septics in Iraq? Aren't they pretty much the same as your International Brigade?'

'They're terrorists,' scoffed Sidney.

'Isn't that what Franco called you?' asked Nick.

'I'm sure young Abdul's mum don't think he's a terrorist,' argued Lenny. 'She probably tells all her mates down the market that he's gone to Iraq to fight for freedom against the Americans.'

Sidney took off his glasses and rubbed the bridge of his nose. 'You're absolutely right again, Mr Knowles. Now be a good chap and gather some firewood while Mr Crick makes a nice wide circle of rocks.'

'What for?' asked Lenny, comfortably numb in the afternoon sun.

'I'm going to roast that chicken,' replied the old man.

If Albacete had been intimidating, the tiny camp at Benimamet on the north-western outskirts of Valencia was downright frightening. Back with the International Brigades, you could always find solace in shared inexperience and comfort in common ideals. Here, on Cobb's ground, there was neither inexperience nor idealism, and it seemed that every *pistolero* and *desperado* too dangerous for service in the army, the militia or the Brigades had found his way to Benimamet. Sullen, unshaven men in drab civilian clothes grunted in response to Cobb's growled greetings, looking upon Sidney like wolves upon a lamb. It was after three in the morning, and the American showed no sign of falling out for the night. He led Sidney into a cold, dark room, checked the shutters were closed and switched on the light.

'Like the desk?' he asked. 'Director of a bank left it to me in his will.'

It was an impressive piece in a room full of loot selected for quality rather than coordination. A Mauser pistol in a wooden holster lay on top of a mahogany sideboard and beside it stood an armoire more suited to the boudoir than the barracks. A narrow pine bed – the simplest furnishing in the room – ran along a side wall and above it hung a giant map of Spain in a thin gold frame. The protective glass surface was smeared with chinagraph markings and it reflected the light from a small chandelier hung directly over Sidney's head. A thick, burgundy carpet was rolled in the corner and another, deep, gold and luxurious, lay on the floor.

'That ammo box is there for a reason,' said Cobb, following Sidney's gaze. 'Goddamn corner won't lie flat. There was a big bloodstain on it, and after the girl had washed it out it went all stiff. Probably have to get another.' He placed a bottle of cognac and two crystal balloons on the leather desktop. 'These came from Toledo and this stuff' – his signet ring chimed dully against the dark bottle – 'I paid for out of my own pocket. That rotgut you were drinking back in Mogente is like straw against velvet compared with this juice. Try a drop – start getting used to quality.'

Sidney accepted and took a seat opposite Cobb. His body felt empty, the nerves deadened and the mind drained of all emotion. Killing men in cold blood was utterly different from shooting them down in battle, and Sidney felt unable to appreciate the full horror of the murder he had committed back there on the dirt behind the tollbooth. The man Cobb had left to supervise him had taken the glass from the sobbing boy and led him from the stable by the hand. He had whispered something into his ear before stepping aside and nodding to Sidney, who had raised the pistol and pulled the trigger, forgetting that he had not yet cocked the weapon. There had been a tiny click instead of a bang, and as Sidney had pulled back the hammer, the boy had turned, his eyes wide with hope. The pistol had gone off and the bullet had hit him under the eyebrow, lifting his scalp as it threw him to the dirt. He had stopped twitching before Sidney could fire the second shot.

'Nice work back there,' nodded Cobb, reading his mind. 'And don't worry. It gets easier every day.'

'Is that what the Field Repair Company does?'

'It's one of our jobs. We try to keep busy.' He opened a drawer, retrieved a cigar and lit it carefully with a long match, as though biding his time. 'This here's a guerrilla training camp. You know what a guerrilla is?'

Sidney shook his head.

'You soon will. It's not your regular army work. We don't answer to the *Ejercito*. We work for General Orlov, and he reports direct to Uncle Joe Stalin. He ran guerrilla units in the Russian Civil War and in Poland. He's a smart guy, and he'd be the first to tell you that the country is finished if it keeps playing the rebels at their own game. You saw how your guys performed up there at the Jarama – they got a snowball's chance in hell against the Regulares – yet the Republic will throw them into the breach time and time again to make headlines. "If every *brigadista* killed gets me two centimetres of column space I shall win this war in the newspapers." Who said that? Don't know? Your boss, André Marty said that. I heard him. And look at that fat asshole Hemingway and his whores on their grand tour of the lines like the fucking Prince of Wales. I saw that bastard in Madrid last year, up at the University City. We were up against the Spanish Legion – tough bastards, but honourable with it – and we had an understanding.' He ran his thick fingers through his black hair and crushed a louse with his thumbnail. 'It was the usual thing: ceasefire an hour before dark, let each other gather our dead and wounded, let the ration limbers come up, take a shit, whatever – and one evening Hemingway shows up with some giggling dame. Passes round some cheap brandy and insists on firing the gun at the enemy – playing at war, you know?' He sucked hard on his cigar, shaking his head. 'We try to tell him there's a ceasefire in effect but he gets his own way and he lets off a couple of dozen rounds. Then he gets the broad to do the same. Then they skedaddle back to their hotel to tell war stories to their idiotic friends. Ten minutes later we get hit by an artillery barrage that kills three men; and after that, no more truce.' Cobb knocked back his cognac and refilled his glass. 'You ain't got the faintest idea what I'm talking about, kid, have you?' he laughed, amused by his own passion. 'You'd think I gave a rat's ass for any of it! Listen up, here's the scoop: three platoons of my guys can keep a division of theirs in the rear on counter-insurgency operations, protecting roads, bridges and telegraph wires. We avoid contact. We move by night. We attack, we

135

disappear, we reappear, we harass, we spy and we melt away. We profit from chaos and we live off the land.' He drained his glass and refilled it again. 'That's where you come in. You were a tracker or some such back in England, right?'

'Gamekeeper,' said Sidney.

Cobb jabbed his cigar towards him. 'That's the one. Most of the brigadistas are city folk – highly skilled with hearts of gold but a fucking liability in the field. You're different, and you're a talented killer, kid. How many do you reckon you might have got on Suicide Hill?'

'Fourteen for sure. Maybe a couple more.'

Cobb blew Havana smoke and chuckled. 'Fourteen confirmed! In France you'd have got the fucking Croix de Guerre for that. Over here you get nada. Unless I find you. Then you get rich.' He leaned forward, as though preparing to share a secret or make a point, but became distracted by something at the back of the room.

Sidney turned to see. There was nothing there but a fleeting memory.

'Pilar!' yelled Cobb. The door opened and a young woman with a face like melted wax walked in. Her left arm ended in a badly swollen stump. She didn't speak. 'Show the comrade to his quarters, then come and take some medicine with Papa Cobb.'

9

Sidney was walking stiffly to the lakeside. Lenny watched him for a few moments, then stretched over the back of his seat and thumped Nick on the thigh. 'Wake up and look at El Sid.'

The old man was naked and was now wading into the mist-covered lake.

'I can't look,' groaned Nick. 'Where the fuck did he sleep last night?'

'The mad old sod made a bed next to the fire.'

'I seriously think I've got frostbite,' announced Nick. 'My feet are numb.' He scrabbled for his cigarettes with violently trembling hands. 'Got to have a smoke to warm up. Want one?'

Lenny fumbled for a Silk Cut. 'What the fuck are we doing here?'

Nick climbed into the front seat, started the engine and slid the heater to the maximum. 'I think we're having an adventure.'

Sidney joined them fifteen minutes later, his skin glowing but a frown on his face.

'El Sid looks pissed off,' noted Nick, and the old man cracked a dangerous, knowing smile as he came alongside the van.

'Gentlemen,' he said, 'I have a question for you.'

'Fire away,' sighed Lenny.

'Right you are. Why are prisons full of idiots?' He glanced from face to face, knowing the pair had inside knowledge.

'Dunno,' shrugged Nick.

'My point exactly. I'll tell you why – it's because only stupid criminals get caught. The smart ones are all around us, free as birds.'

'And your point is what, Mr S?'

'That smart criminals, and criminals is what we are, don't go breezing into Zaragoza driving a bright blue invalid carriage stolen from a cripple in Santander and used in an armed robbery less than sixty miles away.' He tapped the roof of the car. 'We have a serious problem, gentlemen.'

'No we don't,' countered Lenny, pointing along the shore to where two fishermen were launching a boat from the back of a pick-up truck. 'We'll nick theirs.'

They were on the road thirty minutes later, the misery of their cold night melting like hoarfrost as the sun climbed into a cloudless sky. The invalid carriage had been driven deep into the woods along a deeply rutted *camino forestal* and left beside a firebreak at the track's end. The professor's evidence of fascist righteousness in the Civil War remained on the back seat, somewhat creased after spending two nights under Nick; and Lenny performed a careful removal of his fingerprints from the steering wheel while leaving a perfect set on the roof of the car as he leaned in to do so. By the time he had walked back to the lakeside the fishermen had disappeared into the mists and the theft of their dirty red Toyota had been effortless, especially since the owner, with charmingly rural naïvety, had left the keys in the ignition.

'See?' said Lenny, shaking his head. 'Even though they saw the plastic they still left the keys in. No one ever expects the disabled to go nicking.'

They arrived in Zaragoza just after nine, parked the truck and set out in search of a coin dealer. By ten, Nick's coin had been sold for eleven hundred euros, and they were celebrating in a quiet café.

'What now?' asked Nick.

'Now we head to the Maestrazgo,' said Sidney, sipping a muddy-brown *cortado*.

'And you try to remember where the gold is hidden.'

'Correct,' nodded Sidney, 'but you should be aware of something important.'

'Here we go,' sighed Lenny.

'While I am the only person alive to have seen it, it seems that I'm not the only person to have heard about it. There are persistent rumours of its existence circulating in other quarters.'

'Like where?'

'A letter published five years ago in a German newsletter, for example, seeking information pertinent to its whereabouts.'

'What kind of newsletter?' asked Nick, pouring sugar. 'A coin collectors' newsletter? Metal detectors' journal?'

'It's called *Spanienkreuz*,' said Sidney, 'a publication for German veterans of the Condor Legion.'

Lenny whistled up another beer. 'The what?'

'Britain, France and America refused to dirty their hands in the Spanish affair. It was, according to Randolph Churchill – Winston's nephew no less – "a bunch of dagos killing each other". Germany and Italy weren't so snooty. Mussolini needed victory in a foreign adventure to boost his popularity in Rome, and Hitler needed to test his men and machines before he took on the Soviet Union. Spain suited both their needs. The German contingent was called the Condor Legion. It was all a long time ago but the point I'm making is that the whole affair is still very recent history here. The Civil War is far from forgotten.' He jerked a thumb at the barman, an unshaven man of Lenny's age. 'Ask him who the Condor Legion were. He'll tell you. Ask about any one of the dozens of separate factions fighting round here seventy years ago and everyone in here will know. Chances are that this bar has affiliations with one of them. Look at the graffiti out there on the streets: it's not the infantile scrawling we get in Norwich – it's political, and it's not polite.'

'So it takes a long time to get over a civil war,' said Nick. 'So what?'

'So memories are still raw. We must tread carefully in the Maestrazgo.'

'As in?'

'As in we keep our mouths shut and we watch our backsides, Mr Knowles. I fully expect the matter of the gold to be common currency in those parts and a subject of frequent conjecture on the part of the locals. It was always a sparsely populated area and I'm sure that foreigners will stand out as much now as they did back then. In order to quell their suspicions I have devised what I believe to be a convincing cover story.'

Lenny drew his breath and belched. 'Go on then.'

'We're fossil hunters.' He looked up at his team. They looked back.

'What does that involve?' asked Lenny.

Sidney wondered if he was being mocked. He looked at Lenny and decided that he wasn't. 'It involves hunting for fossils, Mr Knowles. The mountains of the Maestrazgo are a dinosaur hunter's paradise. Three men, in a van, with digging tools could as easily be searching for brontosauri and tyrannosauri as they could be looking for gold.'

'They're not called that any more,' said Lenny. He'd seen a documentary on Animal Planet and unusually some of the information had stayed with him. 'Your brontosaurus is now called an apatosaurus, and your T-rex is actually a bit rubbish. Apparently.'

'That's marvellous,' declared Sidney. 'Do you know any more than that?'

Lenny shook his head. 'I thought that was impressive enough.'

'Best refer back to the bit about keeping your mouth shut, then,' suggested Sidney. He opened a copy of the local advertiser, thumbing clumsily to the commercial-vehicle listings and peering closely at the print.

Lenny picked up a tiny aerosol can. 'What's this?'

'Pheromone spray,' replied Nick. 'Makes you irresistible to women.'

'Does it bollocks,' sneered Lenny. 'Where did you get it?'

'Found it in the invalid carriage.'

Sidney looked up from the paper. 'Are you familiar with a Peugeot Boxer, Mr Knowles?'

'Among my many other skills, Mr S. Peugect Boxer? What year?'

'Ninety-five.'

'Mileage?'

'One hundred and sixty thousand kilometres. The seller wants five hundred euros.'

Lenny raised his eyebrows. 'It's not a bad price for the mileage but it depends what state it's in.'

Sidney lowered the paper. 'Shall we go and see it? With luck, we'll be in the Maestrazgo for lunch.'

East of Zaragoza the N232 and the railway followed the south bank of the mighty River Ebro towards Catalonia. A couple of miles past Virgen de la Columna the road forked, its lower tine bending south towards the mountains. The stolen pick-up truck had been left in a supermarket car park, and Nick was now at the wheel of a rusty white van with poor brakes, a loose gearbox, worn-out seating and the words '*se vende*' still painted on the windscreen. Using Sidney as an interpreter, Lenny had persuaded the seller, a fat, taciturn man in a string vest and pyjama trousers, that the problem with your '95 Boxer was the head gasket, especially after 160,000 kilometres, and that he was, in effect, buying a pig in a poke. The seller, seemingly preoccupied with returning to an urgent matter in his bedroom, had agreed to take four hundred euros, and the deal was done.

'This land was once called Ilergetas,' said Sidney. 'It's a lovely

141

spot: protected from the north by the Pyrenees, from the south by the Iberian *cordillera*, watered by both. It was a treasure, and it was lost because Indibilis and Mandonius, the two idiots who ran the place, couldn't agree whose side they were on. That should be a lesson for you and Mr Knowles, Mr Crick.' He glanced to his right, where Lenny was slumped against the passenger window, his snoring fogging the glass and his unshaven chin shiny with dribble.

'Can I ask you a question?' asked Nick.

'You can.'

'This gold – it was Republican gold, right?'

'Correct.'

'And I assume that elaborate precautions were taken to keep its movement secret. Am I right?'

'That's correct. President Azaña and Mr Negrin, the Finance Minister, signed a mandate authorising the transfer of the reserve from Madrid on 13 September. A month later they authorised its shipment to Moscow. At this stage only Azaña, Negrin, Prime Minister Caballero, General Orlov and Uncle Joe knew about the plan, and the only risk analysis that took place was a quick comparison between the devil and the deep blue sea. I've heard that Negrin neither asked for nor received any guarantee from Orlov that the gold would ever be returned. On top of that, Orlov was under strict orders from Stalin to refuse to issue a receipt if asked.'

'How do you know all this? You were just a grunt at the time.'

'I knew nothing of it at the time, but since the end of the war the story of the transfer has become common knowledge. The only mystery, Mr Crick, is what happened to the hundred boxes that disappeared. Some discount the anomaly as a mere account-ing error, a miscount. I know otherwise, because I've seen those missing crates.'

'Who else saw them?'

Sidney stroked his moustache and shook his head slowly. 'No one who lived to tell the tale.'

At dawn on St Juan's Day 1937 the Field Repair Company appeared from the forest like a platoon of ghosts on the road five miles north of Villanueva, just short of the Alfaro turn-off. The patron saint of builders would have been impressed with the speed at which they constructed their roadblock, making barriers from birch trees felled at the roadside and erecting canvas signs painted in the workshop at Benimamet. A team armed with two Lewis guns and supported by a squad of riflemen deployed on the densely wooded slopes overlooking the road while two lookouts sprinted five hundred yards ahead to keep watch. Sidney watched as the men worked, feeling awkward in his new uniform and unaccepted in his new unit. The twelve men of the squad had followed without question as he had led them through the lines and over the hills, fifteen miles into enemy territory, late last night; but now, as a grey day emerged from beneath a colourless overcast, he felt redundant and insignificant. Cobb had not come on the operation, and a short, angry Russian called Sulov with staring eyes and a nervous tic was in command. However, his conspicuous albinism and Sidney's lack of Spanish excluded both from the intelligence-gathering phase of the mission.

As he approached Sidney, his pale blue eyes flashing with insanity, he kicked him on the ankle. 'Those no good.' He pointed at Sidney's gaiters, which had slumped like ill-fitting football socks to spill over his boots.

Sidney slung his rifle and bent down to refit them. The uniform of the Tercio, the Spanish Foreign Legion, was warm, well cut and comfortable, but to be caught wearing it meant that the arbitrary death sentence threatened to all captured foreigners by the Nationalist army would probably be rather slower and more painful than normal.

A whistle pierced the morning gloom and Sulov shoved Sidney off the road. 'You watch,' he hissed, pointing up the slope.

Sidney dropped down behind a fallen tree from where the field of fire covered the area immediately before the roadblock. A tall, pock-marked German called Kreuz strode into the road, adjusting the jauntily tasselled cap the Legion called *el gorillo* before standing with his hands on his hips as though he had every right to be there. Within moments a convoy of three trucks led by a motorcycle stopped at the barrier, flagged down by an enormous Hungarian poet they called El Gordo, who stood in the road holding a red traffic wand. Kreuz yelled over his shoulder and one of his compatriots, a friendly Marseillais with shifty eyes called Simenon, ambled over with a black ledger. The German ignored the motorcyclist's salute and approached the first truck, exchanging military formalities with the driver. He nodded several times, ostensibly bored, then sent Simenon to examine the other two vehicles. When Simenon returned he passed the ledger to Kreuz, who handed it to the driver for a signature, stood back, saluted once more and waved the convoy on.

'Two more, then we go,' said Sulov. 'We go here.' He stabbed the map with a thick finger. 'You make route.'

Two days later they were back at Benimamet, where Cobb found Sidney cleaning his ammunition in the spring sunshine. He dropped his cigar butt in the dust and killed it with his boot.

'How did you like serving in Tercio, kid?'

Sidney shrugged. 'Better uniforms, I suppose.'

Cobb raised an eyebrow. 'Are you saying you're unhappy with your kit?'

Sidney glanced down at his corduroy breeches and worn-out boots. 'It's hardly a uniform, is it?' He tossed a clean cartridge into one wooden box and grabbed a handful of dirty rounds from another.

'What happened to the Hungarian?'

144

'Didn't you hear?'

'I hear lots of things,' replied Cobb irritably. 'I also run a unit that makes the Chicago mob look like a Jesuit seminary. Things happen. So tell me what happened to the Hungarian.'

'He fell out of the train while taking a piss.'

The American looked at him for a long moment. 'That's what I heard.'

'Did we get what you wanted?'

Cobb stuck a finger in his ear, waggled it, and inspected the results. 'Sure you did. There was a big hole in our intelligence about enemy forces in the area. You guys repaired it.'

The road ran due south, rising and falling like a gentle sea, heading straight for a horizon of hills. Nick swept a hand across the landscape, a bare, treeless plain littered with sullen boulders and the whitewashed ruins of abandoned homes. 'It's like a desert,' he said.

'That's exactly what it is,' nodded Sidney. '"El Desierto de Calanda". It hardly ever rains here. What little soil that hasn't been destroyed by centuries of sheep grazing has been blown away because all the trees have been cut down. It's dead ground: nobody lives here any more.'

'Was it like this in '36?'

Sidney watched the empty land go by. 'Exactly the same.'

'Except those houses would have been occupied back then,' said Lenny.

'Not at all. They were deserted then. It was something you couldn't fail to notice, to feel: the utter emptiness of the countryside. One could drive for hours and not see another soul. Not even a dog. And at night the road seemed to be all that existed, like a causeway through limbo.'

'Where did they go?'

Sidney shrugged. 'I don't know. When the war broke out the local fascists set about the local anarchists. Some fled. Many

145

were shot. Then new anarchists arrived from the cities and lynched the local fascists. I suppose with all that going on anyone with any sense thought themselves safer in the villages than out on the *campo*. I'd have moved. Wouldn't you?'

'Too right,' agreed Lenny. 'I'd have fucked off to England.'

'Yes, well, then you would have missed the only decent thing to have come out of the whole dirty, bloody mess.'

Lenny yawned. 'Am I bothered?'

'What happened?' asked Nick.

'They collectivised. They would have a meeting in the village, in what they called the *casa del pueblo*, if it hadn't been burned out by the fascists, or elsewhere, and they would ask everyone to donate everything they owned to the cause.'

'Like what?' asked Lenny.

'Everything: house, livestock, land, if you owned any, tools, money, labour, the whole bloody shebang.'

'The wife?' sniggered Lenny.

'She gave of herself freely. The libertarian anarchists were famous for their teetotalism, abstention and moderation in all affairs. They agreed to ban smoking, alcohol, sexual and racial discrimination. And marital infidelity, which always intrigued me, because they also banned marriage. So everyone surrendered everything to the community, the collective, thus, I suppose, renouncing all the trappings of capitalism.'

'Bollocks to that,' breathed Lenny. 'How did anyone make any money?'

'You're completely missing the point. Money was abolished.'

'So how could I buy fags?'

'Fags were banned, remember.'

'What about sausages? How could I buy sausages?'

'You didn't. You went to the butcher, asked him and he gave them to you. Same for olive oil, flour and milk: you went to the communal store and took what you needed.'

Nick overtook a man in yellow lycra on a racing bicycle, a

single streak of life in a dead landscape. 'Hold up: I can't get my head round this. Where did all this food come from?'

'From the land. *You* produced the food. *You* helped raise the pork for the sausage. *You* harvested the olives for the oil. You and your fellow men, and women, together.' Sidney glanced at Lenny. 'You'd have loved it, Mr Knowles. When the anarchist columns arrived, they chased away the landlords, the *caciques*, the bourgeoisie – all those who had profited from the peasants – and they seized their homes, their land and all their possessions. Religion was abolished so they used the churches as warehouses – in Alcaniz they stored everything in the cathedral. So, when Señor Knowles needs a nice mahogany sideboard for his home, or an attractive oil painting for his wall, or perhaps a fine dinner service, all he has to do is pop into the cathedral and sign it out.'

'Then I can go and sell it down the market?'

'Of course you can't, because there's no money. No markets, either.'

'What about a haircut, or the dentist?'

'Professionals and tradesmen didn't have to pay for their food, or for any essentials, so they didn't need money. Just as you donated your labour to the common good, they donated their skills. Everything was free, if you like, and the advantage of collectivisation on the farms was that the economies of scale and improved yields meant they could buy better seeds and fertilisers—'

'With what? You said they abolished money.'

'Within the community, yes. But each collective existed like an island in a sea of capitalism, and initially they needed cash to trade with the outside world.'

Lenny snorted. 'Sounds like a load of old hippy bollocks to me. Who held on to the money?'

'Whoever was elected to do so.'

'Nice work if you can get it.'

147

'You're very cynical, Mr Knowles.'

'Just a realist, Mr Starman. I've seen these cults and there's always some tosser at the top getting rich.'

Sidney shrugged. 'Well, it was a beautiful experiment. In a little under a year they revolutionised education, social welfare and justice, and yields on well-run agricultural collectives were in some cases eight or ten times higher than the land had given up before.'

'And then the fascists came along and spoiled it?' guessed Nick.

Sidney shook his head. 'Then the Republic came along and spoiled it. Word was getting out to the rest of the world that the people had seized the land, abolished money, banished the priests and what have you, and the government panicked. Didn't want England and France to think that Spain was descending into anarchy, so they sent in the communists to break it all up. And that, gentlemen, was that.'

'Good thing too,' muttered Lenny. 'No fags or booze? Bloody ridiculous way to run a country.'

Ahead, the line between Baja and Alta Aragon was marked by a row of low, dust-coloured hills that rose in successive undulations like the cumulo nimbus of an advancing storm front. Sidney put another sweet into his mouth. 'You may scoff, Mr Knowles, but you're perfect anarchist material yourself.'

'Am I fuck.'

'Do you pay taxes?'

'Course not.'

'Who did you vote for at the last election?'

Lenny paused. 'I wasn't actually in a position to use my vote last time round. Nor was Nicholas.'

'Have you ever voted?'

'Nope.'

'Why not?'

''Cos politics is nothing to do with me. I just want to be left on me tod to do my own thing. I don't harm no one, and no one harms me, and I'm not paying some fat bastard to tell me what to do with my life.'

'I rest my case,' smiled Sidney. 'Man's natural state is one of libertarian anarchism and you, Mr Knowles, are a natural man. Now can we pull over for a moment, Mr Crick? I need to pee.'

The desert plain rose to meet the Sierra de los Moros, a sombre escarpment on the ragged northern edge of the province of Teruel. Plaintive graffiti sprayed across road signs insisted that '*Teruel existe!*' but evidence of human habitation was rarely visible in support of this declaration. Abandoned homes, farms and villages lay by the wayside, their roofs collapsed and their windows broken, the unburied corpses of communities that were born to lose. As the road wound higher and the air became thinner and colder the hard ironworks of bleak coalmining communities rusted in dark valleys, their names – Alacon, Cortes de Aragon – typical of sunny Spain but their faces evocative of Siberia. Lenny was clearly taken aback by the brutal ugliness of the land.

'I thought the same when I first came,' said Sidney. 'To me, Spain was a land of sunshine, oranges and sultry gypsies. Never struck me that it could snow here, that people could die of starvation or exposure.'

Lenny shivered. 'I don't know why you bothered coming in the first place. Should have got yourself a nice little piece of skirt, settled down and looked after your pheasants. Instead you came all the way down here to take pot-shots at Germans when you could have waited until World War Two, got in your bomber and nipped over to Dresden. You could have nailed a thousand of the buggers in a night.'

Sidney nodded. 'I did that as well.'

The road descended the southern slopes of the sierra to the valley of the Rio Martin. Sidney's eyes widened as they approached the junction with the Caminreal road, and he felt a prickle of sweat along his upper lip. 'I've been here before,' he whispered, like a man with déjà vu.

'This where the gold is?' asked Lenny.

'No . . . no, the gold is up in those mountains across the river. Something else happened here . . .' His voice drifted off as he focused on the memory. Then he sniffed, blinked and shook his head. 'Nothing important.'

10

It was April 1937 and Sidney had put on weight. He had not been in the field since Sulov's roadblock operation and had spent the past six weeks teaching illiterate Andalucian *campesinos* musketry and fieldcraft. Cobb had ordered him to instruct them in the art of living off the land, but these men needed no lessons in survival. When Sidney had begun explaining how to make a snare they had stopped him, and asked good-naturedly why one needed a wire to catch a rabbit when one had one's hands. Initially wary of these swarthy men with their thick black hair and rotten teeth, Sidney soon found himself attracted and amused by their warmth, their generosity and their overwhelming gratitude for his assistance in their struggle. He grew flabby on their gifts of fatty *jamon negra*, *queso antiguo* and spicy *sobresada*, and soon developed a taste for the unrefined alcoholic kick of *aguardiente*. Spending days at a time in their company, deep in the forests around Loriguilla, and far from the cold cynicism of Benimamet, he found at last the passion for revolution that Joe had so dearly sought. His Spanish improved through immersion, his face darkened in the spring sun and when his boots could be repaired no more he put on a pair of rope-soled espadrilles.

If Cobb was impressed by his transformation from confused, pale-skinned Englishman to unshaven, sunburned guerrilla, he didn't show it. 'Sid the Kid, you're getting fat,' he said.

Sidney sat in the chair before Cobb's fine inherited desk. 'Not as fat as some,' he replied.

Cobb laughed. 'You need an adventure. Join us tonight – we're going up the coast a ways, and inland.'

A thin white moon hung over the Mediterranean casting a ghostly glow over a dead-calm sea. Cobb drove north at high speed: the road was empty and he was the law. Riding beside him was Klee, an ox-necked brute with a shaven head and tiny eyes whom Sidney had seen around but never previously met. Alongside Sidney in the back sat Kreuz, the tall German from the roadblock operation, his face scarred by smallpox and his long, slicked-back blond hair shiny with grease. The final member of the group was Simenon, who sat and grinned like a spaniel.

'Here's the scoop,' drawled Cobb, 'for those of you who care. I am informed by our leader that the Communist Party can no longer work with the anarchists. Their interests and the interests of the country have diverged.'

'Which country?' asked Klee. 'Spain or Russia?'

Cobb looked at him for a moment, as though perplexed. 'They're the same, aren't they?'

'Gentlemen, please!' smirked Simenon. 'That talk is unpatriotic. You'll frighten the boy.'

'I beg to differ,' replied Cobb. 'I think it's entirely patriotic. Our leaders believe that the militarisation of the army is the key to winning this war, and if I thought this war was winnable, I'd have to agree. Look at the picture: in the blue corner we have the Army of Africa, the Legion, the Regulares, the Falange, the Requetes, the Italians and the Germans – all separate units but all united under one great leader. You take the nigger from Morocco, the attorney from Seville, the spaghetti farmer from Rome, the party activist from Munich, the Carlists or the god-damned singer from the Canaries, and they are all marching to the beat of the same fucking drum. That's why they're going to win, boys, because in the red corner we've got your Marxist

POUMistas, the anarchists of the CNT, not forgetting the anarchists of the FAI, the PSOE, the PCE, the Asaltos, the Ejercito and us. All trying to fight a common enemy and stamp on each other's fingers while we do it. None of us trusts each other, and none of us wants the same thing. That's why the Republic is going to lose.'

'So what we've got to do is unite under one leader and forget our differences,' said Sidney.

Cobb caught his eye in the rear-view. 'So tell us, Sid the Kid, how are we going to persuade our anarchist friends and Marxist cousins to rally under our big red flag?'

Sidney sat back and shrugged. 'You tell me.'

Cobb turned to Klee. 'Show him.'

Klee shifted in his seat to look at Sidney, his big mouth cracked in a cruel smile. He reached into his leather coat, raising an eyebrow like a fairground conjuror, and pulled out a seven-inch stiletto. The blade was blackened, but its honed double edge gleamed in the moonlight. 'We prod them into line with long knives,' he said.

Kreuz nodded. '*Die Nacht der langen Messer*. It worked for Herr Hitler.'

Cobb sighed. 'There's no politeness in politics any more.'

He turned off the coast road at Vinaroz and took a winding route through the Montes de Vallivana, their looming black bulk outlined in silver by the moon. The road curled through dark villages with Catalan names like Traiguera, Chert and Enfoig, where no lights burned and not even a dog marked their passing.

Cobb lit a cigar butt and shook his head in resignation. 'Yea though I drive through the valley of the shadow of Death I shall fear no evil,' he intoned, 'because I am the evillest bastard in the valley.'

Kreuz had fallen asleep, his head lolling as though he'd been cut down from the noose. In the front Klee was quietly cus-tomising rounds for his machine-pistol. Simenon played an annoying game with his hands, pausing to grin at Sidney every time he caught his eye. Cobb half sang, half hummed 'What a Friend I Have in Jesus' for the next hour, until he pulled over on a steep incline. 'Gentlemen, we're here.'

A nervous youth with a wispy moustache emerged from the shadows as the group climbed from the Audi. He dropped his cigarette and shook hands with Cobb, his rapid conversation and jerky movements belying his anxiety. A couple of hundred yards up the hill the road passed through the arched gateway to a fortified village, a hilltop castle with crenellations silhouetted against the night sky. Cobb, whose relaxed demeanour had little effect upon his informant, squatted in the lee of the Audi and balanced his Thompson sub-machine-gun across his knee. With his long leather coat and his brilliantined hair he looked more like a Chicago gangster than a Communist agent, and his men compounded the image. Klee wore an expensive pin-striped suit and Kreuz a tweed jacket and woollen trousers. Simenon was dressed in a pale blue blazer with a black open-necked shirt and espadrilles. One would have taken him for a weekend cruiser to the casinos of Biarritz rather than a hired gun.

'Antonio here says we've got some time to kill, so I'll brief you on the situation,' announced Cobb. 'That's Castellote up there, forward food dump for the whole northern Teruel sector. There's a company of old men and halfwits who are supposed to be guarding the place, but they'll give us no trouble. We're after their boss – Captain Ranzato – and he's nominally CNT. I say nominally because his anarchist pals would lynch him if they knew the racket he's got running from here. His brother-in-law is Comrade Cano. Heard of him?' Only Klee nodded. Cobb continued: 'Cano's a delegate – kind of a major in the anarchist militia – and he's got big influence in the Iron Column. Tell the kid who the Iron Column are, Kreuz.'

The pockmarked blond scratched his ear. 'The Iron Column

is an anarchist brigade. Its members are mostly freed political prisoners. They have no officers, just delegates and committees. They are scum.'

'Just like us, Kreuz, only they're the Spanish variety,' added Cobb. 'They're not all ex-cons. The majority are believers, but one thing they don't believe is that they should abandon their anarchist principles and rally under our big red flag. Cano, indeed, is quite insistent that they should remain apart, as is his comrade Aranjuc, who's on the committee, although for different reasons. Cano will tell you that there are five thousand men under arms in his sector. He draws pay, ammunition and rations for that number.'

'And the real muster is, what, three and a half?' asked Simenon.

'Yeah,' nodded Cobb. He raised an eyebrow at Sidney. 'You get my drift, kid? Cano and Ranzato are making fortunes selling the surplus food down on the coast and I am advised that they're stockpiling the ammunition for use against us at a time and a date to be confirmed. It's rotten, and tonight, gentlemen, we have the opportunity to catch them in the act.' He nodded towards the castle. 'They're up there now, in Ranzato's house, drinking stolen cognac and smoking black-market cigars, no doubt.' Cobb appeared offended by the thought.

'So let's go!' said Simenon.

Cobb held up a hand. 'Easy, Frenchie. We eliminate Ranzato and Cano and we eliminate a pair of corrupt black marketeers. We still have a bleeding heart in the Iron Column.'

'Aranjuc,' muttered Kreuz.

'Now you're getting it. Aranjuc is as clean as a whistle, but he's too honest for leadership. If he told his boys it was in the greater good to join the Communist Party every last one of the bastards would paint his ass red, but he's never going to do it. The sucker truly believes that this war against fascism is a mere distraction, and that the real revolution will continue after Franco's been stood against a wall. We can't be having that crap. I went to see him last week with Lazar from the Ministry. We told him about Cano's scam. He was hurt, embarrassed, but he couldn't refute the evidence, so he asked us to arrest Cano straight away. We declined the offer, suggesting that he make the arrest himself, with us as back-up. Lazar pointed out that after the riots in Valencia it was important for the Iron Column to be seen to be keeping its house in order.' He glanced at his wristwatch. 'I hope he turns up.'

'And he believed you?' asked Kreuz.

Cobb shrugged. 'Doubt it, but what's he going to do? When the Ministry makes a suggestion there is rarely an alternative.'

Sidney looked from face to face and saw not the slightest expression of doubt or conscience. They seemed no more anxious than men setting out to shoot a fox.

'Is this wet or dry?' asked Simenon.

'Ranzato and Cano are coming with me to Valencia,' explained Cobb.

'And Aranjuc?'

'Well, technically, he's done nothing wrong, so we can't hold him.' He nodded at Kreuz. 'He'll go with you. Take the kid with you and drive him as close to the front line as you can get.'

'Then what?'

Cobb's knee clicked as he stood. He reached into the Audi and pulled out a soft black briefcase. 'Give him this,' he said, handing Kreuz a manila envelope, 'and let him go.'

'What's in here?' asked Kreuz, shaking the envelope.

'A map of our front line. Some of the units marked on it are really where we say they are.'

Kreuz raised his eyebrows.

Simenon smiled. '*Ley de fuegas?*' he asked.

Cobb bit his lip, as though considering his response. He nodded slowly. '*Ley de fuegas.*'

★

The arrest was easy. Sidney waited outside with Kreuz and Aranjuc's driver. The German shared his cigarettes then advised the soldier to disappear before he too was arrested for treason, waving him off with enough rumours to scandalise his comrades. Cobb and the others led the handcuffed prisoners from Ranzato's home a few minutes later, the householder shaking his head in disbelief, his brother-in-law bleeding from the mouth and Aranjuc smiling in what seemed to be grudging admiration. The smile dropped as he was separated from his comrades, replaced by breathless, wide-eyed suspicion as he was pushed into his own truck between Sidney and Kreuz.

'Take him home,' snarled Cobb, handing Sidney the key to Aranjuc's cuffs and shaking his head as Ranzato's distraught wife and daughters ran alongside the Audi and tried to pass parcels of food through the windows. 'I'll see you two later.'

The prisoner wore round spectacles on wire frames and kept tipping his head backwards to stop them sliding down his nose. Dark stains seeped across his grubby white shirt and Sidney could smell the sweat as they left the village, the thick, nauseating odour of hope evaporating from a lost soul. Kreuz seemed distracted and withdrawn, merely shaking his head or shrugging in reply to the anarchist's earnest questions. He braked hard twice on the descent from the castle, and each time Aranjuc, his hands cuffed behind his back and bent at the waist to relieve the pressure, fell forward, cracking his glasses on the dashboard.

'Hold on to him, man,' cried Kreuz, but Sidney couldn't bring himself to touch the Catalan.

'*Zapatos aquí*,' he said, pointing at the dashboard.

'I speak English too,' replied Aranjuc, bracing himself with his feet. 'Are you English?'

'Don't answer him,' warned Kreuz. 'They always try to crawl under your skin.'

'And who are they?' asked Aranjuc.

'Prisoners,' replied Kreuz.

'If I'm a prisoner, what is my crime?'

'I can give you no answers, Comrade.'

'I have done nothing wrong. Where are you taking me?'

'You heard my orders. I'm taking you home.'

'My home is in Girona, Comrade. I doubt you're taking me there.'

Kreuz didn't answer.

'You could let me go, you know,' suggested Aranjuc.

'Relax,' sighed Kreuz irritably. 'You'll be all right. Wait and see.'

'Am I under arrest?'

'Would we be taking you back to your unit if you were under arrest?'

'So why am I in handcuffs?' The stains were spreading on Aranjuc's shirt, and the cab smelled of fear and shit. He turned to look at Sidney, staring deep into his eyes and sending urgent, plaintive signals. 'Why didn't you take me with the others?'

Sidney shrugged, the blood rushing to his cheeks. 'I'm just doing as I'm told, Comrade.'

'I think it's best if you shut your mouths now,' growled Kreuz. 'Both of you.'

He slowed to negotiate a hairpin bend and Sidney saw the tail lights of Cobb's Audi for a brief moment, maybe two turns ahead. They drove on in a silence broken only by the manic whirring of Aranjuc's mind. Some men know how to bargain for their lives, others how to beg. Some insist that nothing is over until it's over and others seem to understand that they're dead men walking. Sometimes too much intelligence can be fatal.

They eventually stopped the truck a few hundred yards past the Montalban crossroads. Kreuz jumped from the cab and dashed into the woods, cocking his machine-pistol as he ran. He was breathless when he returned. 'It's clear,' he said, turning to Aranjuc. 'Get out.'

The Catalan swallowed hard. 'Why are you doing this?'

'Orders,' shrugged Kreuz. 'Even an anarchist must understand that. Out!'

The prisoner looked at Sidney. 'You know this is wrong, friend, don't you?'

Sidney avoided his eyes. 'Just get out,' he replied.

Aranjuc was finding it hard to breathe. 'Listen,' he cried, 'this isn't right. I've done nothing wrong. This just isn't right.'

'Since when did right and wrong have anything to do with it?' growled Kreuz, casting one nervous eye westwards. 'Now get out before I drag you out.'

Aranjuc sniffed, shut his eyes tight and shook his head. 'It's not right,' he insisted again.

'Get the bastard out,' barked Kreuz. 'Why do they always make it so difficult?'

When Aranjuc opened his eyes they were wet with tears he couldn't sniff away. They ran from his nose and dripped from his chin. 'Please!' he whispered.

Sidney took a deep breath. 'Just get out, will you?'

'Oh God,' said the anarchist, and a sudden gust of cold wind blew up the valley, shaking the trees and rocking the truck. He shuffled to the edge of the seat and slipped out of the cab, but his legs gave way when he landed and he fell to the road with a sob. Sidney dragged him to his feet, one narrowed eye on Kreuz.

'There must be some way out of this,' gasped Aranjuc. He looked first at Sidney, then at the German. 'This . . . this . . .' Another gust stole his words.

Kreuz touched him on the shoulder. 'One minute to prepare yourself, then you run.'

'Oh God,' moaned Aranjuc.

Kreuz threw Sidney's look back at him. 'We both do it. Understand? Both of us.' He smiled. 'Don't worry: it's allowed under the *ley de fuegas* – the fugitive law. If a prisoner attempts to escape, we're allowed to shoot him down. It's all perfectly legal.'

He glanced at his watch then spat on the road. 'Time's up. Start running!'

'You said a minute,' cried Aranjuc. 'I'm not ready.'

Kreuz took three fast steps and thrust the man forward. He fell to his knees.

'Up!' yelled Kreuz.

'Please don't do this. Please, please, please . . .'

The report of Sidney's Nagant sounded wet and heavy in the damp air. The bullet hit the Catalan in the back, throwing him forward with a gasp. His hands still behind his back, he hit the road with his forehead and tried to scramble to his feet, his shoes scrabbling on the tarmac. Sidney cocked the revolver and glared at Kreuz. The German nodded and fired three rounds into Aranjuc's back.

'Quick,' said Kreuz. 'Get the cuffs off him and turn him over.'

'He's still alive.' The feet were twitching, trying to escape, as though unaware that the rest of the body was dead.

'They all do that. Get those cuffs off. Here's the key.'

Sidney knelt and fumbled with the key as the gas escaped from Aranjuc's body in a long, sad fart. The hands dropped to rest knuckles down on the road as the handcuffs were removed, and Kreuz pushed the body onto its back.

'No dignity,' he sighed as he pushed the envelope Cobb had given him deep into the anarchist's inside pocket. 'The treacherous bastard. Let's go.'

Sidney looked down at Aranjuc's corpse. Behind the broken glasses one eye was shut and the other sat like a stone in the socket. Blood trickled darkly from the nostrils and wet grazes on the chin gleamed. The index finger on his right hand spasmed, flexing as though pulling a trigger, or inviting Sidney to come on down.

'He's wearing a cross.'

'So?' hissed Kreuz. His nerves were trembling like the trigger finger. They were a long way into disputed territory and the shots might have been heard.

'He's an anarchist. They don't believe in God.'

Kreuz looked at him as though dealing with an idiot. He bent down, tore the cross from Aranjuc's throat and tossed it high into the trees. It twisted around a branch, flashing like a firefly in the broken moonlight. 'Happier now?' he asked.

The recollection kept the old man quiet as Nick drove through Montalban and Castell de Cabra to Gargallo, following the shallow, sparkling waters of the Rio Martin. They were skirting the northern edge of the Maestrazgo, jagged mountains that seemed cut from a different rock to the miserable summits of the Sierra del Moro. Sunlight flashed through the trees, as though reflected from the untarnished gold of Aranjuc's crucifix, perhaps still dangling, turning slowly on its chain after all these years. Below it, on the repaved surface of the N211, the beckoning finger of Luis Aranjuc mocked Sidney's memory, the invitation still open. His recall of that night on the road in the pine woods was as sharp today as it had been in 1937, its resolution enhanced by the resin tang on the cold air. It had not been deleted by an autonomic mental mechanism, and he had not knowingly buried it in a shallow grave in the far reaches of his memory. It had always lurked in the shadows at the edge of his consciousness, angry and malevolent, ready to rush into the light and remain on his mind for days or even weeks. As a young truant in Norwich he had wondered why the men wouldn't talk about the war to those who hadn't seen it for themselves; then, in Spain, he had realised that you simply did what you could to keep the memories in the dark. If he cast his eyes into the corners he could see them stacked in perilous piles like unwanted photographs, and scattered like yards of censored out-takes lying in dangerous curls on a slippery floor. Carelessness could bring the whole lot down, burying him in the terror, the horror and above all the guilt of that awful adventure, and yet circumstances demanded that now, after seventy years of neglect, he should

161

root through those memories. He wondered for a cold moment if it would kill him.

'Something bad happened back there, didn't it?' asked Nick. The old man seemed to have shrunk in his clothes, to have become old again, frail and uncertain.

Sidney shook his head. 'Like I said, it was nothing important. I think we take the next left.'

Cobb was gone for two days. When he returned he found Sidney sitting shirtless in the sun, filing bullets blunt. He sucked in his breath in a long, disapproving whistle and shook his head. 'You know what will happen if you get captured with dum-dum rounds, kid?' he asked.

'Pretty much the same as if I get caught without them.'

Cobb sighed. 'You're getting too cynical.' He kicked Sidney's boot. 'Drop that shit and come with me. We need to talk.'

They strolled through the dust in the sunshine towards the low wall that marked the edge of the camp. Klee stood in a circle of seated students, hefting a home-made grenade from hand to hand and watching them pass with undisguised curiosity. If Cobb noticed, he ignored it. He walked with his hands pushed deep into the pockets of his woollen trousers, the sleeves of his khaki shirt rolled up above the elbows to reveal sinewy, suntanned arms. A scar ran from elbow to wrist on his left forearm like a pink worm trapped beneath the brown skin. He said nothing until they reached the wall, then he turned and leaned back with a big smile that suggested nothing but nonchalance to any observer.

'Can I trust you, kid?' Sidney nodded, and Cobb cackled. 'That's kind of unconditional. Most of these bastards would have asked for a little more information up front.' He pulled a cigar from his shirt pocket and rummaged in his trousers before withdrawing a silver cutter. 'You like this?' he asked, holding it up so the sun flashed warnings from its shiny surface. 'I inherited it.'

162

'From those men we arrested last week?'

Cobb looked puzzled for a moment, then shook his head. 'No. This came from some guy who owned a coffee factory outside Reus. Now *there* was a man who knew his cigars.' He lit the cigar with a gold lighter, omitting to explain its provenance. 'Those guys we arrested last week are no longer with us, but it appears that they have taken something very close to our leader's heart. That's why I need to know if I can trust you.'

Sidney waved the smoke from his face. 'I told you already.'

Cobb nodded, and glanced across the camp as though checking for surveillance. 'Remember last year when the Iron Column tore Valencia apart? Maybe no one told you, but what happened was that these guys had been up on the line for months, and they heard that the revolution had been abandoned back in the city. People were going to the movies, going to the track, eating oranges and generally having a ball – acting like there was no war, no revolution, no nothing. Word was that the militiamen came back to teach the Valencianos a political lesson, tearing down the Gran Via, looting stores, beating up diners and burning cars. They attacked the law courts, trashed the main police station, killed a bunch of priests and got themselves a few new recruits from the prisons. Then they came face to face with our machine-guns and the riot came to a bloody end. You never heard about this?'

Sidney shook his head.

Cobb sucked on his cigar. 'Well, it may be that the whole thing was a diversion. One of those guys we took last week – Ranzato – tried to make a deal with me. They always do, and it never does them any good. The smarter ones know they're already dead and they're just trying to save the wife and kids. The dumb and the weak think they can wriggle out of the inevitable. Some of my guys won't give them the time of day, but I always listen. Most of the time we've got nothing on the family anyways, but I make a deal to let the suckers go to their graves with one less worry. They die with the knowledge that they've done their best, and I get a nice car, a new desk or a silver cigar-cutter. It just makes the job more pleasant for everyone concerned. This guy Ranzato was just like the rest of them. I take him for a walk on the beach and he tells me that this is nothing to do with food quotas. I'm all ears, I tell him, and he tells me a tale about a robbery that took place the same day as the Iron Column riots: eight men robbed a fortified villa on the outskirts of town. Now old Ranzato's got me hooked, because this fortified villa is the same place I've been told to deliver him, on Orlov's personal orders.' He blew smoke and scanned the background, his creased eyes narrowed against the sun. 'Let's take a walk while I put you in the picture. Too many goddamned spies in this place. Ranzato told me that late last October two kids watched eight men unload two trucks at the villa. They reported what they'd seen to their uncle, who happened to be the CNT organiser down at the docks, telling him that they'd seen eight foreigners carrying dozens of small but extremely heavy boxes into the villa. The job had apparently taken half the night, and the kids came to the conclusion that these were fascist agents establishing some sort of arms dump in preparation for an operation against the docks.' Cobb raised an eyebrow. 'It was a reasonable assumption – but wrong. Uncle Pedro did the right thing and passed on the intelligence to the militia, who established that the property was on the books of the Interior Ministry and was on loan to the Soviet military mission.' He paused, half turning towards Sidney. 'How did it go with Aranjuc?'

Sidney felt a prickle of sweat as the broken glasses, the bloody teeth and the beckoning finger flashed across his memory. 'Badly,' he muttered. 'He wasn't ready to die.'

'Which of us is?' asked Cobb. 'It was Aranjuc who interrogated those kids and came to the conclusion that what they saw being unloaded was too heavy, and packed in boxes too small, to be war *matériel*.'

'So what was it?'

A rook settled on the barbed wire, his feathers ruffled by the gentle Levantine breeze. Cobb stopped walking. 'Gold,' he replied. 'One hundred boxes of the stuff. Those stupid sons of bitches stole gold from General Orlov and he's going to kill every last one of them to get it back.' The rook watched as Cobb laughed like a rooster. 'It's like one of Aesop's fables: smartass mice stealing from the meanest cat in town.' He grabbed Sidney by the arm and pulled him close, his expression suddenly cruel and aggressive. 'Problem is, kid, that just by knowing this you become one of the mice. Get my drift?' He checked for witnesses, then seized Sidney by the shoulders and threw him into the doorway of a low stone building. 'Soon as anyone finds out that you know this, you're dead. Mention it to the mice and you'll end up like Aranjuc. Tell it to the cats and you'll probably take a week to die, the skin flayed from your back and fucking Slavs watching your lungs through your ribs.' His breath smelled of Spanish garlic and Cuban tobacco. He licked his lips. 'That's not just a threat, kid: it's a goddamned warning. From now on you're either with me or you're dancing a long, slow fandango with *La Muerte*.'

Sidney pushed past him and stood his ground, forcing Cobb to turn to face him. 'So why tell me?' he asked.

'Because I need you to watch my back,' replied Cobb. 'If Orlov knows about my stroll with Ranzato he'll murder me. Even if he only suspects that I know about the robbery I'm fucked. Christ, if I was in Orlov's shoes, I'd probably kill old Cobb just to keep things neat and tidy.' He threw a rueful glance back to where Klee could be heard yelling at his recruits in heavily accented Spanish. 'Maybe the assassins are already here.'

'You mean Klee and Kreuz?'

Cobb ran the tip of his tongue along his teeth, like a snake sniffing the air. 'Why say that? You don't trust them?'

Sidney jumped as the dull crump of a grenade thudded across the camp. 'They're Germans, aren't they?'

'That the sum total of your evidence against them?'

Sidney nodded.

'Kid, you're missing the point,' sighed Cobb. 'The fascists aren't the problem. It's our own people who scare me.'

'I'm just saying there's something about them.'

'Yeah?' Cobb cast his eyes around the camp. 'Well, maybe you're half right. Let me put you in the picture. Kreuz is a fucking hero of the workers' revolution, kid, and if it succeeded, which you and I both know it won't, they'll name a street after the bastard. He's a cold-hearted, humourless bastard but I'd trust him with my life, and that's all that matters. Klee I'm not so sure about, and I'd appreciate it if you kept an eye on him. Fucker makes me nervous.'

There was a glimmer in his eyes that Sidney had learned to recognise. He'd seen it in Joe's face too, as well as in the eyes of the deserter at the roadhouse in Mogente and behind Luis Aranjuc's glasses. Cobb was scared. Sidney watched as he rolled the wet cigar butt between his lips and scratched a meaningless loop in the dust with the toe of his boot.

He spoke slowly, as though to himself, his words stumbling on the trail of his thoughts. 'You know something, kid? You hear rumours in war. I heard they moved the entire Spanish gold reserve to Moscow for safe keeping. I heard something else, too: back in Mother Russia Uncle Joe's been killing people. Lots of people: generals, field marshals, department chiefs, ministers – anyone who looks like they can't be trusted. The Foreign Department guys have survived so far, but I heard that Orlov's name has come up on a Kremlin shitlist and he's not long for this world. He's already moved his wife and kid to France, and if I was in his shoes I'd be looking to follow them. My guess is that the gold was our leader's escape and retirement funds rolled into one and he's going to use every means at his disposal to get it back.' He nodded at Sidney. 'One thing's for sure, kid: I'm fucked, this little detail is fucked and you're fucked. I wouldn't

166

even go back to Albacete, if I was you. Orlov will tell his boys whatever is necessary to get us to Valencia, and then the fun will start. You think that operation with Ranzato, Cano and Aranjuc had anything to do with politics and policy? My ass it did. Orlov wants his gold back, and it won't be long before we've become traitors to the cause and a couple of carloads of goons come for us.' He flicked the cigar butt and pointed a thick finger at Sidney. 'We've got to work out a plan, and the way I see it, kid, we've got three options. Number one, we get what's coming. Number two, we take off to France, and cross as refugees.' He stopped and swung Sidney around to face him, the gleam of fear outshone by the glitter of insanity. 'Number three, we find the bastard's gold and keep it. Now, out of dead, broke or rich, I like number three the best. What do you think, kid?'

Sidney pinched a louse from his scalp and crushed it against his thumbnail. The American had said there were three options, but either he had lied or he had misunderstood the situation. There was no option. Orlov's secret police existed solely to trap deserters and traitors, and since Sidney would soon be falling into both categories he saw no future in attempting to flee. Nor would he wait obediently for his arrest, interrogation and execution. Overhead a Chato biplane turned snarling loops in the cloudless sky, tantalisingly free to fly in any direction. 'What's the plan?' he asked.

'Good boy,' grinned Cobb. 'Ever been to Teruel?'

The target, according to the few newspaper photographs that Gasse, the saturnine company intelligence officer, had gathered, was a worried-looking Andalucian with a gipsy hairstyle and hollow cheeks. His name was Angel Villafranca, and he kept distinguished company.

'Andreas Nin,' muttered Gasse, tapping a group photograph with the blunt end of a pencil. 'Head of POUM – the Marxists. Villafranca's on the far right.'

'In the photo at least,' added Cobb.

Gasse showed another picture. 'And this is our man with the CNT – the anarchists. That's the late Señor Durruti in the leather coat.'

Cobb had summoned Simenon, Klee, Kreuz and Sidney to the briefing. Gasse was present in an advisory role.

Klee looked sweaty and suspicious, his bald head glistening beneath Cobb's chandelier. 'What has this man done?' he asked.

'He's a bad, bad man,' drawled Cobb. 'A bank robber who learned his trade in the south in the late twenties then moved his game to Barca when Andalucia got too hot. Worked as a *pistolero* during the good old days.'

'Could have been one of us, then,' grunted Simenon.

Cobb nodded. 'Could have, but wasn't. He's worked as a freelance for the anarchists and the Marxists. Probably betrayed both and pocketed the difference, but who are we to criticise? Sid the Kid excepted, of course.'

Gasse peered at Sidney over his spectacles. 'You're committed?' He seemed astounded.

Sidney shrugged, once again feeling small and insignificant. 'I just came to kill Germans,' he blurted. It had seemed like a witty retort, but the expressions on the faces of Klee and Kreuz suggested otherwise.

Cobb smiled.

'He means fascists.'

Klee threw a look like a dagger and pointed at Sidney with the stem of his pipe. 'I'm sure your boy can speak for himself.'

Cobb sighed and leaned back against the wall in a manner that inexperienced men would have described as compromising, or even submissive. He pulled a cigar butt from his breast pocket and rolled it between thumb and finger. 'I'm sure he can,' he sighed. 'Now, would you like to talk about it some more, or would you prefer to discuss Mr Villafranca?'

The momentary tension in the ornately appointed office

subsided, but the air still crackled with the static of unfinished business.

'So he was a bank robber, an anarchist and a friend of Durruti,' summarised Simenon. 'So what?'

'That', replied Cobb, 'is none of our business. Our orders are simply to rescue him and to deliver him to Valencia.'

'Which sounds easy,' said Gasse. 'Doesn't it?'

'He's in fucking Toledo or somewhere, isn't he?' guessed Kreuz.

Cobb grinned. 'Close. He's in Teruel. And if we don't get him out of there pretty damn quick we'll be driving to Seville to claim his body. He was captured a week ago, deep inside the neighbours' back yard, and they've charged him with . . .' He paused, rubbing the bridge of his nose like an absent-minded teacher. 'What did they charge him with, Gasse?'

The lean Frenchman shuffled his cuttings. 'Robbery, burglary, murder, robbery, triple murder, train robbery, escape from custody, assault, robbery, theft, conspiracy to defraud and so on.'

'No political charges in there, you'll notice,' remarked Cobb, 'and no mention of his status as a prisoner of war. As far as the neighbours are concerned, Señor Villafranca is nothing more than a common thief with an uncommon charge sheet. He pissed them off when he burgled Colonel Yagüe's villa in '34. There was an incident involving the lady of the house, and the colonel is looking forward to seeing the bastard garrotted.'

'Unless we save the bastard's life,' noted Simenon.

'He may prefer to choke,' suggested Cobb.

Klee sucked hard on his foul-smelling pipe and glared at Sidney. 'So where is he now?'

'In a dungeon in Teruel.'

'And who ordered this mission?'

Cobb took his time to reply. First he flicked the cold ashes from his cigar, then he played his golden lighter over the unburned tobacco. Raising the stub to his lips, he drew hard,

169

sucking an orange glow from the tip and exhaling with a grudging satisfaction, as though the butt tasted better than he had expected. At last he raised his eyes to meet Klee's. 'I did,' he replied, 'and who I get my orders from doesn't concern you, Mr Klee.'

Gasse froze, yellowing newsprint flopping in his fingers. Simenon raised mischievous eyebrows, like a schoolgirl overhearing a scandal, and leaned back against a portrait of the Duc de Guise that had been left to Cobb by a minor Aragonese aristocrat. Kreuz sucked air through his nose, his nostrils flaring like a spooked horse. And Sidney studied the rich Persian carpet, watching tiny columns of smoke rising from the woven landscape like an aviator studying the African bush as spilled embers from Klee's pipe smouldered in the silk. Klee glared back at Cobb, a vein throbbing in his neck, his sidearm heavy and menacing in his waistband. Cobb met his eyes with a smile that was half amusement and half warning, his hands deep in the pockets of his leather greatcoat. Sidney knew that the American's right hand was clasped around the Derringer purchased in Chicago in 1919 by a journalist from Barcelona, now deceased. It had two triggers for its two barrels, and it was designed to fit unobtrusively in a gentleman's overcoat pocket. The two rounds of .32 it fired wouldn't necessarily kill Klee, but they would hurt him, as well as ruining Cobb's coat. As Sidney moved away the German smiled, then laughed out loud, as though recalling a long-forgotten private joke.

'So how are we going to rescue this villain?' he asked.

11

Sixty years later, and 140 miles to the west, the Peugeot van emerged from a dripping tunnel high above a deep gorge. In the narrow space between the jagged peaks of the Maestrazgo wisps of cirrostratus drifted north-eastwards across pale blue sky.

'The road seemed wider when I was younger,' remarked Sidney.

'Are you sure it was this road?' wailed Lenny. 'I can't believe they let people use it. It's got to be against EC regulations or something. They don't have roads like this in England, do they? If you have mountains like these, you should just leave them be – drive round them, not through them.'

Nick's spine was wet with sweat. For once he agreed with every word Lenny had said, only until now he had had no spare capacity to say so. 'Is this the general area we'll be looking in?' he asked.

'I dare say,' nodded Sidney. 'Why have we stopped?'

Nick pointed at a stone archway on a steep drive on the downhill slope. 'It says, "*Hostal*".'

Lenny leaned across Sidney and peered down the slope. 'Looks like a funeral home.'

'It's got a sign saying "*cerveza frio*",' noted Nick.

'What's that mean?'

'Cold beer,' translated Sidney.

'So what are we waiting for?' gasped Lenny. 'Reverse, quick!'

'Now listen to me,' ordered Sidney as Nick drove through the arch and parked in a flagstoned courtyard designed for horses.

'We're fossil-hunters, remember? Gentle, academically minded men with thirsts for knowledge rather than ale. We don't argue, or swear, or fight, and above all we do not talk to the locals. Understand?'

Lenny was nodding. 'Yeah, yeah, whatever. I'll get 'em in. Pint, Mr S?' He hit the ground running and was through the studded door before Nick had killed the engine. He didn't notice the sign proclaiming, 'Hostal La Cerda', and as he emerged in a timbered room illuminated by what little light could penetrate the smoke-blackened windows, he also failed to spot the receptionist slumped behind a dark wooden counter in the entrance. Searching for *cerveza frio*, he glanced around a vast dining room arranged about an enormous circular fireplace in which last night's logs smouldered in a ring of white ashes. Poorly made furniture stood beneath a brown ceiling, seemingly supported by the trunks of several trees arranged in an arbitrary and asymmetrical manner. Grimy windows along the back wall of the room overlooked the valley, and in the right-hand corner, kept company by a single stool, stood the bar. Lenny reached it in three thirsty strides and rang the brass bell. He looked around, then leaned over the sticky wooden surface to peer behind before scratching his backside and glancing over his shoulder. He rang the bell again, and when no one responded he grabbed a glass and flipped the tap on a beer pump labelled 'Mahon'. Above him, the mounted head of a wild boar stared down in mute disapproval.

'Mr Knowles!'

No beer had emerged. Lenny flipped the tap off and turned to lean against the bar in an unconvincing approximation of non-chalant innocence. 'What?'

Sidney was standing in the doorway. 'Are you blind?'

'Er, depends. Why?'

'This man is dead.'

'Which man? Not the barman, surely?'

Sidney pointed at the reception desk.

'Bloody hell!' cried Lenny. 'How do you know he's not just having a kip?'

Sidney lifted the corpse's head by a lank lock of white hair, examined the wizened face, then let it drop with a thud on a blank page in the arrivals book. 'Go and see if there's anyone else here,' he said.

Lenny had gone cold. 'Where's Nick?' he asked. 'I'll send him.'

'Go yourself,' insisted Sidney. 'Quick!'

'Was he murdered? I'm not going in there if he was murdered. I only wanted a quick lager. I'm not going to be the next victim.'

Sidney sighed. 'I'd say he died of a heart attack, a stroke or some other age-related condition. His passing, therefore, was entirely peaceful, and I'm sure that somewhere else on these charming premises there is a member of staff who should be told.'

'Shouldn't we just fuck off?'

Nick pushed through the entrance door, a cigarette hanging from his unshaven face. 'Do you reckon they've got rooms . . .' He stopped, his jaw slack and his eyes wide. 'Which one of you did that?'

'Not me,' insisted Sidney and Lenny in defensive chorus.

'He was like this when we came in,' added Sidney.

'Shouldn't we just fuck off before someone comes?' asked Nick.

'That's what I said,' nodded Lenny.

'Too late,' smiled Sidney as the whisper of rubber on stone betrayed the arrival of another car.

Lenny looked at Nick in disgust and shook his head slowly. 'Nothing's ever easy with you, Nicholas, is it? You can't even choose a sodding hotel without it being like something from the fucking *X-Files*.'

Car doors slammed and low Spanish voices echoed around the courtyard.

'We're just a team of friendly amateur fossil-hunters, remember?' hissed Sidney.

Guadeloupe Serrano Suner was understandably upset at the death of her father, but her uncle Pepe, the corpse's brother, seemed more embarrassed than distraught. He insisted that the three guests should install themselves in the corner of the dining room, then arrived a moment later with a bottle of Vina Fuerte and three glasses. His embarrassment ran deeper when he was forced to admit to Lenny that there was no beer on the premises, an oversight he assuaged with the provision of half a bottle of vodka. His brother was eighty-three, he explained, with a knowing shrug towards Sidney. It was unfortunate, yes, and very sad, but business was business, and if the three gentlemen were in agreement he would have their effects moved into the best rooms in the house right away.

'I haven't decided yet,' announced Sidney.

'Of course,' oozed the proprietor. 'It is an unusual situation. Please enjoy these drinks and in the meantime . . .' He made a pinching movement with his thumb and forefinger that seemed to signify a small but pressing matter that required his immediate attention and departed backwards, sweeping his palm across the wobbly table like an obsequious courtier.

'What do we do now?' asked Nick when the hotelier had gone.

Sidney took off his glasses and polished them with his handkerchief. 'It's a tricky one,' he admitted.

'No shit, Sherlock,' muttered Lenny, pouring oily vodka into a wineglass. 'I say we scarper.'

'And I say we stay,' replied Sidney. 'The place is empty, it's in the right spot and it makes a perfect base from which to begin our search.' He didn't ask Nick for his opinion. 'Mr Knowles, come with me. Mr Crick, park the van at the back of the yard, under cover if possible.'

Lenny tried to pour himself one for the road but Sidney

stopped him. 'No time for that!' he cried. 'We need to negotiate a special rate.'

The Hostal La Cerda was built on the western slope of a
steep valley. A wide staircase of old pine led downwards from the
dining room to the kitchens and the bedrooms. The panelled
walls were lined with faded photographs of blurred hunters in
tweeds and leather. Balding boars stared glassy-eyed from plaques
above inscribed epitaphs too tarnished to read, and prong-
headed deer gaped in surprise as though they had just crashed
through the tongue and groove.

Lenny found the effect unsettling. 'Why can't we stay at the
Holiday Inn?' he muttered as he followed Sidney downstairs.

The old man turned sharply, a bony finger to his lips. 'Shush!
I'm listening.'

From the kitchen the angry words of an unhappy woman fell
like crockery thrown against a tiled floor. Beneath them a man's
voice seemed to urge calm, but his efforts caused the curses to be
thrown with greater force. Sidney crept towards the door marked
'Cucina – Privado', realising with some surprise quite how
dependent he was on lip reading to supplement his failing hearing these days. Until he was close enough to place his ear against
the door the words were merely dull noises of differing pitches,
but then they seemed to crystallise.

'You killed my father!' wailed the woman.

'How, I ask you?' hissed the man. 'I was with you. He was
alive when we left and dead when we returned. It's impossible.'

'Impossible? You pig! You've been killing him for years. This
murder—'

'Don't say that word. I warn you!'

'And what will you do, murderer? Murder me? You'll murder
me too, so you can have the whole place for yourself?'

The hysterics were cut short by the crack of an open palm
against soft skin, and before Sidney could shuffle aside the swing
door was punched open, knocking him flat.

175

Guadeloupe Serrano Suner, a good-looking if somewhat cosmetic-dependent single woman of forty-three, stood over the crumpled geriatric, hands like joints of *jamon iberico* on her wide hips.

'Listening at the eaves, were you, *señor?*'

The door swung open once more, bashing Sidney on the backside as he struggled to regain his composure. Tio Pepe gaped for a moment, his cheek glowing with his niece's palm-print, then bent hurriedly to lift Sidney to his feet.

'*Señor,*' he gushed, 'I'm so sorry! She is insane with grief, you know, this woman. You must excuse her. She says crazy things in her sadness.'

Lenny arrived at Sidney's side too late to be of any assistance. He had been attempting to remove a fox's head from the wall when the accident had happened and had spent the aftermath trying to replace it before the niece noticed. 'You all right there, Mr Starman?' he blustered.

Sidney nodded. Nothing was broken, and that was a bonus at his age. 'Pass me my glasses,' he replied.

'Right you are,' nodded Lenny, stepping backwards. The feeble crack of cheap plastic broken underfoot paid poor homage to the gravity of its consequence. 'Shit,' said Lenny. 'I think I've just trodden on them.' Across the dimly lit passageway, at the foot of the wooden stairs, a fox's head fell to the floor with a dull thud.

'That's very bad luck,' muttered Tio Pepe. 'Those things should never touch the ground.'

Lenny looked up from the floor and met Guadeloupe's dark brown eyes. It was a significant moment. 'Mr Starman?'

'What?' growled Sidney.

'Could you do us a favour? Bit of interpreting?'

Sidney gritted his teeth. 'Go on.'

'Would you ask the lady if she has any cockney in her?'

Sidney sighed, turned to Guadeloupe and made the enquiry. The tearful señorita frowned and shook her head.

'She says no,' explained Sidney. 'She has no cockney in her.'

Lenny nodded thoughtfully. 'Can you ask her if she wants some?'

The argument that followed the destruction of Sidney's only pair of spectacles petered out as each of the antagonists, tired from days without rest or proper food, saw the absurdity of his situation. Still bickering like terriers determined to have the last snarl, they allowed themselves to be led separately to their rooms by the deeply embarrassed sole proprietor of the Hostal La Cerda.

That night Lenny dined alone on fresh trout and stale migas del pastor, an Aragonese speciality that consisted of deep-fried crumbs of day-old bread. He had opted for the de luxe variant of the dish, served with a fried egg, but had been unimpressed until challenged by the wet-eyed Guadeloupe.

'You finished?' she asked in weary Spanish. The Englishman had a strange, musky smell about him.

'Very nice, thanks,' nodded Lenny, in English. There was something very alluring about this big-lipped drunk that invited exploration. He smiled as she whisked away the plate.

'You want dessert?'

Lenny had no idea what she was saying. 'I've got an ashtray, thanks,' he smiled, 'but a lager would be nice.' He tipped a cupped hand towards his mouth.

Guadeloupe frowned. 'Lager?'

'Beerio. San Miguelio. Have one yourself, darling.' He reached into his tracksuit pants and scratched his balls.

'Lager!' sighed Guadeloupe, clenching her fist with the thumb extended like the neck of a bottle and tipping it towards her lips.

Lenny nodded enthusiastically. 'That's right, treacle. A Stella would be nice. Or Carlsberg. Or Carling. Whatever you've got.'

She returned fifteen minutes later with a green bottle and two short glasses. 'Lager!' she declared, tugging the cork from the bottle with her teeth and filling both glasses. She pushed one clumsily towards Lenny, the wine slopping like blood on the tabletop, and raised the other in the air. 'To my poor father, murdered by his own brother!'

Lenny shook his head. 'That's not lager, love. Why don't we go upstairs and open the bar?' He stood.

Guadeloupe drained her glass and stared at him in drunken dismay. 'Drink, *Ingles*.'

Lenny grabbed the wine bottle and leaned on the table. She had a lovely kisser on her, this bird. 'BAR,' he announced, loudly and slowly, in the approved style of English as a foreign language. 'YOU AND ME. BAR. WE GO, NOW. *Comprendo?*'

Guadeloupe poured another glass and held it in Lenny's face. He had the eyes of a *gitano*, she noticed, and the scabbed hands of a fighter. His face, too, showed the marks of recent combat: the bloodshot eyes and bruised skin of a boxer, or a bandit. Since the mysterious death last summer of the intolerably sleazy Paco Escobar, the local specialist in dark deeds done dirt cheap, there had been no one in the Maestrazgo capable of wringing wrongful necks, but this hulk of a man glowed with the promise of a champion, even if he did smell faintly of deer.

'I drink to the man who will avenge my father,' she growled, throwing back the wine in one gulp. She was slurring now, but it made no difference to Lenny.

He glanced at her cleavage and raised an approving eyebrow. She was no spring chicken, but she had a fine pair of lungs on her. He grabbed the bottle before she could pour another toast. 'Shall we go upstairs, darlin'? *UPSTAIRIO!*' He pointed to the ceiling.

Guadeloupe thought she understood his intention. She clasped bejewelled fingers around Lenny's wrist and pulled herself to her feet. 'In my father's house, *señor*, upstairs is downstairs.'

She gave another tug and her face was but inches from Lenny's. 'Come, my gipsy avenger. Let's discuss the terms of your engagement and the means by which you shall be paid.' Her grip was tighter than a monkey wrench, and Lenny winced as she pulled him from the dining room.

Outside a fox barked in the night, its lonely voice rising above the roar of the rushing river of meltwater in the valley below. A half moon shone blue on the crags and silver on the stream, its pale light absorbed by the dense forest of dark pine. Somewhere in that mountainous wilderness lay hidden a fortune in gold, but thoughts of bullion were far from Lenny's mind as Guadeloupe led him past uncurtained windows to her bedroom. From the opposite wall the yellow-tusked head of a long-dead boar watched as she turned the cold iron key and threw open the door, and Lenny caught its frosty eye just as she pulled him through.

'Fuck me, mate,' he confided. 'I think I've pulled!'

The Field Repair Company crossed into Nationalist-held territory at Pozuelo just after 8.30 a.m. on Sunday, 13 June 1937. It was the feast day of Anthony of Padua, patron saint of amputees, animals, the elderly and Lisbon. Neither the time, nor the date, nor the crossing point was chosen by chance. The village was on a quiet sector of the front and occupied by a company of Portuguese troops whose devotion to the saint was greater than that which they gave to their fields of fire.

Cobb glanced at Sidney in the rear-view as the Audi rolled through the rubble-strewn streets of the dusty village. The voices of the enemy escaped from the burned roof of a decrepit church still bearing the scars of anarchist desecration, their songs of praise echoing softly between mean houses occupied only by the elderly and the infirm. 'Wipe the sweat off your lip, kid,' he muttered. 'You're making me nervous.'

Klee swivelled in the passenger seat to throw a look of

mocking disdain at Sidney, then lit his foul-smelling pipe. 'You see the way the devout left their weapons piled outside the church? We could have barred the doors and burned the bastards.'

'Most unchristian,' sighed Cobb. 'They'll get what's coming to them on Tuesday. Big diversion planned to keep them occupied while our side loses a battle elsewhere, and God won't save them.'

'You miss the point, as always,' observed Kreuz.

Like Klee, he wore the curiously formal field grey of the Condor Legion, but the similarity ended there. While Klee was merely a hired gun with the vicious eyes and exaggerated swagger of an overweight bullyboy, Kreuz had once been a believer. A middle-ranking organiser for the Communist Party in Cologne, he had been arrested in 1933 on the orders of Dr Fischer himself and beaten deep into the shadow of death in the *Wilde Lager* at Dachau. Dispatched to dig his own grave in the woods near Wissenburg, he overpowered his executioners and fled south to Switzerland, then to France. His escape became a legend of the Party, but the beatings, the torture and the mock-executions had changed his mind over matters political. He came to his senses in Lyon, three months after his escape, like a man awaking from a deep coma to the realisation that he was utterly alone in the world. When he died, the universe would go out like a light, and no movement, no ideology and no man could stop it happening. The only influence Kreuz could not discount was that of God, whose existence made a mockery of the communist creed.

'That's why the Republic will lose this war,' he announced. 'In all wars in all of history men on each side have claimed that God was on their side – until now. Now they forsake Him. The communists, the socialists, the anarchists, the Trotskyites and the Stalinists might fight like starving rats over all matters, but they agree on one: God is on the enemy's side. God is with the

Carlists, the Requete, the Legion, the Falange and the fascists.' He thrust a long thumbnail into an orange and tore off a strip of peel. 'Nobody is praying for the Republic.'

'You believe in God?' asked Simenon, his bloodshot eyes wide with surprise.

Kreuz pushed half of the orange into his mouth and chewed. 'You miss the point again,' he mumbled sadly. 'What matters is whether God believes in me.'

The deeper they drove into the salient, the less the war seemed to have affected the poor land and its thin people. The mountain villages with their pale pink houses seemed calm and ordered, thought Sidney, compared to the chaos and confusion of towns on the Republican side, their neat streets filled with soberly dressed women and children walking quietly home from church. The kaleidoscope of flags, banners, posters and standards that seemed to be fighting for attention and allegiance from every corner, every lamp-post and every balcony in the Republic was absent from Nationalist territory, save for a handful of carefully positioned exhortations to be vigilant and to remember that bringing in the harvest was as important as fighting a battle. Just one flag flew on this side of the line: the bicoloured bandera of the Spanish crown. In tiny, irregularly shaped fields crowded onto the floodplains of fast-flowing rivers, groves of *empeltre* olives stood shivering in the breeze even as the morning sun swelled their immature fruit. On this side of the line Sunday remained the Lord's Day, and skinny stock waited in vain for human attention. This was the Spain of Sidney's imagination: a simple, pastoral world of shallow waters and dust, of timeless tradition and faith. For a moment he wondered if he might be fighting for the wrong side, and then he remembered he was on no one's side now. He watched as Simenon rolled a cigarette, feeling the acid anxiety burning his stomach and wishing once again that he smoked.

The Audi sped through Gea de Albarracin, provoking stares of envious, yet nervous, curiosity from bent old men who stood on the pavements with their hands clasped behind their backs, then accelerated down the long, straight road out of the Sierra de Penarredonda. Cobb had guessed there would be a checkpoint at the junction with the Zaragoza road, but was surprised by the level of security around the roadblock. He let out a long, low whistle as he slowed down, the Audi's approach already noted by a pair of troopers in the dark green tunics of the Guardia Civil. 'They expecting us or something?' he asked.

'I count two trucks,' called Simenon. 'Twenty, thirty men.'

Klee ran a sweaty hand along the perforated barrel of his machine-pistol, hooking a fat thumb around the cocking handle.

'No shooting, no nerves, no talking,' ordered Cobb. 'We're on their side, remember? He reserved his last glance in the mirror for Sidney and shook his head at what he saw. 'You're sweating like a bride, kid. You're gonna give the game away.'

Three hundred yards ahead the two guards had ambled into the road, their rifles slung and their hands on their hips.

'Machine-gun, my left, eleven o'clock, pointing south,' reported Simenon.

'One of you two smack the kid,' growled Cobb. 'Make him work for a living.'

Kreuz took a deep breath, leaned forward and jabbed his elbow hard into Sidney's face. There was little pain, just the taste of German wool and English blood as his lip was crushed against his teeth. He gasped as Simenon followed up with a blow to the ear that sent white flashes of agony through his head.

'Handcuff him, quick. They're in my briefcase.'

Fifty yards ahead the two guards had been joined by another pair of riflemen and an officer.

'They're new,' shrugged Simenon, slipping a set of brass knuckles into his tunic pocket. 'Had to try them out on some-one.'

'Hold still,' hissed Kreuz.

Cobb rolled to a stop beside the officer. 'Happy St Anthony's Day,' he said. 'What's the deal with all the security?'

The officer ignored both the greeting and the question and peered into the car, his high cheekbones, smooth skin and narrow eyes giving him an Asiatic appearance. He made careful eye contact with every passenger before speaking. 'Papers, please.'

'"Papers, please, *Major*," if you don't mind, Lieutenant.' Cobb reached inside his overcoat and withdrew a leather wallet embellished with a gold shield displaying the crossed pike, arquebus and crossbow of the Spanish Foreign Legion. 'A gift from General Millan-Astray himself,' he bragged.

The officer was unimpressed. 'Are you all Tercio, sir?'

'Just two of Death's fiancés in this car,' replied Cobb. 'Those two gentlemen are specialists from the Condor Legion, but they speak little Spanish.' He jerked his thumb over his shoulder. 'Nor does he.'

'Who's he?'

'Bolshevik. An Englander. Fifteenth International Brigade. He surrendered this morning. Can I leave him with you?'

The officer frowned. 'I don't have the facilities, Major.'

Cobb glanced at the guards, then back at the officer. 'You have a sidearm, Lieutenant, and those men have rifles. All you need is a firing party, for God's sake.'

Klee chuckled and the officer took a pace away from the car. 'Do you have a death warrant for him? Papers?'

'Papers?' sneered Cobb, incredulous. 'Papers? I don't need no stinking papers to shoot a Bolshevik! Do you?'

The lieutenant nodded. 'Yes, sir, I do.'

Cobb waved his hand. 'Forget it then. We'll take him to Teruel and shoot him there. Is this the last checkpoint before the city?'

'It is, sir, for the moment.'

'*For the moment?*'

'We have orders to set blocks on every road junction.'

'Is this an exercise?'

'Apparently not.'

'Must be nice working in this sector,' grunted Cobb. 'Maybe I should ask the general to let my men trade places with yours for a spell. What's going on?'

'Anarchist commandos. We have one of their men in custody and it is believed' – the lieutenant raised a sceptical eyebrow – 'that they may try to rescue him.'

'See?' said Cobb. 'That's what happens when you don't shoot them straight away.' He slipped the Audi into gear. 'Good day, Lieutenant.'

Teruel could be seen from five miles away, its serried skyline of *mudejar* towers stretching above the barren summits of the surrounding hills. Sunshine sparkled from the glazed tiles that clad the spires, lending the provincial capital an air of fantasy and promise that was neither deserved nor appreciated. Sidney was bruised and bleeding, and despite his protests he was still wearing Cobb's heavy handcuffs.

'Keep them on, kid,' Cobb told him through a mouthful of cigar. 'Might play the same scene to another audience.'

'What do we do if Villafranca has left the prison?' asked Klee.

'He hasn't,' replied Cobb. 'We just heard that.'

'So how do we get to him?' asked Kreuz.

'Placing our trust in God and Frankie Cobb is what we do.'

Sidney said nothing, but the plan seemed somewhat feeble. It was an opinion shared by his companions.

'God works for the enemy,' noted Simenon, 'and I trust no one.'

Cobb sighed in irritation. 'Well, hard goddamned cheese, fellas, because if you can't trust God, then I'm all you've got.'

The city looked scared, thought Sidney, as Cobb drove slowly around the walls, the deep valley of the River Turia on his right and the gigantic aqueduct of Los Arcos striding absurdly across the empty street. The few pedestrians on the narrow pavements either ignored the car or watched it pass with the cautious, practised, non-committal curiosity Sidney had observed in the Republic. Over the past eleven months the smart civilian had learned to pass his eyes across the object of his attention as if they were merely on their way to look at something else. These days, too much interest in anything was unhealthy. You kept your head down and you minded your own business; then you woke up one morning to find your city occupied by fascists. Cobb turned right and into a huge arched gateway that was partially blocked by a half-hearted checkpoint. A shifty-looking sentry in puttees and a tasselled forage cap waved the car through after glancing nervously at Cobb's identity papers.

'I guess they're hoping the anarchists will be stopped on the outskirts,' sighed Cobb, shaking his head in weary dismay.

'I hope getting out is as easy as getting in,' muttered Klee.

Cobb parked on a steep, curving street, its cobbled surface shiny with water spilled from an unseen source. The citizenry's new-found skill of ignoring significant sights worked in favour of the Field Repair Company, as no one paid any attention to the big black car with its complement of determined men. Cobb watched the street for five long minutes, switching his glance between the windscreen and the mirrors, before turning to the Frenchman. 'Simenon, you can release the kid now. He's coming with me. You two', he nodded towards the Germans, 'are going sightseeing. We all meet back here at three.'

'What are we looking for?' asked Klee.

Cobb ran a hand through his greasy black hair, scratching the back of his head. 'Damned if I know. Street layouts, escape routes, last-ditch defensive positions. Anything that might help us if the balloon goes up. At six o'clock this evening a guard detail of the garrison will report to Colonel Harcourt's office. His deputy will release unto them one curly-haired gipsy bastard

185

for transfer to the Plaza de San Francisco in Seville, where said bastard is scheduled to die before an invited audience of local dignitaries.' Cobb had been unbuttoning his long leather over-coat as he spoke, and now he removed it to reveal the slightly worn uniform of a major in the Tercio. 'Guess who's going to collect said bastard and deliver him from evil?'

Simenon cupped his hands to light a skinny, hand-rolled cig-arette. 'What am I supposed to do?'

'Stay here and look after my car until I get back. Then you can go for a drink.' He reached out and took the handcuffs from Sidney. 'Keys?'

Sidney pointed at Simenon. 'He's got them.'

The Frenchman returned the keys and Cobb slipped them into his pocket. 'You never know when you're going to meet a classy dame.' He looked around, glancing quickly and uneasily from face to stony face. 'Any more questions, gentlemen?'

'Who's your contact?' asked Kreuz. 'Who told you that the gipsy was being transferred today?'

Cobb narrowed his eyes. 'Don't ask questions that make me suspicious of you. Anyone else?'

'The transport detail,' said Klee. 'How many, and what kind of unit?'

'Again, no idea. Maybe four militiamen, maybe a company of Tercio. Wait and see.' He looked at Sidney. 'What about you, kid? Anything on your mind?'

The whole affair seemed ludicrously fragile to Sidney. 'What do we do with the real transport detail?' he asked.

Cobb smiled. 'We kill as many of them as we can without get-ting caught. That doesn't just go for troops. I'm sure you don't need reminding that this city has welcomed the rebels and as such no civilian can be considered friendly. Nobody we meet outside this vehicle can be trusted, so if they look at you funny, and you can get away with it, drop them.'

★

186

Long shadows fell across the narrow streets of Teruel as the summer sun dropped behind the city walls, but overhead the sky was still bright blue, its cloudless tract criss-crossed by darting swallows and desperate insects. Pavements that had been empty all day filled slowly with women and children walking quietly to mass. Back in the car after a nervous afternoon spent prowling the streets, Sidney watched them pass, the ladies clad in heavy black clothes that seemed a penance in the thick summer heat, their children watchful and wary, as though they knew the huge German car could only carry trouble on its bloodstained seats.

'Pious-looking bunch,' observed Cobb quietly, 'but I bet none of these hypocrites had seen the inside of a church before last summer. Were you ever the church-going type, kid? Before you saw the red light, so to speak.'

Sidney shook his head, but it was ironic that he had spent so much of his youth sitting in a church thinking about Germans only to find himself sitting in a car with two Germans and watching people going into a church. He looked at the back of Klee's sweating skull, noting with disgust the way the rolls of fat cascaded into his thick neck, then glanced at Kreuz, who caught his eye and threw it back. Kreuz seemed to miss nothing – always watching, always appraising. These men seemed drawn from the bottom of the deepest, darkest barrel of society, and their presence sucked the warmth from Sidney's bones. He rubbed his hands on the coarse, itchy wool of the trousers of his Tercio uniform, smearing his sticky anxiety into his aching thighs. The hours of inactivity had finally overcome his resolve not to think about his suicidal situation, and he could feel his nerve crumbling like a glacier meeting a warm sea. He wasn't the only one.

'Damn this,' muttered Kreuz suddenly. 'I'm not doing this again. This is madness!'

'Hush your mouth,' warned Cobb, his voice like a wind across ice. 'Keep your cool.'

He turned slowly to look in the wing-mirror as a snarl of gears echoed between the tall buildings. 'Truck coming. I bet this is the one.'

A covered lorry rumbled slowly along the street, sallow faces under outsized helmets peering from its tailgate. Another passed a minute or so later, then a third. Klee glared at Cobb like a man trying to start a fight, but Cobb ignored him. As the fourth and fifth trucks rolled past the German spoke. 'What now?'

Cobb was still studying the rear-view. 'We wait for Simenon.'

'That's a company of infantry.'

'Yeah? And who says they've got anything to do with Villafranca's transfer?'

'This is very bad,' groaned Kreuz.

Cobb turned to face the criticism. 'Will you shut your god-damned mouth and watch your front? Jesus!'

'Here's Simenon,' said Sidney.

The Frenchman approached the car wearing his usual stupid grin, moving at a lopsided amble through the church-goers, his *gorillo* stuffed through his left epaulette. 'See the trucks?' he asked, lighting a cigarette at Cobb's window.

'So?'

'So that's the bank robber's escort.'

The cathedral bell began to toll.

'I fucking told you,' muttered Klee.

'There's more,' grinned Simenon. 'I asked one of the guys in the front truck if he was looking forward to getting his hands on some Andalucian ass and he told me they were heading north.'

Cobb frowned. 'With Villafranca?'

Simenon shrugged. 'Suppose so.'

'Fuck.'

'Why north?' asked Klee. 'What's north?'

Sidney looked at Kreuz. Kreuz looked back, but said nothing.

'Call it off,' urged Klee. 'We're up against a hundred men.'

'Seventy-seven,' said Simenon.

'Seventy-seven, a hundred, what's the difference? We're still outgunned and outnumbered.'

Cobb drummed his fingers along the steering wheel, his head lowered and his mind whirring. 'That roadblock,' he said at last, 'the one on the Zaragoza road. It had a gun emplacement, right?'

Simenon was watching a dark-eyed woman as she passed, an infant on her hip and a widow's black shawl on her head. 'That's right,' he nodded. 'Thirty-odd riflemen, one machine-gun, three crew.'

'What if we take the checkpoint?'

Sidney swallowed spit, but it stuck in his throat like ashes. He turned to Kreuz. 'Can I have one of your cigarettes?'

The German raised an eyebrow and opened his tin. 'They'll kill you, you know,' he said flatly. There was something nihilistic about Kreuz that Sidney couldn't help liking in spite of the blood running through the man's veins. The German hated everybody and trusted nobody, and his consistency inspired confidence.

Sidney nodded his thanks and choked on the acrid blue smoke, catching Cobb's eye in the rear-view.

'Great fucking time to take up tobacco,' said Cobb. 'Want to go find a billiard hall while you're at it?' He turned to Simenon. 'What do you think, Frenchie? We take the checkpoint and turn the gun on the convoy. Kill the front and rear vehicles and isolate the three in the middle.'

'How do we know which truck Villafranca's on?'

'We don't, but common sense says he ain't on the first, nor the last neither.'

'You haven't told us how we're going to overcome the thirty riflemen on the checkpoint,' growled Klee.

'With my native North American charm,' retorted Cobb. 'How do you think? I'm thinking on my feet here. If you've got a better plan, I'm all goddamned ears.'

'I do have a better plan,' nodded Klee. 'We call the whole thing off.'

There would be no cancellation and no postponement, realised Sidney, as he watched the foul-tasting cigarette burn away in his fingers. The usual rules of time and space no longer applied. There was no beginning, no middle and no end, no past and no future, just what was here and whatever was now. They would live for the moment until the moment moved on, leaving their bullet-riddled carcasses behind. Suddenly he found himself wondering how Tom Leverett was spending this Sunday evening, back in Norfolk. Perhaps he lay even now in the white arms of Mary Foulden, or was sat by her side at a meeting to discuss the war in Spain, the struggle of the international proletariat against the march of fascism and the destruction of liberty. Politics, Mary had once said, was like gutting a rabbit.

'Ludicrous,' spat Kreuz. 'It's suicide!'

'Five of us, with light weapons, against a platoon armed with rifles and machine-guns?' blustered Klee. 'Instant death.'

The bell tolled again. A single elderly man scurried along the street, his head bowed as though against an ill wind.

Cobb looked at Simenon. 'Well?'

'Maybe I'd try it if I was drunk; but sober, I agree with the others.'

'So what do you suggest, gentlemen?'

'We leave it,' insisted Klee. 'Why can't you see that?'

'Yeah,' joined Simenon. 'Why is this bastard so important anyway?'

Cobb ran a hand across his five o'clock shadow, considering his response, and Sidney wondered which way he would vote if the major called for a show of hands. A crash of gears, a metallic gurgle like a lorry clearing its throat, interrupted the debate and saved Cobb from an explanation. Simenon slipped into the car and Cobb moved ahead, his elbow jutting from the window like a Sunday driver. He made eye contact with the drivers of all five trucks, nodding at each before turning a wide circle in the Plaza de Cathedral and following at the rear of the column.

'What are you doing?' asked Klee.

'Just following them,' replied Cobb breezily.

'But why?'

'Nothing better to do.' He flashed the headlights and waved to the troops in the back of the rearmost truck. Several waved back, happy, no doubt, no longer to be last in line. Peering between the seats, Sidney saw the two on the tailgate suddenly look up, and a moment later he too heard the histrionic wail of an air-raid siren.

'Terrific,' growled Cobb.

'Good thing they're ours,' observed Simenon, looking skywards. 'We could get hurt otherwise.'

The convoy turned a corner, rumbling slowly downhill along a narrow street of shuttered shops. The flag of the Spanish crown hung from wrought-iron balconies, and the walls were plastered with posters proclaiming Spain as the battleground in a Christian crusade. Cobb sang softly, not a hymn this time but the anthem of the fascist Falange Española. '*Volverán banderas victoriosas, al paso alegre de la paz, y traerán prendidas cinco rosas, las flechas de mi haz.*' He glanced at Klee. 'You not joining in?'

For a fraction of a second the air seemed to become thinner, the street longer and momentarily out of focus. Then, like a tidal wave, the air came rushing back and Sidney's field of vision seemed to swell as his ears popped and his eyes bulged. The blast sounded like a single beat on a giant kettledrum, its head-cracking reverberation filling the road beside and beneath the convoy in a great rolling cloud of black smoke and grit. Deafened and gaping, Sidney vomited nicotine-tainted bile as the Audi rocked on its suspension, falling debris sounding like hail on the roof. When he opened his eyes the windscreen was shattered and Cobb was staring wild-eyed over his shoulder and through the rear window, blood dripping from his nose and his chin as he sped backwards up the street. The car fishtailed from one side of the road to the other before stopping with a sickening lurch and accelerating forwards, Cobb throwing the steering wheel to full lock to swing through an arched gateway. Killing the engine, he threw open the door, grabbed his weapon and ran back to the arch. Simenon followed, slapping the side of his head as he sprinted to the gate. Kreuz was already gone, leaving only Sidney and Klee in the car. Sidney blinked away the dust, the ringing in his ears too loud to hear Klee's quivering death rattle. A bomb had clearly fallen into the street just ahead of them, and where one fell there would be more. Deafened, he crawled from the car and fell into the courtyard, his rifle landing soundlessly on the flagstones beside him. As he climbed to his hands and knees, vomiting again, he saw Cobb frantically directing him into the cover of the wall. Simenon had edged close to the gateway, his rifle at port, and was snatching fast glances like a kid hiding behind a lamp-post. His hand signals seemed to indicate increasing numbers of enemy gunmen in the street around the bomb site, and as the ringing faded in Sidney's ears they were assaulted again by the tearing blasts of grenades and the uncoordinated rattle of small-arms fire. Above and beyond the street the air-raid siren moaned on.

'. . . hear me? Get a grip!' Cobb was shaking his shoulder. Still stunned, Sidney gaped as Cobb called his men around him with a tap on his head. 'Convoy under attack,' he announced. 'I saw two men throw grenades into the rear of the last truck. Anyone else see anything?'

Kreuz said nothing, Simenon shook his head and Sidney was only hearing one word in four.

'Where's Klee?' barked Cobb.

Sidney pointed. 'In the car.' His voice echoed dully around his skull.

Cobb jabbed a finger at Kreuz. 'Get him.'

The German ran the few paces to the car, his hobnailed boots rattling on the stones. Three white-faced nuns appeared on a balcony and gaped down at the courtyard. Cobb aimed his rifle and yelled at them: '*Andale!*' They took his advice.

'Klee's dead,' yelled Kreuz from the car.

'This is no coincidence,' announced Cobb, still shouting to overcome his deafness. 'Someone else is after Villafranca.'

'Let's hope they killed him,' yelled Simenon. 'Then we can go home.'

'How many men did you see out there?'

'Maybe six or eight, with rifles and machine-pistols. Too much dust and smoke to be sure.'

Cobb blocked his right nostril with a grimy finger and blew hard, dumping blood and snot onto the ground. He did likewise with the left nostril, spat, and wiped his mouth with the back of his hand. 'Let's go get the creep.' He threw a look of disdain at Kreuz. 'Eight men against seventy-seven. That's just three more than us.'

Kreuz nodded. 'Sure, but they had leadership and a plan.'

Cobb ignored the jibe. 'You two, left side. Me and the kid, right side. Let's go.'

Outside the convent the heat from the burning trucks rolled through the narrow precincts in waves that stank of scorched rubber, boiled diesel and seared flesh. Up ahead, where the bomb had exploded, a thick column of oily black smoke twisted into the sky and a confetti of smut spiralled softly earthwards. Across the street Simenon and Kreuz moved cautiously from pillar to post, one always covering the other's careful movement. Cobb walked in front of Sidney with no apparent concern, ambling along the greasy pavement like a rat catcher. He paused to inspect the tailgate of the last truck in line, its canvas canopy shredded by shrapnel and a thin stream of blood draining from its rear end as it sat lopsided on burst tyres. As he rose on tiptoes to peer inside, Sidney swung his rifle to cover a movement from a blood-spattered doorway, his sights swinging across a bearded man in civilian clothes hugging himself in the shallow porch. His blackened face bled from a dozen tiny shrapnel wounds and a leather saddlebag lay at his feet, Mills bombs spilling from its mouth like black eggs. He looked at Sidney with frightened eyes, raising one hand and the wet, red stump of another in surrender. As Sidney took a step towards him, Cobb pushed him aside, firing into the man's chest at close range.

'He was one of us!' cried Sidney as the body slumped open-mouthed against the iron-studded door.

Cobb slapped him round the head. 'Look at your uniform, idiot,' he shouted. 'Grab those bombs.' He waited behind the rearmost truck, his weapon propped on his hip, while Sidney picked up the saddlebag, then poked his nose cautiously around the edge of the bombed-out vehicle. 'Tercio!' he called, identifying himself to the stunned survivors as a Legionnaire. '*Viva Christo Rey!*' Long live Christ the King was the battle cry of the Francoist Spanish Foreign Legion, and it seemed just that a trick that had proved effective for the other side at Jarama should work again. Simenon and Kreuz moved carefully through the battered, half-clothed survivors, calling the same, peering over tailgates and into bullet-riddled cabs for the body of Angel Villafranca.

'Speed it up!' yelled Cobb, dragging the body of an officer of the Regulares from the passenger seat of a Ford three-tonner. Sidney covered him, his heart thumping too fast, too erratically in his bruised chest. The fat, shiny holes in the vehicle's skin had been made by a heavy machine-gun, and he scanned the roofs anxiously for the gunner. The entire front of a building on one side of the street had been reduced to rubble in the blast, exposing rooms with primrose-yellow walls and dark wooden furniture.

'Blood trail!' called Simenon.

Another officer, his skin blackened and his hair singed from his scalp, had seized Cobb's arm and was shouting hysterically in his face. Cobb pushed him aside. 'Kid, take the lead.'

A wounded corporal was staring at Sidney, flecks of pink flesh stuck to his tunic and his instincts telling him that something was wrong. Sidney scowled at him and the corporal shrugged like a man who couldn't care less. Sitting in a shattered street with two broken legs and no eardrums, his uniform splattered with the remains of his comrades, it was as though he had chosen to accept life with no further questions.

'Look,' shouted Simenon, pointing at the wide cobblestones of a narrow alley that ran steeply downhill. 'Blood. There, there and here.'

Cobb slapped Sidney again. 'You deaf or something? Go! Run!'

Sidney ran, his rope-soled shoes silent on the stones, staying close to the sides in spite of the oft-heard warning that bullets followed walls. The explosions had brought the impious onto the streets, but as Sidney dashed past they slipped indoors, crowding into parlours behind beaded curtains as the air-raid siren wailed like a bereaved mother, its howling a muffled hum to Sidney's bruised ears. The alley ran straight downhill, crossed by narrow *callejones* that bent like bows to follow the contours. Sidney paused at each, glancing left and right to where they curved away, aware that he was becoming more isolated with every step. Whoever he was following was losing blood fast. Heavy drops had splashed on the steps and shiny red streaks were smeared along the walls. Just ahead another pool puddled black upon the grey stone, as though the bleeder had paused to catch his breath. Sidney raised his rifle and slowed his pace, taking long, deep breaths himself to steady his hands. Still half deaf, his hunter's instinct raised the hair on his neck and sent a cold trickle along his spine as he closed on the corner, the rifle sling wrapped around his arm and his finger on the trigger. He paused, took two more deep breaths, and stepped into the crossroads. Two men were stumbling away from him, one carried along by the other; in front of them, just disappearing around the corner of the twilit alleyway, were three more. One of these was a boy wearing a beret, the second a tall man with a tan haversack on his broad back. The last, without doubt, was Angel Villafranca. Sidney dropped to one knee and fired a shot. The Enfield went off with a dull thud that dropped the able-bodied man with a violent, crunching thump as it hit him between the shoulder blades. The wounded man fell with him. Vibrations on the cobbles heralded the approach of support, and as Sidney worked the bolt he glanced back up the alley. What was left of the Field Repair Company was close at hand, but as he looked back at his target a bullet ricocheted off the street five feet in front of him, flew over his head with a whizzing crack and clattered onto a tin roof somewhere behind him. The wounded man was shooting back, his revolver lighting up the alleyway in calm, evenly timed flashes. Sidney dropped to his belly, the bag of grenades painful beneath his ribs, the cobbles hard against his elbows. He waited for the next flash, then fired himself. The shooting stopped.

'That better not be Villafranca you just killed,' warned Cobb, dragging him to his feet.

Sidney spat, and wiped the scum from his lips with his sleeve. 'Saw him. Up ahead, going round that bend.'

'Get a move on, then.'

Sidney dashed to the two bodies, his approach covered by Kreuz.

'Slow down,' hissed the German. 'Take your time.'

The men Sidney had shot were motionless, their bodies shrunken in their civilian clothes by the departure of their souls. For a boy used to dropping rabbits and pigeons from great distances, human beings were easy targets. He edged around the bend, felt Kreuz tap him on the shoulder, and moved ahead. Behind them, Cobb walked down the middle of the street like

196

the man who had built the *barrio*, while Simeron covered the rear with slightly more caution. A rifle, Sidney now realised, was the wrong tool for street fighting. It was long, unwieldy and slow to load in a close-quarters environment. If he had been thinking straight, he would have brought Klee's machine-pistol from the car; but then again, if he'd been thinking straight he would have stayed in Norfolk and would never have come to this insane place. Such errors of judgement put men in the ground: carrying the wrong weapon, loading the wrong ammunition, choosing the wrong side.

It had been less than quarter of an hour since that awful blast, yet it seemed like yesterday, or last week, or another lifetime. Klee's lifetime, perhaps. Sidney remembered how quickly the others had reacted to the assault. If he had been on his own, or with a section of Brigaders, he would be as dead as Klee now. These men stayed alive by knowing when to move swiftly and when to move slowly. They were as cunning as foxes, as swift as weasels and as evil as rats. And that, Sidney realised with no little chagrin, was why he was on point and they were behind him. He pointed to a doorway on the opposite side of the alley, glancing back to make sure Kreuz understood his intention before dashing across the narrow street. A ragged boy stood in the middle of the road, his two-year-old sister in his arms and his wide eyes white in his dirty face. The girl stopped struggling as Sidney dashed past and ducked into an open doorway. The smell of garlic and pork fat sent a spasm through his gut as he checked the road ahead through his sights. It was empty, suggesting that Villafranca and his friends were still running, but then Sidney noticed that the boy was pointing. He nodded his thanks, beckoned Kreuz and moved slowly in the direction of the small, grubby finger. A short, dark passageway lit by a flickering gaslight led to a steep flight of stone steps. Villafranca and his surviving escorts had already descended and were slowly crossing a wide courtyard below. Sidney's first shot set them running; his

197

second clipped the shorter of the two, sending him sprawling on the stones. The third turned to return fire, letting off one wildly aimed round before Kreuz dropped him with a shot that made Sidney's ears ring. Suddenly shouted commands from the street below betrayed the presence of enemy troops, and as Sidney and Kreuz tracked them, Villafranca and the winged escort doubled back, dragging the dead man's pack and disappearing into shadows at the edge of the square.

'*Amigos!*' yelled Kreuz. 'We're Tercio! Don't shoot!'

Cobb jogged down the side alley. 'What's going on?' he hissed breathlessly. 'Where's Villafranca?'

'Down there, but there are Regulares there, too.'

An officer and two riflemen came warily into the square and stood beside the dead terrorist. 'Back the other way!' called Kreuz. 'They just crossed that street in front of you. Quick!'

The officer placed his hands on his hips. 'Don't shout at me, Soldier! Get down here and make your report. I want to know who shot this man.'

Kreuz shook his head in sad disbelief. 'Fucking idiot. Now I have to kill him.'

'He can't see us behind the light,' noted Cobb, flipping the sights on his rifle. 'I'll take the stupid-looking one on the right. Kid, you get the fat one. The officer is all yours, Mr Kreuz. Ready?' The simultaneous discharge of three rifles seemed to travel along the roots and shake loose the teeth in Sidney's jaw. He didn't see where his bullet struck the fat rifleman, but when the smoke cleared all three were on their backs. None moved again.

'Keep going,' barked Cobb, 'and watch out for their friends. Simenon, up front.'

The Frenchman pushed past, scuttling down the steps and into the shadows. His high-pitched whistle was Kreuz's cue to follow, and when Sidney joined them they were crouched in a cloister that surrounded the square on three sides and met at an archway on the fourth.

Cobb bent down beside Simenon, his hands on his knees like an old man studying a dead rat. 'That the only way out?' he asked, jerking his head towards the archway on the opposite side of the square.

'How should I know?' replied Simenon. 'You made me wait in the car.'

'That and the stairs we just came down,' replied Kreuz.

'So where's Villafranca?'

'Gone through one of those doors?' suggested Sidney, nodding towards a series of large, arched doorways leading off the cloistered precincts.

'Maybe.' Cobb shouldered his rifle and unholstered his pistol, a big .45-calibre Colt M1911. He chambered a round and tapped Sidney with his boot. 'Want your Luger back?'

'Why?'

'Do you or don't you?'

'Yes.'

'Then you've got to go through that door first.'

Sidney held out his hand. 'I would have had to go first anyway, wouldn't I?'

Cobb dropped the oily weapon into his palm. 'Probably,' he conceded, 'but it's nice to be rewarded. Just remember not to kill the gipsy.'

Sidney licked his lips and swallowed. 'Anyone got any water?'

'Here,' nodded Simenon, passing a bulbous silver flask. 'Armagnac.'

Sidney unscrewed the cap, smelling again the spirit of imminent death. He swallowed and gagged, then swallowed again and rose to a half crouch. 'Come on, then.'

The first door was ten feet away, its handle a black ring of iron cast in the form of two serpents twisting about each other. His Luger gripped in his right hand, he lifted the handle with his left and pushed the door. 'Locked.' He moved silently to the next, its handle a rat king. 'Locked again,' he whispered, his relief overwhelmed by the fear of shortened odds. Three doors remained. He crept to the third, its handle a crown of thorns. His pulse thumped in his ears and the pistol felt unfamiliar and untrustworthy in his hand. He lifted the crown and pushed, but this door too was locked. The fourth handle was a ring of fire, the tips of the black flames worn shiny by generations of human hands.

Simenon stopped him before he could try the door, his spaniel smile on his lopsided mouth. 'You've used up your luck,' he said. 'I'll take this one.'

Sidney moved aside as the Frenchman raised the ring and pushed. The door swung stiffly inwards and Sidney noticed a smear of fresh blood on the threshold. Simenon winced at the creak, but his pained expression turned to shocked surprise as a hollow metallic clunk heralded his end.

'*Merde!*' he cursed.

It was a fitting last word. The grenade exploded with a flat bang and a flash that lit up the square. The blast threw Simenon against a pillar, the chunks of shrapnel perforating flesh and chipping bone, killing him before he had time to bleed. His body slumped at the foot of the pillar, his trousers shredded, his tunic smoking and his eyes wide open.

Sidney had been blown onto his backside and he rolled against the wall, furiously pulling a Mills bomb from his saddlebag. Cobb gripped his wrist before he could pull the split pin, shaking his head angrily. 'Get a fucking grip, kid!' He pulled a pistol magazine from his pocket and gripped it between his teeth before rolling into the doorway and firing eight rounds into the ceiling. Then he was gone, swallowed by the shadows, the only proof of his presence the snap and the click of the new magazine going home. 'Come on!' he yelled from the darkness. Another eight rounds kept Villafranca's head down, and as Sidney darted through the door he could have sworn that he saw the figure of Death, fifteen feet high with a six-yard scythe, grinning in the stroboscopic muzzle flash of Cobb's automatic. 'Why couldn't it have been somebody's fucking kitchen?' seethed Cobb as Kreuz slithered alongside, his belt buckle scraping on a stone floor still hot from the explosion.

'It's a statuary,' whispered Kreuz, indicating a menacing crowd of oversized silhouettes.

'It looks like hell,' replied Sidney.

'Angel Villafranca!' yelled Cobb. 'My name is Frank Cobb. I'm with the Fifteenth Battalion of the International Brigades. I've been sent to rescue you. You hear me?'

'Brilliant,' sighed Kreuz. 'Now he knows where we are. If he tosses another grenade, we're finished.'

'Shut your goddamned mouth, Kreuz,' hissed Cobb, 'and take cover behind Jesus over there.' He pointed to a grotesque crucifixion scene, complete with dicing legionnaires and weeping handmaidens, their shiny colours glinting wetly in the semi-darkness. He took a deep breath. 'Listen up, Angel. Two choices: live or die. Simple as that. My men just killed three rebel soldiers in the square. More will arrive any moment, and then we're all dead.' He cocked an ear, licking his lips, then poked Sidney in the upper arm and pointed to his right.

Leaving the bag of bombs, Sidney crawled silently around Death's dominion and slithered past a ten-foot Salome, her ruby-painted lips parted in frozen ecstasy as she beheld the blood-spattered head of the Baptist at her bejewelled feet. The floor smelled of dust and rat shit, and Sidney realised with a curious detachment that the last thing Simenon had seen was that giant statue of Death, lit up in the flash of the detonating grenade. The thought made him want to laugh, and he bit his lip as he rested in the cover of a tapestry-sided tableau that seemed to represent a station of the cross on the Via Dolorosa. Above him towered a bony, bloody Jesus, his back bent beneath the cross he was born to bear, his bearded face furrowed with fear and pain. Near by, someone was sobbing, their agony an echo of those emotions.

'Angel,' continued Cobb, dropping his voice to what he thought was an urgent plea, 'I don't have to be here, pal. I could leave now and tell my commander that you were killed in the crossfire, that I couldn't find you or that those other cocksuckers got to you first. I'm certainly not willing to die for you, so if it's all the fucking same to you I'll just call my boys off and go home. What's it to be?'

Sidney heard faint, panicky whispers from near to where he sat, his back against the Via Dolorosa. He wiped the sweat from his face and wondered if he could move closer, maybe finish off Villafranca's wounded comrade. If he moved the right way it would take him to their rear, but if he chose wrong he would crawl right into their sights. Villafranca saved him from having to make the decision.

'*Señor*, how can I trust you?'

'I'm from Indiana,' quipped Cobb. 'You can't trust me.'

The joke fell on barren ground.

'Listen,' called Cobb. 'I'm American. My men are British and German. We're wearing Tercio uniforms because we have to, but we're as committed to the fucking revolution as anyone. Now quit stalling and come on out. There's ten of us and two of you. If we wanted to kill you, we would have done so already.'

The urgent whispers melted to become resigned monosyllables.

'All right,' called Villafranca at last. 'I'm coming out. My comrade needs medical attention.'

'Halle-fucking-lujah,' muttered Cobb.

The bank robber's comrade was bleeding badly. The beret she'd been wearing when Sidney had shot her was gripped in her hands and pressed against the exit wound just above her right hip. Her dark curls were lank with sweat, her smooth skin pallid and her lips the colour of deadly nightshade. Sidney saw immediately and with stomach-churning certainty that no doctor could save this girl, and Cobb confirmed it with a glance. 'She's fucked,' he bellowed. 'That bullet from your private reserve?'

Sidney smarted as though slapped. His carefully customised hollow-point round had hit her in the back, entering below her right shoulder blade before spinning through her body to ricochet off her pelvis and tear a ragged exit wound the size of an orange just above the waistband of her coarse woollen trousers. It had done far more damage than one could reasonably expect of a rifle bullet, performing above and beyond the call of duty. The average ball round would have punched through the shoulder and emerged on the other side, leaving little more than scar tissue, but this one had taken the girl's future with it.

She looked at Sidney, the pupils huge in her dark brown eyes. 'You have a drink of water?' she called.

Sidney shook his head. 'Sorry.' He ripped open a dressing, pulled aside the bloody beret and pushed the brown cotton wad into her wound.

She smiled, a faint flicker across her lips. 'You've been to Andalucia. I hear it in your voice.'

'Not true. I learned Spanish from Andalucians, that's all.'

'I can't hear you. The explosions . . .'

'I said I learned Spanish from Andalucians. I've never been there.'

Cobb's dark shadow fell across her. 'Who are you?'

She looked at him, considering his rudeness and balancing it against whatever she had left to lose. 'Durruti Commando. All of us from Teruel. We volunteered to rescue Villafranca.'

'You know why?'

'He's a hero. We weren't going to let the Nationalists treat him like a criminal.'

'How many of you are there?'

The girl sagged, wincing. 'Just me, I think. Something went

wrong back there. I believe the Asturians put too much dynamite in the car.' She patted the haversack she had taken from her fallen comrade.

'Which car?'

'The car that blew up. They packed explosives in the trunk, but when it exploded it blew up our own people.'

Cobb raised his eyebrows. 'You used a car as a bomb? I like your style, doll-face.'

'Most of our people were hiding in the house opposite the bomb. The blast blew the wall down on them.'

'And how the hell did you think you were going to escape from Teruel?'

The girl was staring at Sidney, blinking hard against the darkness, a sad and knowing smile lying faintly on her blue lips. Her head lolled to one side.

Cobb caught it, squeezing her chin hard in his hand. 'Escape route, doll-face?'

But for Villafranca, she would have told him to go to hell. 'The sewer,' she said. 'My comrade Salazar out there in the square was the engineer for the city. He was leading us to the sewer. The fascists shot us both. Did you see?'

A hot rush of something more caustic than shame scorched Sidney's cheeks. He leaned harder on the compress, now black with blood and as slippery as warm soap.

'Yeah, honey, I saw everything,' nodded Cobb. 'We killed the bastards. Now where's the sewer?'

She closed her eyes, as though holding back the tears. 'It's a strange thing that's happened here, isn't it?' she whispered. A chill seemed to rise from the floor, creeping like bromide through the bones of those upon it. 'I would never have guessed it would end like this.'

'We don't have time for this, honey,' sighed Cobb. 'If we don't get Villafranca out of here, it really will have been for nothing.' He leaned close enough to whisper in her ear. 'Help me out, doll-face. Make my life easy, and when the time comes, I'll make it as painless as I can for you. OK?'

She licked her lips, her eyes still closed. 'Across the square. Through the arch, a manhole on the main street. It was supposed to be left open – a workman's tent and a barrier. It's not far.'

Cobb gripped her shoulder. 'You're an angel already.' He turned to Kreuz. 'Ready?'

'Eh?'

'I said, "Ready?"'

Sidney ripped a strip from the dusty shroud of the risen Christ, screwed it into a ball and pushed it into the girl's wound.

She smiled at him, her eyes full of tears. 'You mustn't leave me for the soldiers to find. You must shoot me.'

Sidney shook his head. 'We'll take you with us.'

'Forget it,' said Kreuz.

'I'll carry her,' insisted Sidney.

'She'll be dead before we get her across the square,' said Cobb.

'He's right, *hermano*,' nodded Villafranca.

'Shoot me,' whispered the girl. 'Please.'

Sidney drew back, but she grabbed his hand, squeezing his fingers in a clammy grip. 'Can't do that,' he stammered. 'Why can't we take her with us?'

'I'm counting to three,' warned Cobb.

'I can't shoot you,' insisted Sidney.

'Damn right,' agreed Cobb. He pushed Sidney aside, placed one hand over the girl's mouth and thrust his narrow Toledo stiletto into her heart. She squirmed beneath him as he twisted the blade, fighting as if she'd suddenly realised that she'd made a terrible mistake. 'Hush now, doll-face,' he whispered. The dagger hissed as he withdrew it from her corpse, wiping the blade on her bloodstained shirt. 'Now can we go?' he asked, looking up at Sidney. 'And don't look at me like that. You killed her. I just shortened the agony. Clean up your own mess in future.'

He opened the haversack, nodding in approval as the sweet odour of high explosive seeped out.

'Dynamite,' he muttered, tossing the bag to Sidney. 'Take this and keep it dry.'

Kreuz leaned against Pontius Pilate and pushed a charger into his rifle, shaking his head. 'Christ Almighty,' he sighed. 'And now I have to crawl along the stinking sewers.'

12

Nick felt sick. It was either Lenny's smug demeanour or his driving that was churning his stomach; or both. Of course the oily, poorly fried egg he had eaten for breakfast was a contributing factor, as was the rollercoaster pitch of the road, but for the most part it was Lenny Knowles who was making him sick. 'Slow down,' he groaned, as Lenny accelerated through a sheer-edged hairpin. 'We might miss something.'

'Yeah, I know what I'm missing,' nodded Lenny with lascivious grin. 'The old ones are the best, you know.'

'She wasn't that old,' protested Sidney, wedged between his two employees and squinting through a pair of antique spectacles Lenny had appropriated from the inn.

'Not to you, maybe, Mr Starman.' Lenny pulled as close to the edge of the road as he could to let the white-faced driver of a petrol tanker squeeze past. 'Don't get me wrong – I'm not knocking it.' He inched forward. 'I was fucking cross-eyed when I woke up this morning.'

'Oh, for God's sake,' groaned Nick.

Lenny raised a jaunty eyebrow. 'Jealous, are we, Nickle-Arse? How long's it been since you've had a Melvin? Two years, is it? I'm surprised it hasn't dropped off, mate. You've sort of evolved into a non-sexual organism.'

'Asexual,' said Sidney.

'Hold up, Casanova,' called Nick. 'You haven't exactly been putting it about these past few years.'

'That's 'cos I've been faithful to my ex-wife, Nicholas. Some of us have morals, you know.'

'There's no answer to that,' retorted Nick. He glanced at Sidney. 'Sorry about this, Mr Starman.'

Sidney took off his new glasses and rubbed his eyes. The frames were too large, the nosepiece too narrow, and squinting through the greasy lenses gave him a headache. 'No need to apologise, Mr Crick,' he sighed. 'You worry about offending an old man because you fail to consider that an old man might have seen much, much worse than the likes of you two.'

'Have you?' asked Lenny.

'Oh yes,' nodded Sidney, 'but I'm not telling you about it. Let's concentrate on the job in hand.'

The task was to drive through the mountains until Sidney saw something he recognised. Almost seven decades had weathered his recollection, eroding its features and turning solid fact to rubble. The soaring, sparkling crags and their enclaves of black forest were both familiar and alien, as though reality were the mirror image of memory. There had been a road junction just after the pass: that was fact. There had been several miles of narrow, twisting roads and then another road junction where there had been yet another bloody incident. Then there was the forest track, the *camino forestal*, which climbed up and away from the spur road and into the mountains, its surface choked with broken boulders and fallen trees. Sidney had studied the pre-war map on his living-room wall for twenty-five thousand nights and he could draw its impressionist topography from memory. Here was the Puig Montsant, the Garganto de la Balsa, the Sierra de las Cabras, the Loma del Fuente del Rayo. That red dot was the Majada de Marin, that one the Caserio La Alcaria and these two the Casas El Penitente. They were all here, in this valley, distributed above, below, left and right of this winding road, their aspects imagined rather than remembered, but nevertheless concrete features of a real valley on an accurate map. The only problem was that Sidney couldn't be entirely sure that this was the *right* valley.

'What about that track?' asked Nick, breaking in on his doubts.

Sidney shrugged, then nodded. 'Try it,' he said.

'Here we go,' sniffed Lenny. 'Magical mystery tour.' He swung the van from the frost-shattered tarmac onto a rough track of broken rock.

Progress was slow and difficult until the van squeezed between a pair of outcrops that guarded the track like the Pillars of Hercules. Thereafter it became worse, with boulders the size of television sets and water-worn ruts that were knee-deep.

'We're going to bottom out,' warned Lenny.

Nick gripped the dashboard with white knuckles. 'Can't have been this one, Mr Starman. If we can't get up it now, there's no way you'd have made it back then.'

Sidney winced as a rock scraped along the bottom of the van with an angry rumble. 'Could be any track in these parts,' he replied. 'You'd be surprised what we accomplished back then.'

The trail began to resemble a mountain stream as it climbed higher, twisting through dank, still forest that sometimes saw sunlight for three hours a day. No living thing stirred, and when Nick stepped down to drag storm-broken branches from the track the silence was deep enough to induce agoraphobia. 'It's prehistoric out there,' he muttered as he climbed back into the cab.

'Perfect for dinosaur-hunters, then,' observed Sidney. 'You remember our cover story, gentlemen?'

'Every time I look at you I think of dinosaurs, Mr S,' nodded Lenny. He turned to see how the jibe had been taken. 'Blimey! Are you all right? Look at how pale he is, Nick.'

Nick looked at the old man and repeated the question.

Sidney took a deep breath and nodded at the track. 'Don't you worry about me. Keep your eyes on the road.'

Nick shook his head. 'I think we should stop and you can have a rest. There's no rush. We've got plenty of time.'

Sidney grimaced. 'Plenty of time is what we don't have, gentlemen. I'm having a funny turn, that's all. I'll be fine in a minute, so keep driving.'

Nick shrugged and lit a cigarette.

Lenny was aghast. 'Nicholas!' he barked. 'You really are a selfish bastard, aren't you?'

Nick gaped. 'What?'

'Put the sodding salmon out, for fuck's sake! Have you no brains at all? Passive smoking causes heart disease – let's give El Sid a fighting chance, eh?'

'One fag won't make a difference,' argued Nick, winding down the window.

'At his age it could be the straw that breaks the donkey's back,' insisted Lenny.

'Camel,' interjected Sidney.

'Silk Cut, actually, Mr S, but it makes no difference. He should know better. Now put it out, Nicholas.'

The Peugeot slipped and skidded, wheezed and whined its way along the track, zigzagging through the dark woods until it emerged above the tree line and into the pale morning sunlight. Heavy drifts of wet, stained snow lay in north-facing hollows, dripping sullenly onto bare rocks that were rimed with ice. From here the track ran straight and level, following the contour along the north-eastern side of a ridge that gnawed the cold, blue sky like reptile teeth.

'Any of this ringing bells?' asked Lenny.

Sidney shook his head. 'Difficult to say with these glasses. Where did you get them from?'

'The dead bloke,' admitted Lenny, his voice rising in self-defence. 'I never nicked them. I asked.'

'How?' challenged Nick. 'You can't speak Spanish.'

'Sign language. Those glasses . . . for him no good now . . . for my old China . . . very bleeding useful . . . *mucho gracias*. She'll give me anything now, that bird. I'm fluent in sign language and the language of love, both of which are a fuck sight more useful than your Latin or whatever poncey stuff you learned in school, Nicholas.'

'I didn't do Latin,' protested Nick, but he knew it was just Lenny's chip talking.

'Bet you did,' replied Lenny. 'Anyway – how are they?'

'Very good,' nodded Sidney. 'They'd be even better if I could see through them.'

'Should have gone to Specsavers, then,' sniffed Lenny. 'Listen: is there any chance at all that we're on the right track?' The van lurched violently as it slipped into a pothole.

'Very hard to say,' replied Sidney. 'I mean, what I can make out looks familiar, but then everywhere round here will look exactly like this.'

'How far was it from the turn-off?' asked Nick. 'Do you remember how long it took you to get there?'

'An hour, perhaps an hour and a half.'

Lenny looked at his imaginary watch. 'And we've been up here, what, half an hour?'

'Forty minutes,' nodded Sidney.

'Well it's not here,' decided Lenny. 'I've got a very good sense for these things and I'm telling you that there is no gold in these here hills. You know why? Because you would never have got seven tons down this track without falling off the bleeding mountain. Obvious, innit?'

The valley was still in shadow by the time they returned to the tarmac road and Lenny was itching to call it a day. He wanted to go back to the hotel, have an early lunch, a siesta, and leave his options open for a second sortie later in the afternoon. He was outvoted.

The next track, as Sidney had predicted, was identical to the first, only it was in a worse state of repair. The Peugeot bumped and crashed against the rutted, rocky bed, and the cab filled with the familiar smell of burning clutch as it picked its way along a route built for *burros*. Conversation evaporated as each man came to realise the enormity of the task before them and the ludicrous odds of a successful outcome. Every mountain looked similar to the last, a looping layercake of overlaid sediments rising out of a dense forest of wet pine. The looping crags were riven with fissures and chimneys, their bases hidden in a mess of boulders and scree. Seven tons of gold could disappear for ever in this wilderness.

Just as the primeval landscape disheartened Lenny, it disturbed Nick. He stared through the open window, holding back his nausea and trying to see the reason behind his fear. Reduced to its elements, what lay beyond and beneath the van was prosaically benign: rock, wood, water, earth and the deep blue sky. Yet there was something else that could see but not be seen, that could touch and not be touched. Something wicked, something malevolent, detected by a sense long unused. Its dominion over the land explained why no man lived here, why no birds sang and why no goats wandered the eponymous Sierra de las Cabras. If the gold truly lay buried in these mountains, then whoever had brought it here had chosen his hiding-place well, knowing that it wouldn't be found by chance.

'We're doing this all wrong,' he announced. 'Let's finish this track off and go back to the hotel. There's got to be a better way of searching.' He neither invited nor received dissent.

Guadeloupe had been waiting for Lenny to return all morning. She had washed and dressed her father's corpse and left him lying in a bed covered in fresh sprigs of rosemary. Prieto, the undertaker, was expected later that day but she would tell him nothing. After cleaning the rooms, washing the floors, laying the fires and feeding the boars she had changed into a tight dress, piled her hair high on her head and applied two layers of lipstick before seating herself at reception to await her avenger's return.

'What's she saying?' asked Lenny as he followed Sidney into the foyer.

'She's asking if we found any bones this morning.'

'Tell her I've got a nice one for her.'

'No, I will not. She wants to know if we want lunch.'

''Course we do. What's on the menu?'

'Er, trout for Mr Crick and myself, and apparently a steak for you,' replied Sidney with some dismay. 'I quite fancy a piece of beef myself. Is there only the one steak?'

'Just the one,' nodded Guadeloupe. 'For him only. I need him to be strong.'

'Er, quite,' nodded Sidney.

Lunch was taken on a cantilevered wooden terrace that hung high above the white water in the valley below. Sidney and Nick ate grilled trout with *migas del pastor*, flat lemonade and a jug of vitriolic rioja while Lenny tucked into an enormous char-grilled steak encircled by the same fried breadcrumbs and topped with the essential fried egg. Guadeloupe watched him eat, filling his glass with specially ordered lager and smiling every time he swallowed.

'*Postre?*' she whispered when he pushed away his plate. Lenny pulled his cigarettes from the sleeve of his T-shirt and shook his head. 'Got one here, darling.'

'*Postre* means dessert, Mr Knowles,' explained Sidney. 'Ashtray is *cenicero.*'

'I know,' lied Lenny. 'I'm just having a fag before I get my dessert.' He took a long drag and rose from the table. 'If you'll excuse me, gentlemen. England expects and all that.'

Nick and Sidney turned to watch him follow Guadeloupe to her boudoir.

'Does he really have to wink like that?' sighed Sidney.

'He'll be whistling when he comes back,' warned Nick. 'Tell me more about the gold.'

Sidney raised his eyebrows and pulled his flask from the inside pocket of his tweed jacket. He shook it at Nick in invitation.

'Don't drink, remember?'

'Ah yes. Remarkable.' He poured a shot of Armagnac into his wineglass. 'My understanding is that a rather charming gipsy named Angel Villafranca stole the gold from Orlov's house on the orders of the anarchist command. The FAI, if they admitted it, would have said they were repatriating bullion stolen not by a foreign power but by a foreign individual. Orlov, you see, was lining his own pockets. Stalin's purges had begun – too many witnesses to too many crimes – and Orlov knew his name was writ large on that list. He deliberately muddied the count on the manifests, claiming that there were two hundred boxes less than the Spanish count, when in fact there were only one hundred less. He gambled on the Russians being so pleased to receive what was, in effect, a free gift that they wouldn't think to pursue the other hundred boxes. Those were transported to Valencia and stored in the cellar of the local Russian intelligence head-quarters, where they were to remain until Orlov had planned his escape. You don't need me to tell you what happened to the poor sods who drove the lorries and helped unload the bullion. I've heard Orlov planned to sail to Mexico and then to travel overland to the USA, but in the event he lost his retirement fund and ended up defecting penniless to Canada. Most annoying, I'm sure, and no less so for the anarchists who realised shortly after the heist that Villafranca was a thief without honour.' He took a sip of Armagnac and chuckled. 'You only had to look at him to realise he was a thoroughly untrustworthy type. Long hair, unshaven, tight trousers – you know the sort. He took the lot and hid it out there somewhere.' Sidney waved his glass at the mountains. 'Deep behind enemy lines, so to speak.'

'And how did you find it?'

'Villafranca showed me,' smiled Sidney.

'That was nice of him.'

The old man raised his eyebrows as he studied the past. 'He didn't really have much choice,' he said. 'Now, I'm off for a kip. Don't leave me too long – we don't want to overwork the undertaker, do we?'

With Lenny preoccupied and Sidney asleep, Nick spent the afternoon pacing the terrace and looking for inspiration. He knew there had to be an easier way of finding Villafranca's hiding-place than driving up and down random mountains on the off-chance that an octogenarian would remember the view. The problem was that the witness wasn't telling the whole story, and the parts he *had* told were, for the most part, entirely useless. Sidney was being selective with the truth, trying to entertain rather than inform, and recounting history as though he hadn't been there. He'd done that from the beginning, Nick realised, explaining the war from an objective point of view that entirely ignored his own part in events. Nick flicked his fag end over the rail and marched to Sidney's room.

'Let me in. It's Nick.'

'What do you want?'

'I want to talk. Let me in.'

'I'm trying to get some sleep, Mr Crick.'

'No time for that. You can sleep when you're dead.'

Nick could hear the old man's bones cracking as he shuffled wearily across to the door and drew the bolt.

'What?' growled Sidney.

'I'm Nick Crick, pleased to meet you,' announced Nick. 'Two years ago I got drunk at a party, lost control of my car and crashed into the river Bure. I killed my wife and daughter and served eighteen months for it. In my opinion I should have done a lot more time, but then again, as the judge said, I'm doing life in my head. That's why I don't drink, Mr Starman. That's my secret. Now, why don't you show me the same respect and tell me your secret?'

215

Sidney looked at him for a moment, licking his moustache and blinking fast behind his new spectacles. 'Fine,' he nodded at last. 'Shall we go for a walk?'

They didn't walk far. Sidney was clearly in pain as they followed the dirt path down to the river, and when they reached its rocky banks he leaned back against a boulder and declared that he would go no further. 'I feel as though I'm fading fast,' he said. 'This trip has taken it out of me, you know.'

Nick kicked a pebble into the rushing torrent. The sun was sliding behind the western peaks, and even though it was not yet three in the afternoon a twilight chill was creeping up the valley. 'Are you scared?' he asked.

'Of dying? Of course I am.'

Nick shook his head. 'I'm asking if you're scared of confessing what you did over here. It was a dirty war, wasn't it?'

Sidney stared at the water. 'I came to Spain to kill Germans. I made no bones about it – never pretended to be political, to care about the plight of democracy, about the workers' struggle and what have you. What I'm saying is that I didn't come down here for the right reasons.'

'You were in the International Brigade,' nodded Nick. 'It was a noble cause – you said so yourself.'

Sidney shook his head. 'I left the Brigade after Jarama. I joined a unit called the Field Repair Company under the command of Frank Cobb. He took his orders directly from General Orlov. We were supposed to be a special-duties unit but we were really little more than a death squad. I killed more Spaniards than Germans, and more Republicans than Nationalists . . .'

'You actually killed people?'

Sidney sighed. 'Your generation sees the likes of me as either benign grandparents or crotchety old pensioners. You don't consider for a moment the horrors we've seen and the atrocities we've committed. Of course I bloody killed people. I killed children, girls, old men who I thought were incapable of

216

murder. I've shot men in the back, put bullets through their heads when they were down on their knees begging. Doesn't seem so noble now, does it?'

Nick ran his gaze along the eastern ridge, its peaks still warm with sunlight. 'I don't really care who you shot,' he said. 'You were probably following orders and if you felt so bad about what you had done I doubt you'd have come down here to fetch your ill-gotten gains. All I want to know—'

Fast, angry footsteps were coming along the path.

'Mr Knowles, I believe,' guessed Sidney.

'Aye-aye,' called Lenny. 'What's this? Secret meeting for the intellectuals, is it?' Nick sighed. 'We're just talking.'

'About me? About the gold? What could be so private and important that you have to come all the way down here to discuss it?'

'Mr Crick was just telling me about his prison sentence for, what was it, causing death by dangerous driving?'

'Yeah,' said Nick, meeting Lenny's indignant eyes. 'Someone told Mr Starman that I'd been inside and I thought it was time to clear the air. I thought you were otherwise engaged.'

Lenny wasn't sure whether he was pleased or not. He'd been certain that they were conniving against him, plotting to cut him out of the deal, and here they were having a heart-to-heart like a couple of girls. He twitched a little. 'Yeah, well, she's loading her old man into the undertaker's van. What does *tio* mean?'

'"Uncle,"' replied Sidney. 'Like Tio Pepe, the owner.'

'Uncle,' repeated Lenny thoughtfully. 'And *mi* means "my", right?'

'Correct.'

'And *matar*?'

'*Matar*?'

'Yeah, *matar*.'

'*Matar* means "kill".'

Lenny drew a little circle in the dirt with the toe of his trainer. 'Oh shit.'

'No wonder she's feeding you up,' grinned Nick.

'Not now, Nicholas,' growled Lenny. 'I've got issues.'

'So has Mr Starman. He was about to explain his part in the recovery of Orlov's gold.'

Lenny stood open-mouthed for a moment as though slapped. 'Er, I think I've got slightly more important things to do than stand around listening to a history lesson, Nicholas. That mad cow wants me to kill her uncle.' He made a mouth with his hand. '*Matar mi tio, matar mi tio* . . . I didn't know what *matar* meant but I was hoping *tio* was "arse".' He shook his head. 'I need a bleeding drink. Fill me in later.'

They watched him wander back up the path, mumbling and shaking his head.

'You were wrong about the whistling,' observed Sidney.

13

It didn't take Angel Villafranca long to realise that he was not among friends. It might have been Sidney's refusal to give him a weapon, the punch in the head he took from Kreuz, or Cobb's heavy handcuffs that betrayed his predicament. But he took abuse with the nonchalance of one long used to negotiating with angry authority figures and worked hard on selling his natural, gipsy charm to his captors.

'You stink of shit, you know that?' he grinned as they sped north in a delivery truck that said '*Jamones el Carrascal*' on the side.

Cobb had stolen it from a poorly locked garage near the sewer outfall down on the River Turia. 'Hit him again,' he said. 'Then gag him.'

Kreuz cracked Villafranca on the ear with the butt of his pistol and stuffed a bloodstained bandanna into his mouth.

'Although he has a point,' conceded Cobb. 'We do stink of shit.'

'So does he,' noted Kreuz.

'At least we're out of the sewers,' muttered Sidney. 'Simenon is still down there.'

'Hey, quit the sentimentality, kid. A sewer's as good as a grave – you just get eaten by rats and not worms. What do you think the enemy would have done with his carcass if we'd left it in the square?'

'What about Klee?' asked Kreuz.

'Nothing I could do,' admitted Cobb. 'At least he was wearing

Condor Legion uniform. Maybe he'll be repatriated to the Fatherland and given a hero's funeral.'

'You joke too much,' warned Kreuz.

'Yeah? Well, here's one that'll crease you up: I'm not running the roadblock with Villafranca in the truck. You and the kid are going to escort him on foot up and around the checkpoint. I'll pick you up on the other side at the Albarracin turn-off. Can you cope with that, kid?'

Sidney moved his shoulders in a non-committal fashion. 'S'pose so.'

'If he gives you any crap, knock some teeth out or break some ribs or something, but for Christ's sake don't kill him. Not yet.'

A few miles later, Cobb refused to stop the truck, so they climbed down while it was still moving. Only Sidney lost his footing, falling heavily onto the cobbled road, dropping his rifle and skinning his knees. Villafranca raised his eyebrows and performed a little dance as Sidney climbed to his feet, wordlessly boasting of his innate grace. Midsummer's night was eight days hence, and dusk was only now falling across the campo. Millions of unseen crickets chirped like a crowd in a busy beer garden, suddenly falling silent every now and then as though disturbed by the arrival of strangers.

'This way,' hissed Kreuz, dragging Villafranca into the rocky bed of a dry watercourse. He pointed across a flood plain of stone and shrub to where the shadow of night fell down the slopes of the western sierra. They walked in single file for thirty minutes, climbing short walls to cross *fincas* of stout olives, feeling the heat rising from the parched soil. A prowler's light lay across the plain, the few minutes of dusk that guarantee invisibility, and as Kreuz led them up a goat track into the hills Sidney fought to hold back the numbness of nervous fatigue. A fork in the path led north, following a low contour through the boulders and running parallel with the road, a mile or so to the east.

It was now dark enough to see the braziers glowing at the checkpoint, orange dots that seemed to float in the black summer heat.

Kreuz waited for Sidney to catch up and wiggled his hand like a swimming fish to indicate the route they would take. 'But first we rest for five minutes,' he said. He pushed Villafranca into the lee of a boulder and squatted beside him, chewing on a hunk of bread he drew from his tunic pocket. He offered some to Sidney, who refused, and none to the prisoner, who smiled and shook his head with aristocratic disdain.

Kreuz turned his back on Villafranca and spoke to Sidney in English. 'So how long do you think we last with this man Cobb?'

Sidney shrugged.

'I think he'll kill us both, and him.' Kreuz jerked his head towards the gipsy.

'What for?'

'Ach – come on. Surely you've realised this mission is unofficial.'

Sidney looked towards the distant fires. 'Don't know what you're getting at,' he mumbled.

Kreuz laughed. 'Cobb doesn't deserve such loyalty, believe me. You think you're bringing this idiot to Orlov, don't you?'

'That's what I've been told.'

Kreuz tore off a piece of bread and ate it slowly, staring at the ground. 'I used to be like you,' he said at last. 'Naïve, loyal, brave. It took the fascists to beat some sense into me, but for every thing they gave me, they took two things. Give up your naïvety and your loyalty, Sidney, and I'll give you wisdom in return. The gipsy will never make it to Valencia. Cobb is working to some private agenda. And we're being used.'

'I'm just following orders,' argued Sidney.

'Fine. Tell Orlov that before he has you shot for treachery. I hope you're as brave when they kick your backside into the courtyard.'

Sidney felt his cheeks burning. He wasn't sure he could lie to Kreuz.

The German studied his face, chewing mechanically. 'Why do you think we've got Villafranca?'

Sidney squirmed. Did Kreuz know about the gold, and if so, was Cobb aware that he knew? Had Cobb confided in Kreuz too? Was this just a test? He kicked a stone down the slope and scraped his tongue along his teeth. 'I don't know,' he replied. 'I don't care, neither. I just do as I'm told.'

'So you'll follow this man to your death?'

'I hope not.'

'Even if he's acting illegally?'

Sidney raised his eyebrows and snorted – a short, sharp expression of sardonic surprise. 'What's legality got to do with anything? We killed our own allies in Teruel rescuing a man who by all accounts is nothing but a common criminal.'

Kreuz smiled at him. 'Exactly. Show me the papers ordering that action, for what they'd be worth before a tribunal.'

Sidney shook his head. 'Look, Kreuz, don't ask me for explanations. Cobb tells me what to do and I do it. No questions.'

'Do you know what happened in Madrid?'

'What's that got to do with anything?'

'You should know, that's all.'

'So?'

'So Cobb's entire team was captured during an assassination attempt. Two died in the firefight, and they were the lucky ones. The rest were taken to Salamanca for debriefing where they say two more died under questioning. The rest were garrotted. Only Cobb escaped.'

Sidney met Kreuz's eyes. 'What are you saying?'

'Exactly what you heard. No more and no less.'

'We should get going.'

'And if I was forced to remove Cobb from his command, could I count on you to follow me?'

'Is that what you're planning?'

Kreuz tossed his crust down the hillside and stood up. 'I'm planning nothing. I'm merely trying to do my duty as you are doing yours.' He laid a heavy hand on Sidney's shoulder. 'I hope I can rely upon you, should the necessity arise.'

'Why should I trust you?'

'Why should *I* trust *you*?' retorted Kreuz. 'And why should either of us trust Cobb? He's already deceived us both and I think it prudent that whatever confidence we had in him we should share among ourselves.' He brushed crumbs from his lap. 'It's up to you to decide for yourself, but if I were you, boy, I'd choose wisdom.'

Cobb was sweating as they reached the truck, pacing up and down on the roadside, running his fingers through his brilliantined hair and puffing nervously on a cigar butt. 'I didn't know you were going via fucking Toledo,' he growled, dragging Villafranca to a rear door that unnervingly depicted a smiling pig dressed as a butcher. He unlocked the cuffs, smiled at the prisoner's gratitude, then passed them through a steel ring on the wall and snapped them shut again. Villafranca looked disappointed. 'Well, what the hell did you think I was doing?' asked Cobb. He took a map from his jacket pocket and laid it before the prisoner. 'Tell me where.'

'I already told you where when I thought you were my friend.'

'Yeah – I remember asking you back when I thought you were smart. Now tell me again.' Cobb traced his finger along the map. 'Cella . . . Celadas – you sure that road is passable?'

The gipsy turned his head in haughty disdain.

Cobb slapped him. 'Is this road passable?'

Villafranca nodded.

'OK, Alfambra, Escorihuela, back southwards to Cedrillas then east to Villaroya and Fortunete to this junction here.

Where does this take me?' He placed a hand over the map.

Villafranca understood why. 'It takes you to the bend in the Villarluengo road.'

'And that better be the place, Angel-face.' Cobb stuffed the gag back into the gipsy's mouth and turned to his men. 'Anyone see you?'

'Of course not,' sighed Kreuz.

'So let's go. We've lost an hour already. Kid, get in the back with the prisoner.' Cobb climbed into the cab and started the engine.

It was blacker than night in the back and it smelled of blood and wood shavings. Sidney sat over the rear axle, wincing with every rut and pothole, feeling Villafranca's eyes probing his face for an opportunity. Unlike Luis Aranjuc, this wily gipsy faced Death with a matador's bravado and a daredevil's curiosity, dancing through its shadow with one eye on the audience and another on the door. Villafranca had long ago judged the margins within which escape remained possible and he affected an air of intelligent amusement at his predicament. Sidney couldn't see his face, but he knew the bastard was grinning at him from across the van. Cut the fool's head off and like a farmyard rooster he would still try to run. He wondered what Cobb and Kreuz were discussing in the cab, realising that he might have become as much a prisoner as Villafranca, only more dispensable.

Until two hours ago the only man he felt he could trust in the whole world was Cobb. Now he trusted no one, and the loneliness scared him. Death scared him too, not for its aftermath but for its passage. He'd grown up preoccupied with his father's slow end, bleeding to death in a queue outside the hospital in Rouen, and had imagined the creeping chill that had steadily claimed his numbed limbs, the terror of Death's cold grip and the misery of wasting a life unfulfilled. Now he knew that the reality was much, much worse, and that when *La Muerte* came calling she sent *La Soledad* ahead of her to clear a path, to ensure that her victim had eyes for her alone. He remembered the hatred, the inexplicable disgust he had felt for his comrades on the Jarama when they had fallen mortally injured. Joe had sensed the distance between them, the revulsion Sidney had been unable to hide as he had bled to death on that blasted hillside. And when he had passed on, he had done so alone, his vital reputation besmirched and his living character assassinated by *La Soledad*. Villafranca, it seemed, had made a friend of that solitude and, suddenly unable to bear the weight of his thoughts, Sidney reached across and pulled the bandanna from the robber's mouth.

'Thank you,' croaked Villafranca. 'You have some water?'

Sidney recalled Kreuz's warning about prisoners trying to get under your skin and immediately regretted removing the gag. 'No,' he replied.

'*Hombre*, you must have some water, for the love of God. My tongue is like leather.'

Sidney felt in his pocket for the flask he had taken from Simenon's body. 'Here,' he said.

'My hands are tied,' said Villafranca. 'Pour it into my mouth.'

'It's not water.'

'What is it?'

'Armagnac. It belonged to the man you killed with that grenade.'

'I never threw that,' insisted Villafranca. 'It was the girl, whatever her name was. God rest all their souls.' He said it with sincerity, then tipped back his head to receive the spirit. He licked his lips as Sidney stopped pouring. 'Very fine. Have some yourself.'

Sidney took a sip, then another. 'It should have been me at the door. He pulled me back and opened it himself.'

'Why would he do that?' asked Villafranca.

'I don't know. I'd tried the first three doors and they were all locked. He told me to stand back, that he'd take this one.'

'What was his name?'

225

'Simenon. He was French.'

'*Hermano*, pour a little more on my tongue, in memory of your friend Simenon.'

Sidney tipped the spirit down the bandit's throat and took another long pull for himself. 'Did the girl really throw the grenade?'

'As I sit here before you. She was hurt and she was scared.'

'Then she should have killed me,' breathed Sidney.

'She didn't, though,' said Villafranca, 'so thank God for that. Have you been to Andalucia?'

'No.' Sidney saw him nodding in the gloom, his teeth seeming to glow.

'You've got a bad accent, *hermano*. You'll never get a job with an accent like that. Maybe you won't need a job. Do you know where we're going?'

'To get your gold.'

'I feel it is no longer mine, if ever it was. I have been merely its courier, as you may be, if indeed you are still alive to see it.'

'You don't scare me,' growled Sidney. 'You make one move . . .'

'*Hermano*, I'm not threatening you. I'm warning you. Your boss is not the only man in Spain who knows what I've got to offer in exchange for my life. After all, what is gold without life? What good would all that bullion have been to me if I'd been garrotted in Teruel, or Seville? To weigh my pockets down, maybe? To keep me still while the wheel was turned?'

Sidney lost the point in Villafranca's heavily accented slang. 'What are you saying?' he asked.

'I'm saying that, unfortunately, and due to circumstances entirely beyond my control, we are not the only people heading to Villarluengo. I made a deal with a German officer in Teruel. Herr Oberst Claus von Wittenburg. The Regulares were taking me to his headquarters when the anarchists attacked the convoy.'

★

Cobb was furious.

'Don't hit him,' protested Sidney.

'Don't fucking tell me what to do, kid,' hissed Cobb. He launched a kick at the handcuffed prisoner, catching him below the right kneecap and dropping him to the bloodstained floor of the truck. 'What were you thinking, you gipsy halfwit?'

Villafranca retained his dignity even in agony. He bit his lip until the pain passed, then raised his head. '*Señor*, if I had known you were coming, then I would have said nothing. You should have sent word.'

'Very fucking funny,' seethed Cobb. 'Now the whole fucking place will be crawling with fucking square heads.'

'I don't see why the presence of enemy forces should be such a surprise,' mused Kreuz, leaning on the back of the van. 'Surely you anticipated contact as we recrossed the line?'

Cobb rounded on him. 'Shut your goddamned mouth!' He pointed to a dark knoll rising from the roadside. 'Get up there and watch out for headlamps on the road.'

Kreuz frowned. 'Why not send the boy?' A full fat summer moon was rising over the eastern sierra, plating the ridge with silver and illuminating the wide valley.

''Cos I'm damn well sending you,' yelled Cobb. 'Jesus! One fucking anarchist is enough already.'

Kreuz shrugged and threw a warning look at Sidney before shouldering his rifle and ambling onto the clinking shale. Sidney had seen potential witnesses sent away before, and his stomach filled with acid as he wondered what sudden, life-threatening betrayal he might be about to commit that Cobb could use as an excuse for his murder. The ability to determine his part in events seemed to have been snatched away and he felt as helpless as a drowning man in a flood-swollen torrent, swept along by forces too powerful to resist. He watched as Cobb scratched his head and wondered if the American would even bother devising a justification for killing him. These days such an effort had become

227

a redundant social nicety, like a long letter apologising for failing to attend a party at which you hadn't been welcome. Kreuz wouldn't give a damn how or why he'd been killed, despite their pact. Less than five seconds had passed and Sidney suddenly knew that if he was to be executed, it wouldn't be now, not while the four of them were being hunted by the Condor Legion.

Cobb wiped his mouth and looked at Sidney. 'Get down,' he muttered.

Sidney jumped onto the road. Cobb stood in the rear doorway, his leather coat flapping about his legs.

'He only told them what he told us,' noted Sidney, speaking English.

'Whaddya mean?'

'He only told them about the bend in the Villarluengo road.'

Cobb ran his fingers through his thick brown hair. 'Kid, I'm struggling to keep track of this operation. Is that good or bad?'

Sidney shrugged. 'He's keeping the specific location to himself. It's all he has to bargain with.'

'So?'

'So the Germans know only to go as far as the bend. As long as we've got Villafranca, we can stay one step ahead.'

Cobb looked at Sidney in frustration then hauled the prisoner to his feet. 'Where's the fucking bullion?'

Villafranca didn't hesitate. 'It's near Villarluengo but I could never tell you where.'

Cobb glanced at the roadside knoll he'd sent Kreuz to climb, then back at Villafranca. 'So draw me a fucking map.'

Villafranca shrugged apologetically. '*Señor*, I regret that I am no artist.'

Cobb reached for his sidearm, murderous intent creasing his face. He stared hard into the gipsy's eyes for a long moment, then threw him to the floor. 'I hate you, Villafranca,' he spat. 'I hate you so much that I think I'm going to take the personal risk of delivering you to Seville myself, you sorry son of a bitch.'

Villafranca looked up at his captor, his brown eyes big and wet in an unshaven face. 'I must confess, *Commandante*, by the same token, that I am little enamoured of you.'

'Bloody women!' cursed Lenny. He had, with Sidney's assistance, just lost his first argument with Guadeloupe. 'I can't believe you let her say all those things to me, Mr S. I mean, you just stood there and let her call me a coward and, and . . .'

'A hypocrite.'

'Yeah . . .'

'And she said you were a disappointing lover.'

'All right,' cried Lenny, 'leave it out.'

'Disappointing were you?' asked Nick

'And you smelled odd,' added Sidney.

Nick sniffed. 'Are you wearing that pheromone spray?'

Lenny reddened. 'If you'd been there, Nicholas, which you weren't, and you could speak Spanish, which you can't, you'd know that what she actually meant was that I was totally drum and bass in the sack but that she was disappointed in my refusal to murder her uncle. Am I right or what, Mr S?'

'Oh, er, absolutely, Mr Knowles,' nodded Sidney.

'So you're custard pied, then?' asked Nick.

Lenny glared at him. 'Leave the rhyming slang to the cockneys, Nickle-Arse. And no, I am not chucked. No one chucks Lenny Knowles. Lenny Knowles does the chucking.'

'Except when he's in prison and then Mrs Knowles assumes responsibility.'

'Are you trying to wind me up, Nicholas? You know very well that Hazel and me reached the mature decision that we were no longer compatible as man and wife and decided to go our separate ways.'

'After she chucked you out,' insisted Nick.

'You're really annoying me now,' warned Lenny. 'You want to watch your back before you start criticising others.'

Sidney stamped out the smouldering resentment he had watched kindling between Nick and Lenny before it could burst into flames. His attempts at diversion, however, were less successful, as he led them up two more steep and unmarked tracks high into the Maestrazgo. He was all but certain before they had even left the metalled road that neither would lead to the gold, but the similarity of one *camino forestal* to another was confusing and, he feared, even overwriting the faint memory he retained of the last time he had been here. Darkness came early and fell fast, the starlight falling through the black trees as they turned wordlessly, irritably, back to the inn.

A mile from the road the van skidded on black ice and slipped deep into a rut.

'Fucking brilliant,' declared Lenny. 'Now what?'

Nick slumped over the steering wheel and stared at his reflection in the windscreen, idly wondering if he shouldn't just get up and walk away from the whole adventure. He was cold, tired, depressed and unaware that Lenny was thinking exactly the same thing. That afternoon Nick had tried to drag the whole story from Sidney but the old man had sidestepped like a politician, answering questions with questions and preaching sermons when he should have been confessing. Nick had learned little in jail, but he had become adept at detecting the odour of bullshit, and Sidney stank like a Norfolk cowman. Lenny's less than jocular slap on the arm jerked him back to the present crisis.

'You going to lend a hand or what?'

Nick looked out into the night, wishing for a moon. The forest seemed to throb with dark malevolence, setting traps within its shadows and false promises where its lie could be seen. 'What's the plan?'

Lenny lit a fag and squatted by the nearside front wing. He

was always at his best when preoccupied by practical matters. 'See this? We've got to lift this clear and get something – rocks and stuff – under the wheel so she can get some traction.' He puffed on his cigarette, making it bounce between his lips as he looked around. 'And that's what we're going to lift it with.'

Nick looked to where he was pointing. 'That's a tree trunk.'

Lenny looked at Sidney. 'See, Mr S? They teach them some pretty clever stuff at college these days.'

'How are we going to lift this van up with a tree trunk?'

'Lever, Nickle-Arse. We're going to make a big lever.'

'I see,' nodded Sidney. 'Using this boulder as a fulcrum, I presume?'

Lenny looked at him. 'I don't know what you're going on about Mr S. We ain't using that boulder for nothing because I need it to rest the lever on. Now you stand back while Nicholas and me shift that log.'

It took fifteen minutes to move the tree trunk into position, and another quarter of an hour to balance it on the boulder. Lenny stood by as Nick collected ballast, wondering if he could persuade Sidney to help him talk Guadeloupe around upon their return. Obviously he wasn't going to accede to her demands that he murder her uncle Pepe, but she might settle for him giving the old sod a slap. That option, he decided, was something best left to sign language, as he couldn't see Sidney translating an offer to beat up a fellow pensioner. Ideally she would let the whole matter drop and he could concentrate on seeing to her more urgent needs, but the longer he spent away from her, the harder it was going to be to penetrate her defences. If there was one thing Lenny Knowles knew in life, it was women. It was a gift that was frequently a curse but one he had learned to live with. He watched Nicholas pissing about with a handful of stones until he could stand it no longer. 'Are you ready yet?'

Sidney stood to one side, peeing, as he seemed to every half hour or so, against a pine tree. He was like a lost dog after the rain, thought Lenny, pissing up every tree so he could find his way home. Shame he hadn't done it seventy years ago.

'Now what?' asked Nick, visibly disturbed by the mud on his hands.

'Now we put our backs into it and lift the bugger up. When it's up, and only when I say, you nip over and shove your stones under the wheel while I hold the fort. Ready?'

Perhaps the lever was incorrectly positioned, or maybe it was too short, but it took considerably more effort than Lenny had anticipated to raise the van. Finally, after twenty minutes of panting, cursing and sweating, and the addition of another football-sized rock to the fulcrum, the wheel lifted clear of the rut.

'Now!' yelled Lenny, throwing every ounce of his weight against the lever. Nick dashed across to the van and scooped his pile of sticks and stones into the rut. There was a sudden crack and the van dropped back, its front now eight inches clear of the track.

'Well done!' cheered Sidney.

'Sorted!' grinned Nick.

'Oh fuck,' wailed Lenny. 'I've done my sodding back in.'

Nick and Sidney lay him in the back of the van and drove slowly back to the inn. Lenny stared at the steel ceiling, gritting his teeth and auditing the advantage to be gained from his injury. As it happened, it was just a minor twinge, but properly managed it would get him off work for an indefinite period, leaving him free to pursue the psychotic Guadeloupe. He was guaranteed her sympathy, and disability would grant him freedom from the obligation to commit homicide. He reached for his cigarettes, realising as he did so that as a wounded hero he enjoyed a celebrity status of indeterminate duration during which he had no need of his own money, booze or cigarettes.

'Nicholas,' he groaned.

'What?'

'Light us a fag, mate. I'm dying back here.'

Nick lit a Winston, Sidney passed it back and Lenny smoked it with the satisfaction of a man who had copped a Blighty wound. Not quite buggering up his back was the best thing he could have done, and the manner in which the injury had been sustained was immaculate. Falling downstairs while pissed would have achieved the same end but without the honour that over-flowed from his heroic, one-man effort on that icy Spanish mountain. Lenny had single-handedly saved the cause and every-one in the van knew it.

Guadeloupe, however, was not as impressed as he would have hoped. She watched with a disgusted curl on her lip and a sar-donic hand on her hip as Nick reversed the van up to the reception and opened its rear doors.

'What happened?' she asked Sidney.

'Poor chap's wrenched his back.'

'Impossible,' she sneered. 'He has no backbone to wrench.'

'What she say?' asked Lenny.

'Nothing,' replied Sidney. 'Now how are we going to move you?'

'Can't we just leave him in there?' asked Nick. 'Chuck in some blankets and some vodka – he'll be fine.'

Lenny shook his head. 'You see, Mr S? He's nasty, isn't he?'

'Can you stand?'

Lenny sucked air and shuffled painfully along the floor of the van on his backside, breathless with slightly overplayed suffering and exhaustion. 'I honestly don't think I can,' he replied, crying out as he shook his head. 'Think I've done me neck in as well. Christ! I hope this doesn't mean I'll never work again.'

'What do you mean "again"?' asked Nick.

'I suppose we could move you into a chair and manhandle you down to your room,' suggested Sidney.

'Or even just as far as the bar,' offered Lenny, trying to be helpful.

Guadeloupe returned from the bowels of the deserted hotel to watch as Sidney fetched an oak chair from the restaurant. Lenny felt her critical gaze burning through his crew-cut as he sat awkwardly in the back of the van, his head cast down like an unwanted puppy's.

'Come on then,' urged Sidney. 'Mr Crick? Take your friend's other arm.'

Nick looked aghast at the suggestion. 'I'll just nip to the bog first,' he said, and dashed into the hotel.

Lenny looked at Sidney. 'See? He wants me to suffer, the bastard. If I had time I could list the number of times I saved that git's arse inside. Bloody jailbait he was when he turned up on the wing. You should have seen the looks he got from the old lags as he minced through.'

'I know the feeling,' smiled Sidney.

'Didn't know you'd been inside, Mr S.' Lenny's eyes widened at the prospect, then narrowed as he remembered that he was supposed to be in agony.

'I wasn't,' replied Sidney. 'I was far too smart for that. I don't think Mr Crick is coming back. Do you want to try to walk?'

Lenny thought for a moment, then nodded bravely. 'I'll give it a go, Mr S. I don't want to be no trouble.'

As far as Lenny's riverine view of life extended, this was the delta. The hard work was done, the rapids, the falls, the dams and the cataracts were far behind, and all that lay ahead was a gentle meandering towards the sea. He rose slowly and unsteadily to his feet, conscious of Guadeloupe's sceptical stare and trying to achieve that tricky combination of hero and victim. To show too much pain would make him a pansy, and too little would dilute her pity. As it happened, he thought he'd brought exactly the right combination of noble suffering and grim determination to his slow walk into the bar, an opinion confirmed by Guadeloupe herself.

'Give him these,' she muttered to Sidney, dropping a brown

bottle into his bony hand. 'One or two will stop the pain. Twelve or more will kill him. Dinner is at nine-thirty. Trout, with *migas del pastor*.'

'What did she say?' asked Lenny. 'She feels guilty, doesn't she? I know women.'

'She brought you some drugs,' replied Sidney.

'See? When they bring you drugs it's a sign that they care. What she bring?'

Sidney held up the bottle. 'Can't tell. The label's faded. All I can read is "1986".'

'Old drugs,' exclaimed Lenny. 'I'm well in here. She must have got them from the cellar. Give 'em here.' He snatched the bottle with perhaps a little too much dexterity and immediately compensated with a mighty groan. 'Oh shit!' he gasped. 'I'm my own worse enemy, I am. Don't know my own strength, see.' He unscrewed the cap and tipped two large, white pills into his palm. 'Want one, Mr S?'

Sidney frowned and shook his head. 'Absolutely not, and you should go easy on them. No drinking – that's an order!'

They were both utterly wrecked by dinnertime. When Nick came into the bar, he was astounded to hear his colleagues breathless with laughter, their faces shining in the candlelight. Two bottles stood between them – one tall, green and all but empty and the other short, brown and plastic.

'You're both pissed,' said Nick.

Lenny's giggles exploded from his red face. 'Look at him, Sid,' he guffawed 'He looks right miffed.'

Sidney turned to inspect Nick's expression and found it just as amusing as Lenny had. 'I say, Mr Crick,' he slurred. 'Will you join us for a little drink? Just a little, tiny, sociable tipple?'

'We've got nibbles,' added Lenny, offering the pill bottle. 'They're very moreish. Just nip over to the bar and sign us out another bottle of vino.'

Nick shrugged and picked a bottle from the rack behind the bar.

'Where's your glass?' asked Sidney.

'I don't drink, remember?'

'Balderdash, man! Get a bloody glass. Here, I'll fetch you one.' He wobbled towards the bar. 'Good God Almighty – the floor feels like it's made of India rubber.'

Nick glared at Lenny. 'What's he on?'

Lenny shrugged. 'Couple of glasses of wine and a couple of those.' He pointed uncertainly at the pill bottle. 'They go rather well with the wine, Nickle-Arse. Have one.'

Sidney sat down heavily and tried to look serious. 'So tell me, Mr Crick, why do you persist in this self-flagellating abstention?'

'You know why.'

'Because you got drunk and killed your wife and child. Very sad, I'm sure, but why the teetotalism? If you're punishing your-self, then it's a very weak retribution. Swearing off a luxury for life? How noble. And if you're staying sober on the off-chance that you might accidentally make the same mistake twice, then don't worry, old boy. You are so utterly dull and self-absorbed in your self-imposed sobriety that no woman in her right mind is going to marry you and bear your children.' He reached out to touch Nick's arm and shook his head sadly as the younger man snatched it away. 'Listen, Mr Crick. Your sorrows are destroying you. You've let them steal your appetites, your verve, your con-trol over your own life, because you think you owe them something. You owe your sorrows nothing, and I know what I'm talking about. I let my sorrows and regrets have the best years of my life and I know better than any man here what you should do with your sorrows.'

Nick sighed. 'Go on.'

Sidney picked up the bottle and poured a glass of thick, red wine that sloshed like spilled blood onto the worn tabletop. He raised his own. 'Drown the bastards! Now drink!'

236

Nick looked at the glass, touching it with one finger. 'Drinking won't solve anything,' he protested weakly.

'Murder rarely does,' agreed Sidney, 'but never mind that. Drown your sorrows now.'

'Yeah,' slurred Lenny, proffering the pill bottle, 'and have one of these babies while you're at it. They're bloody marvellous.'

Nick raised his glass and took a reluctant sip.

'I said drink, man,' cried Sidney. 'This isn't bloody communion!' He crashed his glass into Nick's. '*Salud!*'

Lenny refilled his own and raised it. 'Cheers, Nickle-Arse. Welcome back to the land of the living.'

Nick took a deep breath and drank, trying to swallow all the regret, guilt and apprehension that came with this sacrilege. He had sworn never to drink again as penance for his crime, but perhaps the old man was right – maybe it was too light, too easy and too convenient to be an appropriate punishment. Blaming the booze for the crash had always seemed a little like holding a gun responsible for a shooting. And, as Lenny often said, guns didn't kill people; men with moustaches killed people. He closed his eyes as he swallowed the dregs, realising as he did so that the last time he had been happily drunk had been a moment before he lost control of the company car. He held out the glass. 'More,' he demanded, wondering if this potent Priorat would dissolve the hard shell he'd built up around his emotions and let them come flooding like spilled acid through his mind.

Sidney poured. 'One for the road,' he smiled. 'One for the road to recovery. Well done, Mr Crick. You drop your principles like the worst of us.'

Deep down a warning bell was ringing, and Nick watched with alarm as Lenny leapt to his feet, remembered he was injured and collapsed back into his chair.

'That's the dinner bell,' he cried. 'I'm bloody starving.'

Nick's head swam as Guadeloupe and Tío Pepe wordlessly

delivered three plates loaded with a pink fish and a pile of fried breadcrumbs.

'No egg tonight?' asked Sidney.

'No egg,' growled Guadeloupe. 'Tomorrow I go.' She jerked a painted thumbnail at Pepe. 'The murderer will attend to your every need.'

'What she say?' asked Lenny when she had gone.

'I think she's still angry with her uncle,' replied Sidney, not wishing to spoil the party. He turned to Nick. 'I've been meaning to ask you – and it's none of my business – but how do you intend spending the money you'll earn from your share?'

Nick shrugged. 'I'll retire.'

'Like Razumov?' asked Sidney.

'Like who?' countered Nick.

'Never mind,' sighed Sidney. 'And you, Mr Knowles?'

Lenny picked fish bones from between his lips. 'Usual stuff, I suppose. Nice motor – Beemer or equivalent – get the kids everything they need, like quad bikes, Xboxes and all that palaver, then fuck off to Florida.'

'So you don't see yourself moving back in with your ex-wife?' asked Sidney.

'Nah. It's over. Just be nice to do right by the kids.' He took a slurp of wine. 'I mean, she's been begging me to come back, but you know how it is, Mr S. Life moves on, don't it?'

'And you Mr S?' asked Nick, 'what are you going to spend it on?'

The old man leaned forwards, keen to explain his plan. 'I was wondering when you would ask what an old man, at the very end of his life, could possibly do with a fortune. I'll tell you: I want to build memorials to the Brigades. I want to raise one on every battlefield, from Madrid to Jarama to Brunete to bloody Teruel and the Ebro.'

'Why?' asked Lenny.

'Because they were the last of their kind. Sacrifice like theirs will never happen again for so noble a cause and so thankless a task.'

'But you lost,' belched Lenny.

'So you keep reminding me.'

'What sort of memorials?' asked Nick. 'You can't use crosses.'

'Here,' said Lenny. 'My mate Trev bought a load of statues of Lenin or someone in Russia a few years back. Dozens of them – he thought he could sell them to yuppies as garden ornaments but he got stuck with them. They're in a hangar out in the Fens. They'd do you a treat, they would.'

Sidney stared at the tabletop. 'I was always a consumer rather than a creator of memories. I've had this idea for years now, and I've never been able to visualise exactly what I want to erect.'

'You thought about materials?' asked Lenny.

Sidney shook his head.

'Bronze isn't cheap, you know.'

'It's cheaper than gold.'

Lenny took a slug of wine and nodded. 'Fair enough. I could price it up for you, if you like.'

'Mr Knowles, I had no idea you were familiar with sculpture.'

'That Roger Moore is one of my favourites.'

'You are a constant source of amazement.'

'Anyway,' declared Lenny, through a mouthful of breadcrumbs that had the taste and consistency of oily grit, 'even if we don't find the gold we're quids in. Your house alone has got to be worth a hundred and fifty.' Since there was no gold and this trip was merely a last dash down memory lane, Lenny had for some days been anxious to ascertain the veracity of the pledge Sidney had made in the Bay of Biscay. Now, when the old geezer was wrecked on booze and pills and was unlikely to remember a word he had said come morning, seemed the ideal moment. He watched as Sidney removed his glasses and rubbed the bridge of his nose.

'I meant what I said, gentlemen. You're both welcome to

share between you everything I own, but I can't give you the house.'

Lenny held up his hands in horror. 'Blimey, Mr S, don't get the wrong end of the stick. We wouldn't make a move on your gaff until you'd popped your clogs or been put in a home or something. God, no. Lenny Knowles does not turn OAPs out of their houses. Can't speak for Nickle-Arse, of course.'

Sidney shook his head. 'I thank you for that, but you're missing the point. I simply can't give you the cottage.'

A dark cloud drifted over Lenny's face. He reached for his wallet and removed the carefully folded envelope. 'I'm sorry, Mr S, but there seems to have been some misunderstanding. This letter clearly states that you are making Nick and me the sole beneficiaries of your entire estate.' He thrust the document at Sidney. 'Look.'

Sidney nodded. 'I did, and I stand by that, but the house is not part of my estate.'

'Course it is,' argued Lenny. 'You said it was.'

Sidney shook his head. 'Mr Knowles, I never said the house was part of my estate. As I recall, you asked me what my plans were for the house and I told you it was part of the estate.'

'Exactly,' cried Lenny.

'Not my estate – the estate.'

Lenny suddenly looked very worried. 'What are you talking about?'

'The house was given to my mother, rent free, for the duration of her and my natural lives on the understanding that after our deaths it would return to the Rutherford family. The house simply isn't mine to give you, Mr Knowles.'

Lenny went white. He reached for the pill bottle, tipped another two into his shaking palm and washed them down with wine. Then he lit a fag and stood up, only just remembering to wince. He shook his head, grabbed the bottle and limped into the darkness.

Sidney watched him go, his head wobbling under the weight of the wine, then poured himself another drink. 'Oh dear,' he said. 'I think our party is over.'

'You shouldn't drink so much, Mr Starman,' warned Nick, wiping the table before laying out his map. 'You'll forget the details.'

Sidney glanced at his glass, then back at Nick. 'I don't think so. I've had seventy-odd years to remember the details.'

'Fine. Give me some pictures to work with.'

Sidney took a slurp. 'I don't see how this will help.'

'You describe what you saw, what you passed, whether there was a river, a waterfall, a cliff or anything physical, and I'll find them on the map.'

Sidney nodded thoughtfully, as though acknowledging that he could no longer reasonably conceal the truth. He looked at Nick for a long, drunken moment and sighed. 'All right,' he said at last. 'There was a house.'

'You said a mine – a Roman mine.'

'That's where the gold was, it's true, but there was a house. I spent some time there.'

'Brilliant!' enthused Nick. 'What did it look like?'

Reminiscence repressed for seven decades surged forward like a mob of freed prisoners, each clamouring to be heard, yet when Sidney opened his mouth the words came slowly and uncertainly, as though his body had not yet accepted his mind's decision. 'A valley,' he made a sweeping gesture with one hand, 'wide and sloping. Olive trees, some almonds, and, just there, right in the middle, these cypress trees. They looked like the sort of thing you'd expect to see growing around a Roman villa, but there was just this little white house, and a track.'

'Was this before you got to the gold?'

Sidney shook his head slowly, mesmerised by memory. 'It was afterwards. I came down from the mountains and there was an enormous moon hanging over the valley. I was hurt,' he tapped his shoulder, 'an infection had set in and I was feverish. I saw those cypress trees sticking up like great black spires, like one of Gaudí's churches, and I remember walking and walking and never getting any closer. The whole front line was lit up by artillery, and the next thing I knew I was inside the house.'

Nick lit a fresh cigarette and then a candle, dragging the wax-encrusted wine bottle onto the map to shed light where the feeble bulbs failed. Five minutes earlier he had been searching for one ancient mine among hundreds. Now he was looking for one that was within walking distance of a wide, south-facing valley with a single small house in a circle of cypresses. The trees would not be marked on the map, but the other features warranted inclusion in the survey, and finding them was simply a matter of scanning the grid, square by square.

'What else do you remember?'

'The olive trees,' yawned Sidney. 'They looked wild and unkempt, growing here and there like survivors rather than standing in neat rows like you see lower down.'

Olive trees didn't help. 'What else? Was there a stream or a bridge? A road?'

'There was a cliff,' he offered, 'and lots of boulders.'

Nick looked up. 'A cliff?' he said. 'And lots of boulders? In mountainous terrain? Gosh, Mr Starman, why didn't you say?'

Sidney stood up, gripping the table. 'I can't see the point in this. I understand the theory but I don't think you have any idea how much land is out there. There are probably thousands of houses like the one I remember, just like there are hundreds of holes in the rock that might or might not be mines. Who's to say the house hasn't been demolished, or the trees cut down?' He straightened, grimacing as a sciatic spasm seemed to stab his right thigh. 'Good luck, Mr Crick. I'll see you in the morning.'

He lay awake on his thin mattress, listening to the roar of the river below and wishing it would drown the clamour in his head. Like Nick's renunciation of the bottle, this return, so late in life, was a pale penitence. He had promised her he would return, and he had broken that promise. He had failed her, and he had failed to make good that failure. He fired cold reason into the guilty thoughts crowding his head, trying to calm their riotous mood by pointing out that even after all these years he had returned, but he knew his argument was as irrelevant as it was insincere. What really mattered was whether she had waited for him. He stared at the ceiling, as he had done for so many nights and so many years, willing sleep to take him away from his thoughts. Sleep, like a cruel jailer, demurred, leaving the prisoner to be tormented by his conscience.

He was still awake when Nick hammered on the door. He climbed out of bed painfully, slowly wrapping his dressing-gown around his pyjamas and fumbling in the weak light of the bedside lamp for his glasses. When he opened the door Nick was puffing on a cigarette, red-eyed and flushed with excitement.

He pushed past Sidney and strode in to the room, placing the map on the bottom of the bed. 'Check it out, Mr Starman,' he grinned, stabbing a nicotine-stained finger at the map. 'Mountain there, cliff here, wide, south-facing valley in front of it and, bang in the middle, the Cortijo de Los Cipreses!'

Sidney stared at the map, unable to focus on the words written beside the black dot, but understanding their meaning. They provoked a frantic fluttering in his belly – the feeling of chickens coming home to roost. 'Well, I'll be buggered, Mr, Crick,' he said weakly. His last excuse had just expired.

14

What remained of the Field Repair Company made contact with the enemy an hour before sunrise on St Elisieus Day 1937. Hernando Sabar Solas had been a baker before reluctantly volunteering to serve in the Nationalist army and as such he was accustomed to being at work before dawn. Special orders, telephoned from Teruel, forbade the passage of any vehicle through any checkpoint on the front. All drivers and their charges, with no exceptions, were to be held until their mission and their identity had been verified. There was a brand-new German machine-gun in the stone shelter to add weight to their authority, but no one knew how to use it. Solas was relighting his cigarette when he saw the headlights of an approaching truck. By the time he had woken his three companions the grind of gears could be heard in the twilight.

'Maybe we can impose a war tax on them,' mused the veteran of the three, a forty-year-old corporal and the only professional soldier in the squad. He slid his bayonet into its scabbard and scratched his unshaven throat.

'Might be a truckload of officers' supplies,' called one of the recruits, a butcher's boy from Alicante.

'Whoever they are, they go no further tonight,' observed the corporal.

'A troupe of French dancing girls, lost and looking for somewhere to lie down,' grinned Gilberto Mendez Segura, a cunning young man with a strawberry birthmark who had left a seminary to fight for freedom, a cause that Solas, a devout Catholic, thought must have been one of considerable convenience. Six months earlier Segura had been looking forward to a life of celibate ministry in a church that had been stripped of its glory. Now he was free to rape, loot and pillage in the name of the Holy Father.

'Stand in the road and wave it down,' the corporal called to the butcher's boy. Then he glanced at Mendez. 'Lower your weapon, Private – you'll hit the boy.' He slung his own rifle and wandered casually along the roadside, following a lamp that cast yellow light and black smoke from an untrimmed wick. When the truck was fifty yards away the corporal flashed his torch on and off, then straightened his cap and tunic on the off-chance that an officer was abroad at this time of night. As it pulled alongside he noted that it was a civilian vehicle, from Teruel, and it was driven by a pock-marked foreigner in a Condor Legion uniform. He stood on tiptoe to shine his beam into the cab. It slid across another face, narrow and angry beneath a shadow of stubble and a head of slicked-back black hair.

'Turn that light out, Corporal!' it barked. Another bloody foreigner.

'Sorry, sir,' replied the corporal evenly. He had a good nose for officers. 'I'm under orders to let no vehicle pass tonight.'

'I know you are,' replied the passenger. 'I'm the exception. Move that barrier.'

'There are no exceptions, sir. I have orders.'

'Show me your orders.'

'They came by telephone, sir. I have nothing in writing. May I respectfully ask you to step down from the vehicle and accompany me to my post?'

'For the love of God!'

The German was drumming his fingers on the wheel. The corporal took a step into his blindside and unbuttoned his holster. 'Is there anything in the back, sir?'

245

'Jamon Serrano, *sobresada* from Majorca and some fresh *morcilla*. Care to look?' The officer climbed wearily from the cab, his leather greatcoat hanging like a cape from his shoulders. He came around the front of the truck, ignoring the recruit, and walked past the corporal. 'I'm extremely tired and extremely late. Come with me and I'll give you something nice that will prove I'm the exception.'

The corporal followed, setting his face for a hard bargain and noting with some distaste that the officer smelled like a latrine. The morning star had risen above the eastern ridge as the night entered its darkest hour. The officer smiled at him in a conspiratorial fashion. 'Help yourself,' he said.

The corporal pulled open the door and leaned inside, smelling sawdust, sweat and garlic before he felt the rough hand across his mouth. Wisdom flickered like a lost dream and the sudden certainty of his death made him gasp as his head was pulled backwards and a rough hand that smelled of dried blood, human excrement and Cuban tobacco clamped his mouth shut.

'How many at the post?' breathed his murderer into his ear.

'Fuck your mother,' snarled the corporal. And this is how it ends, he thought. He relaxed as Cobb's blade sliced through his throat, letting his weight fall against his killer as the blood drained from his body in a lazy spray, sending him to his death with the uneasy feeling that he'd wet himself.

'Out,' whispered Cobb to Sidney. 'We're at a roadblock. There's a soldier in the road with a lamp, and a barrier maybe twenty yards behind him. I don't know how many men are at the barrier. I'm going to try to drive right up. You go wide on the flank and cover. Go!' He stood aside and glared at Villafranca. 'One word from you, gipsy boy, and I'll cut your balls off.' He laughed out loud, but not for the prisoner's benefit, as he heaved the twitching, steaming body of the corporal into the rear of the truck before heading back to the cab. 'No need, Corporal,' he cried jovially. 'Jump in and I'll drive you up.' He waved to the butcher's boy, still standing in the road with the lamp at his side. 'Move out of the way. Delivery coming through!' He slid the corporal's pistol across the seat to Kreuz. 'You take the left, I've got the right and the kid's covering our asses from the flank. Kill them all.'

The boy with the lamp had turned his back on them and was walking back to the barrier. The lorry crawled along behind him, its feeble klaxon wailing weakly as Segura yawned and Solas began to wonder what was happening.

'Move that barrier,' ordered Cobb, leaning out of the cab.

Solas walked slowly to the driver's side, aware that something was wrong but unable to recognise any specific threat. As he hesitated at the very edge of his life his dusty boots rested on a step worn by the feet of thousands before him. The average man, ignorant of instinct, merely paused before stepping over the edge into oblivion. Only those few equipped with a special gene, that animal talent which cannot be learned, withdrew from the abyss. Solas was just an average man.

'What's going on?' he asked the driver, his fingers tight around his rifle sling.

'Damned if I know,' shrugged Kreuz, firing two shots into his face.

As Solas whirled backwards the soldier with the lamp froze, seeming to expand in Sidney's sights. He dropped him with a bullet that hit him square in the spine an inch below his belt. Segura saved his life by stepping into the shadow of the roadside hut they had used as a sentry post. Open-mouthed, his legs leaden with fear, he yelped as Cobb emptied his automatic at him, the bullets cracking the air as they ripped past. He darted behind the hut, searching for pools of darkness into which to dive on the slope behind, hearing the enemy yelling at each other in what sounded like English. 'Kid! I've lost one. Find him and kill him! Kreuz, cover me in the hut.'

247

Sidney ran past the fallen recruit, his feet bruised and aching in his rope-soled shoes.

Cobb waved him past. 'He went thataway. Don't take any chances.'

Sidney checked for backlight then ducked into the shadow in the lee of the hut. Behind it a steep slope, still bathed in the waning moonlight, rose up to a ridge that was pale against the starry sky. He turned an ear towards the mountainside, listening for the clatter of scree and scanning the foreground for the trail of his quarry. There was neither movement nor sound. Breaking cover, he moved fast and low to the bright side of a boulder as big as a house, biting his lip and holding his breath to listen for movement. All was quiet, suggesting that the soldier was dead, wounded or lying in wait. Tensed against a sudden shot in the dark, Sidney glanced around the rock and saw Segura's rifle lying where he'd dropped it. Smiling now, he stood up and advanced like a gamekeeper approaching a wounded fox, his fear replaced by a cautious confidence. Segura was wedged under a rock a few feet beyond the abandoned weapon, dreadfully aware of the mistake he had made and listening in terror for Death's footsteps. The rattle of a kicked stone told him the end was at hand and he scraped his face on the rock as he turned, quivering, to face his killer. He saw a skinny young man, probably no older than himself, with fair hair and old eyes in a suntanned, unshaven face, crouching on one knee and aiming a rifle at his head. His expression was that of a Catholic icon: blank, unfeeling and as hard as stone. Here knelt a man doing his duty without passion, a Godless Bolshevik who had embraced reason without hearing it. There would be no negotiation, no pleading and no mercy. Numb with fear, Segura closed his eyes and started mumbling Hail Marys, the liturgy becoming stronger and more urgent as he waited for the end. But it didn't come, and when he opened his eyes, the young man was gone.

Sidney Starman had just made his first conscientious personal decision of the Spanish Civil War.

Cobb was not happy about the soldier's escape. 'You're getting flaky, kid,' he warned. 'I used to think you had potential.' He walked back past the truck to where the butcher's boy lay gasping in the road.

'You renounced the dum-dums?' he called, bending down to examine the wounded sentry. Sidney shook his head. 'I ran out. I'm using ball.'

Cobb shook his head. 'Like I said – you used to have talent and now you're losing it. Drag that corpse from the back of the truck while I deal with this one.' He crouched down to speak to the boy. 'My colleague's bullet has smashed your spine,' he explained. 'If you don't bleed to death, or die of infection, you'll never walk again. Never dance, never fuck – I bet you've never fucked, have you? – never take a stroll in the park.' He cocked his pistol. 'You'll never teach your kids how to fish or how to play ball, and you'll never walk your daughter down the aisle. Life would be pain and misery from here on, young man, and I'm going to spare you the suffering.' He stood up and fired the pistol into the back of the stricken boy's neck. The impact of the bullet lifted the body from the ground before it flopped back, shrunken and lifeless.

'That's two you owe me, kid,' nodded Cobb, holstering his weapon. He turned as Kreuz emerged from the stone hut. 'Where the fuck have you been?'

The German stared at him. 'Destroying the telephone. In case the man you both failed to kill returns.'

Cobb ignored the jibe. 'You see that '34 in there? Let's take it with us. Never know when you're going to need a machine-gun.'

From behind a rock, high above the checkpoint, Segura watched, trembling as the truck rumbled northwards, the grotesque smiling pig in its butcher's apron diminishing in the pale light of dawn. He waited until he was sure it had gone then set off unsteadily along a goat track to the next checkpoint, whispering promises to God.

Nick switched off the engine, leaned on the steering wheel and lit a cigarette. They had left the inn two hours earlier after the worst breakfast yet, the deterioration of which was due to the fact that Guadeloupe had gone to town, ostensibly for her father's funeral. Lenny had not reported for work, so Nick and Sidney had set off for Cortijo de Los Cipreses without him. Nick took a long, thoughtful drag and exhaled slowly, blowing smoke into the cool, clear morning. Then he looked at Sidney. 'This is the place, isn't it?'

Sidney swallowed nervously. 'It is.'

'There's someone home.' Nick pointed through the trees to where a burgundy Seat was parked outside the tiny stone house. He opened his door.

'What are you doing?' cried Sidney.

'Going visiting, Mr Starman. Come on . . .' He tapped his foot on the road. 'Take a stroll down memory lane.'

'Get in!' hissed Sidney. A lone crow was already sounding the alarm. How long before the dogs joined in?

Nick stared at him, half a smile on his face. 'What's the problem? Don't tell me you massacred the family living here.' It was meant as a joke but suddenly seemed quite possible. 'You didn't, did you?'

Sidney shook his head. 'Of course I didn't.' Strictly speaking. 'Now get in.' He hid in his overcoat as the rough wooden door of the house was pulled inwards.

A young woman appeared on the threshold, shielding her eyes against the morning sun as she squinted to recognise the van.

'She's coming over,' said Nick.

'Oh God!' groaned Sidney, but God had never been on his side.

He had, however, clearly been on the side of Anita Romero Molino, if only in the matter of looks. She stopped at the edge of the property, her hand still on her brow as though in salute and her straight black hair flying in the wind like an anarchist's flag.

'Let's go, Mr Crick,' urged Sidney, but his driver was already halfway to the house.

'Can I help you?' asked Anita.

Nick swallowed nervously, grinding his dog-end underfoot. Her eyes were as green as grass after rain. 'I'm sorry,' he said. 'I don't speak Spanish.'

The girl frowned. 'English?'

'Yes. Is this your house?' She's beautiful, thought Nick. Utterly, unspeakably gorgeous.

'Why you ask?'

It was a good question. He glanced at the van, then back at the girl. 'There's an old man in my van who once stayed here.'

The girl shook her head. 'Not here, *señor*. Never here.'

Nick raised his eyebrows. 'Well, he seems to think so. It was a long time ago, in the summer of 1937.'

Anita squinted, both hands now on her hips, as she looked from Nick to the van and back again. 'Who is he?'

'He's an old soldier. His name is Sidney Starman.'

Anita stared at him, then nodded, her suspicion turning to anger. 'He has come for his gold, I suppose?'

'Wow!' cried Nick. 'How do you . . .'

The girl strode past him, her fists clenched by her side as she crossed the rocky track to the van. She stopped beside the passenger window, knocking on the glass, her head tilted to one side. 'So you have returned?' she cried.

Sidney fumbled to lower the window, a red heat creeping up his neck. 'I beg your pardon?' he replied.

'You are Sidney Starman?' She was still speaking in English.

Sidney took a deep breath. The hour of reckoning had arrived. '*Si. Soy Sidney Starman.*'

Anita took a step back and spat in the dust, shaking her head. 'You left it too late, *Ingles*. We buried her last Friday.'

Sidney's feet went numb in his brogues and a creeping chill seeped up his spine. Cracks were splitting the levee and the dam was breaking, but even though his lip trembled at the news no tears came. He stared ahead, shrunken in his clothes. 'Oh God,' he murmured.

'Why now?' challenged the girl. 'You stay away until she died and then you come back for your gold?'

'Oh God,' repeated Sidney, his breath only reaching his breastbone and his heart hammering in his chest.

'You promised to return, and she believed you. Her family, her neighbours, everybody laughed at her but she always believed you'd return. She didn't even have a photograph of you, Sidney Starman, so she drew pictures of you.' Anita whirled about, raising a tiny dust devil, and strode back through the cypresses to her own car. She pushed past Nick moments later, smelling of jasmine and honey, a cloth-bound book in her hands. 'Look!' she cried, opening the book. 'Drawings of you, Sidney Starman!'

She was wasting her breath. Sidney had collapsed.

The vending-machine repairman watched as Lenny leaned over the bar and lifted a bottle of Larios gin, took a long swig and stuffed it inside his jacket. This man looks like trouble, thought the repairman, quickly taking in the bruised face, wild eyes and slightly disconcerting twitch. He looked as though he was trying to uncrick a knot in his neck while glancing at an imaginary watch, and he dressed like an English football fan. The repairman absently tapped the contact switch on the cigarette machine and wondered how a man who looked like an escaped convict could have ended up skulking around this place. He belonged down on the Costa Brava, surely, in some English pub where they sold all-day breakfasts and Sunday roasts, not out here, in the middle of nowhere. The thug tried to lift a stag's head from the wall, forcing it until a cracking sound advised him to leave it alone. He lurched back to the bar, popping a pill with one hand and lighting a cigarette with the other, before farting loudly and chuckling in a self-satisfied way. He picked his nose, flicked the result and scratched his arse. Then he saw the repairman.

'All right, mate?' he winked.

The repairman nodded back. 'Hello,' he replied in accented English. 'How are you?'

'Bad back,' grimaced Lenny. 'Done it in digging holes.' He mimed like a gravedigger.

'That is nice,' nodded the repairman.

'You work here?' asked Lenny.

'Excuse me?'

'Do you work here?'

'Yes.'

'Seen Guadeloupe around?'

The repairman hadn't seen her around and was disappointed by her absence. Guadeloupe was the only reason he bothered driving out here to repair the machine. If he'd known she wasn't going to be here, he would have sent his son. He unscrewed a floppy microswitch and shook his head. On second thoughts, he could never send his son out here. The consequences were too enormous to consider and he accepted that he was doomed to repair vending machines at Hostal La Cerda for ever. 'She is not here,' he replied. 'She go.'

The Englishman was swigging gin from the bottle. 'Where's she gone?'

'Town. Montalban. I hear she go for ever. Her father die, you know.'

'What do you mean "for ever"?' blurted Lenny, letting the repairman know what he had already suspected. 'You mean she's not coming back?'

'It is no problem, *señor*. Her uncle he is renting a new cook.

253

She is very good. Very old and very fat and she make very good *migas del pastor*. You know this dish?'

Lenny took another mouthful of gin and stared red-eyed into a bleak future. The whole job had turned to bollocks. The hoard of gold was a figment of Sidney's imagination and it turned out that the refurbished cottage on the market for £275K was a figment of his. The old man's will amounted to no more than a few grand's worth of the sort of collectables Lenny could pick up in a month of house clearances – hardly enough to cover his fines and his CSA obligations, let alone his rent and the payments he was obliged to make to his friendly neighbourhood loan shark every week. He could even see himself coming out of this half-arsed adventure poorer than when he went in, and now the only chance of a backrub in this miserable excuse for a boarding house had fucked off in a strop. Not normally a man predisposed to violence, he was overtaken by a sudden desire to punch someone. He glared at the vending-machine repairman.

'I take you to town if you please,' stammered the Spaniard.

'I'll get me stuff,' growled Lenny.

'Where is his medicine?' cried Anita, her hands still on the old man's lapels.

'Medicine?' repeated Nick.

'Pills. Tablets. What he takes for this.'

'I don't think he takes anything for it. I've not seen him do it before.'

'How long you know him? All your life?'

Nick frowned. It was an odd question. 'About a fortnight, actually.'

'You not his grandson? His nephew?'

'God, no. Do you think he's all right?'

Anita turned an ear to Sidney's pallid face. 'He still breathes.' She patted his pockets. 'Are you sure he has no medicine?'

'Never seen any. Maybe it's in his room at La Cerda.'

Anita twisted her face in disgust. 'You're staying La Cerda?'

Nick shrugged. 'We like it.'

'Well, you must take him back there. Maybe his medicine is in his room.' She loosened Sidney's tie further and lifted the collar of his raincoat to protect his face. 'He is very old,' she said, staring coldly at his features. 'Perhaps it is his time to die.'

'Perhaps it is,' nodded Nick distractedly.

This woman moved with a beauty and a warmth that her caustic exterior could not conceal. She closed the passenger door carefully, walked past Nick and went into the house. Moments later she returned, a black bag in her hand. 'You know this thing?' she asked, as though he should. 'It's a bota. I put water inside it. The old man may need it.'

'Thanks,' said Nick. 'And sorry. If he gets better, we'll come back. Something important—'

'Don't bother,' said Anita, shaking her head. 'I'm going back to Barcelona tonight and he didn't come all this way to see me. *Adios.*'

Her words lingered like perfume in the van as Nick drove away, her husky Catalan accent and her green-eyed stare from beneath that low, dark fringe causing an uncomfortable tightening in his chest. He lit a cigarette, glanced at Sidney, and shook his head. The old man was dying and he had no idea what to do with him. He had grown to like and respect him, and until a few minutes ago he had felt he had been travelling not with the worn-out, ground-down geriatric in the flat cap and mackintosh who needed to pee every twenty minutes but with the man living inside that rotting carcass. He'd met a mind that had grown stronger and wiser as the shell it occupied had declined, and now he was probably going to have to dispose of the body. He'd long been aware that it might come to this, but Death was just another face in a crowd that Nick had chosen not to acknowledge. He was becoming proficient in denial, but recently he had noticed that he was allowing those things he had

255

forsworn to approach, to smile, to discuss possibilities. Sidney Starman had plied him with rough wine in an effort to make him confront what was left of his life, and if Sidney Starman hadn't pegged out back at the farmhouse he would no doubt be encouraging Nick to adjust his orbit around that green-eyed girl. Whatever her name was.

She hadn't introduced herself. Nick flicked his dog-end from the window. It didn't matter what her name was.

Sidney came round an hour later, his face blotchy, his breath short and his lips blue. He sighed long and low, like a man too far gone to moan, gasped in a lungful and turned to Nick. 'I think I just suffered a minor heart attack,' he announced.

'I'm taking you to hospital right now,' nodded Nick. 'Try not to move.'

'Don't be bloody daft. I'm not going to hospital.'

'You're not well.'

'I'm fine, you idiot. I'm nearly ninety bloody years old.'

'You just had a fucking heart attack, Mr Starman. You're going to hospital, and that's final.'

'You take me to hospital and I'll never come out. It'll be the end of me and the end of this adventure.'

Nick stared at the road and swallowed. 'Don't care,' he said at last. 'You're going to A&E.'

Sidney laughed, his voice a dry croak. 'You've got a good heart, Mr Crick.'

'Better than yours, Mr Starman.'

'In all ways. But don't mistake quantity for quality in the consideration of life. As I said, I'm nearly ninety, and I'd rather die out here, in the sunshine, than beneath a fluorescent tube in some God-awful hospital. Do you understand?'

Nick sighed. 'It's your life.'

'Thank you, Mr Crick. Now, give me your copy of the will.'

'Don't be daft.'

Sidney licked his lips with a yellow tongue. 'I might not come back next time. Let me sign that paper.' He fumbled in his jacket for a pen, the effort leaving him breathless.

Nick handed him the brown envelope, watching with one eye as Sidney scratched his name across the bottom. 'There,' he said, capping his pen. 'It's done. You can add a witness later. Is there any water?'

Nick passed the *bota*, the little black camels around its neck tinkling against the tarnished silver collar, and nearly gave Sidney another seizure.

'Did the girl give you this?' he gasped.

Nick nodded. 'Recognise it?'

'It came from the checkpoint,' muttered Sidney, turning the smooth black bladder over and over in his hands. 'It's Moroccan . . .' His voice trailed off.

'Keep talking,' urged Nick, fearing a relapse. 'Tell me about the checkpoint. Tell me how you got the bota.'

Gilberto Mendez Segura stumbled into Company HQ an hour after sunrise and blurted his carefully rehearsed story to Lieutenant Ernesto Zapata Jimenez, the sad-faced, narrow-eyed duty officer. His uniform stained with blood he had soaked up from his comrades' bodies to bear testament to his courage, and his trousers stained with urine that attested to his cowardice, Segura reported that a truck loaded with ten or more anarchist commandos had rammed the checkpoint and engaged the guard in a desperate gunfight shortly after three in the morning. The lieutenant called the major and the major dispatched a motorcyclist to Battalion HQ before telling Segura to take a seat.

An hour later three truckloads of German troops arrived and Segura was beginning to wish he'd kept his mouth shut. He leapt to his feet as an officer wearing the immaculate uniform of an *Oberst* of the Condor Legion strode irritably into the commandeered farmhouse, returning the Spanish salute with a wave of his hand.

'Colonel Claus von Wittenburg,' he announced in unaccented Castilian. 'Is this the man?'

The major nodded. 'Make your report, Private.'

It had all happened very quickly, explained Segura. He had been off duty, but had stood to when he heard the first shots.

'Good,' nodded the German approvingly. 'Then what?'

Segura replied that he had then engaged the enemy, killing three and wounding two as his own comrades were gunned down on either side.

'On either side?' asked the German, clearly impressed.

'Er, yes, sir,' confirmed Segura.

Von Wittenburg nodded slowly, then waved at the lieutenant. 'Paper, please, and a pencil.'

Segura added that he had personally witnessed the execution of a wounded recruit, explaining that the enemy had taken their casualties with them, speeding in a north-easterly direction deep into the salient.

'Draw the position,' interrupted the German, handing Segura a sheet of flimsy mimeo paper and a chinagraph pencil. 'Well?'

'Nowhere to rest the paper, sir.' Suddenly Segura knew that the Oberst saw right through his story. He felt the flush of guilt hot on his cheeks and wet along his spine.

'Get on your kneees and use the chair,' suggested von Wittenburg. As Segura sketched he lit a cigarette and leaned over his shoulder, blowing smoke at the drawing. 'So you left the safety of the billet and crossed the road to engage the enemy from there, you say?'

'Yes, sir.'

'Very bold.' The German looked at the Spanish major. 'A very brave man you have here.'

He offered Segura a cigarette and invited him to sit down. There was a half-empty bottle of Bobadilla brandy on the cluttered kitchen table but the officers chose not to share it, in spite of the private's shattered nerves. Segura had heard that there were no ranks on the other side and that officers were elected by committee. It sounded like a much fairer system.

'Where is your weapon?' asked the German.

'My weapon, sir?' replied Segura.

The officer nodded.

Segura floundered. 'I, I, er, I lost it, sir. I mean, I didn't lose it, but it was broken. I think it was hit by an enemy bullet and it just sort of broke.'

The corporal, the tough veteran whom Segura had last seen going to the rear of the enemy truck, had once told a story about a friend of his whose rifle had been broken in half by a communist bullet. It was possible.

The *Oberst* looked at him. 'It broke, you say?'

'Yes, sir.'

'Where?'

Segura mimed holding a rifle. The farmhouse suddenly seemed cramped and overheated, its oppressive atmosphere a nauseating mix of sweat, paraffin, garlic and black tobacco. 'Here,' he said, indicating the hand guard.

'And was that when you fled?'

'Yes, I mean no, sir. I was in cover and unable to reach another weapon. I held my position until they drove away.'

'That would be the five remaining anarchists?'

'That's correct, sir.'

'And you personally accounted for every one of the five casualties.'

'I believe so, sir.'

'Can you describe those you didn't succeed in killing?'

'Yes, sir,' blurted Segura. 'One was thin and blond. He looked like a German. He ran away when he saw me.'

'A German?'

'Yes, but they spoke English to each other.'

The officer raised his eyebrows. 'English? Do you speak English?'

Segura blushed. He was talking too much and was losing the plot of his carefully crafted tale. 'A little, sir,' he conceded.

'But can you be sure it wasn't German, or Russian?'

Definitely not, thought Segura. One of them — he hadn't seen him but he'd heard that movie-star accent — had been American: a gangster. He nodded. 'No, sir. I can't be sure. They destroyed the telephone, too.'

'Did you see a Spanish man with long hair?'

Segura shook his head.

'Are you sure?' asked the German.

Two hours earlier, Segura had been certain that his survival and his irrefutable account thereof would win him a medal and a week's leave. Now he would settle for a few hours' sleep and a little sympathy. He watched miserably as the German conferred with the Spanish officers.

'You will be issued with a replacement rifle, Private,' announced von Wittenburg with a weary sweep of his hand. 'The one you lost will, I'm sure, be deducted from your pay. I've also sought your temporary attachment to my unit. I have a job for you.'

Segura felt his mouth drop open. 'Sir?'

'I need you to lead us to these anarchists.' He smiled cruelly. 'After all, Private, you're the only one who knows what they look like, and I'm sure that your soldier's honour needs avenging.' He raised his hands in mocking imitation of a small man holding a large rifle and swayed back and forth like a midget dancing with a big girl. 'They killed your fiancée, remember?'

Sidney felt the truck lurch to a stop and heard Cobb come around the side of the van singing the Fred Astaire song 'I'm Putting All My Eggs in One Basket'. Cobb pulled open the rear doors, letting cool morning air rush in, and the smell of fear, death and uncertainty trickle out to seep into the stony ground. The dead corporal's blood remained on the floor, a neat black circle in the sawdust. Villafranca shook his head in dismay as the American performed an impromptu and decidedly amateur tap dance routine on the gravel road, singing, 'I've got a great big amount saved up in my love account, honey/And I've decided love divided in two won't do . . .'

'He's a fucking clown,' sighed Villafranca as Cobb paused for breath, a lunatic grin on his face.

'So I'm putting all my eggs in one basket, baby/I'm betting everything I've got on you!'

'Very good, *señor*,' nodded Villafranca. 'May I sing for you now?'

Cobb stuffed a cigar between his teeth and nodded. 'Like a canary, Angel. Where to from here?'

'Can you see the Alto Maestrazgo from out there?'

'How the fuck should I know? What does it look like?'

'If you unlock me, I'll show you.'

Sidney slid to the edge of the van and jumped to the ground. A pale light lit a steep-sided, pine-clad valley, its bottom buried beneath a thick blanket of rolling mist. Early crows flapped from west to east, heading towards the sunlit ridge high above them. Kreuz was peeing against a tree on the other side of the road, a tiny, dishevelled figure against the black bulk of the mountain. This was the bend on the Villarluengo road, where perhaps a dozen forest tracks descended from the sierra, their entrances like cave mouths between the dripping trees.

Cobb laughed at Villafranca's suggestion. 'I was born at night, Angel, but not last night. I'm not unlocking you. Describe the mountain.'

Villafranca sighed in exasperation. 'Tall, stripy, grey at the top, white in the middle and green at the bottom. Lots of rock.'

'Ha fucking ha. You'll have to do better than that.'

Villafranca looked him straight in the eye. 'That's the best I can do. I'm a bank robber, not a poet. You want a poet? You should have saved Lorca. Now please let me out. I need to pee.'

Cobb scowled. 'One move out of you . . .'

'Yeah, yeah, whatever you say, Major.'

'You're staying cuffed, creep.'

'You're too generous, Major. I presume you will hold my dick for me while I pee?'

Cobb climbed stiffly back into the truck. 'No, I'll cut it off and pass it round the back so you can hold it yourself,' sighed Cobb.

'Such kind words. If only you meant them, *señor*.'

'Shut your mouth and hold still . . .'

Sidney heard Cobb cough and belch at the same time, and as he turned he saw the American bent double in the sawdust, his arms across his gut. Villafranca pushed him away, pointed a pistol at Sidney and pulled the trigger. The air split as Sidney was spun around, seeing the mountains, the forest and then the blue sky. His shoulder smarted as though kicked, his knees buckled and his head hit the road.

'I'm hit,' he heard himself gasp. 'The bugger's shot me.' He looked up, saw Kreuz sprint past him, then saw Cobb stagger from the rear of the truck, sawdust like fresh snow on his coat. 'Cocksucker stabbed me,' he yelled, his hand crimson on his belly. 'Where did he go?'

Sidney sat up, stunned and shaken, not quite understanding what had just happened.

'Kreuz, you fucker,' panted Cobb. 'Get that bastard back here now!'

The German appeared at the rear of the truck, his rifle in one hand and a Spanish bandolier in the other. Sidney felt as though an enormous weight had collided with his left shoulder, leaving a numbness in its wake that stretched from his ear to his elbow. He touched the wound, a furrow through wool and flesh slick with blood.

Cobb swept his hair back with one hand, and threw Sidney a furious look. 'He get your legs?'

Sidney shook his head.

'Then get after him. Bring that bastard back!'

The gipsy hadn't gone far. A precipitous flight down a goat track had been too much strain on legs atrophied by incarceration and numbed by long hours of confinement in the truck. He slipped on a rock, twisting his ankle, and discharging another round from Cobb's pistol that nearly took his own nose off. He limped on for another twenty yards or so and fell again, weeping tears of pain and frustration. Then he heard his pursuers and backed off the track to lie in the cover of an acacia bush. He saw the German trotting down the path with his rifle aimed cautiously ahead of him, pausing every five paces to look around nervously. Villafranca had already dropped the English boy, and with luck he'd kill this one too, allowing him to move back up to the road, finish off the major and escape in the truck. The American's pistol was a real gangster's piece, a heavy nickel-plated Colt firing bullets as big as acorns. Hit a man in the right spot with one of those at close range and the shock would break every bone in his body. He waited for Kreuz to fill the sights, aiming at a point below his sternum, licking the sweat from his moustache and taking short, shallow breaths. Freedom was but a shot away. Then, suddenly, there was a gun barrel poking into his left ear.

'Don't shoot!' smiled Angel Villafranca, slowly placing the Colt on the dusty ground. 'We can negotiate!'

Cobb was in no mood to negotiate when they dragged him back to the truck. Stripped to the waist, his braces hanging by his knees, the major was sitting in the cab, winding a bandage around his midriff, a cigar fuming between his lips. He took his pistol from Sidney without a word and swung it hard and fast into Villafranca's face, sending him sprawling in a splatter of spit and blood. Then he leaned low over the cowering gipsy, brandishing a bayonet in his face. 'Where did you get this, you sneaky, conniving bastard? Where'd you get it?'

'From the man whose throat you cut,' admitted Villafranca, flinching as he spoke, but nevertheless succeeding in making Cobb seem like the bad guy. 'It was on his belt.'

Cobb kicked him, groaning with the effort. 'You double-crossing son of a bitch! Look what you've done.' He stepped back, holding his hands apart to reveal the dark spot swelling slowly on his dressing.

'I'm sorry,' mumbled Villafranca.

'And don't add insult to injury by lying to me, neither. You've just fucking guaranteed your execution.'

Sidney glanced at Kreuz, expecting to see his own concern reflected on the German's pock-marked face. He was surprised to see what looked like optimism instead.

'We need to tend to that wound,' said Kreuz.

Cobb dismissed his suggestion with an angry wave. 'Forget it. We'll head for the hills, find somewhere to lie low and recover until the heat dies down.' He glared at Villafranca. 'Know any good spots?'

15

The vending-machine repairman was glad when he finally dropped the shell-suited hooligan in Montalban's Plaza Mercador. His only regret as he drove away, his windows wide open to fumigate his car of Lenny's flatulence, was that the Serrano girl had stooped so low. She was friendly and fun but, with one obvious exception, she had absolutely no taste in men. He drove home to his wife feeling older, wiser and a little sadder.

Lenny, on the other hand, felt young, hopeful and, in spite of the twinges from his back, quite extraordinarily virile. He was dressed in a nearly original Nike leisure suit, bright white Reeboks and a moody Burberry baseball cap. Pausing to take a swig from the Larios he'd lifted as a leaving present from La Cerda, he pulled his gold coin from his pocket and kissed it. He had known it would come in handy from the start – an instantly redeemable insurance policy that would buy fun, food and lodging anywhere in the world. A stylised, three-masted ship looking like some floating castle was on the reverse, long pennants snapping in the wind. The obverse showed a shifty-looking bloke with a beard, probably some Spanish king. Tonight, the drinks were on him. Nick's coin had sold for eleven hundred euros, but that had been in a city, in a specialist coin shop. Out here in the sticks Lenny knew he would probably get only scrap value, but he would hold out for five hundred minimum. That would be enough to buy him a night on the town and a bus ticket to the Costa Brava when it all went wrong. He had no idea just how wrong it was about to go.

It was late afternoon and already dark, but within moments he'd spotted the modest premises of Cruz y Hijo, noting the foil tape of the alarm system peeling from the window and the velvet-lined trays of cheap rings and flashy watches displayed on dusty glass shelves. Inside the shop, surrounded by discounted clocks of dark wood and cut-price necklaces of thin silver and cheap gold, Hermann Gutierrez Cruz was unaware that a prophecy was moments away from being fulfilled. He was reading a TV listings magazine and idly wondering if the future might be in consumer electronics when the security buzzer sounded. He checked the CCTV and saw an individual he assumed was a truck driver absently scratching his backside on the threshold. Earrings, he guessed, for some roadhouse tart, and he pushed the button to open the door.

'*Señor*, please, no food or drink in the shop,' he called, but the lorry driver ignored him, advancing on the counter in a haze of alcohol fumes. He was carrying a bottle of Larios, noticed Hermann, and was clearly a drunk. He spread his fingers to inch closer to the panic button that was wired directly to the police station, and almost pressed it as the drunk seemed to lunge at him. There was a rattle on the counter and when Hermann looked down his heart skipped a beat and left him giddy and weak-kneed. He glanced nervously at the drunk, then back at the coin, and closed his eyes in breathless wonder. '*La profecia*,' he murmured.

'The Prof is indeed here,' belched Lenny in reply. 'I'm a dinosaur bone-hunter, from a university in England. What will you give me for this little number?'

English, realised Hermann. That explained the alcohol and the outfit. He fought to regain his composure, struggling against the urge to snatch up the coin and run screaming to the church.

'Welcome to Montalban, *señor*,' he beamed.

'Yeah, lovely to be here, Pancho,' nodded Lenny. 'What's it worth, then?'

What was it worth indeed? Almost seven decades of waiting, three generations of patience and the best part of two adult lives spent scouring the hills in defiance of a witch's prophecy and a mother's desperation. Hermann felt his eyes well up with tears and the feeling evaporate from his short, fat legs. A miracle was happening before his eyes and the Englishman wanted to know what it was worth. He sniffed, waving a finger in the air. '*Señor*, please wait here. Please do not move – let me fetch you a chair and something to drink, although I see you have brought your own.'

'No matter,' shrugged Lenny. 'We can lay into your stock. Got any beer?'

'I regret not. I have a bottle of *coñac*, if you please?'

'Sorted,' nodded Lenny. 'Don't get this treatment in Ernest Jones, you know.' Locals probably didn't receive this treatment either. The jeweller had obviously mistaken him for a visiting academic, thus explaining the red-carpet treatment. Lenny decided to play along.

'Please,' said Hermann, placing a bentwood chair. 'My name is Hermann Cruz. You are?'

Lenny tapped his nose. 'Lenny Knowles, mate. Professor Lenny Knowles, dinosaur-hunter.'

'Please make yourself comfortable, *Profesor*. I must just, er, look up this coin in my reference.'

'You take all the time you like, mate,' nodded Lenny.

He poured tobacco-brown *coñac* into a smeared glass and looked around the cluttered shop. Someone cleaned the glass display cabinets once in a while, but whoever did so was either short or careless, or both. From where he sat, Lenny could see narrow swaths of clarity bordered by curving corners of dusty opacity, hiding the details of a stock that looked unchanged for twenty years. The watches came in big plastic boxes lined with faded satin, their gaudy metal bracelets often accompanied by a matching ballpoint pen or a pair of cufflinks; or even, in a couple of instances, a tiny bottle of aftershave bearing the name of some optimistic designer whose goods you'd be hard pushed to shift in Norwich market, let alone from a proper shop. If you could call Cruz y Hijo a proper shop. Lenny had never found a timepiece he really liked, he realised, checking his unadorned left wrist. Nothing kept time like an imaginary watch.

He swigged his *coñac* and topped up his glass, wondering if there was anything else in here that he could ever desire. A counter display of crucifixes, St Christopher charms and other weird Spanish saints ranged from the mean to the outrageous in size and price, and it struck Lenny that the proprietor would probably end up soldering a chain on to that gold coin and selling it as a medallion to some hairy-chested local yokel. Cheap wall clocks from China suggested that the world had stopped at ten-to-two as Lenny took another swig and sighed. It was all a bit Harry Big Buttons, as they said down the East End, and it had to be the first jewellery shop he'd ever been in that wasn't worth robbing. Faded photos, some framed, some simply pinned up, lined the space between the cobweb-draped picture rail and the cracked ceiling, in bleached black-and-white and garish, seventies Kodacolor. The only subjects of these snapshots were a fat, incapable-looking boy who grew older in each successive shot and a seemingly ageless bald man who either scowled from a wheelchair or smiled grimly from the back of a mule. The landscape was always the same: the layered peaks and dark forests of the Maestrazgo. The fat, useless kid, guessed Lenny, was now the man he could hear half whispering and half shouting into a telephone behind the beaded curtain to the rear of the shop. He looked up as the shopkeeper returned from the rear. 'What's the Bobby, then, Pancho?'

The twin roots of Hermann's heritage had suffused him with an innate understanding of Englishmen that was as clichéd as it was true. They were friendly, condescending, patient and stupid, but prone to explosions of medieval fury and violence when perceived slights finally percolated through their thick skulls and into their alcohol-muddled minds. This Englishman – the witch hadn't guessed that bit – was the first who'd ever entered Cruz y Hijo, and Hermann was keenly aware that if he managed the affair correctly, he would be the last. '*Profesor*,' he began, observing that if this hooligan was typical of Albion's academic establishment then one could hardly blame their perfidious youth, 'I would like to pay you seven hundred for the coin . . .' Lenny's eyes narrowed, so Hermann adjusted his estimate. 'Plus three hundred for the gold content. Making a total of one thousand euros, which I'm sure you'll agree is a fair, even a generous, price.'

Lenny stuck out his lower lip. If the dago was up for a grand, he'd certainly go to twelve-fifty. 'Sorry, Pancho,' he smiled in a friendly but condescending way. 'Fifteen's my arsecrack.'

Hermann's English didn't stretch to invented cockney rhyming slang. 'Arsecrack?' he repeated.

'Arsecrack,' nodded Lenny, drawing a pair of buttocks in the air and indicating the gap between. 'The bottom line. Fifteen K's my bottom line.' He poured himself another two fingers of *coñac* and lit a cigarette.

'I have to make a call,' said Hermann.

'Tell you what,' suggested Lenny. 'If you can't make the decision, why not let me speak to the man who can?'

'I do make the decisions,' replied Hermann, archly. 'But I do not hold that kind of money on the premises.'

Lenny stood up, and Hermann's heart leapt in panic. 'You go make your call,' said the Englishman with a patient smile. 'I'll be over there in that bar.'

Sidney had been surprised by the lack of pain in his wounded shoulder. The .45 round had ripped a chunk of flesh from the scalenus muscle, passing less than an inch above his collarbone and perhaps three from his throat. After the punch of the impact all he had felt was a leaden numbness, similar to that caused by a heavy pack or a blow from a blunt instrument. It had seemed a minor, trifling injury at the time. But now it hurt. Dressed with a bandage that passed over the wound and under his right armpit, the raw, torn muscle throbbed with a deep, depressing intensity that reached from his fingertips to his buttocks and sent his jaw into spasm. Alternating waves of cold sweat and nausea rippled through a head that felt as bruised and as swollen as a football. Lying alone in the sawdust at the rear of the truck, he stared wanly at the bloodstained walls, struggling to save himself from further injury as they lurched up a rutted mountain track. Villafranca was now in the front between Cobb and Kreuz, and the German was doing a good job of looking after the wounded, stopping regularly to check that Sidney was still alive. Sidney had tried to tell him that it was only a flesh wound – it was a superbly heroic thing to hear himself say – but his fragile countenance seemed to suggest otherwise.

'How's Cobb?' he asked, as Kreuz dusted sawdust from his tunic.

'He says the same as you, but his is a deep wound. He needs medical attention.' He swept a pile of shavings onto the ground, catching Sidney's eye as he did so. 'Fucking sawdust!' he cursed, swinging the door shut. 'I'll check on you again soon.'

The lorry moved on, gears grinding and wheels slipping on the wet rock, and as he drifted into half consciousness, Sidney remembered a story his mother had told him as a child. There was once a woodcutter who lived in a forest, and one day he felled a tree to find it occupied by an elf. He caught the elf and placed him in his hipsack, planning to hand him over to the king for a reward. 'I'll reward you,' cried the elf. 'I'll give you much, much more than the king, if only you promise to let me go.' The woodcutter asked the elf to prove it, and the elf directed him to a hollow stump in the dark heart of the forest. He urged the woodcutter to lower a lantern and take a look, and deep in a chamber beneath the forest floor the astounded woodsman saw a fortune in gold. The only problem was that he didn't have a rope or a ladder with which to reach the hoard.

'Go home and fetch one,' suggested the elf.

'But how will I find the stump again?' asked the woodcutter.

The elf scratched his head. 'Fill your bag with sawdust and leave a handful at every path junction.'

'But if I fill the bag with sawdust, I'll have to let you go.'

'That', said the elf, 'was the deal.'

'You'll move the piles,' said the woodcutter.

'I give you my word that I'll neither move the gold nor the sawdust,' promised the elf, and it's well known that elves cannot lie.

Sidney awoke as the truck stopped, then lurched into reverse, tipping him onto his good side. As he pulled himself upright the hoarse whine of the engine changed in pitch and volume, becoming louder and deeper, its urgent revving accompanied by the agonising screech of steel on rock. Sidney watched in dismay as the roof of the truck shivered, sending flakes of paint spiralling downwards before it bent and split, punched by a fist of over-hanging rock. At last the engine cut out, shaking like a wet dog, and all was quiet. The door opened to semi-darkness lit only by the orange glow of Cobb's cigar.

'You OK, kid?'

'Where are we?'

'Ali Baba's place. Bring your weapon.'

Villafranca limped past. 'It's a Roman mine. I left a lantern here somewhere.'

Sidney studied Cobb's face in the gloom. 'How's your gut?'

Cobb sucked on his cigar, his unshaven upper lip shiny with sweat. 'Hurts like a New Jersey whore.'

'Where's Kreuz?'

'I'm here. You want to talk to me?'

Sidney shook his head as Villafranca shuffled to the rear of the truck.

'There is just one lamp' – the gipsy shook it – 'and it's only half full.'

'Quit stalling and show me the goods,' growled Cobb, touching his lighter to the wick and throwing a yellow light over the rough stone walls. The truck had been reversed into a low, narrow tunnel, its sides still bearing the shell-like marks of hand-hewn tools and its fragile-looking roof riven with deep fissures. The man-made section was perhaps thirty feet long, opening out into a much wider space littered with fallen rocks.

'Smells like shit in here,' observed Cobb.

'Could be us,' suggested Kreuz. 'From the sewers.'

'Could be them,' countered Cobb. Two bodies lay huddled like cold lovers against a crack in the wall, as though they had tried to crawl inside. 'Your work, Villafranca?'

The gipsy crossed himself as the lamplight rippled across black fingers, bent like claws on the dung-splattered floor. 'God grant them peace in the hereafter. They could not be trusted.'

'Unlike yourself, of course.'

Ten yards from the tailgate Villafranca set the lantern on the ground and lifted the corner of a tarpaulin. Even from close up the uneven pile lying in the shadows looked like no more than another heap of fallen rocks. Cobb extended his .45 at arm's length. 'OK, Villafranca. You've just outlived your usefulness. Get over here.'

The Spaniard sighed and let the tarpaulin drop, stepping to one side like an indignant child.

'Kid, get that tarp.'

Sidney bent and lifted the corner, its canvas oily and stiff with dirt. He smelled dry cedar and his knuckle brushed smooth, planed wood. The lamplight fell on a stack of narrow wooden crates. Right now he would have expected Kreuz to be demanding to be told what was going on, but the German remained

272

almost breathlessly silent. Sidney dragged a single box clear of the pile by its rope handle, the effort sparking a blaze of pain across his back, and looked at Cobb. 'Want me to open it?'

Cobb looked at Kreuz, the pistol gleaming in his hand. 'I suppose you're wondering why I brought you here today, Mr Kreuz.'

The German glanced at the two corpses, then at Cobb. He licked his lips and smiled. 'It's not my job to wonder, Major. I just follow orders for the greater good of the workers' revolution.'

'You know what's in those boxes?'

Kreuz looked him straight in the eye. 'I do not.'

Cobb nodded to Sidney. 'Crack it, kid.'

Sidney used his bayonet to lift the wooden lid and raised the lantern to illuminate the contents. The box was heaped with loose coin, a glittering mess of gold bullion that glowed like lava and seemed to radiate its own feverish heat in the dim light.

Cobb's enjoyment of the moment was spoiled by a surge of pain and he fell back against the wall, gasping like a man winded. Kreuz gasped too, but not in distress, and Angel Villafranca merely smiled sadly at a prize he would never enjoy.

'What are we to do with this?' asked Kreuz evenly.

'Why, we deliver it to Orlov, of course,' exclaimed Cobb, 'together with this idiot.' He took his hand from his belly long enough to relight his cigar. 'Unless you have any other suggestions, Mr Kreuz.'

'If they are our orders . . .'

'Exactly. See if you can back the truck any closer. There are one hundred boxes here and it looks like it's you and the gipsy doing the loading.'

Sidney watched Kreuz squeeze between the truck and the wall, and spoke only when he had gone. 'Something's up with him.'

Cobb frowned. 'Don't complicate things, kid. You're almost useless to me now and I need him.'

'Did he ask you why we turned off the main road? Did he ask why Villafranca was guiding us? I'm telling you: he knew about the gold. He's planning something, and we're going to suffer for it.'

Cobb grimaced. 'If I want my fortune told, I'll ask the gipsy. Stick to what you know, kid, and quit messing up the water. If he wanted to make a move, he could have done so back at the turn-off when we were both down.'

'No, he couldn't,' insisted Sidney. 'He needed Villafranca. He's biding his time.'

The truck rattled into life, coughing like a smoker and filling the low tunnel with acrid exhaust fumes as Kreuz tried to drive closer to the bullion.

'Christ Almighty!' coughed Cobb. 'Let's get out of here before we choke.' He prodded Villafranca past the truck, out of the mine and onto a narrow, grassy ledge high above the valley. 'I couldn't have got the truck up here,' he remarked, 'and you can't even drive. Frankly, I couldn't have done it without Kreuz, so let's try to treat him as part of the family until he proves otherwise.' He threw Villafranca a sour look. 'How the hell did you find this place?'

The gipsy shook his head, his lank curls rolling in the breeze. 'I'm not talking to you any more. I need to make peace with myself.'

Kreuz switched off the engine and jumped from the cab. 'I'm as close as I can be,' he called to Cobb. 'What now?'

'Now we load up,' said Cobb. 'I want to get out of here.'

'What should I do?' asked Sidney, fearful of being left alone.

'Go fill this up,' replied Kreuz, tossing a goatskin bota from the cab. Tiny silver camels dangled from the collar around its neck and they jingled as Sidney lifted it from the ground. 'From Morocco, the Regulares,' said Kreuz. 'It'll last a hundred years.'

'We ain't got that long,' muttered Cobb.

Sidney grabbed his rifle and walked slowly to the edge of the slope, scanning the thin woodland below for a watercourse. His left arm was stiff and inflamed as far as the elbow and the hurt came on like a buzzard, making great, swooping attacks that left him weak and nauseous. His shirt was black, his fingers sticky and his hair matted with blood, and as he set off, his rifle in his good hand and the empty canteen over his uninjured shoulder, he realised he was hot with fever. For a moment he wondered if he might bleed to death, on his own, on this ugly mountain, and the certainty that this would not happen was tempered with a deep shame that so minor an injury should have brought him so low. He stopped to rest against a pine, breathing in the deep, antiseptic smell of the resin, promising himself that he would wash and redress the wound when he found a stream. Then he heard a whistle, and the pain and self-pity were washed away on a flood of adrenalin. Dropping to his belly and crawling to the downhill side of the track, he peered over the edge and down to where the trail switched back through the denser woods of the lower slopes. A gentle westerly rustled the firs, their branches creaking and their cones cracking in the warm sunshine. A horsefly flew in crazy circles before settling on his bloody shoulder. He slapped it away and it circled before landing again. He wiped sweat from his eyes and his lip and slipped a pebble into his mouth to give him enough spit to wet his parched throat. Down below, nothing moved. Smaller, darker flies found him now, buzzing in his ear as they swarmed on his wound, rising an inch and resettling as he tried to brush them away. A black beetle climbed up his hand and over his rifle as he stared through the sights, searching for the movement he had heard.

Three minutes later, he saw them. Two came first, walking slowly up the track, the sunlight glinting from their rifles. Six more followed, some bareheaded and others, their caution apparent even at extreme range, hunched beneath heavy steel helmets. Sidney's alarm intensified as he saw a three-man machine-gun team emerge from the trees in the wake of the riflemen. He looked back to the first pair, counting slowly as they moved along the track. If they kept advancing at that pace, they would be at his position in less than an hour, loping like beagles from one pile of sawdust to the next. Sidney counted thirteen, the last clearly an officer, before crawling away from the roadside and back to the others.

'Where's the water?' demanded Kreuz, his shirt dark with perspiration and his scalp glowing pink through his sweat-soaked hair.

Sidney threw the empty bota to the ground. 'Bugger your water, Kreuz,' he panted. 'We've got company.'

Cobb, bent double on a bench made from bullion boxes like a man with loose bowels, raised an eyebrow. 'Who, and how many?'

'I counted nine riflemen, an officer and a gun team before I came back.'

'Did they see you?'

Sidney treated the question with the contempt it deserved.

Cobb struggled to his feet. 'How the hell did they find us?'

'Ask Kreuz,' suggested Sidney, drawing his Luger. 'Ask him about the sawdust.'

Kreuz smiled and turned his back on Sidney, pushing a crate onto the truck. 'I think the boy is delirious,' he told Cobb.

The major raised an eyebrow. 'Yeah? Well indulge him.'

Kreuz wiped his hands on the seat of his pants. 'I have no idea what either of you are talking about. Now can we continue loading?'

'I asked you to tell us about the sawdust,' repeated Cobb, his voice the low, dangerous growl of a crouching leopard. 'I saw you tipping that shit into the road at the checkpoint and I thought you were being careless. Then I saw you do the same on the Villarluengo road, and I got suspicious.'

'And then I caught you sweeping great armfuls out on the track every time we stopped,' added Sidney.

Kreuz gaped. 'Don't be ridiculous. Every time someone

opens this door the stuff pours out.' He kicked the truck bed. 'Look: it's full of it!'

'Don't fuck with me, Kreuz,' warned Cobb. 'It's over. Who are you working for?'

Sidney knew the German was going to run in the same way he could tell when a crouched hare was going to make a break.

'Who are you working for?' barked Cobb again.

'Does it make any difference?' asked Kreuz coolly.

Cobb shrugged. 'Might do to me.'

Kreuz laughed, short and fake. 'Right now I'm more use to you alive than dead. There's no need for any of us to die here. Give up now and I guarantee you won't hang.'

'Why?' drawled Cobb. 'You got influence?'

The German nodded fast, his eyes on the slowly moving muzzle of Cobb's .45. 'I have enough influence, yes.'

Cobb smiled. 'You really are one of us, aren't you, Kreuz? A fully paid-up, senior fucking member of the Self-Interested Bastards' Society. Beats me how the likes of us ever got together, but you know as well as me that there's only one way to leave. I suppose I'm wasting my time asking you to call the dogs off. I doubt you've got *that* much influence.'

Kreuz shook his head. 'No man is more important than one ton of gold, and there are seven tons here.'

'How do you know?'

'We were aware of the raid on the Russian house in Valencia.'

'*We?*'

'Abwehr.'

'Who?' asked Sidney.

Cobb grinned. 'Abwehr, kid: German intelligence. Kreuz here is a German spy.'

'You bastard!' cried Sidney. 'After what they did to you in that camp? After they nearly killed you? Or was that all lies?'

Kreuz scratched his ear and smiled. 'All true, little man. But now you know why they let me go.'

Cobb drew a breath. 'OK. End of story.' He raised the Colt, aiming at Kreuz's chest.

Suddenly the German leapt from the rear of the truck, landing lightly and lunging at the lantern with his boot. He had just a split second to extinguish the light, and failed, but he retained the advantage of surprise. He spun on his heels, darting behind Sidney and barging him towards Cobb.

Sidney dropped to his knees as Cobb fired, the bullet howling as it ricocheted from the opposite wall. 'You nearly bloody shot me!' he yelled at Cobb.

'Shut up and get after him,' spat the American. 'And don't be discharging firearms out there, neither. Use this.' Sidney looked down at the Toledo dagger he had last seen coming out of a girl's heart in Teruel. Even Cobb recognised the dilemma. 'Come on, kid,' he urged. 'It balances out in the end.'

Sidney snatched the dagger and squeezed past the truck. The rattle of scree gave Kreuz away, and as Sidney reached the edge of the grassy ledge he saw the German fifty yards below, moving diagonally to his right. Sidney jumped onto the slope and set out on an acute course to intercept him. Kreuz heard his footfalls and turned to look over his shoulder. As he looked back, he stumbled, landing on both knees and slapping the steep slope with his hands. He slid before rolling and regaining his feet, moving now with an injured lope, losing ground to his grim pursuer. At last he turned, smiling, his hands half raised in almost playful surrender. 'I think now is the time to relieve Cobb of his command,' he panted. 'I trust I can count on your support.'

Sidney switched his grip on the dagger, preparing for an upward thrust. 'Shut up and turn around,' he ordered.

Kreuz was walking backwards, his hands out in front of him, his elbows protecting his ribs. 'Don't do this, Sidney,' he urged. 'You owe no more loyalty to anyone than I do. Think for a moment. You're wounded. I'm not. I could take that knife from you and cut your dick off.'

278

'Try it,' hissed Sidney, lunging like a swordsman. The blade cut a furrow along Kreuz's lifeline and sent a ribbon of blood splashing on the scree.

The ferocity of the attack alarmed the German, who leapt backwards, clutching the wounded hand to his chest. 'Listen to me,' he insisted. 'Just listen for one moment.' He lurched to the left to avoid the thrusting blade.

The Andalucians had taught Sidney how to use the knife, always moving forwards, slash, slash, stab, never letting the enemy recover and waiting for the moment when he fell on his arse.

'We can go back up there, you and I . . .' panted Kreuz.

Sidney changed his grip again and slashed, feeling muscle tear beneath the steel as he sliced the German's triceps, smelling the blood now as it sprayed from the wound. Kreuz was almost running backwards now, slipping to the right with every rearwards step. With nowhere to hide, he stepped onto a boulder on the very edge of a cliff, suddenly no more than a little boy taking refuge from a wild animal. 'You'll die in that cave,' he cried, his blood dripping at his feet in fat, scarlet splashes. 'Come with me and I'll guarantee you live.'

'Is that what the Nazis promised you?' asked Sidney. 'They were lying to you, Kreuz.' He punched the blade towards the German's thigh and Kreuz leapt backwards, fixing Sidney with a stare that seemed to go right through him to rest on a thing far more terrible, far more horrific, that dwelt inside. His eyes widened in shock, blinked in the briefest acceptance, and then, with a rattle of rocks, he was gone. 'Christ!' breathed Sidney, peering over the cliff edge. Kreuz had already hit the bottom, one hundred feet below, and as Sidney watched, the broken body rolled slowly to a halt on the scree.

In Montalban Lenny was enjoying a truly blinding night out. He'd noticed that the bleakest locations often offered the best drinking establishments, as though the lack of opportunity and hope was reconciled by well-fitted boozers – Wales being the obvious exception – and the bar they called Ke Tal was one of the finest examples. The only drag had been Hermann, who had joined him early in the evening, trading the coin for an envelope containing ten fresh hundred-euro notes and what appeared to be an IOU for a further monkey, to be paid after the banks opened in the morning. Lenny's delight at netting the full fifteen hundred was immediately tempered by the realisation that the short, fat Spaniard would undoubtedly have paid more if pressed, but it was still three times what he had expected. He clinked his glass against Hermann's, looking over the jeweller's shoulder at a right little raver stood sucking on an alcopop by the payphone. It was still too early for most Spaniards to be abroad, and other than the barmaid she was the only girl in the bar.

Hermann followed his gaze, then winked at Lenny. 'Perhaps I could introduce you?' he suggested.

Lenny licked his lips. 'Perhaps you could, mate.'

'I think first you should join me in the toilet.'

Lenny speared his host with a watery eye. 'Steady on, Romeo.'

'I have something you might enjoy.'

'I'm sure you think you do, mate.' He pointed at the miniskirted girl. 'I'm more of a ladies' man myself.'

Hermann bristled, vowing that the lout would regret his insinuations later. He fixed a smile to his face and nodded towards his palm.

Lenny glanced down, his eyes widening in delight. 'Is that what I think it is?'

'It is, *Profesor*. For you, just fifty euros.'

Lenny snatched the paper square from Hermann's sweaty hand. 'Got any more? Do us three for a ton.' He slapped a hundred down and hoisted himself from his bar stool. 'Nice one,

Pancho. You can always rely on a shirt-lifter to have a bit of the old Gianluca.'

When Lenny returned, snorting and blinking like a turned-out bull, the girl was sitting in a booth with Hermann.

'*Profesor*,' called the shopkeeper. 'Come and meet Mercedes. I've been telling her you're something of an Indiana Jones.'

'And you're something of an Ernest Jones,' quipped Lenny. He loved the way cocaine accelerated his wit. 'Ernest Jones is a chain of jewellers' in England,' he explained.

'I know,' nodded Hermann. 'Glass of cava?'

'What's that?'

'It's like champagne.'

Lenny made a face. 'Fizzy piss. I'll stick to my lager.'

Hermann waved to the barmaid. 'I was telling Mercedes about the coin you found.'

'There's a lot more where that one came from,' winked Lenny.

'Everybody knows about the treasure,' smiled the girl. 'Or they think they do.' She crossed her legs, smoothing her skirt over her fishnets. Lenny couldn't help but notice.

'There is no treasure,' declared Hermann. 'You think seven tons of gold could remain hidden out there all this time?'

'There's much older treasure still lost in the Maestrazgo,' insisted Mercedes. 'What about El Cid?'

'You know El Sid?' asked Lenny.

'Of course,' replied Mercedes. 'He's a legend in these parts.'

'Well, I'll be buggered,' exclaimed Lenny, shaking his head.

The Spaniards looked at him for a moment, then Hermann smiled. 'I love this English humour. And rumours, my dear, of treasure in the mountains are just that. Yes, it's probably true that someone pilfered a small amount of bullion from the gold reserve in '36 and stashed it in the hills, but I'm talking about pennies.' He sipped his *cava*. 'That's why these bone collectors turn one up every now and then.' He looked at Lenny. 'Where did you find the coin you sold me?'

Lenny shrugged. 'Out and about.'

A deeply tanned man with tattooed arms and shoulder-length hair leaned across the table to greet Hermann and Mercedes. He smelled of aftershave and marijuana, and the silver bracelets on his thick wrists tinkled as he shook their hands.

'Enrique Pinsada,' announced Hermann. 'A business associate.' He spoke to the new arrival in Spanish and Pinsada offered Lenny his hand.

'He wishes you an enjoyable stay in Montalban,' explained Hermann as Pinsada pulled up a chair. 'Do you mind if he joins us?'

As it happened, Lenny did mind. Pinsada had the hawkish good looks of a proper gipsy and offered unwanted competition for the key to Mercedes. 'Not at all,' he lied.

'So, you were saying about your coin,' continued Hermann. 'You found it where?'

'Didn't say,' smiled Lenny. He sipped his beer, feeling Pinsada's eyes on his face.

Hermann shrugged. 'Almost every man in this town wears a crucifix made from coins found in the Maestrazgo. Show him yours, Enrique. My father made that one. I get people bringing baubles they've found into the shop every other month, but yours was in particularly fine condition.' He winked at Mercedes. 'Maybe I'll make your wedding ring from the *profesor's* coin.'

'You getting married?' asked Lenny. She really was a stunner.

'Not yet,' she replied, a promise implicit in her answer. 'No one around here is rich enough.'

'She thinks that one day someone will find the treasure and she wants to be the first to congratulate him,' laughed Hermann, translating the comment for Pinsada's benefit.

The gipsy lit a cigarette and said something in reply. He didn't seem especially amused.

'He says she'll die an old maid,' explained Hermann. 'He says

282

there is no treasure in the hills. Just idiots out looking for it.'

'I heard there was seven tons hidden in an old mine,' said Lenny.

Hermann raised his eyebrows and told Pinsada. Both laughed.

'Is this the tale of Orlov's gold?'

'That's right. I think that was his name. Russian bloke from the war.'

Hermann nodded. 'Orlov. It's a myth, *Profesor*, a legend. A fairy story for the gullible. It never existed.'

'I know a man who's seen it,' insisted Lenny.

'Know,' asked Hermann, 'or knew? Anybody who claims to have seen it would be dead by now.'

Mercedes had leaned forward, one hand on her glass and the other in her bleached blond hair. She was captivated, noticed Lenny, and Pinsada was looking increasingly marginalised.

'That's where you're wrong, Pancho. This old boy is alive and kicking, and he's seen it.' He stubbed out his cigarette and lit another, wiping his nose with the back of his hand. 'Seven tons, in one hundred boxes, in a cave in those hills.'

Mercedes gasped. 'So that's why you're here!'

'He's pulling your leg, dear,' said Hermann. 'So where is this old man now?'

Lenny sat back and swigged his Heineken. 'Not far.'

'In Montalban? I'd like to meet him.'

'I'm sure you would, mate, but he's not here.'

'And what is this ancient man's name?'

'El Sid,' grinned Lenny, rubbing his nose.

'I think you're teasing us, *Profesor*,' said Hermann slowly, with as much latent menace as he could muster.

'Course I am,' nodded Lenny. 'Having a laugh, ain't I?'

Mercedes stood up. 'I don't think it's funny.'

'Hold on, darling,' urged Lenny. 'Where you off to?'

'I'm going home. You're all making fun of me.' She pointed at Hermann. 'He says I'm a fool, you pretend there's some old man out there who knows where the treasure is and him . . .' She threw a look of disgust at Pinsada and shook her head. 'Excuse me, gentlemen.'

Pinsada stared at the floor as she strutted away, and Hermann shrugged. 'She is very passionate, that one,' he explained. 'Dynamite in the sack, I've heard, but a short fuse. Shame. She liked you.'

Lenny held up a finger. He knew women inside out. 'If you'll excuse me, lads . . .'

He caught up with Mercedes as she was going into the ladies'. She turned to face him, putting a hand on her hip and tipping her head to one side. Lenny could see straight down her top.

'I was only having a giggle, sweetheart,' he explained. 'Didn't mean to upset you.'

'So who is this man?'

'What man?'

'The old man. He doesn't exist, does he?'

'El Sid? Course he does,' insisted Lenny. 'Just didn't want to tell you in front of those two.'

'So what is his name, this old man? He is not El Cid. El Cid has been dead for centuries.' She licked her lips, looking up at Lenny with eyes that could light fires.

Lenny felt himself go hot and cold. He swallowed. 'You're too young to remember David Bowie. There's a Starman, looking at the sky. He's forgotten where the gold is and he can't remember why.'

'You're drunk,' said Mercedes, turning away.

Lenny caught her arm and turned her back. 'I'm off my head, darling,' agreed Lenny, 'but that's his name: Sidney Starman. El Sid.'

Mercedes looked into his eyes, searching for a glimmer of truth, then glanced quickly around the bar. 'Want to go somewhere else?' she asked. 'We can get away from the others.'

'Go on, then.' Lynyrd Skynyrd's 'Freebird' was playing – an

apt tune, thought Lenny, considering he'd just pulled without even buying a drink.

'Wait here,' she said. 'I have to use the toilet.'

'I'll get my bag,' said Lenny. He strolled back to the table like a vaudeville performer, bending down to grab his holdall. 'You'll have to continue without me, gents,' he leered, winking at the gipsy. 'You've either got it, mate, or you haven't.'

'Bullshitter,' muttered Pinsada, watching Lenny sashay back to the bar. 'Waste of my time.'

Hermann shook his head. 'He may be full of shit, but he's the real deal. I've seen the proof. The whole thing happened as foretold.'

Pinsada groaned. 'Leave out the supernatural stuff, Cruz.'

Hermann raised his eyebrows. 'The witch told me that one day a fool would walk down off the mountain and hand me a golden coin, and that, my friend, is exactly what happened. I'm sorry if it scares you, but there it is.'

'Did your witch tell you how we were going to find this great hoard after the fool had gone?'

'I've got great faith in your sister,' replied Hermann. 'I'm sure she can squeeze most things out of most men.'

The gipsy moved his eyes slowly across Hermann's face. 'Don't ever make remarks about my sister, fat man, and don't be wasting my time. I've got a crew sitting outside costing me money.'

'You mean your brother,' sighed Hermann.

'And Escobar.' The gipsy was on the edge of his seat, bent almost double. He lit a cigarette and looked intently at Hermann.

'Escobar? Who's Escobar?' Hermann had told him to bring known faces.

'Paco Escobar.'

'I thought he was dead.'

'So does everybody.'

'So who fell overboard?'

Pinsada shrugged. 'Some gay guy from Barcelona. Escobar owed him a favour. Bought him a cruise.'

Hermann shook his head in dismay. Paco Escobar was an associate of the Pinsada brothers who had played on his name to develop a reputation as the meanest bailiff in Aragon. Moving on from debt recovery and repossessions, Escobar had become an expert in the resolution of planning disputes and was chief suspect in the murder of a lawyer from Castellon who had opposed a thirty-million-euro marina project. The case against him had collapsed when Escobar was reported missing, believed drowned, after falling overboard from a Mediterranean cruise ship. Now he was back, and his timing was perfect.

'What the fuck were you thinking?' hissed Hermann.

Pinsada stretched out his hands. 'Escobar doesn't take orders,' he insisted. 'And if there are necks to be wrung, he's the man. I need him gone – he's got family in Colombia – and I made a deal.'

'You made a deal? With a fucking psychopath? With what?'

Pinsada took a drag on his cigarette. 'I cut him in on the gold.'

'There is no fucking gold yet. Jesus!'

'Yeah, well, that's not what you told me on the phone. Way I heard it, there was seven tons waiting to be squeezed out of an Englishman. I told Paco that if he got blood on his hands, he would have the cash to wash them in Medellin.'

'And the way I understood it, this was between my family and yours, like always.'

Pinsada opened his mouth to reply, but Hermann stopped him with an outstretched palm as his phone crab-walked across the table. He flipped it open, yelling to make himself heard over the loud music: 'Cruz.'

'It's me, Mercedes. I'm in the toilet. Can you hear me?'

The jeweller frowned. 'What are you doing?'

'I'm peeing. The Englishman told me a name: Sidney Starman. Heard of him?'

Pinsada raised his eyebrows as Hermann Cruz went very pale. 'Where is he?'

'Outside the toilets.'

Hermann leapt to his feet, knocking his drink into the ashtray. Pinsada still looked perplexed.

'What's he wearing?'

'Who?'

'Sidney Starman.'

'How should I know?'

'You said he was outside the toilet.'

'Not him, stupid. The Englishman.'

Hermann slapped a flabby palm to his shiny forehead. 'Now listen to me, Mercedes. I need to know where Sidney Starman is. Do you understand? You do whatever it takes to find out, and I'll buy you a car.'

'You'll buy me a car? Are you nuts?'

'I'm serious. I need to know where that old man is, right now. You tell me, and I'll buy you a car. That's the deal.' He snapped his phone shut and slumped into his seat as though slapped. 'Holy Mary, mother of God,' he whispered, staring into space like a man touched by fate. 'Holy fucking Christ!'

Pinsada scratched his chin. 'You're buying my sister a car? Who the hell is this Sidney Starman?'

Hermann was pouring *cava* with trembling hands.

'Hey, Cruz,' called Pinsada. 'I asked you who Sidney Starman was.'

Hermann took a sip of wine and turned his head very slowly to look at Pinsada. 'I want Escobar with us tonight,' he breathed, 'and I want him to take his time.' He pointed a wavering finger at the gipsy. 'You tell Escobar I want him to bring the full horror of the fucking Inquisition with him tonight. You understand?'

Pinsada nodded.

287

'Good,' grinned Hermann. A fat bead of sweat rolled down his cheek. 'There's going to be screaming, bleeding and pleading tonight, Enrique. Do you think you can handle it?'

'Two things,' said Pinsada. 'Number one: don't fucking insult me, fat boy. And number two: who the fuck is this Sidney Starman?'

Hermann drained his wine. 'Sidney Starman is a corpse,' he said quietly.

'Freebird' came to an end and 'Honky Tonk Woman' began, as though the barman had known that Guadeloupe Serrano Suner was about to walk into the bar. She breezed in wearing high heels and weeds, dragging a paunchy playboy in her wake. Lenny was at the bar, trying to explain that he wanted twenty-four bottles of Heineken, a litre of vodka and a couple of Bacardi Breezers for the lady. He didn't see Guadeloupe come in and he didn't spot Mercedes emerging from the ladies'. Mercedes reached up and stroked Lenny's cheek before giving his rather large backside a playful squeeze, delighted by the prospect that there was a car out there with her name on it. She was less pleased, however, when Guadeloupe, twenty years her senior and twice her bodyweight again, slapped her in the chops. Hermann watched as Guadeloupe followed up with a straight right to Lenny's jaw, knocking him flat.

'I've just saved myself the price of a car,' he murmured to himself, then he turned to Pinsada. 'Drink up – I know exactly where to find Sidney Starman.'

16

'Why the hell did you toss him over a goddamned cliff?' seethed Cobb. 'Why the fuck couldn't you just cut his throat like a normal guy would?'

'He fell,' insisted Sidney. He was sweating from exertion, shock, pain and fever, the gash in his shoulder smarting like an acid burn. He was thirsty, and the cave was cold, and he desperately needed to rest.

'Sleep when you're dead,' suggested Cobb. 'What are we going to do about the body? Can you get it back?'

'Why?'

Cobb sighed angrily, leaning forward on his golden throne, his coat draped around his shoulders and the pistol in his hand.

Villafranca moved slowly in the background, carrying gold coin with cuffed hands from an open crate on the floor of the cave to another in the back of the truck, using a helmet as a bucket.

'Why do you think? Give me a break, kid, I'm not at my best.' A black stain stretched from armpit to halfway down his thigh. 'One minute you're telling me the mountain is crawling with troops. Next you're telling me you've left Kreuz on the rocks like a fucking signpost. Then you're asking me why we can't leave him there. Get a fucking grip!'

'Oh bugger,' murmured Sidney.

'You've killed us all, kid,' announced Cobb. 'Hey, Villafranca! Quit loading. There's no point any more. Someone light me a last fucking cigar.'

'We'd better prepare our positions,' suggested Sidney.

'Our position is un–fucking–tenable, to use the correct military terminology,' hissed Cobb. 'The bastards will burn us out. They'll throw half a dozen grenades in here and they'll suffocate us.'

'So let's go. Leave the bloody gold. It's not worth dying for.'

Cobb coughed, vomiting blood, and then hawking to clear his throat. 'Course it's worth dying for, fool. It's probably the only thing worth dying for. We either take it with us or we die protecting it.' He bent down, gasping, and picked a coin from the floor. 'See this? It's the only fucking cause I ever believed in.' Shrunken, drained and dying, the last of Cobb's life seemed concentrated in his eyes. 'You leave if you want to, but me and him' – he jerked his sidearm towards the gipsy – 'we'll go down defending this cave.' He turned to Villafranca and explained his fate in Spanish.

The gipsy nodded. 'I thank you for including me in your last stand.' He didn't look so grateful.

Sidney chewed his lip, his jaw aching from the throbbing in his shoulder. His thirst felt like a disease and his body felt poisoned with fatigue. If death promised a long, painless, dreamless sleep, he would welcome its embrace. 'I'll stay,' he heard himself say.

Cobb didn't thank him. He pointed instead at a crack in the cave's ceiling, a fist–sized fissure thirty feet long that would one day bring the roof down. 'Fetch that bag of dynamite from the truck and jam a bunch of it in there. Stick a few seconds' worth of detcord on it and let it hang.' He raised his eyebrows in a mirror of Sidney's expression. 'Might work,' he said. 'Last man standing lights the fuse.'

As Sidney kneeled on the roof of the truck and began wedging the dynamite into the cleft, Villafranca made his pitch. 'Let me die like a bandit, Major,' he urged. 'Give me a rifle.'

'Shut up,' replied Cobb, 'and carry on loading.'

'But what is the point if we're not getting out of here?'

'Because it warms my heart to see you sweat. Now get loading.'

The gipsy dropped to one knee. 'Major, I'm sorry I stabbed you, but I was only doing what you'd have done in my place. You and me, we're the same.'

'Don't insult me.'

'At least let me dress your wound. I'm a gipsy. We have healing hands.'

'You're a snake on a goddamned stick.'

'Take off your coat.'

Sidney pushed the single, short length of detonating cord into the centre stick of explosives, crimped it and let it hang. He peered over the edge of the truck to where Cobb was being attended to by Villafranca, his Colt buried in the gipsy's curls.

'Cord's too short,' he called.

Cobb looked at the booby-trapped crack, his gaze following the line to where it ended a few inches beneath the cave roof.

'Looks fine.'

'But you'd have to be right underneath the stuff to set it off.'

Cobb yelped and cracked the gipsy on the ear with the butt of his pistol. 'I swear I'll kill you, Villafranca. Healing hands, my butt.' He looked sadly at Sidney. 'Kid, I'm not sure you've grabbed the concept of the last stand. Leave the fuse dangling. I wouldn't want it any other way.'

The enemy troops arrived half an hour later. They approached the cave from the east, scurrying cautiously along the track and squinting into the afternoon sun. Sidney lay between the front wheels of the truck, his position protected by a double wall of bullion crates. He shot two soldiers as their comrades stood and gaped. Cobb hit a rifleman dressed in Spanish uniform in the belly with a burst from the machine-gun, dropping him to his knees with one hand on his wound and another groping for his rosary. Sidney thought he recognised the soldier – the birthmark

291

on his right cheek seemed familiar – and then he was gone, knocked backwards in a pink mist as Cobb's next shot hit him in the throat. The sulphurous stink of cordite lingered in the cave as the enemy withdrew.

'German gunners,' called Cobb. 'You'd have thought they'd have sent infantry. Jesus must love you, kid.'

'They can only get at us from the flank,' replied Sidney. 'They're exposed before they can get a shot from the front.'

'Think we can kill them all?'

'Not enough ammunition.'

'Listen: let the next guy get close enough to grab before you drop him. We'll have his canteen and his weapon.'

Sidney gave a thumbs-up and looked to his front, thankful for the small mercy that the gipsy had shot his left shoulder and not his right. Pain from the wound still dominated his consciousness, preoccupying him like a chill wind from which no shelter could be found, but since Villafranca had cleaned and dressed his handiwork with Armagnac and a soiled shirt sleeve it felt a little better.

'Cover the front,' called Cobb. 'I'm going to recruit Villafranca.'

'You what?' protested Sidney. 'Are you barmy?'

'What have we got to lose? They'll kill him too if they find him here.'

'But what if he runs?'

Cobb jingled the handcuff keys. 'He won't be running nowhere.' He paused, as though considering the consequences of an unexpected idea. 'If by some miracle you get out of here, kid, Frankie Cobb's recommendation is that you leave the country.'

'What about you?'

'I'm going nowhere without my gold.'

'And Villafranca?'

'He gets my second-last bullet. Listen to me: there's a ship called *La Esmeralda* leaving Tarragona on the fourth. Captain's a guy called Allnut. Tell him I sent you – he'll understand if I'm not there. The ship's bound for Veracruz in Mexico. Ask the captain nicely and he might drop you in Algiers. If you can't make it by the fourth, there's a bar by the docks called Racine. The owner's a Belgian broad named Grace. Give her my regards and she'll sell you an exit visa.'

'What am I going to buy it with?'

Cobb looked disappointed. 'What do you think?'

Sidney shrugged. 'Gold?'

'You don't miss a thing, Sid the Kid. Fill your boots. Take as much as you can carry.'

Sidney closed one eye. It eased the nausea. 'Why do you think I'll survive?'

'I'm not saying you will, just that you deserve to.'

'Why me and not you? Or Simenon, or that girl in the beret?'

'Cos you're not cut out for this line of work. You're the only one in the neighbourhood still fighting for a cause. And unlike gold, which is real, and can buy a man fine clothes, beautiful women and exotic alcohol, there ain't no cause in this world worth dying for.'

'Those Germans out there wouldn't agree.'

'Oh yeah? You think the fucking Condor Legion is here because we're republican? Wrong. They're here because of the gold, because Gipsy fucking Rose Lee in there cut a deal with their boss and because the late Mr Kreuz left them a trail.' He swept a lick of hair from his face, leaving bloody streaks on his forehead. 'Couple of days ago you told Klee you came to Spain to kill Germans. You've just nailed two – three if you count Kreuz – so that's your ambition fulfilled. Give up while you're ahead. Go home or go to Mexico, marry a plain girl, get yourself a pretty mistress, some kids and a dog and live the rest of your life in peace. It's what I should have done twenty fucking years ago.'

★

A good night at Ke Tal had turned into chaos. Guadeloupe had arrived out of nowhere and decked Lenny. As he went down he dropped his takeouts, spilling lager, vodka and broken glass all over the floor, and as he struggled back to his feet he met a barstool coming the other way that sent him back down again. It was, he realised drunkenly, the second time he'd been flattened by an older woman in a week, and he wasn't having it. He jumped up and grabbed Guadeloupe by the wrists, but Victor Velasquez, a haulage contractor who had escorted Guadeloupe from the wake, wasn't prepared to stand by and see his lady friend attacked by a hooligan.

'Hey, hey, hey,' he shouted, pushing between the pair, bravely attempting to separate them until Lenny felled him with an elbow to the throat.

Guadeloupe shook herself free, lifting glasses from the bar and hurling them at Lenny. Several missed, hitting other drinkers, whose indignation was drowned beneath the flood of inventive invective gushing from Guadeloupe's carefully painted, but indescribably foul, mouth. A short-haired woman with an earful of rings tossed a bottle of San Miguel that hit Guadeloupe on the forehead, stunning her into silence for three long seconds before she hefted another barstool that flew over Lenny's head and knocked her attacker flat. The short-haired woman's long-term companion, with even shorter hair and more earrings, pushed Lenny aside and threw a punch at Guadeloupe. Victor, his tight black trousers and loose white shirt stained with spilled beer, struggled to his knees and threw his arms around Lenny's waist in a gesture that was somewhere between a rugby tackle and a prayer. The short-haired woman, now recovered from her stool strike, waded forwards to assist her girlfriend and tripped over Victor, who sank back to the floor, taking Lenny's tracksuit pants with him. Everyone froze as Lenny stood at the bar with his trousers around his ankles, until Guadeloupe pointed breathlessly at his naked crotch and said, 'All this violence, all this trouble, over that little thing?'

Then the police arrived.

Montalban was a small town, far from the coast and the hedonistic nightlife of Barcelona. Madrid was even further away, and apart from the hikers, bikers and bone-collectors who passed through every summer, the commune had seen few of the tourist euros enjoyed by so many municipalities in the kingdom. Police Chief Pablo Menendez Berrueco, however, could see that changing, and the evidence was now being escorted to the back of his car. He felt quite excited and rather proud that he had just arrested his first English lager lout, and while the charges were nowhere near as serious as those laid by his CNP colleagues down by the sea, he still felt that a drunk and disorderly with criminal damage, indecent exposure and resisting arrest was an honourable welcome to the British Tourist Club. As two of his constables forced the confused and emotional prisoner into the patrol car he spotted Cruz leaving the bar. 'Hermann!' called Pablo. 'Your professional services are required.' In addition to his jewellery business and his money-lending operations, Hermann Cruz served the community as interpreter for the town hall. 'Ask him if he's on any medication, will you?' A soft drizzle was falling, as though a cold cloud had slipped down the mountain.

'Of course,' nodded Hermann. He leaned into the window of the patrol car, his back to the chief.

Lenny raised his eyebrows in an expression that seemed to accept no responsibility whatsoever for his arrest. He was, thought Hermann, a most irritating man, and he was overwhelmed with a desire to grind his face into the shit. He had known the idiot for less than five hours and yet in that short time he had been insulted, patronised and belittled by that caustic and typically English arrogance.

'I have to ask you if you're on any medication,' he announced coldly.

'Only the stuff you sold me, Pancho,' winked Lenny. 'Tell you what: have a word with Plod – I'll bung him a wad – and I won't mention where I got the Boutros Boutros from.'

Hermann felt his throat swell. He took a deep breath. 'My name's not Pancho. It's Hermann Gutierrez Cruz, and I want you to remember that. I'm the official interpreter in this town. I speak German, French and English, and I'm the one they'll send for when it's time to talk. I'm going to your hotel now, with a few special friends, and when I've finished with your friend Mr Sidney fucking Starman I'm going to break his fucking back.' He leaned closer to Lenny. 'Several witnesses will say you were the last man they saw him with, and if you want to say any different you'll have to say it through me.' He nodded to the policeman. 'He seems very disturbed, Pablo. He's ranting, making no sense, but he's not on any meds.'

'You snidey little wanker,' spat Lenny.

'See what I mean?' shrugged Hermann. 'I'll be on my mobile if you need me.'

The chief drove the prisoner to the station, deciding, with some disappointment, that while undoubtedly as strong and as stupid as an ox, this was not a dangerous man. 'Sit here,' he said, pointing at a plastic chair. He called for a custody officer to fill in the forms and a recruit to act as guard. 'Process him, cross-reference him and lock him up to sleep it off. I'll see him in the morning.' He scratched his armpit, handed Lenny's passport to the recruit, and went home for supper.

Lenny sat on the wipe-clean chair and tried to think like a river. He'd managed to lose two wraps of cocaine down the back of the seat in the patrol car and he had enough cash to pay any reasonable fine they wished to impose. As far as he knew, he was being charged with D&D and causing an affray, neither of which seemed that serious. But they were going to bang him up overnight and *that* was disastrous.

'You come with me, please,' said a humourless-looking young

policeman, and Lenny followed him into a windowless office divided into six little interview suites. There was a calendar pinned to the frayed partition: it was St Agatha's Day, patron saint of jewellers. Next to it was a dog-eared poster warning of terrorism. Beside that, just above the cop's left shoulder, was a computer printout, one of dozens of daily bulletins hanging from a bulldog clip. It seemed to show Europe's most wanted, and there, next to Mohammed Bin Masoud and below Felix Ottermeier, was the slightly bemused face of Leonard Arthur Knowles, caught on a cheap CCTV camera waving a tube of Pringles as though he were in some cut-price commercial.

Lenny stifled a gasp as he saw himself in black and white, feeling as though his heart was packing its things and walking out on him. The cop called a colleague for assistance as Lenny attempted to project an air of confused innocence.

'Do you have anything sharp in your pockets?' asked the first cop.

Lenny shook his head and the officer searched him, dropping his cigarettes, lighter, wallet and a tiny aerosol of pheromone spray into a plastic basket. 'OK, sit down, please,' said the cop.

'That's not mine, mate,' insisted Lenny, pointing at the aerosol, his hands still in cuffs.

The colleague left and the first cop leaned over a computer keyboard, studying Lenny's passport. 'Look at me please,' he said, pointing a digital camera at the prisoner. He checked his screen. 'OK, one more. Look at that wall . . . thank you.'

Lenny looked around the office as his name was tapped with agonising slowness into the ancient computer, his mind whirring like a Pentium processor. The police station was all but empty – every couple of minutes he heard the faintly echoing, deeply bored farewells of officers clocking off for the night and all the time the death-row ticking of the keyboard as the cop filled in the form with the alacrity of a dyslexic monkey. Lenny tried to remain calm, but the unfairness of the situation was making him angry. All he'd wanted to do was cash in his coin, have a few beers and sod off to the coast for a few days. They were decent, honest, straightforward intentions, and if it hadn't been for bloody Sidney Starman changing his will at the last minute, he would never have walked off the job, and this disaster would never have happened.

El Sid had also never bothered to mention that he was already known in these parts and right now that fat jeweller was on his way to La Cerda, with his special friends and murderous intent. Nick was incapable of defending himself, let alone anyone else, and Lenny could see exactly how some smart-arse Spanish brief would tell the story. Two heartless jailbirds befriend a frail old man and intimidate him into paying for a lager frenzy on the Costa Brava. They blaze a trail of crime and destruction across northern Spain before reaching Zaragoza, where they force the old man to sell an heirloom to fuel their depravity. On the way back to the coast something goes wrong: they argue, and Leonard Arthur Knowles kills his partner and the old man. A vending-machine repairman would be wheeled out to recall giving an agitated Englishman a lift into town. He would remember the accused mentioning that he had hurt his back while digging. Guadeloupe, anxious to keep her own murderous conspiracy under wraps, would either remember nothing or accuse him of coercing her into the sack by threatening to *matar* her *tio*. Finally, upstanding Montalban citizen Hermann Cruz would recall buying a coin from the accused, and then bumping into him in a local bar where, he would recall, the prisoner seemed anxious, drug-addled and predisposed to violence. The best Lenny could hope for was to be sectioned under the Spanish equivalent of the Mental Health Act.

The office seemed to telescope as Lenny suddenly became acutely aware of his own breathing, of the pulse in his ears and of the true depth of the shit he had fallen into. Sidney and Nick were in mortal danger – not from Hermann, who looked incapable of slapping a puppy – but from that wicked-looking gipsy. The 'special friends' were likely to be closer to Enrique Pinsada than to the fat jeweller on the social scale, and Lenny was more than familiar with the cruel creativity of the Pikey mind.

Behind the desk Officer Lorenzo Aceitunilla was cursing Windows and wielding the mouse like a student with a pointing trowel. It was all a matter of cross-referencing the arrest form with the database on the mainframe and Lorenzo was wrestling with a total mental blank. Some speccy kid with a goatee had been in the commissariat only a month ago, running a refresher course that Lorenzo had attended with no enthusiasm whatsoever. He knew it was a matter of opening something and typing a password and then entering the prisoner's name, but he was damned if he could remember how to do it. He rose wearily from the desk and pushed his head around the partition to consult with his colleague. 'Tell us how to cross-reference collars again, will you?' he asked. PlayStation he could do. PCs he couldn't. He was a crime-fighter, not an IT geek.

His colleague sighed. 'Watch,' he said. 'You go into Cynet and you enter your password. Simple as that.'

'Then what?'

'If you look at the screen, it's pretty obvious. You go File, Open, and then you enter the arrest-form reference.'

'Which is where?'

The other cop looked at him. 'You've got to learn this, man. The arrest-form reference is at the top of the screen when you save the form.'

'Hang on,' said Lorenzo. He returned to his desk and copied Lenny's reference onto a Post-It note. 'Two minutes, OK?' he told Lenny.

His colleague typed in the reference. 'Then you hit this button here, and sit back and wait. This one will take a bit longer because he's not Spanish.'

299

It was not Lenny's lucky night. Down in Teruel, in the main police station in Calle Cordoba, red lights started flashing. An automated message flew back along the copper cables requesting human verification of what the computer already knew to be the truth. A man arrested for minor offences in Montalban was almost a perfect visual match with one of two men wanted for the armed robbery of a petrol station in La Rioja, and according to Lorenzo's arrest sheet his name was Leonard Arthur Knowles.

'Holy shit,' gasped Lorenzo's colleague. 'We'd better call the chief. He arrested him – he needs to be in on this.' He looked up at Lorenzo. 'Where's the suspect now?'

'At the custody desk,' replied Lorenzo, peering around the partition to check. 'Oh fuck!'

Lenny had gone.

'I'm wondering what your fondest memory of this insignificant little war will be,' called Cobb.

The two remaining members of the Field Repair Company, supported by Angel Villafranca, had just repulsed a frontal attack by a section of enthusiastic, brave and ultimately incompetent German artillerymen. Two lay dead in the gathering gloom, and another was dragging himself on his elbow towards the lip of the escarpment.

'I haven't had my fondest memory yet,' replied Sidney grimly. He winced as Cobb fired a burst from the machine-gun that broke the man's back, killing him just inches from cover. 'Bastards are getting closer all the time,' noted Sidney, his voice a thirst-ravaged whisper. 'Soon as they attack in force we're buggered.'

'They're gunners,' said Cobb, 'not infantrymen, and they're green as grass. We'll hold them off as long as our ammo lasts. But they'll never let us leave.' He hawked a gob of bloodstained scum onto the floor. 'Christ, but I'm thirsty. Think you can reach that fellow in the doorway?'

The nearest German corpse was ten yards away, sprawled like a dropped doll in the mouth of the cave.

'Probably,' nodded Sidney, his head swirling as if he were drunk. 'I'll try to get his canteen.'

'Try to get the whole body, rifle and all.'

'The whole body?'

'That's what I said, kid. He'll be carrying food. ammo, water, field dressings, dirty pictures from Berlin and all sorts in that uniform, and if they see you going through his pockets out there they'll skin you alive. Drag him back here. If he's wearing a nice watch, I'll let you keep it.'

It took Sidney twenty minutes to drag the corpse into cover, and for all his effort the felt-covered canteen on the dead man's belt held just a couple of mouthfuls of sour water.

'He stinks!' complained Villafranca, reloading the machine-gun magazine from the German's pouches.

'He's crapped his pants,' explained Cobb, rifling the dead man's uniform. 'Too much meat in his diet. Look: a sausage! Want a bite?'

'I want water,' croaked Sidney.

Cobb's eyes glittered in the darkness. 'Think you could find some?'

Sidney swallowed bile. Every muscle ached like a dose of the flu and his jaw throbbed like tetanus. He blinked slowly. 'Find some what?'

'Water, kid. Cool, clear, mountain water.'

'Where?'

Cobb waved weakly, dismissively, towards the night. 'Out there. In a well, or a stream bed, or a tinkling fucking spring in some enchanted forest clearing. The Hun has probably pulled back to the tree line to wait for daybreak and reinforcements. What do you reckon?'

They swayed like two alcoholics, mumbling and stumbling over the rank body of a German volunteer. Sidney reckoned he would trade every ounce of Orlov's gold for a goatskin of water, and would never regret the transaction.

'Leave your rifle,' said Cobb. 'Take the Luger and the bota, and fill your haversack with gold. You might have to buy your way out of trouble.'

Sidney didn't say goodbye. He was only going out for water.

Cobb called him back. 'Here,' he said, pushing a wristwatch into Sidney's hand. The strap was sticky with blood. 'I told you I'd get you a nice watch. Keep a close eye on the time – we'll be waiting for you.'

'He wanted me to go,' explained Sidney to Nick, 'and he never expected to see me come back, with or without water.'

The bota, with its necklace of tarnished silver camels, lay on the table between them. The menu that night had featured *lomo de cerda*, a welcome change from the usual trout and the only other recipe in Tio Pepe's portfolio. Unfortunately, by the time the pair had presented themselves for dinner the pork loin was all gone.

'Gone?' asked Sidney.

Tio Pepe shrugged and nodded.

'We're the only bloody guests! Who ate it?'

The aged proprietor wiped his chin. 'I'm sorry, gentlemen. It's very difficult trying to provide a high-class service on one's own. The generator has gone down and I'm cooking on a woodstove. May I offer a bottle of wine as compensation?'

'You may,' agreed Sidney, 'and what's to eat?'

Tio Pepe cringed. 'Perhaps a trout, grilled, with *migas del pastor*?' Nick watched him shuffle away and wondered what Lenny was eating that night.

'Do you think he'll come back?' asked Sidney.

'Hard to say. Depends if he's gone on a bender or made a serious attempt to get home.'

Tio Pepe returned like a ghost in the gloom and silently

placed a dusty, unlabelled bottle on the table. Sidney poured, sipped and winced. 'Mr Knowles has no money. I can't see him going on a bender.'

Nick raised his eyebrows. 'Lenny has never let the lack of cash stop him drinking. He used to get Special Brew smuggled into prison. I reckon if he's gone drinking, he'll be back, and if he's gone hitching, he won't.' He shrugged. 'We'll manage.'

An hour later Sidney pushed away his untouched plate. His appetite had gone now, as though his body saw no point in processing further nutrition. He took a slurp of the harsh black wine, feeling the acid shrink his gums. The end, he felt, was very near, and his memories were projected on a mind that seemed clearer, cleaner and sharper than ever before. His life, he realised, was under review, like a book of done deeds to be presented to St Peter. There was much to admit.

'I remember sliding down a cliff on my backside, then seeing way down below me that great big circle of cypresses and thinking there must be a grand house there. The whole valley was lit up by an enormous yellow moon, and I saw a squadron of their bombers flying across it like a flock of Canada geese. That's the way to fight a war, I thought: have your tea, nip out and bomb something, and get home in time for last orders.' His voice was quiet and his speech slow, as though his batteries were all but exhausted.

'That's why you joined the RAF?' said Nick.

'No chance of being executed by your own side, you see,' replied Sidney, as though he'd given the same explanation countless times before. 'A pilot flies above the fog of war.'

'So what happened?'

'Well, I was weighed down with a sack of gold, wasn't I? And I was weak from the gunshot wound in my shoulder. I remember I made it as far as the outermost olive tree, and I sat up against it for a moment, just to catch my breath. I saw flashes, like summer lightning, reflected in the leaves and along the silver branches of the tree, and when I looked round the whole northern horizon was lit up. Cobb had told us there would be an artillery barrage, a feint, and by God he was right! The front was only eight miles away, and you could feel the ground shaking from the explosions. I turned around to watch it and must have passed out. They found me under the tree the next morning.'

'The Germans?'

'Wearing this?' Sidney tapped his watch. 'I wouldn't have been here now if they'd caught me wearing this! No . . .' He paused, his voice dropping to a mournful murmur. 'No, Mr Crick. Someone else found me.'

Nick heard the purr of an engine moments before the headlight beams probed the candlelit dining room. It could have been anybody – locals, tourists, even the generator repairman – and Nick was surprised that the first thought to come unbidden to mind was that the new arrival might be the girl from Los Cipreses. He was to be sorely disappointed. The visitors were Hermann Cruz, the Pinsada brothers and their pot-bellied assassin, Paco Escobar.

'They've locked the door,' whispered Nick.

'I noticed,' replied Sidney.

'Shit,' said Nick. 'Where's fucking Lenny when we need him? Do you think they're bandits?'

Sidney raised his eyebrows and drained his glass. When he put it down, Hermann Cruz was standing beside him, extending a podgy pink hand. 'Mr Sidney Starman, I presume?'

Sidney refilled his glass, took a reflective sip and then turned to face the fat jeweller. 'And you are?'

Hermann dropped his hand and smiled. 'I'm sorry – we've never been introduced, but I've been waiting to meet you all my life.'

'Delighted, I'm sure,' muttered Sidney.

'You knew my father very well.'

'I did?'

'Oh yes, Sidney Starman, you did. His name was Alberto Cruz. Does that ring any bells? No? Well,' Hermann licked his lips, hamming it up, 'in England his name would have been Albert Cross, and in France they would have called him, let me see, Albert Croix.' He placed his hands on the back of Sidney's chair and tipped it backwards, spinning it on its rear legs so the old man faced him. 'In Germany, Mr Sidney Starman, my father was known as Albrecht Kreuz.' He let the chair rock forward, stopping it with a finger in the centre of Sidney's forehead. 'Does that jog your memory, old man?'

Sidney glanced at Nick. 'You owe me nothing, Mr Crick. Save yourself.'

Even if Nick had been capable of escape, he had missed his chance. Paco Escobar stood behind his chair, gently squeezing his shoulders in a massage that only increased the tension.

'Who's that?' demanded Hermann.

The wild boars looked down from the walls like expert witnesses.

'He's no one,' called Sidney. 'Just a hitch-hiker. Nothing to do with this.'

'I don't believe you,' said Hermann, 'and there's no time for deceit, Sidney Starman. Do you have any idea how long I've waited for you to come back?'

Enrique Pinsada's brother Octavio, a tall, short-haired man with a narrow face wasted by prison and cocaine, was strapping the old man to the chair with silver duct tape while Enrique held him down. Sidney stared ahead, affecting bored resignation. Escobar studied Nick's neck, rolling his tongue along the back of his teeth and feeling the sap rising.

'Two lifetimes,' announced Hermann. 'That's how long I've waited for this day.'

'Just ask him where the fucking gold is,' said Enrique.

'I know what to ask him, thanks,' nodded Hermann irritably. He held two fingers in Sidney's face. 'Two lifetimes . . .'

'There's nothing wrong with my hearing,' snapped Sidney.

Enrique shook his head in dismay and turned to Tio Pepe. 'Get me a bottle of Scotch,' he ordered.

Octavio tore off a six-inch strip of sticky tape to cover Nick's mouth.

'Wait,' said Escobar, picking up a marker pen. 'Check this out.' He drew a wide, toothy grin on the silver tape and slapped it over Nick's downturned mouth. 'That's brilliant,' he grinned. 'Enrique, look at this: is this funny or what?'

'Two lifetimes,' repeated Hermann. He'd spent all his life rehearsing this speech. 'How do you pay back two lifetimes?'

'Yes, yes, I've got the two-lifetimes bit,' sighed Sidney. 'Get to the point.'

Hermann felt his breath shortening and his cheeks flushing. He stood over Sidney, staring down at the old man in petulant rage. Sometimes words were inadequate, he decided, striking Sidney hard across the face with the back of his hand. Sidney rolled with the blow, tears streaming down his face as his aged flesh swelled. He knew what was coming, and took his time before looking back at his tormentor. Hermann's thick gold ring drew blood on the second blow, splitting Sidney's cheek.

'You have all of your father's cruelty and none of his imagination,' said Sidney.

'You crippled him,' hissed Hermann.

'I was trying to kill him. He was a traitor.'

'He was serving his country. You and the American were the traitors.'

Sidney raised an eyebrow. 'That depends on your point of view, but I'm sure you didn't wait two lifetimes to tell me that. I take it Herr Kreuz is dead now?'

'He died in '77.'

'I'm amazed he survived the fall.'

'He was unarmed. He wanted to surrender. You pushed him off that cliff.'

Sidney took a deep breath. 'He fell, he jumped, he was pushed. What difference does it make?'

'It broke his back. Fractured his skull. If it hadn't been for our troops he would have died there.'

'But he didn't, did he? He lived a long and happy life and raised a delightful son.' Sidney cast a critical glance at Hermann's clothing. 'Although I take it he didn't find the gold.'

Hermann leaned close to Sidney, grabbing his little finger and bending it backwards. 'I want you to try to understand the pain he went through. Forty years of mental anguish and physical suffering, searching his mind and these damn mountains for that mine. The last thing he remembered was the drive from Teruel. Do you recall that journey? Can you imagine the agony of knowing that you'd seen, touched, a fortune, and forgotten where it was?' He increased the pressure on Sidney's finger, wanting to hear it snap but lacking the strength. At last he let it go and dragged up a chair. 'My father used to tell me a story about a goatherd who captured a wood sprite. The sprite said that if the goatherd let him go, he would lead him to a great treasure. Wood sprites, as you know, are honest, but cunning. They cannot lie, but they'll cheat. The *Nisse* took the goatherd to a cave stacked with gold and asked the goatherd to release him. Knowing that the sprite could not take the treasure back, the goatherd let him go. It seemed a deal well done, and when the sprite produced a silver flask and two tiny cups, they drank a toast to celebrate. The goatherd took what he could carry, and went home to fetch a donkey cart, unaware of the secret effects of the wood sprite's spirit. By the time he reached the village, he remembered nothing.' Hermann pulled his chair closer, his face shiny in the lamplight. 'All he had was a pocketful of gold that he couldn't explain. It was soon spent, and he passed the rest of his life wondering where he'd got it. Years later he caught the same wood sprite stealing milk from his goats. It resurrected a long-dead memory and he asked the sprite if he remembered him. The *Nisse* looked at the goatherd and apologised. 'It's the stuff we drink,' he explained. 'It ruins the memory.'

Sidney stared at Hermann and shook his head. 'I'm too old for fairy tales, Mr Kreuz.'

The Pinsadas frowned as Hermann punched Sidney hard in the face, tipping the chair backwards and dropping the old man to the floor. Nick yelled from behind his grinning duct-tape gag, struggled to his feet with his chair strapped to his back like a parachute and collapsed as Escobar threw a roundhouse at his ear.

'You're a fucking animal, Cruz!' announced Enrique. 'He must be ninety. Are you trying to kill him?'

'You're never too old for justice,' spat Hermann.

'For fuck's sake, man,' said Octavio, looking at the bleeding pensioner. 'That's harsh.'

Hermann glared at Tio Pepe. 'Get me some water.'

Enrique put a hand tattooed with a spider's web on Hermann's shoulder. 'Hold up, Fat Boy. You smack granddad up any more and you'll kill him. It doesn't take much at that age.' He glanced at Octavio. 'Remember that old bastard who sold us that Merc?'

His brother nodded. 'One minute he was here. The next, gone.' He snapped his fingers.

'See? Is he the only one who knows where the treasure is?'

'He's the only one here who's seen it,' nodded Hermann.

'So the young one is surplus to requirements?' Enrique was pointing at Nick.

'That's correct.'

'So we work on the young one and let the old one watch.'

'We should butt-fuck him,' grinned Escobar, 'and leave the smiley face attached.'

'Get the old fella upright first,' ordered Enrique.

Tio Pepe shuffled up with a glass of water on a tray. 'I'm afraid we have no ice, *señor*,' he mumbled. 'The generator . . .'

Hermann snatched the glass from the tray and threw it in Sidney's face. 'Where is it?'

Sidney shook his head. 'Don't know.'

'OK,' grinned Escobar. 'Watch this.' He grabbed Nick's ear-lobe between a fat finger and a thumb and stretched it. Then he opened his knife and dragged the blade across Nick's cheek, the steel rasping against the stubble. 'This is what it will feel like when I cut your throat,' he whispered, and Nick's eyes widened as the knife sliced through his ear, cutting through the cartilage and drenching his neck in hot blood. 'Look!' said Escobar, showing Nick the severed flesh. He peeled back the gag with its manic grin and pushed Nick's ear into his mouth. 'Eat up!'

Hermann suddenly felt quite ill. He called for more water and turned to Sidney. 'Where did you say the gold was?'

'I didn't,' replied Sidney calmly, 'and I won't until you release that man.'

'Oh no,' said Hermann, shaking his head. 'That's not how this will work. I'll release what's left of that man after you've told me where the gold is. I'm sure you're more than aware that you won't be leaving.'

'Your father would be proud of you.'

'Thank you. So where's the gold?'

Nick's ear was heavy on his tongue, like a slice of warm pork fat. He could feel spilled blood running down his arm and he was terrified that he would choke on his own vomit. His body went rigid as Escobar seized his left hand and pinned it to the tabletop. Octavio held the chair still as Nick's little finger was unpeeled from the fist and laid like a puppy-dog's tail against the grain.

'This is nothing to what Orlov would have done to you,' noted Hermann. 'Just days after you disappeared with Villafranca he closed down the POUM and arrested Nin. History tells us Stalin wanted the anarchists and the Marxists to disappear, but you know why Andreas Nin died, don't you, Sidney Starman?

309

You know why Orlov had the skin peeled from his body, don't you? No man ever dies like that for politics, not even here. Now where's the gold?'

'If I knew, I wouldn't tell you. I'm so sorry for this, Mr Crick.'

Escobar stabbed the point of his knife into the tabletop, the blade just touching the outside edge of the tip of Nick's little finger. He winked at Nick and pressed downwards, using leverage from the table to slice through the flesh. The pain came on like a siren and Nick screamed through his gag as he felt the steel brush bone.

'Put your hand over his mouth,' grunted Escobar.

Octavio shook his head. 'No way, man. That's fucking nasty.'

'Just stop the fucker yelling,' insisted Escobar.

'Get it over with Escobar, for fuck's sake,' cried Enrique, gulping back his whisky. Nick fell silent, horror-struck as he watched his nail point upwards under the pressure of the knife. A thick pool of dark red blood appeared on the tabletop. Then, with a sound like a snapped carrot, his fingertip was severed.

'Open up,' said Escobar, peeling back the gag.

Hermann looked away and sipped his water. 'This is as difficult for me as it is for you,' he told Sidney as Escobar wiped his blade on Nick's face.

'I'm going to have a drink and then I'm going to pour him one,' he announced. He slapped Nick around the head. 'You look like a man who needs a drink.'

The goatherd's dog found Sidney at dawn. All night the mountains had echoed with the thunder of artillery, but at first light the bombardment had lifted. One or two shells had landed very near, thought the goatherd, and he wondered what the Reds had to gain by blasting an uninhabited mountain range. He threw Sidney over his shoulder and carried him back to the house. His daughter watched him approach, the early sunlight painting the cypresses pink.

'I think he's dead,' said the goatherd, dropping the body on a narrow bed. 'Feel the weight of his haversack.'

His daughter yelled at him to lift the injured man before he ruined the bedspread, then she unfolded a grey blanket from a painted chest at the foot of the bed and laid it beneath him. 'He's been shot,' she said. 'Bring that hot water from the stove.'

For a day and a night Sidney lay on the shore between life and death, ebbing and flowing with the tides. The goatherd's daughter washed the gash in his shoulder with hot soapy water and dressed it with a poultice of honey, pine resin and thyme. She spooned a watery garlic soup between his chapped lips and washed the blood from his hands with a bucket and a brush. She stripped him bare and washed his clothes in the stream, rehydrating the thirsty lice which lived in the seams. And as he lay on her mother's bed, mumbling in his delirium, she wondered where this pale young man had come from. He was clearly a foreigner, yet he dressed like a bandit. His heavy bag lay untouched at the foot of his bed and the ugly black handgun was hidden beneath it. He wore no crucifix, there had been no papers in his pockets and the goatherd's daughter had a dark feeling that this man was trouble. She sketched him as he slept, filling in the dark hemispheres beneath his eyes with charcoal. On the third day he rose, stumbling from the house wrapped in his blanket, blinking in the sunlight and startling her as she chopped wood.

'Where's my gun?' he asked. He spoke Spanish like a southerner, like a bandit.

'Under the bed,' she told him. 'I'll fetch your clothes.'

She heated onion stew while he dressed and filled his bota from the stream. He came to the table as though ready to leave.

'I'm sorry to have troubled you,' he said. 'My name is Sidney Starman.'

The girl smiled. 'I am Izarra Romero. Will you eat?'

'Can't,' replied Sidney, shaking his head. 'I left my unit last night

311

to fetch water. Must have passed out. I have to try to get back.'

Izarra looked at him. The glitter of fever was still in his eyes. 'You came here three days ago,' she said. 'My father found you on the mountain. It was the night of the bombardment.'

His mouth dropped open. 'Oh God,' he mumbled. 'Oh my God. I'm sorry. I have to go.' He heaved his haversack onto the table, spilling the stew, and fumbled with the buckles as the sweat bubbled on his lip. 'Look,' he said, exasperated by the effort, 'just keep the whole bag. It's for you. Thank you.' He stepped outside, through the shadows of the cypresses and into the sunshine, marching uphill with his bota over his good shoulder and the pistol in his hand.

Izarra grabbed bread and goat's cheese and wrapped them in a tablecloth before running after him. 'Take these,' she insisted.

'Thank you, Isabella,' nodded Sidney. He looked weak.

'It's Izarra,' she replied. 'Where are you going?'

'Back to my unit.'

'Are you a German?'

'God, no,' cried Sidney. 'I'm English. I'm with the International Brigade.' He was taking long strides and Izarra was running to keep up.

'But they're . . .'

'The enemy. I know. I'm on the wrong side of the lines. Please don't tell anyone you've seen me.'

'You think I would?' asked Izarra. 'After nursing you? I thought you were a bandit.'

Sidney stopped and faced her. The little strength he had regained had just drained away. 'I suppose I am,' he admitted. Then he collapsed.

He slept for another thirty-six hours, writhing in the sweaty grip of a murderous fever. It was dark when he awoke, his throat raw with thirst and his pulse pounding in his ears. Izarra was sitting beside the bed, a rosary clasped in her hands.

'What's that noise?' croaked Sidney.

'My father,' said Izarra. 'He's been drinking, and he always sings when he drinks.'

'I meant the other noise, like chopping.'

'He is digging your grave. He said it would be easier to do in the cool of the night and we would be able to bury you as soon as you died, before the flies found you.'

The waning moon shone through the window, its pale light white on Izarra's face.

'I have to go,' said Sidney. 'My unit . . .' He sat up and swung his legs out of bed.

'I'm sure your unit thinks you are dead,' declared Izarra. 'You stay here.'

When her father returned he said the same thing. 'They're long gone,' he announced. 'There were soldiers on the mountain early in the week but they pulled out on the night of the barrage. They've left you for dead, *Inglés*.'

'You don't understand,' insisted Sidney. 'Those were German soldiers – Condor Legion – and they were looking for us. We were holed up in a cave, an old mine, way up the mountain. They wouldn't have pulled out before they'd killed us.'

'Then that's what they did. Consider yourself lucky.'

Sidney shook his head. 'I can't do that. I promised I'd bring water, and that's what I'll do.'

'You'll never make it. You're too weak to make it up the hill, let alone climb the crags.'

'So I'll die trying.'

The goatherd poured himself a drink and laughed softly. 'You're an idiot, boy. Are all the Reds this stupid? Have a drink, but don't spill it on the bed.' He knocked back his *aguardiente* and poured another two shots. 'Where is this cave?'

Sidney hesitated. 'Why do you ask?'

'You think I'd betray you? You rest in my house, you eat my food, you drink my liquor and you think I'd betray you? Mother of God!'

313

Sidney closed his eyes. 'I don't think you'd betray me, *señor*. The cave is high above the trees. It faces south, and there's a track winding up to it from the eastern valley. It's not a cave, but an old mine. That's all I know.'

The goatherd nodded. 'I'll find it.'

'Listen,' said Sidney. 'My officer is badly injured, and he has a prisoner. You'll be fired on if you don't identify yourself, so tell them Sid the Kid sent you.'

'Sid the Kid?'

'You'll be well rewarded.'

The goatherd looked at his daughter. 'This man is either very rude or very stupid. I choose to believe the latter. I'll leave the dog with you.'

17

Maybe it was the booze, maybe it was the anaesthetic effect of the cocaine, but Lenny felt no pain at all as he landed in a rhododendron bush at the back of the police station. He was taking his escape attempt one step at a time, not really believing he could get away with it but utterly determined to keep running until they caught him. He'd once been banged up in a prison van with a serial escaper called Jimmy the Flea. The wiry Glaswegian never travelled in short sleeves since they couldn't be rolled down to conceal the handcuffs he was invariably wearing when he made his breaks, and on a long, hot trip between nicks he had talked at length on the philosophy of escapology before doing a runner at a motorway service station. The secret of the art of flight, said Jimmy the Flea, was to be like Spencer Davis: keep on running. Never stop, never give up and never, ever, consider yourself to be caught. Lenny's attempt to stroll out of Montalban police station by the front door had been thwarted by a security gate so he'd turned around and gone upstairs. The station was deserted and he'd heard abandoned personal radios on untidy desks crackle with the breathless news of his escape. An open window in a stained kitchenette had led to a flat roof and a leap of faith from that had dumped him in the rhododendrons. Staying deep in the shadows he peeked around the side of the building, ducking back as a patrol car roared into the car park, its beacons flashing. Another arrived moments later and four cops ran into the station. Lenny gave them a few moments, then walked quickly across the brightly lit compound, his head down as he passed the unmanned gatehouse. Out in the street comfortable lives went on in warm houses, the flickering blue of their television screens reminding Lenny of what he was missing. He headed uphill, towards the black bulk of the rain-washed mountain and out of town, his priorities losing the handcuffs and procuring a car. Behind him he heard the sirens as the cops left the station like angry wasps, buzzing through Montalban on a street-by-street search. At the edge of town he turned onto a broken track, walking briskly in the darkness past unkempt houses on his left and a steeply sloping paddock on his right. Dogs barked as he passed, raising the alarm across town as mongrels yelled and sirens wailed and law-abiding citizens peered out through drizzle-smeared windows into the wet night. It seemed likely to Lenny that one of these houses would be empty – as good as a building site with tools left on the job with which he could break the cuffs – but luck had a far better prize in store for him.

He had been on the run for forty-five minutes when he encountered a chain-link fence and followed it into the forest until it turned parallel with the N211, going east. He found the breach a hundred yards along and squeezed through, tearing his tracksuit pants and scratching his leg on the wire. He was now in a compound between a hangar-like building and an elevated fuel tank. The air smelled of diesel, and as he approached the building security lights triggered by infrared sensors bathed the yard in halogen light. Lenny slipped into the shadows, and three minutes later he was inside the building, broken glass in his hair and bleeding from a cut on his forearm. He couldn't help but smile. A Renault G300 tanker truck was parked inside, its cab painted with the words 'Transportes Velasquez'. Lenny shook his head in self-admiration. 'Does Lenny bleeding know or what?' he grinned. He'd once spent six months on remand with a haulier from Hornchurch who'd been charged with drug smuggling. The haulier's brother used to send copies of *Trucking*

International magazine, the second-last page invariably impregnated with LSD, and Lenny had thus developed a psychedelic appreciation of lorries. He squeezed past the tanker and found a greasy workbench running the length of the right-hand wall. Still humming 'Keep on Running', he found a bench-mounted grinder and switched it on. The twin wheels reached full speed in seconds, whirring with a soft hum on well-oiled bearings. Lenny looked around for a bucket, found an old Swarfega tub and filled it with water from the washbasin at the back of the workshop. By grinding and dipping he cut through the cuffs in half an hour, and ten minutes after that he was heading for the coast.

In a petrol tanker.

All things being equal, Lenny would have dumped the truck at the first airport he passed and bought a one-way ticket to Blighty. His passport, snatched from the station prior to his flight, was on the dashboard, and he had nine hundred euros in his pocket. He could fly home first class if he wanted to and take his chances with the British judicial system, an institution he had always seen as tertiary education for the underprivileged. The problem was that there were some people on earth – doctors, nurses, legal-aid solicitors and Lenny – who were born to help others. It was in their nature, and between them they made the world a better place. Lenny shook his head like a weary but indulgent father and swung off the shiny N211 and onto the meandering Villarluengo road, realising as he did so that there was a serious leak in the brake lines. 'Leave it to Lenny,' he muttered, wondering if he could handle Hermann's special friends. He was unarmed, but that wasn't a problem. Lenny had long since learned that it was what was in your head that counted in a scrap, not what was in your hand, and if push came to shove El Sid's antique firearm would probably be available. He accelerated up a long, straight incline, changing down to take the corner, and narrowly missing Guadeloupe Serrano Suner, who was

317

striding along the verge, a bag over one shoulder and her thumb hanging over the road. Lenny stopped with some difficulty, leaned across and opened the passenger door. 'Hop in, love,' he said.

Guadeloupe was delighted to see Lenny, but she didn't let it show. She had drunk far too much *coñac* at her father's wake and she felt that she might have overreacted when she saw Lenny and that gipsy tart together in the bar. She couldn't understand a word the big hunk was saying, but the mere fact that he had driven after her proved that he hadn't taken offence. She bit her lip, dropped the bag and put a hand on her hip. 'So you're a lorry driver now?'

Lenny had no idea what she was talking about. 'Get in out of the rain, you daft cow!' he called.

Guadeloupe tossed the bag up and climbed in.

Lenny was astounded. 'That's my holdall,' he cried.

Guadeloupe leaned forward to squeeze the rain from her hair. 'That's your bag,' she said. 'You left it in the bar. I nearly threw it in the river.' She rummaged through it for her shoes and her handbag, then studied herself in a compact mirror. Her hair hung like a horse's tail and her eyes were like a panda's. 'Mother of God!' she gasped. 'I look like a witch!' She glanced at Lenny, suddenly curious. The last time she'd seen him he'd been chatting to sleazy Hermann Cruz from the back seat of a police car. 'How did you get here?'

'Renault G300, darlin',' nodded Lenny. 'Almost a classic, although the brakes are fucked.'

His sleeves had sagged to reveal the halves of his handcuffs, hanging like gipsy bracelets on wrists burned raw by red–hot splinters.

'My God!' she whispered, touching the scorched skin. 'You escaped!'

'No one ties Lenny Knowles down, love,' nodded Lenny.

'And you came for me!'

'I'm heading for your gaff. Going to get that fat jeweller and cut his fucking bollocks off.'

'That's so sweet! This road goes past my father's house. Give me two minutes to grab my things and we can flee together, like Bonnie and Clyde. Maybe you can kill my uncle while you're waiting.'

Lenny heard three words he understood and threw a warning glance. 'Don't start that *matar mi tio* nonsense again.' His eyes lingered on her thigh and he licked his lips. 'Although, if the opportunity arose . . . But don't push me on it. I'm not promising anything.'

Guadeloupe's eyes widened in terror as the truck fishtailed around a hairpin, scraping a steel safety barrier and crunching along the roadside scree. 'Slow down a bit, lover,' she cried.

'Sorry about that,' replied Lenny, through clenched teeth. 'I told you the brakes were fucked. Bit of a bugger on a petrol tanker.'

Guadeloupe lit a cigarette with shaking hands. Lenny snatched it from her mouth and puffed hungrily. She nodded and lit another, blowing smoke and sniffing the air. 'Is there a petrol leak in here?'

Lenny smiled and nodded. 'Jumped out of a window. Landed in a bush.'

She poked his arm then pointed to her nose and sniffed. 'Petrol?'

'That's right, treacle. Petrol. This is a petrol truck. I nicked it.' He jerked his thumb over his shoulder. 'Look out back.'

Guadeloupe checked the wing-mirror, her breath misting the glass as she craned to see the trailer. 'Oh my God!' she gasped, winding down the window and tossing her cigarette. 'I didn't notice.' Lenny was grinning as she leaned across and took his, sending it the same way. 'Oi!' he cried.

'You fucking crazy bastard,' she cried. 'And you drive like you've got no brakes.'

The driveway to La Cerda was too steep, too twisted and too narrow to take a truck down, so Lenny parked at the top, switched off the engine and killed the lights. 'You nip in and tell me how many geezers are in there,' he said. 'You . . .' he pointed, 'go in . . .' he let his fingers do the walking, 'have a butcher's . . .' he pointed two fingers at his eyes, 'count, *uno, duos, treos, fouros,* then come back and tell me. Got it?'

'Exactly,' nodded Guadeloupe. 'You wait here . . .' She pushed an open palm towards him. 'I'll go in and get my stuff . . .' She nodded fervently, encouraging Lenny to understand through mime that she was going in to pack a couple of suitcases and she'd be right back in *fouros minutos,* maximum. She leaned across and kissed him hard on the lips, running her long fingers over his battered face and pouting before slipping out of the truck.

'Good girl,' said Lenny.

Twenty-five years of coming home late had made Guadeloupe an expert at covert entry. Staying deep in the shadows on the edge of the drive, she ducked left close to the building and took a steep and well-worn path through the shrubs to her bedroom. Moments later, her skirt hitched around her waist, she was in, and she heard the shouting. She crept along the corridor and tip-toed up the stairs to peep through the banisters, into the dining room. What she saw made her flee in panic.

Lenny grabbed her as she thundered past, a cigarette hanging from his lips.

'Oh my God!' gushed Guadeloupe. 'My poor father's not a day in the ground and they've started.' She grabbed his sleeve. 'You've got to see this. They're having some kind of party in there. Your friend, the young guy, he's got his head in a bucket, and where the hell Paco Escobar came from I can't imagine. He's supposed to be dead! Oh God! Do you think they're worshipping the Devil?'

Lenny looked at her. 'I haven't got a fucking clue what you're

320

rabbiting on about.' He pushed past and waddled down the drive like a saddle-sore sheriff.

Guadeloupe caught up with him and steered him through the shrubs, over her balcony and into the corridor.

'Wait here,' he whispered, and crept to the foot of the stairs, hiding in the shadows as Tio Pepe shuffled past with a mop. Yelps, barks and grunts came down the stairs as though the beasts of the forest had made dinner reservations. He could hear Sidney protesting loudly in English, crying, 'For the love of God, stop him, Kreuz. This serves no purpose,' and a scraping noise, like a table dragged across a floor. Signalling for Guadeloupe to stay put, he crept past the stairs to Sidney's room, timing his movement across the creaking floorboards to coincide with the racket above. The door was locked, but as he turned Guadeloupe was at his side, her pass key in her hand. Sidney's canvas rucksack was empty, but a fast and thorough search of the room revealed the Luger, still wrapped in its greasy cloth and hidden on top of the wardrobe.

'My God!' gasped Guadeloupe.

'Shhh!' hissed Lenny. 'How does this thing work?'

'Give it to me,' whispered Guadeloupe, working the action and chambering a round. She pointed at the safety lever. 'Be careful.'

Lenny was halfway up the stairs before Octavio Pinsada spotted him. The Spaniard stared for a moment, a bottle of Scotch in one hand and a cigarette in the other, before opening his mouth to yell a warning. Lenny shot him in the belly before he could find the words, knocking him onto his backside with an expression of surprise only slightly greater than Lenny's. The Luger hadn't been fired for sixty-nine years, but it had kept its promise: all Lenny had to do was point it and pull the trigger. It was simple and effective, and he suddenly understood the popularity of the firearm with the criminal classes.

He bounded up the stairs, overlooking the whisky bottle

Octavio had dropped, and entered a candlelit torture chamber. El Sid was strapped to a chair with gaffer tape, his eyes angry and defiant in a face bruised like a thundercloud. Nick was face down on the table, his head overhanging and what seemed to be blood dripping from his hair. A fat skinhead with cunning eyes in a shiny face was stood over him, pinning him down with a bejewelled hand. Hermann Cruz had ducked behind Sidney's chair and the gipsy from the nightclub was standing perfectly still in the middle of the room, his hands outstretched to show he was unarmed and his body casting four shadows. The sour smell of cheap wine and black tobacco hung in the air and the floor was crunchy with broken glass. Lenny circled the room, passing through pools of darkness and light and pointing the pistol like a professional. Then he saw the bucket.

'Fucking hell, Nickle-Arse,' he exclaimed. 'I've heard about falling off the wagon but drinking it by the bucketful?' He shook his head and kept moving, his gun hand a distorted shadow on the wall. 'You all right, Mr S?'

'Delighted you dropped by,' replied Sidney. 'These gentlemen have been attempting to break Mr Crick's aversion to wine by drowning him in the stuff. I'm not sure it's the most effective approach.' Lenny shuddered. A gang of tarmac tinkers had tried the same with him once, using draught Guinness rather than wine. Lenny had thwarted the attempt by the simple expedient of drinking the entire bucket, but he could only begin to imagine the psychological consequences of bringing excess wine consumption and death by drowning together again in Nick's fragile mind. Suddenly angry, he pointed the Luger at Cruz. 'You get your boys and you line up over there,' he growled, flexing his fingers around the grip. Hermann nodded, muttering to his crew. Nick rolled off the table as he was released from Escobar's grip, falling to the floor with a thud and curling into a foetal position.

'You all right, Nickle-Arse?' called Lenny.

Nick shook his head, coughed and threw up a torrent of frothy wine.

'Nick,' shouted Lenny. 'Get the fuck up off the floor. You're getting puke all over your strides. Tell him, Mr S.'

'We need you at our side, Mr Crick,' called Sidney. 'Have you seen the hotelier?'

'Don't worry about him Mr S,' said Lenny. 'He's too old to give us any trouble.'

Enrique Pinsada was babbling, seemingly begging for his life.

'What's he on about, Mr S?'

'Wants to tend to his brother – the one you shot.'

'Tell him he can fucking wait. I want him alongside the others. Tell them to empty their pockets and drop their pants. I want shooters, knives and the Cheddars for that pick-up out front.' Lenny kept moving, swinging the pistol to aim at the top of the staircase as Guadeloupe announced her arrival. There was a thud and a squeal as she tripped over Octavio, lying bleeding in the dark.

'I'm afraid you've lost me,' confessed Sidney. 'Did you say Cheddars?'

Lenny sighed. 'Cheddar cheese. Keys. It's cockney.'

'Right you are.'

Somewhere in the shadows Guadeloupe was murmuring, 'Oh my God. Oh . . . my . . . God,' over and over again, her voice rising like an ill wind.

'Nick,' called Lenny. 'Stop puking and come and help me. I can't untie Mr S on my own.'

Nick climbed to his feet, his mouth wide in a grimace of pain and disgust. 'Look what they've fucking done to me!' he slurred, holding his bloody hand in the air. 'Look what they've done!'

Lenny nodded. 'Looks a bit sore, Nick,' he agreed. 'Can you just untie El Sid?'

Nick stumbled past Sidney, his face black with blood, and streaked with wine and tears. 'Give me that fucking gun!' he yelled.

'Steady on, Nickle-Arse. Be a good lad and unwrap Mr S.'

'Give me the gun,' insisted Nick, swaying drunkenly.

Lenny moved aside. 'No,' he said gently. 'I'm not giving you the gun.'

Nick stared at him for a long moment, and Lenny bit hard on the urge to tell him that his suffering at the hands of the sadistic Spanish psycho had probably done him the world of good. It just didn't feel like the appropriate moment.

Hidden from view in the darkness below floor level, Tio Pepe stood in the stairwell, his heart thumping hard, his mouth dry and his double-barrelled Benelli twelve-bore in his clammy hands. His fame as a marksman was undiminished by age, and the flea-bitten trophies adorning the walls of the establishment attested to his accuracy. His first shot would bring down the lout with the pistol and the second would disable his skinny accomplice. Hermann Cruz could go to hell, but Paco Escobar was a very powerful man and the Pinsada brothers were better as grateful friends than as disappointed enemies. He moved up a step, seeing the top of his niece's head to his left and the white stag on the far wall he had brought down at a measured range of nine hundred metres on that sad day in 1975 when Franco had died. He winced as the stairs creaked, and then he saw the Englishman, his face yellow in the candlelight and his black pistol held at arm's length. His sidekick was attempting to untie the old man with his one good hand, and from some-where in the shadows he could hear Octavio Escobar groaning in agony. The range was less than ten metres, the light reason-able and the target large. As Tio Pepe stepped up to take his shot the only thing standing between Lenny Knowles and sudden death was Octavio Pinsada's dropped whisky bottle. There was a blinding flash as the old hunter slipped on it, dis-charged the left barrel, and was thrown backwards by the recoil, tumbling down the stairs and breaking his neck with a crack that was drowned out by the blast of his weapon. Across the room the white stag hit the floor in a cloud of blue smoke and Escobar made his move, charging Lenny like an out-of-shape wrestler. Lenny pointed the pistol and waited for the approaching hulk to fill the sights. He pulled the trigger at a range of six feet, and at five, and at four, the Luger clicking like a disappointed woman each time. Then Escobar cannoned into him. Clasping each other, the two men rolled across a table and onto the floor. At that moment Enrique Pinsada decided to withdraw from the affair. He walked slowly past Nick and Sidney, stepping around the fight with his hands where everybody could see them, and knelt at his brother's side, nodding his thanks to Guadeloupe, who had staunched the bleeding belly wound with a bunched-up bar towel. Lenny and Escobar were throwing ineffective, short-range punches at each other's head as they rolled across the floor. They called it bitch-fighting in prison, and Lenny had once been on remand with the Queen of the Bitch-Fighters, a gay gang leader from Eltham who had taught him that using one's teeth was the secret of breaking the stalemate. Lenny chomped on Escobar's left ear, grinding his teeth as he shook his head from side to side like a demented terrier. Escobar screamed, his immense strength suddenly diluted by intense pain, and tried to roll away.

Nick ripped the last of Sidney's bonds from him, then helped him from the chair and towards the door as Hermann Cruz darted from the shadows and down the stairs. Guadeloupe screamed as she watched the fat jeweller wrench the twelve-bore from her uncle's death grip, point it at her and pull the trigger. The shot missed, and as Hermann rummaged through the dead man's pockets for more shells, Enrique Pinsada handed Guadeloupe the keys to his pick-up. Whispering her thanks, she dashed across the room, pressed them into Nick's hands and pushed him to the door. Seizing Sidney's bloodstained chair, she swung it over her head and smashed it down on Escobar's back, slamming the splintered remains against the side of his head. Lenny followed through with a knee in the groin and rolled clear, spitting flesh from his bloody mouth.

Hermann reached the top of the stairs as Lenny pushed Guadeloupe through the door, his poorly aimed shot bringing an avalanche of ancient plaster cascading from the ceiling. There was another ear-splitting roar as he fired again, breaking the mirror behind the bar. He reloaded as he waddled across the room and reached the door just as Nick, driving one-handed, sped away. His last shot went high, splattering harmlessly against the petrol tanker parked at the top of the drive.

'Don't go to town, for fuck's sake,' panted Lenny from the back seat.

Nick ignored him. His head was spinning but he knew exactly where he was going.

'Fuckers!' yelled Hermann as the pick-up turned left, heading away from Montalban. 'I'll kill you all!'

He stormed back into the hotel. The room smelled of gun-smoke, sweat and spilled blood. 'On your feet, gentlemen. Let's go!' he barked.

'Fuck you, Cruz,' growled Enrique. 'You're on your own.'

'I said let's go,' shrieked Hermann. 'Get up!'

Enrique shook his head. He was sitting on the floor, his legs splayed, holding Octavio around the waist. 'Fuck off, Cruz. I've retired.'

Hermann wondered for a moment if he should shoot them both, but he could see only pleasure and no purpose in the deed. 'You're out of the deal,' he hissed. 'You hear me? You're out!'

'So what?' muttered Enrique, looking down at his mobile phone. 'I just lost a quarter share in nothing.'

Escobar grabbed Hermann before he could reply, snatching the shotgun and shoving him towards the door. They could have taken the Peugeot van, but the keys were in Nick's pocket. They could have taken Tio Pepe's rusty old Mercedes, but he'd

326

locked it in the garage, so they took the petrol tanker parked at the top of the drive.

'Put your fucking foot down, Cruz, you pussy,' shouted Escobar, his neck drenched in blood from his mutilated ear and the shotgun resting between his legs. 'You want to catch them or what?'

The tail-lights of the pick-up could sometimes be seen far ahead, disappearing and reappearing in the black folds of the mountain. The petrol tanker swung back and forth across the road, and Escobar leaned forward to catch the passport sliding along the dashboard. He studied the photograph and read out the name: 'Knowles, Leonard Arthur. You know what I'm going to do to Knowles, Leonard Arthur, Cruz? I'm going to take this shotgun and stick it up his arse and I'm going to get his friend to pull the trigger. What do you think about that?'

Hermann didn't reply. He'd just realised that the brake pedal was as floppy as an old shoe underfoot and that consequently he had no control over a speeding tanker carrying twenty thousand litres of premium unleaded. Escobar noticed the look of horror on Hermann's face and checked the speedo. 'One hundred and ten,' he noted. 'That's pretty fast, Fat Boy.' The road ahead seemed to vanish into a black hole, the tanker's momentum echoing from the low safety wall as a whirring rush. 'You probably want to slow down a bit for the tunnel,' advised Escobar, but deceleration was no longer an option. Hermann kept the truck on track until he emerged on the other side, where his nearside wheel clipped a fallen rock. 'Fuck this,' muttered Escobar, tossing Lenny's passport into the slipstream and reaching for the seat belt. 'I'll kick your arse for this, Cruz.' The belt was stuck, and as Escobar tugged it Hermann clipped the safety wall. There was a flash and a wet explosion as 168 lead pellets exploded from the right barrel of the Benelli at 1400 feet per second, reducing Paco Escobar's bald head to a mush resembling five kilos of puréed strawberries. With crunchy bits.

Soaked in blood and brain tissue, unable to see through the red-washed windscreen, Hermann careered against the cliff in a streak of orange sparks before recrossing the median. The tanker then crashed through the low safety wall and over a sheer drop of 266 feet. Hermann was alive for the entire nine seconds it took to hit the bottom. Then he died, his body and that of his headless companion reduced to ashes in a fireball that lit up the valley like a sunrise.

The goatherd returned before dawn, focusing on the flickering flame in the window of his home as he trudged through the night's darkest hour. Sidney and Izarra were waiting for him in the parlour. He unloaded his shotgun, took off his hat and poured himself a drink. Then he looked at Sidney.

'Your cave has gone, *Inglés*. I knew the spot – it's an old mine – but it is no more.' He drained his *aguardiente* and poured another. 'Just a huge pile of rocks. Looks like the roof fell in during the Red bombardment the other night.' He raised an eyebrow. 'It's what footballers call an own goal, is it not?'

Sidney shrugged. It was over. 'Thank you for looking, *señor*. I'll leave tonight. I have to get back to my lines.' Except he had no lines. He had no unit, no loyalties and no excuses. He had nowhere to hide in Spain, and no idea how he was going to escape.

The goatherd seemed to know it, too. He poured them both a drink. 'They'll shoot you if they catch you, *Inglés*. You know that, don't you?'

Sidney nodded. 'I'll take my chances.'

Izarra glanced at her father. They had lived side by side for seventeen years and had little need of words. The goatherd nodded. 'Izarra will show you the secret path out of here. Where do you want to go?'

Sidney shook his head. 'I'll manage on my own. It's too dangerous for her. If they catch me, they'll shoot me. If they catch her . . .' He let the awful possibilities hang in the smoky air.

The goatherd ignored them. 'Where do you want to go?' he asked again.

Sidney stared at the tabletop, looking for guidance in the grain, and then he looked at the goatherd. 'I don't know,' he said at last. 'Can I tell you a story?'

As the sun rose over the mountain its rays came through the cracks in the door and found Sidney's share of Orlov's gold, stacked on the parlour table in glittering towers. The American's apparent death had shaken Sidney, proving that his sixth sense for a survivor could not be trusted. He'd always been able to picture Cobb as an old man, as he had himself, and now that the American was gone he was suddenly aware of his own fragile mortality. Izarra reached over and picked up a coin.

'Put it back,' barked the goatherd. 'It's not yours.'

'It's all right,' nodded Sidney. He watched as she held it up to the light, following the buttercup reflection as it flowed across her smooth skin.

'You know what I'd buy if I had one of these?' she asked.

'A new axe?' guessed the goatherd, unbuttoning his fly. 'We could do with a new axe.' He stepped outside to pee and Izarra watched him go.

'I'd buy a looking-glass,' she said. 'A big one.'

Sidney glanced around the house. 'You don't have a mirror?' he asked.

Izarra shook her head.

'So how do you know what you look like?'

She shrugged. 'I don't. I've seen my reflection in the pool out back but there's little detail.' She looked up at him, a twinkle in her eye. 'You tell me what I look like, Sidney Starman.'

He bit his lip. 'You're quite beautiful,' he said.

His words startled her and the smile fell from her lips. 'You shouldn't have said that,' she said, and then she walked out, her cheeks burning.

Sidney split the gold into two piles, packing one half in a

pillowcase and stowing it in his haversack. He took half a round of hard goat's cheese and two loaves of bread, making room at the top for a bottle of the goatherd's home-brewed *aguardiente*. Izarra had repaired his espadrilles, darning the torn soles with coarse hemp that smelled of straw.

It had been agreed that Sidney would set off at moonrise and that Izarra would accompany him until dawn, when she would leave him to head for the coast on his own. Throughout the day she moved around the tiny house in an awkward, self-conscious manner, avoiding Sidney's eyes and making him wish he could leave her behind. He reassembled his Luger, stuffed it into his waistband and went out into the early evening to help the goatherd bury his share of the gold.

'It's good that you know where I'm hiding it,' grunted the goatherd as he rolled a boulder over Sidney's grave. 'If you ever come back, and I am gone, you can take it.'

'It's not mine to take,' insisted Sidney. 'It's yours and Izarra's.'

The rock rolled into place with a gentle crunch and the goatherd straightened his back. He swept a hand across the valley, across his olive trees, his hives, his chickens, his stream, his vegetable garden and his goats. 'What in the name of Christ the King do I need money for, hombre?' He smiled like a millionaire, and then he frowned. The dog let out a low, rumbling growl and Sidney followed their gaze to where the track slipped off the hill. A faint cloud of pale dust rose above it, drifting westwards on the evening breeze. The goatherd slapped him on the shoulder. 'Get your things, Ingles. Izarra!'

They heard the trucks long before they saw them, the whine and grind of low gears on a steep road. The goatherd broke his shotgun and stuffed a cartridge into the breach.

'What are you doing?' asked Izarra.

The goatherd placed his weapon on the table, took his daughter's face in his hands and kissed her forehead. 'Go now,' he said, 'while you've got a head start.'

Izarra shook herself free. 'What are you talking about?'

'Come with us,' added Sidney, even though his tactical judgement disagreed.

So did the goatherd. 'None of us would stand a chance,' he said. 'You two go and I'll hold them off awhile.'

'No!' shouted Izarra. 'They'll kill you!'

'They'll kill us all, Daughter, if they catch us.'

Izarra turned on Sidney. 'This is your fault, Sidney Starman,' she hissed. 'It's you they want, and it's you who's brought this misfortune on our house.'

'You're wrong, Xigueta,' said the goatherd gently. 'It was I who brought him into our house and it was you who healed his wounds. It was we who harboured an enemy soldier and it's us they'll shoot. I'm charging you with this man's life.' He placed a hand on her head. 'Go with my blessing. Let me do this one thing for you.' He turned to Sidney. 'You go now, *Ingles*, and take care of my daughter. Or stand here and fight.'

'I'll take care of her,' promised Sidney.

The goatherd nodded. 'Take the dog. He knows the trails better than any of us.'

They moved fast and low through the shadows beneath the scattered olive trees, taking a wide route through the dead ground on the slopes. The dog led the way, and Sidney pushed the sobbing Izarra before him, urging her onward when she stopped to look back. The trucks stopped after the first shot was fired from the house. Riflemen spilled from the canvas awnings and took cover beside the track. Sidney, Izarra and the dog reached the scree and started their traverse on a goat track as a gun team set up a '34 and laid down suppressing fire. A rifle squad trying to outflank the building came under fire from a side window and took cover in the stream bed. From the mountain-side the machine-gun fire sounded like impatient fingernails drummed on a tabletop, the dry report echoing along the valley. Sidney pushed Izarra higher, heading for the spot where the stream gushed between two spurs. Far below, the gunfire was punching chunks of rock from the house and a poorly thrown grenade had unearthed the goatherd's onions. The squad in the stream bed laid down cover for a second group to rush the blind side, but as they began their assault the machine-gun hit the bee-hives, scattering wood splinters, honey and indignant bees across the garden. As the second group fled the swarm, grenadiers sprinted into cover behind the cypresses at the front of the house, unscrewing the caps from grenades and fumbling for the drawstrings. Inside the house the goatherd poured a last glass of aguardiente. He was down to his last cartridge, and God would-n't forgive him for using it in the way he wanted to. He walked slowly into the bedroom and took down the picture of his wife – Izarra's mother – then took a seat at the kitchen table. Short bursts from the machine-gun were flying through the house, coming through the front door and going out through the back to pin down the flanking party. Outside all was chaos, but inside there was a moment of serenity. The goatherd lifted his shotgun and pointed out of the window, looking all the time at the pic-ture of his wife. 'A few more minutes,' he promised, firing his last shot through the shattered glass. He drained his *aguardiente* in one long draught, stood up and threw his weapon through the window. Then he glanced around the parlour with the wistful expression of one leaving a much-loved home to go to a better place. Outside the firing died away and the clatter of small arms was replaced by a clamour of shouts in a language the goatherd didn't understand.

He was bleeding when they brought him before the colonel. Five years from now, almost to the minute, Herr Oberst Claus von Wittenburg would die in a Russian air strike on his armoured column on the Don, taking to his shallow grave the real reason why he was interrogating a peasant goatherd on a Spanish mountain. He knew before he started speaking to the man that he would be wasting his time, but he indulged the prisoner with the opportunity for mulish defiance. Five minutes later his sergeant stood the goatherd against an olive tree and fired his pistol into the back of his head.

Safely into the sierra, Izarra never heard the shot.

18

Anita Romero Molino didn't hear the pick-up approaching along the same dusty track. She had meant to leave at nightfall, but her old car had refused to start, so she'd eaten one last meal with the ghosts of her ancestors before falling asleep on her grandmother's bed. The clunk of car doors and whispered voices woke her at 1.20 a.m. She rolled out of bed and pulled on her jeans, wide awake and fearful. There was no one alive who had business up this track, at this time of night, and only bad news came visiting at this hour. She picked up the blunt axe that stood beside the door, wondering what to do next, and the knock startled her. She recognised the voice as that of the pale Englishman who had visited that day, the man who had driven Sidney Starman here, sixty-nine years too late to make any difference.

'What the hell do you want?' she cried. 'It's nearly two in the morning.'

'I know,' replied Nick from the other side of the door. 'I'm really sorry but we're in a bit of a mess out here. We didn't know where else to go. Can we come in?'

Anita bit her lip and looked at the ceiling. Back home, in Barcelona, she'd have told him to fuck off, but here, with the fragrance of her green-eyed grandmother still lingering, she could hardly refuse those who begged sanctuary. She replaced the axe and opened the door. There were four of them, and they looked like they'd crept out of the grave. 'Holy shit!' she cried. 'Have you been in a road accident?'

Nick smiled weakly and shook his head. 'Just feel a bit faint, that's all,' he said. Then he fell over.

'Loss of blood,' explained Sidney as Lenny carried Nick into the house. 'Er, these are my colleagues. This is Mr Knowles and this is Miss Suner. You and Mr Crick are already acquainted. Do you mind if I put the kettle on? A strong, sweet brew is what this man needs and I've got my own bags. Is there honey, for the tea?'

'There have been no hives here since 1937,' replied Anita. 'The bees never came back.' She gaped as a woman with wild hair, bloody feet and black-ringed eyes shook her hand. 'Call me Guadeloupe,' smiled the banshee. 'This is my fiancé Lenny. Have you got anything to drink?'

Anita felt the parlour swirling around her, but it was all too weird to be a dream. She pointed at Nick, slumped on a wooden chair. 'Get this man on the bed,' she said, 'and fetch water. We need to get the stove going.' She repeated herself in English as Lenny lifted Nick and dropped him on the bed.

'Where are the matches?' he asked. 'I'll get a blaze on the go.'

'I'll fetch the water,' said Guadeloupe, but Sidney stopped her.

'I'll get it,' he said. 'I know where the stream is.'

Anita watched him limp from the house. She offered a cigarette to Guadeloupe. 'What the fuck is going on?' she asked.

Guadeloupe shrugged. 'I have no idea. We just rescued those two from some sort of drinking party. I think the young one is quite badly hurt.'

'Have you called the police?'

Guadeloupe glanced at Lenny, kneeling before the cast-iron stove, feeding kindling into the ashes. She took a drag on her cigarette and shook her head. 'I think that would be the wrong thing to do.'

Anita looked at her for a moment, then nodded. 'Nothing ever changes, does it?' she said. 'I've got a first-aid kit in the car. There's a bottle of *aguardiente* on the dresser.'

Lenny was visibly shocked by the extent of Nick's injuries. Anita was horrified to discover, as she tended his wounds with a bucket of hot water, a ripped towel and the tiny motoring first-aid kit, that he had lost the tip of his left little finger, his left earlobe and a lot of blood. Sidney felt like a ghost as he watched the girl mop the young man's brow in the same bed upon which he had once been saved. The rush of adrenalin that had sustained him that night had long since gone, drifting away like a wind-blown smokescreen to reveal an advancing sense of urgency. The beating he had sustained back at the hotel had left him with damage that would never heal. He'd peed blood outside the house, and as he had fumbled with his fly he had noticed that his right arm, from elbow to fingertips, was completely numb, as though it had already died. He could no longer hear more than muffled mumbles in his right ear and his tongue felt fat and heavy, as though it was suddenly too big for his mouth. Furthermore, he had the distinct physical impression that some-thing was perched on his left shoulder – there to whisper in his one good ear that time was very short.

Anita was wringing a facecloth in the bucket when she sud-denly looked up, her eyes flashing in the candlelight. 'I think you should tell us exactly what's going on here, Señor Sidney Starman,' she said.

Sidney stared at her for a long time, his bruised face bathed in the moon's pale glow. He sent her a smile that she returned, unopened, and then he sighed. 'I came to Spain in 1936,' he said.

Nick listened from the bed, the pain rising and falling like a storm swell as the old man told his story. Pausing only to sip from his flask, Sidney spoke of Figueras and Albacete, the Jarama and Mogente, Benimamet, Valencia and Castellote, his voice very quiet as he recounted the Teruel affair. Anita kept up a low translation for Guadeloupe, whose wide-eyed reaction to every turn of events was counterbalanced by Anita's fierce indifference.

336

Lenny, hogging the bottle, was utterly enthralled and interrupted frequently, seeking clarification and explanation. As the *aguardiente* took hold he insisted on proposing toasts in appreciation of every daredevil caper and death-defying escape, an action Sidney acknowledged by raising the hip flask he had inherited from Simenon in recognition of Lenny's own gallantry.

'Without you, Mr Knowles, I would probably have been telling this story to Hermann Cruz by now,' he declared.

'Whatever,' shrugged Lenny modestly, choosing not to increase the enlightenment by explaining exactly how the fat jeweller had found out they were staying at La Cerda.

For his part, Sidney considered sparing Anita the details of her great-grandfather's death, then rejected the notion. The truth, he had learned, could only hurt when it was hidden, so he described the goatherd's end exactly as he remembered it. He'd neither seen nor heard the execution, but he presumed the man had been murdered.

'He was,' nodded Anita. 'He was buried outside the cemetery walls in Pitarque. My grandmother had him disinterred and brought within the walls in 1977.'

'I'm sorry she had to do that,' said Sidney, standing up. A shadow seemed to fall across his mind, disturbing his sense of balance, and he swayed for a second before steadying himself on the table. He crossed to the parlour window to breathe in some fresh air. Outside the stream up which he and Izarra had escaped sounded like a round of applause.

'You haven't finished yet, Mr Starman,' said Nick.

The old man watched the moon set, feeling the same wistful sense of departure the goatherd had experienced as he sat in this room with his photograph and his glass while Death hammered on the door. He had reduced his Spanish adventure to a short lecture, describing the horror, the terror and the shame in a few quiet words. The exercise was easy and worthless but for its value as entertainment. What really mattered, and what no one

337

wanted to hear, was what had happened every day since he had left Spain. That was where the lessons of life were to be learned, from a man who had lived in the squalor of shame and cowardice. He took a last deep breath of mountain air and turned back to the smoky room. These people weren't interested in guilt, regret and self-hatred – they wanted romance and adventure, their common precedents. He pointed over Anita's head, past where Nick sat on the bed with a bloody towel wrapped around his left hand, past the grave the goatherd had dug for him, and beyond the olive tree where he'd found him. 'We went that way,' he said. 'We followed a goat track that brought us down to the road by the stone bridge on the Montalban road. It took us all night – I was still very weak and Izarra was distraught. I built us a hide in the woods and we passed that first day in silence. She could have left any time, but I suppose being anywhere, with anybody, was better than going back home.'

'Poor cow,' muttered Lenny as Anita translated in a low voice.

'The poor child!' echoed Guadeloupe.

Izarra sobbed all day, but as darkness fell she dried her tears and led Sidney northwards through the forest, following rushing streams and dusty goat tracks over the brooding crags. They crossed the lines that night – exactly where and when they couldn't tell – but Sidney knew he was back on Republican ground as they crept past a huddle of conscripts, mere boys and old men, sitting on a river bank, their faces faintly illuminated by the glow of their cigarettes. As Sidney, Izarra and the big dog crept past the men were singing '*El Corazón de Pena*', passing a flask of *vino mosto* around and hoping for a quick end.

Sunrise found the fugitives a good ten miles behind the lines, sleeping on a bed of rushes in an abandoned watermill while the dog kept guard. They sent him home that night after Sidney had secured a lift from an American ambulance group, explaining to the young volunteers that he was an injured soldier of the

International Brigades and that Izarra was his nurse. The naïve Americans gave them coffee and chocolate and didn't ask how a casualty and his carer came to be wandering around the rear by night. They were dropped at dawn at the aid station in Chiprana. Izarra was horrified: she had never been anywhere quite so crowded or so squalid.

'This is nothing,' said Sidney, stealing the identity card from an unconscious volunteer and tucking his own papers into the dying man's shirt. 'You should have seen the hospitals after Jarama.'

The Teruel front was quiet, for the moment, but the jagged juxtaposition of conflicting ideologies produced a steady stream of casualties. Tuberculosis, trench foot, dysentery, gunshot and shrapnel trauma were the principal reasons why soldiers came to Chiprana and two out of every ten patients lay in fear that their self-inflicted wounds would be noticed by the commissars. Sidney took Izarra by the hand, leading her towards the railway station through rubbish-strewn streets filled with bandaged drunks and filthy children. Izarra was scared, and suddenly dependent on Sidney. In the mountains and the forests she had been in charge, but out here, in the human world, she deferred. Two soldiers gave them their table in the overcrowded station café, and they shared a slice of tortilla and a bottle of beer while Sidney peeled the mortally wounded soldier's picture from the stolen ID and replaced it with his own. Outside a captured Italian airman was being paraded through the streets, his hands tied to a donkey's tail, his Errol Flynn moustache dripping with blood and half his scalp hanging off. Jeering militiamen threw rocks and bottles and aimed kicks at him as he passed, many of their ill-directed missiles hitting the increasingly irritated donkey. Sidney watched, with mounting queasiness, and shook his head. 'Do you want to go home?' he asked Izarra.

She waited until she had finished chewing before answering. 'I'll go back tonight,' she said quietly.

'I asked if you wanted to.'

Izarra ran her fingers through her hair and stared at the table-top. When she looked up, her green eyes were swollen with tears. 'I don't know,' she sobbed. 'I don't know what I'm supposed to do.'

Out on the platform an NCO was blowing a whistle, and the rattle of iron-shod boots echoed through the station. Spanish soldiers moved in perfect time and in close order, but somehow subverted the martial effect by maintaining lazy, good-humoured conversation as they marched. A legless cripple, still in uniform, had dragged himself into their path, holding up a carefully written placard stating, 'Here, but for the grace of God, go thee.' His forage cap tinkled with coin as a distant fusillade marked the demise of the Italian pilot.

Sidney pushed away the tortilla and swallowed back the nausea. He reached out and took Izarra's hand. 'Your father entrusted me with your care,' he said softly. 'I'm taking you to England.'

They took the train to Tarragona, arriving in the late afternoon of St Barnabas's Day – the patron saint of protection against hail. When dozens of dirty soldiers started jumping from the train as it approached the docks and made its way into the station, Sidney and Izarra followed. On the enemy side Nationalist soldiers were considered to be on leave from the moment they fell out from their unit, whereas the Republicans, under pressure from the unions, decreed that it began when they reached their destination. It was one of the few advantages of fighting against Franco. Wily troops soon realised that if they could avoid the checkpoints on the station, they would remain officially in transit. As long as he reported to the military authority within a reasonable period, a rifleman could feasibly double the length of his leave. The traditional response from a soldier arrested for being drunk and disorderly was to thank the policeman for reminding him that he had to get his permit stamped.

Sidney, however, had no intention of being arrested. Armed guards patrolled the tracks and the wide Passeig Maritim, but they were impotent against the ragged, bearded bands who rushed across the street like rats to disappear in the bars, brothels and alleyways of the port.

Tarragona was a city mute with fear and troubled by suspicion. It had been seven weeks since the bombing of Guernica in the Basque country, and daily raids on the docks by Italian squadrons based in Mallorca were grinding on nerves already frayed by the fear of street-fighting between the squabbling factions of the Republican coalition. Earlier that week a bomb on a bus had killed two, and suspicious blasts along the railway line had been attributed not to fascist but to communist saboteurs. Aware that the heavy pack on his back was of Moroccan manufacture and of a type frequently used by Tercio sappers to carry explosives, Sidney grabbed Izarra's hand and slowed his urgent pace to a casual, carefree stroll. Passers-by looked away as they scurried home, or stared at the pair with open suspicion and undisguised hostility. Faith in the revolution had drowned in blood, dragging hope down with her, and there was precious little charity left for meddlers from overseas. Realising that his falsely cheerful demeanour was inappropriate, Sidney drew Izarra closer and affected a drunken gait, as though he had just come from a wake. The papers he had stolen identified him as John Longbottom, a twenty-four-year-old volunteer with the American Abraham Lincoln Brigade, and while adequate to survive a cursory check, they would not save him in the event of a search. He was dressed in civilian clothes, carrying an enemy-issue haversack and armed with a German pistol and a Legionnaire's dagger. Furthermore, he was wearing a German watch and carrying all that remained of the Spanish gold reserve. Shooting, he realised wryly, would be too good for him.

They turned into a piss-stinking alley scattered with the rat-chewed remains of uncollected garbage and emerged on a boulevard leading down to the docks. The Basque flag, the *Ikurriña*, flew from sandbagged shopfronts and balconies in a display of solidarity with besieged Bilbao, but its similarity to the Union Flag merely reminded Sidney how far he was from home.

'I think we're safe now,' he lied, still holding Izarra close. 'I'll get us a place to lie up for a spell while I find us a boat.'

He stepped into a jewellery shop, where he sold three coins for two hundred pesetas, and then into a cavernous department store with no customers and little stock, where he bought Izarra a new dress and himself a shirt and a razor.

They tried several hotels, but all were fully booked except for the Hotel Torre del Vella, a narrow and crumbling lodging on the Nou St Pau. Single occupancy was no longer possible under emergency regulations, stated the clerk. Clients were respectfully requested to accept double occupancy and to agree to share with strangers, if necessary. He ran a disapproving eye over the couple and told them bathing was permitted between six and eight, and that dinner was served at nine. Neither porterage nor room service was available due to the current situation in the country.

'Sod their rules,' whispered Sidney as they squeezed into their attic room. 'I've fought for this country and I'll say when I can bathe. You go first, then get some rest. I'll be back later.' He waited until she had gone down the corridor to the bathroom before pushing back the bed and lifting a board with the tip of his dagger. A knock at the door raised his hackles, but it was Izarra.

'I don't know what to do,' she said.

Sidney laughed and led her back to the bathroom, where he ground a block of soap into the plughole and explained how to use the taps. 'And look, Izarra,' he smiled, 'a mirror!'

Back in the room he took six gold coins out of the pillowcase, then stuffed it back in his pack and hid it beneath the floor-boards. Armed with pistol and dagger, he headed downhill to the sea, presenting his false papers to a checkpoint of *carabineros* near the dock gates.

'Where's your uniform?' asked a sullen corporal.

'They still haven't given me one,' sighed Sidney

'Where are you going?'

'To the *estación maritime*.'

'Why?'

'I'm meeting a girl there. She's coming down from Barcelona.'

'Yeah?' asked the corporal, returning the papers. 'Bring her back this way so I can check her out.'

'Sure thing, Corporal,' smiled Sidney. He found the Bar Racine a few minutes later. Almost opposite the dock gates, it was a low, shady burrow where daylight rarely shone. Inside, drunken sailors sang, slept or sulked at the zinc or sat sullenly on low stools at stained tables. La Niña de los Peines was singing songs of pain and betrayal from an unseen gramophone, reminding Sidney of the night he crossed the lines with Izarra.

'Frank Cobb sends his regards,' he told the overweight *patronne* as she set a small beer before him.

'He does?' she replied with little interest. 'How nice. Are you American?'

'English,' replied Sidney. 'Are you Grace?'

'Every gorgeous gram of me.' She walked away to serve a bearded sailor. Five minutes later she was back. 'Got any snapshots?'

'Of Cobb?'

'Of whoever: Cobb, your sweetheart, your mother. I don't care, but there's a fellow at the end of the bar who works for the military police – and I'd like him to think we are just having an innocent chat. Seeing as Frankie Cobb sent you, I take it the nature of your visit is anything but.'

'I need a passage on a boat . . .'

'Whoa there, soldier,' cried Grace 'Not so fast. Show me

what you've got: loot, souvenirs, anything to make it look like you're bragging and not begging.'

Sidney pulled out Simenon's flask. 'How about this?'

Grace ran her plump fingers over the beaten silver. 'That's lovely. How many of you are there?'

'Two.'

'And how are you going to pay me?'

'In gold.'

'Mmm . . . silver *and* gold. How's Frankie? Still working underground?'

'You could say that.'

'What's your name?'

'Sidney Starman.'

'OK, Sidney Starman. Show me the gold.'

Sidney glanced at the plain-clothes cop and pulled a coin from his pocket.

'Nice,' smiled Grace, 'but not enough for one, let alone two, sweetie.'

'How much is it?'

'How much have you got?'

'I asked first, Grace.'

'Now you sound like Frankie. It's two of those each. Half to me now and half to the man I introduce you to.'

'When?'

'You just want out of Spain? Or have you got a specific destination in mind?'

'A boat going to England would be good, but anywhere will do.'

'Ships try to sail before the air raids, but you're too late for today. Come back tomorrow at half past five. What's in the flask?'

'Armagnac.'

'I'm impressed. You're the second of Frankie's boys drinking Armagnac. I hope the culture's rubbing off on the old bastard.'

344

She laughed out loud and banged the flask down on the zinc. Then she leaned in close. 'One more thing: leave your friend outside. No bags. It's a short walk from here to the dock gates but it's far enough for trouble. Two of you walk in, and the deal's off. You come with luggage, the deal's off. Go on, take your flask back and I'll give you a drink on the house.'

Izarra was sitting on the bed wearing her new outfit when Sidney returned. 'You look beautiful,' he told her. 'Come on, I've got an idea.'

Across the street from the hotel was a photographer's studio with faded pictures of pre-war brides and long-dead grooms propped up in its taped windows. Dogs were howling as they crossed the street. The chorus had started a few minutes earlier with one spooked mutt on the outskirts of town and now it had spread down every street in every quarter. Drinkers in a corner bar glanced at their watches then at the sky before paying their bills and heading for home.

'Together or apart?' asked the photographer. 'It's four pesetas a shot, or ten for three.'

'One each of us on our own, and one of us together,' replied Sidney, delighted to see the faintest smile emerging from Izarra's eyes. He placed a ten-peseta note on the counter. 'You go first.'

The photographer nodded at the money. 'Keep that,' he said. 'You pay me tomorrow when you collect the prints. Have you had your photo taken before, *señorita*?'

Izarra shook her head.

'It's not difficult,' explained the photographer. 'You see this . glass eye here? You look right at it, you try to look as sweet and as pretty as you can, then there'll be a bright flash. That's all there is to it. Ready?'

Outside, the low moan of the air-raid siren rolled over the rooftops, quickly becoming a strident cry of alarm. Sidney glanced fearfully into the street, watching the Guardia de Asalto policemen and the drinkers run from the bar as the roar of approaching aircraft filled the air.

'Don't worry about it,' said the photographer. 'They're Italians, from the base in Mallorca. They come every day at this time and drop firebombs on the docks. They never bomb the city. Now smile at the big glass eye, *señorita*. Ready? One, two, three . . .'

There was a bright flash in the street followed by a flat bang and a rush of dust and broken glass.

'They've never done that before,' remarked the photographer coolly. 'I think we'd better head for the shelters.'

The thump of flak from the dockyard batteries provided a bass rhythm to the howling of the siren and the whine of desynchronised aero-engines. A huge twin-engined bomber, its wings painted like a leopard, flashed overhead, silver incendiaries tumbling from its belly to roll down roofs and explode in gutters. Sidney watched one fall onto a balcony where a bare-chested man took a broom and swept it into the road. It burst with a brilliant whiteness as it fell, engulfing a plane tree in flames and sending a scorching wind along the street. Sidney, Izarra and the photographer sheltered in the doorway until the bombers moved on like a passing hailstorm. 'They've never done this before,' repeated the photographer in disbelief as he locked the shop. 'What have we done to them? Listen – come back tomorrow and we'll carry on. It's ludicrous trying to take memorable photographs with all these distractions. I'm taking my cameras home. Good evening and good luck.'

The bombers didn't return, and as fires, shouts and bells broke out across Tarragona, Sidney and Izarra returned to the hotel for dinner.

Later, as Sidney dozed in a chair, Simenon's flask in his hand and the asylum howls of a terrified city splitting the night air, he felt a soft hand on his face. Startled, he opened his eyes and saw Izarra standing beside him.

'I'm scared,' she whispered.

Sidney took her hand. 'You're not alone,' he replied.

'Is it like this in England?'

He pulled her to him, gently kissing her forehead. 'Oh no, Izarra. It's nothing like this.'

They slept late the following morning and Sidney only just made it to the studio before it closed for the afternoon.

'Can't charge you for that,' said the photographer gruffly, 'Look at it.'

The picture had been taken at the exact moment the incendiary had gone off in the street, and instead of looking into the lens, Izarra was staring to her right, her startled eyes reflecting the flash of the explosion. 'Come back on Monday morning and I'll shoot you both – all three for eight pesetas.'

'I can't,' said Sidney. 'I'll be gone.'

Down the street, the baker laughed at him when he tried to buy bread. 'Xico, you've been at the front too long,' he said. 'You've got to be here at six in the morning if you want bread. By nine it's all gone. Haven't you heard about the flour short-ages? I suppose you're used to getting the best of everything in the army, but it's bloody hell being a civilian these days.'

Sidney was told a similar story wherever he went, and he returned to the room empty-handed.

'Don't worry,' said Izarra. 'We can go a day without food. Tell me more about England.'

Sidney lay back on the bed, his head in her lap. 'We've always got plenty to eat,' he said, 'and you can buy bread all day long. We've got all sorts of meat and game, and there's always fish on Fridays.'

'And?'

'The houses have thatched roofs. It's like straw, and it keeps the rain out.'

'You have lots of rain in England, I know.'

'More than here, that's for sure. But it's good for the fish. Brings them close to the surface.'

'You like to fish?'

'Never done much, but I'd like to get better at it.'

'Will we get married when we get to England?'

'Blimey!' gasped Sidney, pulling himself upright. He looked into her green eyes. She stared straight back, biting her lip. 'Would you like that?' he asked.

She nodded.

'It won't be easy being a gamekeeper's wife.'

'I don't care.'

'You'll have to raise pheasants and gut rabbits.'

'That's not so hard.'

'And keep house and bring up children.'

'I'll be a good wife to you, Sidney Starman.'

'Then that's what we'll do!' He pulled her tight against him and kissed her. 'Now it's settled. Last night was our engagement. We'll get married in St Giles as soon as we get back.'

They left the hotel at five in the afternoon. Sidney had paid for two nights in advance so anyone who saw them leave would assume they were going sightseeing. It was not a good day to be a tourist in Tarragona. But for the knots of *asaltos*, the roving patrols of *carabineros* and the prowling, unmarked cars of the secret police, the city seemed deserted, and rather than being the easy stroll down to the sea he had anticipated, it was suddenly extremely dangerous to be on the streets.

'How far are we going?' asked Izarra. She was young and green, but she could smell trouble.

'To the next alleyway,' muttered Sidney. 'Then we run like hell.'

The next alley didn't come soon enough. The car, a black 1933 Citroën 10, cruised slowly past and then stopped a few yards ahead.

'Oh bugger,' said Sidney.

The doors opened and two men, one thin and unshaven and the other fat and shiny, stepped out. Sidney noticed that neither was expecting trouble – the thin one was lighting a cigarette and the fat one had his hands stuffed into his trouser pockets.

'Papers,' called the thin one in a playful, singsong voice as they passed.

'Yes, sir,' nodded Sidney, imitating Cobb's most heavily accented Castilian. The thin cop looked at him curiously.

'American?' The jocularity had gone from his voice.

'Yes, sir,' said Sidney.

The fat cop took a step towards Izarra. 'Why so nervous?' he asked.

'I'm not so nervous,' replied Izarra nervously.

'So show me your papers.'

The thin cop was staring at Sidney's identity card. 'This is not valid,' he said. He perceived a movement, heard the rustle of clothing, saw startled pigeons explode from a window ledge, smelled something familiar, saw the bright blue sky, and died without hearing the shot.

Sidney turned, the Luger at arm's length and pointing straight at the fat cop's face. The fat cop raised his hands, a loose gold watch sliding down his arm as he did so, his mouth opening more in surprise than fear as the bullet entered with a loud crack just below his left nostril and exited, in a spray of blood and bone, just in front of his right ear. He staggered backwards for four paces, sinking to his knees with rolling eyes as Sidney stepped forward and fired a second bullet into his forehead, blowing the green fedora from his shaven scalp.

Sidney turned and grabbed Izarra's arm, suddenly aware that she was screaming. 'It's OK,' he said, his ears ringing. 'He'd have missed his partner and taken it out on his wife. Let's go.'

Three hundred yards ahead a squad of carabineros were approaching curiously, as though uncertain of the facts. Sidney doubled back, leading Izarra down the Nou St Pau. As they passed their hotel the clerk was talking to the photographer and both stopped to gape as their clients sprinted past. The asaltos followed a moment later, their boots like hammers on the cobblestones.

'Through the park!' cried Izarra.

'No cover. Just stay on the curve,' panted Sidney. 'This way!' They ran along a narrow, stinking *callejone*, its stones slippery with spilled rubbish and heavy with the smell of urine. Even here the communists had plastered the walls with their slogans, and the peeling corners of the propagandists' posters flicked against Sidney's elbow as he passed. 'Downhill,' he gasped. Whistles were being blown in nearby streets as the troops tried to establish a cordon, and alarmed faces were appearing open-mouthed in shadowy doorways. 'Stay indoors,' yelled Sidney. 'Fascist parachutists!' He pulled Izarra into another narrow alleyway, scattering a family of cats as he did so. Pausing to adjust his hair and his dress at the end of the alley, he took Izarra's hand and strolled into the next street. A drunkard, locked out of his house, looked away in shame as they passed.

Five minutes later they crossed the railway bridge and turned onto the Moll de Costa.

'The bar's up ahead,' said Sidney. 'They told me to come alone, so you'd better wait at the tram stop on the corner. Keep watching the door. I'll be coming out with someone else – he'll be from the ship. Follow us until we call you forward. Is that all right, my darling?'

Izarra took both his hands in hers, smiled sadly and nodded. 'I understand, Sidney Starman. Don't leave me behind.'

'I won't. God! How can you say that? Of course I won't leave you. Do as I say and in five minutes we'll be gone. I promise.'

'What happens if something else goes wrong?'

'It won't.'

'You can't say that. What happens if, if . . .'

Sidney cupped her face in his hands. 'Izarra, listen to me.

350

Nothing will go wrong. Have faith. If we get separated, go home. I'll come for you, my darling. I promise.'

'You promise?'

Sidney took her hands. 'A day, a week, a month, a year, or a lifetime – no matter how long it takes, I'll come for you. But it won't come to that. Five minutes, that's all.'

She looked long and hard into his eyes, then nodded.

He kissed her and walked into the Bar Racine. A wave of heat, smoke, sweat and beer-soaked song hit him as he entered a room filled with maudlin afternoon drinkers. Grace was behind the bar, watching her waiters and looking too good for her own dive. She frowned as Sidney reached the bar.

'I said no bags,' she said.

'But these are my things.'

'Things will get you shot. You've broken the rules, and you're covered in blood.' She sloshed a caña down in front of him and walked away.

Sidney looked down, noticing for the first time that his shirt was splattered in secret policeman's blood. He leaned into the bar, hiding his front from a multinational fraternity of seafarers, who, in their drunken, classless unity, put the Third International to shame.

A pretty girl in an orange dress shook a tin full of change at him. 'Will you give something for the children of Bilbao?' she smiled.

Sidney shook his head.

At last Grace came back. 'I should throw you out,' she said.

'I'm sorry,' replied Sidney, 'but I need these things. I didn't think it would matter.'

'Cemeteries are full of men who didn't think things would matter. I'm doing this for Frankie Cobb, not for you, and I'll tell him when I see him. Where's your friend?'

'Outside.'

'At least you got that right. Your man is standing at the end of

351

the bar. He's the first mate on the *Myrtle* and his name's Bob Owen. Off you go.'

Bob was a genial sort, but he played by the rules.

'You'll have to leave the bag, chum,' he smiled. 'It's their customs men, see? They're on the lookout for chaps on the docks with luggage. We have to make you look like a stevedore, and they don't carry bags, see?'

Sidney shook his head. 'I've got to take it.'

'Why's that, chum? Got state secrets inside? The Crown Jewels?' He smiled and poured back his drink. 'Leave it here, down by the bar there, and we'll get you aboard before the bloody Eyeties come.'

'I'm sorry, Mr Owen,' said Sidney, 'but I can't leave it behind.'

The burly, bearded sailor shrugged. 'If you get caught that's your lookout, chum, and the final decision rests with the old man. He's a Quaker, my captain, and if he says no, it's no. We've been boarded before by the dago navy looking for contraband, so be warned, and the bag will cost you double.'

Sidney nodded. 'That's fine.'

'So pay up.'

'Here?'

'Yes, chum.'

'Why not when we're on the ship?'

'Because I want it here. That's a sovereign each for you and your mate, and another for the bag.'

Sidney pressed the gold into his hand. 'Let's go.'

'Blimey, you are in a hurry, aren't you? Your mate outside – did you tell him to follow us at a safe distance? The dockyard gateman will let you and me and the next bloke following through. He mustn't let anyone else get in the way. Is he clear on that?'

'I think so,' nodded Sidney, 'I told her to follow . . .'

Bob frowned. '*Her?*'

'Yes.'

He shook his head and pulled the three gold coins from his pocket. 'Here, mate, take them back. This is not on.'

Sidney pushed his hand away. 'You've got to take us! We've got no one else.'

'There's plenty of ships coming through, mate. You'll manage. Although you'll be hard pushed to get a woman on board.'

'Why?'

'They don't belong on ships, chum, especially not in wartime. The crew won't have it, neither. Women are jinxes, Jonahs, and we've got to cross the Bay of Biscay. Sorry, old son, but I can't help.'

The dockyard air-raid siren started wailing, much closer and much louder than the day before. Bob Owen checked his watch and finished his beer. 'Good luck, chum,' he nodded.

There was a sudden rush to the bar, and the few men who left did so with the mild resignation of workers heading home before the rain. The secret policeman was the first to leave, followed by a French matelot who paused on the threshold and yelled something into the bar. All those who understood shrugged, except Grace.

'This your doing?' she snapped. 'There's police everywhere outside.' She shook her head and bustled around the bar, crossing to the front door and surveying the street with her hands on her hips. After exchanging words with persons unseen she turned and addressed her clientele in seven languages. English was third on the list. 'Gentlemen! There's a control outside. You are requested to leave one by one and cross the street with your hands in the air. Apparently there's been a shooting. The *carabineros* will call you forward for an identity check. Please pay your bill before you go.'

Bob Owen looked at Sidney, at the sweat on his lip and the blood on his shirt. 'They after you, by any chance?'

Sidney nodded.

'Must be quite a price on your head.'

'Done for, aren't I?'

Bob rubbed his beard and banged his empty glass on the bar. 'Grace, me old darling! Get us a bottle of rum and another glass.' He winked at Sidney. 'We'll think of something, old chum.' Then, as the siren screamed and sailors muttered, he punched Sidney hard in the mouth.

19

It took Lenny six days to clear a passage through the pile of boulders blocking the mouth of the mine. Alone, stripped to the waist and glistening with sweat in the pale sunshine, he worked against the rockfall like a river, flowing around the slabs he couldn't move, cutting a serpentine route along the path of least resistance. Rising at five, he and Nick drove to the foot of the crag and walked for two and a half hours to reach the mine. Lenny would then drink a litre of beer before attacking the giant heap of calcareous scree, going over, under and around chunks of rock as big as vans, digging with an ancient brown spade, levering with a black iron bar and pushing with his own bruised and bloody bare hands. Anita or Guadeloupe would arrive at lunchtime, with bread, cheese, tomatoes and more beer, and Nick would loiter around the edge of the heap, picking blackened brass bullet cases from the dirt and doing what little he could to help. Lenny, he had noticed, was a changed man since his timely return to the inn that night. Maybe it was Guadeloupe's influence, or maybe it was simply that he had needed one good night on the town, but his argumentative, overbearing and incompetently authoritarian attitude had vanished, leaving a straight-faced team player who cheerfully compensated for his fellows' shortcomings. He still drank like a thirsty fish, swore like a psychotic soldier with Tourette's and smoked like a fire in a rubber factory, but against all expectation he had proved himself to be the right man at the right time.

'Cometh the man, cometh the hour,' Sidney had noted one

night as Lenny had staggered outside to throw up after downing a pint of vodka. The old man had also observed a fundamental change in Nick's behaviour, spotting a spark in eyes that had previously seemed as dead as stones. He seemed to spend every spare minute deep in serious discussion with Anita, and when he wasn't talking he was fetching water, gathering kindling, and following the Catalan around like a lost lamb.

Sidney lay awake at night, listening to their quiet conversation, and when Anita finally retired to her great-grandfather's bed and Nick fell asleep in the threadbare chair, he wondered if this was what it was like to have a family.

In the mornings, while Lenny worked and Nick watched him, Sidney remained confined to Los Cipreses. He spent his days outdoors in the armchair and his nights propped up in the same bed in which he had dozed with Death back in 1937. Anita remained aloof, treating him with compassion but little warmth until the day she watched him cry. It was the third day of the dig, and Sidney was sitting in the shade of an olive tree, studying Izarra's faded sketchbook. She had created a secret, fantasy world with a sharp pencil on cheap paper, one where Hispanic churches dominated English villages, wherein the thatch on the roofs grew upwards and indolent donkeys loitered in rain-washed streets. In one a soldier in full dress uniform with medals, sword and sash was cheered by a happy crowd of top-hatted folk as he left the church with his shy new bride. In another the same couple, now with children, lunched in the shelter of an oak tree while a summer shower rippled the surface of the river. As Sidney stared at the sketch the tears he had trapped inside for nearly seventy years finally came, dripping onto the washed-out picnic like real drops of rain. First he wept, and then he sobbed, a shrunken old man shaking in the shadow of an olive tree. Anita watched him from the house, waiting for the sorrow to subside, and when she walked through the weeds towards him she kicked stones ahead of her to announce her arrival.

Sidney took a deep breath, shut the book and wiped his eyes. 'Lovely sketches,' he sniffed. 'She was quite the artist.'

'I wish I had half her talent,' nodded Anita. 'Take this stick. Can you walk awhile? I want to show you something.' She took his arm and led him uphill, to the edge of the property, stopping beside a faded sign that read 'Coto privado de la casa'. She pointed to a rocky knoll a couple of hundred yards up the mountain. 'We're going to that hill. Can you make it?'

'Course I can, if we take it slowly,' wheezed Sidney.

It took twenty minutes to reach the knoll. 'I thought you should see this before . . .' Anita's voice drifted on the wind.

Sidney smiled, leaning hard on the stick and sucking in air. 'Before I die,' he panted. 'Quite right too. What is it?'

Anita knelt beside a bronze bonsai, eighteen inches high and fixed to an exposed limestone slab. 'It's an olive tree. It's too small, isn't it? I made it for Izarra, as a memorial, as a symbol of faith and longevity, and I set it up here to overlook Los Cipreses. It's why I came back. I'm a sculptress, and I thought this was so much more apt than a stone in a cemetery where nobody went.' She dusted the trunk with her shirt cuff. 'I made it too small, didn't I?'

Sidney shook his head. 'It's perfect, my dear.'

'The metal is cheap, but the process is too expensive. It cost me five hundred euros just to make this.'

Sidney didn't hear her. He just stood and stared at the tiny brown tree, its leaves immobile in the gentle easterly.

Despite his best efforts Montalban police chief Pablo Menendez Berrueco could find no grounds upon which to lay charges against the Pinsada brothers. Octavio was in a serious but stable condition at Teruel's Obispo Polanco Hospital and Enrique was sticking to his story. He claimed that the fugitive Englishman had burst into the run-down Hostal La Cerda on the Villarluengo road at approximately 11 p.m. on the night he had escaped from custody and had shot Octavio Pinsada in the belly. Pablo hadn't believed a word of it until patrol officers, responding to a report that the safety wall had been damaged just after the Puig Ansenia Tunnel north of Villarluengo, looked over the edge and saw the remains of what appeared to be the petrol tanker Victor Velasquez had reported stolen from his depot. The sceptical police chief bought Enrique a *café cortado* in the hospital canteen and demanded the truth in return.

Pinsada leaned back on his chair, his body language promising honesty. 'I told you before. We was having a drink, talking about this and that, and suddenly he's there at the top of the stairs. I recognised him from the club, didn't I, and I knew he'd been nicked. He's come up the stairs and then *bang!* No warning or nothing. Shot Octavio right in the guts.'

'Then what?'

'Then the old bloke who ran the place appears with his shot-gun. Starts blasting away from the top of the stairs.'

'Where were you?'

'On the floor, mate, trying to get to Octavio.'

'And who else was there?'

Enrique had been expecting this question. The last he'd seen of Hermann Cruz had been when Paco Escobar had been kicking him out of the door. 'Why do you ask?' he replied.

'Because I'm investigating a fucking gun battle and I'd like to know who was involved, you daft bastard.'

'Fair enough,' nodded Enrique. His hand had slipped over his mouth.

'So who else was there?'

Enrique tipped his head back and stared at the ceiling. 'Now, let me think . . .'

Pablo shook his head. 'I haven't got time for this. Was Hermann Cruz there? Yes or no?'

The gipsy rubbed his earlobe. Clearly Hermann was denying having been there. Maybe the cops knew about Escobar. Maybe the two other English guys had filed a complaint. Enrique scratched the back of his neck. He and Octavio had taken no part in the torture, and if they were honest, the Englishmen would admit that. However, they had stood by and watched, so that made them accessories to charges of kidnap, torture and grievous bodily harm. These serious offences would pale into utter insignificance if Escobar had been arrested, but Enrique's guess, based on the fact that he was facing the cop over a coffee and not over a barrel, was that he was still at large. He frowned and leaned forward, doubled up like a man with an ulcer, sipped his *cortado* and looked up at Pablo. 'You know what, Chief? I think I might be suffering from that post-traumatic stress disorder. My mind's a blank after the first gunshot.'

'Oh, for fuck's sake, Pinsada. You remember at least as much as the second shot because you mentioned Pepe Serrano firing his shotgun.'

'See?' said Enrique. 'I forgot I said that. I probably need counselling.'

'Look: my men have found a burned-out petrol tanker at the foot of the Ansenia Gorge. There are the remains of two bodies inside. We've identified what's left of one of them by his dental records. It was Hermann Cruz. The other has no head.'

'What about fingerprints?' asked Enrique, suddenly keen to assist.

Pablo sighed. 'Wake up, Pinsada! Have you any idea how little there is left of the human body after it's been toasted over twenty thousand litres of unleaded? However, just before the tunnel, we found a British passport. We suspect the other body is that of Leonard Arthur Knowles. Can you confirm whether Hermann Cruz was at the hotel when the Englishman started shooting and whether the two left together in the petrol tanker? That's all I'm asking.'

Enrique raised his eyes to heaven and thanked God for His mysterious mercies, silently promising to leave 5 per cent of the takings on his next big cocaine deal in the poor box at Santo Nino. Escobar was out of his life for ever, and even Octavio would agree that a small-calibre bullet in the belly was a low price to pay for freedom. 'Listen,' he said. 'I haven't told you this, but before he got arrested that Englishman was talking to Hermann about gold. Hermann had promised him a lot of cash for information about some cave up in the mountains . . .'

'Yeah, yeah, yeah,' nodded Pablo. 'Hermann the German and his famous crock of gold.' He remembered asking Cruz to speak to the prisoner. They'd had quite a chat, but it had seemed unimportant at the time. Obviously there had been more to it.

'Anyway,' continued Enrique, 'the Englishman shoots at old Pepe Serrano, grabs his shotgun from him and runs out the door. I gave chase and saw him climbing into this petrol tanker outside. Guess who's sitting in the cab?'

'Tell me.'

'Hermann Cruz. On my life. He ducked down when he saw me but I saw him.'

'We know he was in the truck. Would you testify that the other man was Leonard Arthur Knowles?'

'Course I wouldn't,' replied Enrique, leaning back on his chair. 'Unless there's something in it for me.'

'And why would Leonard Arthur Knowles break into the Hostal La Cerda to shoot your brother? Were you associates?'

'Never seen the man in my life before, I swear. I reckon he was doing a hit for Hermann. Cruz owed me and my brother a lot of money – all legit – and I think he was trying to get out of paying.'

'By shooting one of you?'

Enrique shrugged. 'Maybe he meant to get me as well.'

Pablo picked up his receipt and folded it carefully before

360

putting it in his wallet. 'I'm done with you for the present, Pinsada. Counselling's on the fourth floor.'

He walked back to his car, spinning his keys on his finger. One unreliable witness had confirmed seeing Leonard Arthur Knowles climb into the petrol tanker. DNA sampling from blood found at the Velasquez garage would probably match with whatever the British police could offer. Quite what Hermann Cruz was doing at the wheel of a stolen petrol tanker had not yet been adequately explained, but Pablo knew when he was wasting his time with Pinsada. He drove north out of Teruel, past the Dinopolis theme park and into the Maestrazgo. The case against Leonard Arthur Knowles was now virtually closed and all outstanding warrants cancelled. All that remained was to establish whether that creep Hermann Cruz had been a victim or a willing accomplice, and that could wait until Monday.

His deputy called. 'Are you on your way back, Chief?'

'I'm going straight home,' he replied. 'I've got a semi-positive ID on Leonard Arthur Knowles as the second body in the Velasquez truck. The heat is off.'

'There's something else, Chief.'

'Go on,' sighed Pablo.

'The forensic team at La Cerda have found personal effects in two of the rooms, and a fingertip and two earlobes on the dining-room floor.'

'Fuck it!' spat Pablo, swinging a U-turn and heading back to the hospital. He missed the Pinsadas by ten minutes.

The night before Lenny broke through, Sidney called Nick to his bedside. He was slipping away fast, drifting between peaks of brilliant lucidity and troughs of near-comatose introspection. He hadn't eaten for five days, and his bowels had stopped working. The fingers on his right hand were blue and the bruises on his face were the colour of rotting aubergines. His skin seemed

361

jaundiced and gave off a faintly repulsive odour; his tongue was a maggoty yellow. Nick poured him a glass of Armagnac from the near-empty flask and pulled up a stool.

'I've had a splendid idea, Mr Crick,' said Sidney. 'Anita is a sculptress.'

'I know,' nodded Nick. 'Have you seen her olive tree?'

'That's my point. I was thinking about the boys in the Brigades being like the last trees standing on the battlefield, and that's what I want.'

'An olive tree? It's a bit small, isn't it?'

Sidney glanced to see if Anita was in earshot. 'You're right,' he nodded. 'I thought that, but I didn't say anything. Imagine, though, if it were life-size?'

'Good idea. Especially with its overtones of peace and all that.'

'Exactly. I want you to take my share of the gold and go with her. Commission five trees—'

'And raise them in Madrid, Jarama, Brunete, Teruel and Ebro – the sites of the five biggest battles fought by the Brigades. I'm ahead of you, Mr Starman.'

'Good lad. Do you mind?'

'Got nothing better planned. What makes you think she'll agree to it?'

Sidney sipped his Armagnac and sighed. 'She'll do it, Mr Crick.'

Bob Owen wasn't sure if one punch in the face was enough, so he hit the kid again, just to make sure. Then he threw a glass of rum in his face and poured another.

'Drink up, old son.' He pinched Sidney's bleeding nose and tipped the spirit down his throat. 'And another. Let's have this haversack off as well.' Outside the siren sounded like a fat lady singing as behind the bar a real one looked on with dismay. 'Hold him up, Grace old girl,' asked Bob, forcing a third glass between

362

Sidney's bloody lips. 'He needs to be wearing my coat and hat.'

The last few staggeringly drunk Russians were stumbling out of the bar, their papers in their hands.

Bob Owen threw the haversack over one shoulder and Sidney's right arm over the other. 'Cheers then, Grace love,' he nodded. 'I'll see you again.'

'*A bientôt*,' replied the landlady, as Bob dragged Sidney into the street.

A queue had built up at the checkpoint, much to the annoyance of the uniformed *carabineros* and the plain-clothes secret police. They yelled to make themselves heard over the wailing siren, dispatching riflemen to head off wandering Russians. Semi-conscious through drink and concussion, Sidney scanned the crowd behind the barriers for Izarra. He could hear himself mumbling her name, over and over, but the faces across the street had merged into a smear of flesh against a whirling background. Suddenly the anti-aircraft batteries opened up to the north of town, their barrage sending a wave of shock through the crowd. People started running – when the guns began firing the bombers were only moments away. As the crowd thinned, Sidney closed one eye and caught sight of her, standing by the tram stop, scanning the line of sailors. An *asalto* officer was trying to steer her away, pointing to the shelter entrance. Down by the checkpoint the secret policeman was pointing at Bob Owen.

'Oh, bloody fiddlesticks,' muttered Bob. 'Here comes trouble.'

The dockyard guns started firing, their thunderclap reports drowning out the screaming siren as the *carabineros* glanced nervously skywards. Sidney looked left, up the street, and saw a scattering of dots approaching like a murder of crows. The *asalto* was dragging Izarra to the shelter, and what was left of the queue broke up, sprinting in the same direction, as a sequence of seven huge detonations rolled down the street, straddling the railway line. The blast waves rushed past like a hot, oily wind, blowing grit and litter as the first planes roared overhead. The soldiers were now firing into the sky, and as the queue disintegrated three more explosions engulfed the dockyard. Bob dragged Sidney through the confusion, waving his papers at a terrified soldier and passing through the dockyard gate. The wharf was choked with smoke and confusion, with freighters sounding their horns and casting off into a harbour churned by high explosive.

'You're not that bloody drunk,' said Bob, letting Sidney go. 'Follow me.' He glanced over his shoulder. 'Mind your back.'

The secret policeman from the bar was following them, disappearing and reappearing among the throng of panicked stevedores and drunken sailors, emerging blinking but determined from screens of grey smoke. Bob caught Sidney by the collar and dragged him onwards. 'That's our *Myrtle* up ahead. Once we're on board he can't do a bloody thing about it. That's British sovereign territory, that is.'

A hissing incendiary slammed into the quayside and rolled into the sea yards in front of them. Fire bells yelled like trapped children while the siren wailed like a new widow as red-hot shards of shrapnel rained down, starting fires on the dockside and sinking in clouds of steam in the water. The steady hammering of the flak batteries was dogged but ineffective, their ordnance exploding high above the raiders who came in three waves. Then, suddenly, they were gone.

As the last explosions echoed across the city and the batteries fell silent, Sidney dropped to one knee behind a waist-high coil of smouldering coir. Bob hurried on and the secret policeman followed, spotting his crouching killer just a moment too late. Sidney thought he detected a sense of failure in the agent's eyes as he shot him twice in the head and twice in the chest, dropping him on the quayside. His head swimming from the effects of the rum, the punches and the bombing, he stumbled to the corpse and rolled it awkwardly into the harbour. In the smoke and confusion no one saw a thing.

As Sidney turned Bob appeared at his side with a couple of serious-looking shipmates. He pointed at a rusting, salt-caked coaster tied up to the wharf. 'This is her,' said Bob. 'Up you go, quick.' He glanced around for the agent. 'Where's the copper gone?'

'He's been repaired,' slurred Sidney. 'I'm going back to get the girl.'

Bob grabbed his arm. 'Oh no you're not, chum. You're coming with us.'

Sidney struggled to free himself from the sailor's iron grip, drunkenly aware that one round remained in the Luger's magazine. 'I can't leave her,' he mumbled. 'I promised her.'

'Oh well,' shrugged Bob, 'you'd better go back then.' He released Sidney's arm. 'Off you go.'

'Thanks, pal,' nodded Sidney.

'You're welcome, chum,' smiled Bob, before felling him with a straight right to the jaw. 'This one'll never make a sailor,' he told his shipmates as they carried Sidney up the gangplank.

'She spent two years in Montjuic,' said Anita.

Sidney lay propped against the bedstead, the last of his Armagnac gripped in his bony fingers. The window was open and the candles flickered when the breeze took a shortcut through the house. Outside the moon glowed like a distant iceberg in a dark sea.

Anita pushed a cigarette between her lips and Nick lit it for her. 'They never charged her. Just locked her up on suspicion of terrorism and forgot about her. When the fascists came she was denounced by a fellow prisoner and transferred to the camp at San Pedro de Cardeña. You have no idea what went on there. You thought the concentration camps were all closed down in 1945, didn't you? They kept her there until 27 April 1950. My mother was twelve when Izarra was released. It was the feast day of the Virgin of Montserrat, and she'd spent her childhood in prison.' She took a bitter drag and blew smoke. 'Did you know you had a daughter, Sidney Starman? Did you know you had a granddaughter?'

Sidney closed his eyes. 'I had no idea,' he said slowly, 'until the first time I saw you. Then I knew.' He reached for her with a trembling hand, but she turned away, her elbows on her knees and her hands before her face. The old man's fingers stretched into space, seeking contact before flopping onto the blanket.

'What is she like, your mother?' he asked.

'You mean your daughter? Sad. Alcoholic. Prone to long bouts of hysterical laughter followed by weeks of dark depression. Like her mother, she never married. Unlike her, she never believed in the future. She jumped from the balcony of our apartment in Sant Marti when I was sixteen. She'd waited up for me – I'd been drinking, getting high – and we argued. I left her with her bottle and went to bed. The police woke me up.' She stubbed out her cigarette and lit another. 'My father was an artist, a proper one, not a dreamer like my mother, but he moved back to Chile when I was six. I didn't know about Izarra, my grandmother, until after my mother was buried. I've been coming here for the last nineteen years, and, like her, I always knew you'd show up some day to dig up your own grave.' She brushed back her fringe and looked Sidney straight in the eye. 'So how was your life, Grandfather?'

20

Lenny broke through on the feast day of St Joseph – the patron saint against doubt – rolling away a final boulder to reveal a black hole between the rock pile and the roof of the mine. Then his nerve failed.

'Your turn now, Nickle-Arse,' he said.

'My turn for what? I can't dig.'

'Nothing else to dig, mate. Just crawling now, and you're much better at crawling than me. Off you go, Indiana – here's El Sid's torch. Quick as you can.'

'I think you should be first in,' protested Nick. 'You did all the work. It doesn't seem right that I should take the credit.'

'Why change now, Nickle-Arse? Anyway, I'm too muscular to squeeze through the gap. Might get stuck.'

Nick paused at the entrance to the tunnel. 'It's a bit tight.'

'You'll be all right.'

'Stay here and listen out in case something happens.'

'Of course I will,' promised Lenny, walking down the slope to fetch his beer.

Deep inside the passage Nick grazed his head on the ceiling and his chin on the floor as he inched forwards, wondering if he should have wrapped a bandanna around his face to protect himself from tomb fever. By Sidney's account there were five corpses in the mine – three Spanish, one German and one American – and God only knew what kind of bacteriological curse they would unleash upon him. Scarcely breathing, he pushed through the black hole, feeling cool, dry air on his face as the spoil fell away. The torch light spilled over fallen boulders, throwing grotesque shadows on the far walls before resting on the smooth surface of a wooden box. Something glistened in the beam and Nick felt an adrenalin surge numb his legs and snatch his breath. Holding the torch in his bandaged left hand, he dragged himself forwards with his right, until he was clear of the tunnel and could stand. The rock pile shifted treacherously underfoot, the long slabs of limestone sliding away with a series of hollow clicks. There was no truck, and, as far as Nick dared look, no calcified corpses. The beam yellowed, and Nick shook the torch until it regained its brightness. The darkness was absolute and the silence complete, but for his fragile, breathless presence. Scarcely daring to move, he shone the torch at a desiccated canvas tarpaulin. The treasure was clearly hidden beneath it, and he inched slowly towards it, terrified that a sudden movement would set off a seventy-year-old booby trap and bring the whole mountain down on his back. The crate he'd spotted from the tunnel mouth was partially open, its contents exposed to the dead air. Nick reached out to touch it, his heart like a trapped rabbit's and his pulse loud in his ears.

'Hands off!' roared a deep and demonic voice.

Nick leapt backwards, dropping the torch and scrabbling in the darkness in blind panic. Lenny's disembodied laughter echoed around the cave.

'You bastard!' yelled Nick. 'You nearly gave me a fucking heart attack!' He snatched up the torch and pointed it at the tunnel.

Lenny grimaced in the beam. 'Settle down, Nickle-Arse. Is it all there?'

Nick crept forward, more confident now Lenny was watching over him. 'There's one open box here.' He bent down and scooped up a handful of bullion. 'Jesus Christ! It's gold, all right!'

'How many more are there like that?'

Nick pulled away the tarpaulin and started counting. It didn't take long.

It was dark when they came down the mountain, carrying one of the two remaining boxes of coin between them. Lenny had calculated that his share was just about adequate to sort out a new passport and a new life, in Florida with Guadeloupe, far away from his old existence in Norfolk. He was unaware that the Spanish police were no longer searching for him and that earlier that day a death knocker from Norfolk Constabulary had visited his ex-wife Hazel at home and asked her to sit down. As far as Hazel was concerned, it was the best gift she had ever been given. She immediately made plans to move herself and the kids in with her new lover, an American Air Force captain due to rotate back to his home state, Florida.

'So what's your plan, Nickle-Arse?' asked Lenny.

Venus had risen over the valley, glowing like a stricken bomber in the red western sky, and the pair were resting on a slab beside the trail, sharing their last cigarette. Nick bent down to pick a Peruvian reale from the box and turned it in his fingers. There was a fairy tale he had once heard about a couple of chancers who left a trail of treasure all the way down a mountain before coming to a bad end. He couldn't remember the details.

'Going to Barcelona with Anita,' he said. 'She's going to make olive trees out of bronze and we're going to raise them up in memory of the International Brigades.' He shrugged. 'We'll see how it goes.'

The lamps had been lit at Los Cipreses and the house glowed in the distance like gold under moonlight. Lenny shook his head in weary dismay. 'Nothing's ever easy with you, is it? Why couldn't you fuck off to the Costa Brava and open an English bar like any normal geezer?'

Nick shook his head. 'Can't see myself behind a bar. I'm not really into drinking.'

Lenny shrugged. 'Not a bad thing in a barman. Never get high on your own supply and all that.' He looked at the crate and shook his head. 'All this hassle for two poxy boxes.'

'That's two more than you thought there'd be.'

'Yeah, and ninety-eight less than El Sid said there was.'

Far above them, back in the cave, a pile of rock undisturbed for sixty-nine years until that day settled into place, the slabs of limestone sliding over each other to reveal a small square of dented steel.

Neither Nick nor Lenny heard the movement.

'What do you reckon happened to the rest of it?' asked Nick.

Lenny blew smoke. 'You are a thick twat, Nickle-Arse,' he sighed. 'There wasn't any more – El Sid told you there was a hundred boxes to get you excited, and you fell for it.'

Deep in the cave the rockpile subsided a little more, exposing the faded pink ear of a long-buried pig still wearing, somewhere under the rubble, a butcher's apron and a psychotic grin. The movement was too slight and too gentle to be heard outside the old mine, and down on the path Nick looked at Lenny. 'When we go back to get the other crate we dragged out, do you reckon we should go back inside for another look round, just in case?'

Lenny looked back at Nick, his expression a mixture of sadness and disappointment. 'No, I do not, Nickle-Arse. There's fuck all in there except rocks and bodies. You should be grateful for what you've got. Take it from me.' He tapped his nose. 'Lenny knows.'

Anita met them outside the house. 'He's slipping away,' she said. 'I think he's been hanging on to see you both again.' She touched Nick's arm. 'I think you have to say goodbye.'

Nick nodded, letting her hand rest on his wrist. 'What about you?'

She smiled as though she might cry. 'We've been talking all day. Now it's your turn.'

'How do I look, chaps?' called Sidney weakly as they entered the house.

Guadeloupe squeezed Lenny's hand and slipped outside. The two men placed the box of coin on the table.

'It looks like a deathbed scene by Goya,' commented Nick.

'Nicholas!' scolded Lenny. 'You're so insensitive.'

Sidney seemed to be breathing in without exhaling, as though his lungs were taking everything he could give them. 'Is that gold I smell, boys?' he whispered.

'Two fucking boxes, Mr S,' nodded Lenny. 'Talk about a bleeding lost cause.'

'Now you know how I felt,' retorted Sidney, his voice just a hoarse croak. He swallowed hard and frowned. 'Two boxes? Did you look properly? There were a hundred of the buggers when I left.'

'Whatever,' sighed Lenny. 'That's one of them on the table. We tipped half of it out and it still weighs a bleedin' ton. We'll go back tomorrow for the rest.'

Sidney shook his head. 'I don't understand. Are you certain of this, Mr Crick?'

'Two boxes,' confirmed Nick. 'And this, stuck in the open one.' He pulled a four-inch-long aluminium cylinder from his jacket pocket and handed it to Sidney. 'It says "Sid the Something" on the side. It's written in pencil. We didn't open it because it looked like a flare canister or a booby trap or something.'

Sidney looked at the canister, then at Nick. 'You silly sod,' he said. 'It's a cigar tube.' He handed it back. 'Open it up.'

Nick twisted the top and the rich, toasty smell of Cuba filled the room. He tapped the tube against his palm and the cigar slid out, speckling his hand with flecks of aged tobacco. A three-inch square of paper was wrapped around the cigar, and Nick passed both to Sidney. 'It's a cigar with a note wrapped round it,' he said.

'I can bloody see that. Get me a light and a pen and pass me my glasses,' he said. 'And Mr Knowles, let me sign your copy of the will.'

Lenny performed a brief charade of having forgotten about the legacy, thought for a moment, then shook his head. 'Don't worry about that, Mr S,' he said. 'I was never in this for the money.'

'I know that, Mr Knowles. You were in it for the house, and I'm sorry for the misunderstanding. Now give me the bloody will before it's too late.' He scrawled his name with a trembling hand and handed back the document, his jaundiced eyes meeting Lenny's as he did so. 'Thank you for your help, Mr Knowles.'

'Pleasure, Mr S,' mumbled Lenny.

'I want you to bury me in the grave outside. Anita knows where it is. There's a little more gold buried there, too, but that's for her.'

Lenny nodded. 'Right you are, Mr S.'

'You'll need to get me seen by a doctor beforehand.'

Lenny frowned. 'It'll be a bit late for that, won't it?'

Sidney sighed. 'You'll need a death certificate for a grant of probate, you bloody fool. Anita knows what to do.'

Nick brought the lamps closer and polished the spectacles with the hem of his T-shirt before placing them on Sidney's face. Lenny cut the end from the cigar and lit it from a candle, grimacing as he sucked the aged tobacco into life. 'Fuck me, that's foul,' he gasped, passing the cigar to the old man.

Sidney took a series of puffs and held the note up to the light. 'It's from Frank Cobb,' he said, smiling as he read it. Then he chuckled, the cigar like a chimney in the corner of his mouth. The chuckle became a cackle, then, as tears welled up in his eyes, it became a giggle. The last embers of life twinkled in his eyes as he reread the document, suddenly exploding in a choking, gasping gale of uncontrollable laughter that racked his old bones like a tubercular convulsion. He sucked on the cigar, shaking his head as he scanned the note for a third time, his shoulders shaking as though he'd just read the funniest joke in the world. Howling now, he tipped his head back, bit his lip and struggled to contain his mirth long enough to explain it, but his failure merely started off the others.

In moments all three were giggling helplessly, tears of laughter streaking their grimy cheeks. Breathless, Nick looked at Lenny, his hand over his mouth. 'Why are we laughing?' he cried.

'Buggered if I know,' spluttered Lenny. 'Ask El Sid.'

But it was too late for that. El Sid was dead.